Lobster Trapped!

W.J. GOGUEN

PublishAmerica
Baltimore

© 2004 by William Goguen.

All rights reserved. No part of this book may be reproduced, stored in a retrieval system or transmitted in any form or by any means without the prior written permission of the publishers, except by a reviewer who may quote brief passages in a review to be printed in a newspaper, magazine or journal.

First printing

ISBN: 1-4137-4318-8
PUBLISHED BY PUBLISHAMERICA, LLLP
www.publishamerica.com
Baltimore

Printed in the United States of America

This book is dedicated to my sister:

Doreen Goguen (1955-1979)

I would like to acknowledge the following people in the writing of this manuscript:

William Cote, who originated the idea.
Loretta Michals, who gave me the confidence.

Chapter I

November 21, 1718

Salt water broke over the bow of the large sloop situated in the Ocracoke Inlet off the coast of North Carolina, and the surge thoroughly doused the lens of young Matthew Peddigrew's calfskin telescope as he peered off of the starboard side of the ship; temporarily causing him to lose sight of the objects he had just spotted. He pulled the vellum tool down, drew a cloth from within his jacket and wiped the lens clean then placed it against his eye once more.

"Damn!" he exclaimed, attempting to focus. The instrument was not all that extraordinary, but it served its purpose, and it was certainly better than the wooden one which replaced it. He closed his left eye, peering through the device with his other.

There was no doubt about what he saw! The masts of two sloops teetered in the waves in the distance. The young navigator instantly knew who it was and determined that there was no time to waste. He must tell the captain, thus he shoved the telescope away into his jacket and ran across the deck of the enormous vessel towards the door which accessed the deck below.

The storm which had recently passed caused the waters in the inlet to grow somewhat rough. The wooden boat creaked in the wind, and it rocked as he hustled to his destination. He acted in a panic; dodging the other sailors on board as he went, who all politely got out of his way, uncertain of his hurry. It was very uncommon for him to act like this; after all, they were in a friendly port—a spot that Blackbeard himself had generously paid for!

The good Governor Eden of the North Carolina province welcomed the well-known pirate with open arms—and open pockets! He shared in the vast amounts of treasure that Drummond acquired ('Drummond' was one of the many names Blackbeard held and it was the one that Eden preferred to call him). It was a safe harbor for the pilferers. The governor took no shame, since the king himself had issued Blackbeard a letter of marque, allowing him to plunder or do whatever he pleased, but of course, it was all for a fee.

Eden saw no harm in this, but he did anticipate his share and as such, the pirates were welcomed into the ports of North Carolina. It was only a miscue by Blackbeard, or Drummond or Tech or Teach (his real name), that drew the governor of Virginia to despise him. He had gone ashore on the province of Virginia and met a young girl, fifteen years of age, the daughter of a close friend of Governor Spottiswood. Blackbeard took the girl (with her consent), and brought her to North Carolina, where Governor Eden himself performed the marriage ceremony (not that he needed another wife, he already had thirteen!) Once completed, Blackbeard and his many followers held several nights of revelry; drinking and gambling with no thought of the girl.

She was devastated and, as such, returned to Virginia through the aid of a concerned captain anchored at Ocracoke who had met the pirate but was completely sickened by his total lack of tact or respect.

When Governor Spottiswood heard the story, he became infuriated and issued a proclamation to apprehend the pirate, where a reward was posted—one hundred pounds! It was a hearty sum! This was administered on the eleventh day of November and posted in all churches and public areas.

During the previous storm, many ships had sought refuge in the inlets to Ocracoke, near where the pirate ship had anchored. The news of the reward had spread from ship to ship and, finally, to Blackbeard himself. At one time, there were as many as a dozen ships posted up in the inlet. The storm had passed and many of those vessels departed, fearing the imminent, leaving only three now along the coast—another sloop and a small coaster which hailed from Boston, commanded by a Captain Burley. Blackbeard knew the men and had caroused with them often on shore.

Peddigrew raced down the stairs, holding on to anything he could until he got to the captain's chamber. He pounded on the door furiously.

"Aye! What it be?" The voice was so boisterous and loud that it scared the young navigator, who jumped backwards when he heard it. He stepped to the door once again and placed his cheek on the outside, as close as he could get, speaking in a low but assertive voice.

"Captain, it's me, Matthew Peddigrew. I've news, sir!"

"News? Ye got news? Well, then come in, boy, and let me hear it!" he bellowed.

The lad turned the knob on the door to the cabin and entered. The room reeked with foul, disgusting odors and he pulled the kerchief, which he usually wore on his head, out of his jacket and placed it under his nose to block the nasty air. The room was small, as it should be aboard a ship, but it was the captain's quarters and as he looked throughout it, he felt it should have been larger. Blackbeard stood up from his desk, where he was fondling through charts and maps. The quarters appeared even smaller with the contrast of the large man before him.

"What it be, boy!" He saw the young man was trembling. "Why d'ye shake? Ye got news? What is it, come on with it! Speak, boy!"

The young gentleman removed the cloth from below his nose and spoke, without breathing, avoiding the stench emanating from within the small cabin.

"I saw 'em, sir!" He quickly placed the kerchief back over his face. He was wearing a jacket in the cool air, his legs covered with pantaloons and stockings and his shoes buckled up with one strap holding them onto his feet.

Blackbeard was an ominous figure, standing nearly six feet high. The jacket he wore was blue and the bottom of his pants fell well short of the top of his shoes, which also only held one buckle each. His hat was off, showing his long, mangled hair, and his beard encircled his whole face in an almost gruesome fashion—protruding down his chin, but also swirling around his eyes. He didn't look human.

He leaned back as he stood, curling his spine. "Saw 'em, did ye? Who'd ye see?"

"The English Navy, sir! They have two ships stationed on the mouth of the harbor. They're here, Captain!"

Blackbeard growled. "So, they've come!" He fondled the twisted plaits of his beard, which hung down his chest, ending just above the weapons stuffed into the belt on his pants. "That damned Spottiswood sent his bullies down here! Who does he think he is? He ain't got no right! He ain't got no jurisdiction in the Carolinas!" There was contempt in his expression. He was chewing on tobacco and spit towards the back of the room.

"So they mean to have a fight, the fools!" He twisted the hair between his fingers and lowered his head in contemplation. "They can't get through the shoals. They'll ground out on the sandbars. I've got time!" The cabin rocked with a surge from the receding storm, and the boy fell against the door behind him, which shut with the unexpected roll.

Blackbeard placed his right hand on his head in reflection. "How many vessels are left in the inlet?" He turned quickly to the boy cowering in his presence.

"Three friendly ones, sir, including ours, but not counting the two English ships."

"Two more than mine, ye say? Good. Good. That be to me liking!" He grabbed his mustache and twisted it while thinking. "The fella from New York still here?"

"Yes, sir, and the ship from Boston." The boy had done his job as best he could. The information had been reported.

The pirate swiveled, placing the palms of his hands down on the paperwork on his desk. "Good boy, now fetch me some Hollands!"

The lad placed his hand against his chest. "Aye, sir!" He reeled towards the door behind him and opened it. "I'll fetch ye Hollands f'r ye now." He kicked the small sill on the door. "It don't look good, does it, Captain?"

Blackbeard laughed and rubbed his belly. "Boy, they ain't got nothing I can't handle. I got cannon. I knew they were comin', but they can't navigate these straits and inlets and I can. They don't know these waters. They be the ones committing suicide. They be the lost souls!"

"Ah, yes, sir. I'll get ye Hollands, sir." The lad began to exit until he heard Blackbeard yell once more.

"Boy!"

Peddigrew stopped. "Yes, Captain?"

Blackbeard was staring at the far wall. "Where be ye glass?"

"I keep it here, sir." He patted the top of his jacket.

"I'll take hold of it and have a look for m'self!"

The lad fumbled through his jacket until he found the telescope and pulled from beneath, holding it out to the waiting hand of the pirate. "Will that be all, Captain?"

Edward Teach grabbed hold of the instrument. "Nay, that ain't be all. Meet me on deck when I look at the situation. I've business to tend to and ye be me mate to see it done. I'll follow ye up. Come along, now!"

"Aye, sir! I'll bring the Hollands to ye there." The lad opened the door and left with Blackbeard behind, patting the six pistols tucked into his belt as they ascended out of the dingy, dark and stinky quarters.

The light shone brightly in his eyes as he reached the top of the steps, and he squinted looking into the sunshine, but the sun was setting in the west and his visual objective was definitely to the east.

"Where be they, boy?" he asked, twirling the telescope in his hands. A strong wind blew from the southeast, making the walk to the bow awkward.

"I saw 'em over there, on the horizon." The lad pointed in the direction of Ryals Shoal, north of Pamticoe Sound.

Blackbeard drew the telescope to his face as he approached the front of the ship and looked through. The sloop rocked and rolled while he evaluated the situation. The boy left his side. "I'll fetch ye Hollands, sir."

"Aye, aye, aye!" He waved to him in indifference. The scope proved the young navigator correct. Two masts could be detected over Ocracoke Island and now, in the abating mist he could see the yardarms of the two vessels; one a sloop and the other a schooner. Their sails were down.

"They be spankin' new!" he spoke aloud. "Damn, if that ain't Parker's work!" He pulled the scope from his eye and dropped his head, pondering at the thought. "They ain't got no right to be here!" He paced about the deck in a curious manner, thinking. "But they can't get in—it's too shallow for 'em!"

He thought for several minutes, simply assessing the situation. The boy rushed up to his side with a mug. "Your Hollands, Captain." He handed the blackjack to Blackbeard, who accepted it fondly and took a long quaff, then placed the mug on his hip.

"Have someone fetch me a boat, boy, I've got to talk to the fella from New York!"

"Aye, aye, sir." The lad ran towards the stern, when the bearded man spun around to him, holding his hand near his mouth to direct his voice.

"And tell Tully to get up here!" he screamed and stamped his foot at the boy, who stopped and turned around.

"Sir?" he said.

"I said, tell Tully to get up here! If they mean to have battle, they'll have it, I say!"

"Aye, aye, sir." He turned back around and flew down the remainder of the deck with a reckless abandon.

"And fetch me more Hollands!" His complexion was anxious, uncertain and definitely furious.

The wind blew stronger and it was getting dark as Peddigrew returned with the new mug. "There be a boat waiting for ye, sir."

The captain took the mug and handed the empty blackjack to the young navigator. "Where's Tully?" he yelled as the boy attempted to return to the galley.

"He's on his way, sir. He said he'd be a minute, getting ready for that party and all."

"That'll be fine then. Get off." He picked up the telescope again and looked at the objects lurking in the water. "They've dropped anchor, so there ain't no rush. I think I'll join that party!"

Tully passed the boy as he approached the captain. "Ye called for me, sir?" The man was completely trimmed, from top to bottom, wearing a full dress uniform and a clean shave. A stately man, adorned with all the dressings of a fine sailor, thin and tall. He stood stately. "What ye want?"

Blackbeard turned around. "Ah, Tully, Tully, we got rounds t'make."

"Rounds, sir?" He seemed disoriented. "I'm off duty now, and I've a party to attend to on shore."

"Aye, and so do I! But ye never be off duty on this vessel! First, though, we shall see the boat from New York anchored to port side. I need a talk with the captain, and then we go ashore." He struggled with his message. "Maynard is out there!" He pointed to the two boats in the inlet.

The boatswain looked to the direction indicated. "So!" he said. "Spottiswood means his word. It's all around the inlet, ye know."

"Aye, I know! He's got no right to be here and that man just can't be bought! This is the Carolinas, for God's sake, not Virginy! But I'll take care of 'em. I got a boat awaiting." He tucked the telescope into his pocket. "They're gonna be sorry they found me! Now ye follow me." He pushed Tully aside and walked down the starboard side of the ship to where the boat awaited while the boatswain followed.

"Do you know his full purpose?" Tully asked.

Blackbeard stopped short and turned to the mate who halted directly behind him. "Aye! Aye, aye, I know!" he said. "I know his purpose; 'tis to *kill* me!"

Tully spun, shocked by the response, then he looked out to the ocean. "I see! It may very well be that he really means to do so."

"'Tis!" Blackbeard laughed a long and serious laugh. "'Tis, me matie! Now come aboard, get ye along." A boat had been drawn to the stern of the sloop. Young Peddigrew pulled up as they looked over the rail.

"Drop the ladder, boy, before the sun sets!"

"Aye, sir! You want me to get ye more Hollands for the ride?" He lofted down the rope that managed their drop to the dinghy.

"Nay. They'll be plenty on the New Yorker's vessel."

First, Blackbeard boarded and then Tully. The two stepped gingerly down the rope to the waiting boat where a steward eased it into position as they stepped on. "Ev'ning, Captain. I heard ye need to speak with the fellow from New York, and ye need a ride." He was a bit stalky, and spoke with a thick English accent.

"Yes, yes. Ye know where the vessel be. Take us there!"

"Aye, sir, right away, sir!"

The wind had calmed slightly, blowing gingerly from the south and the sea had settled somewhat. They rowed to their destination, a small sloop anchored nearly 100 yards from the massive *Queen Anne's Revenge*. The steward began to speak as he rowed. "Your captain ain't on the ketch anchored there. Where ye want me to take ye?"

"What?" replied Blackbeard. "That's his boat!"

"Aye, Captain, but he went aboard the coaster from Boston about an hour ago."

"Well, why didn't ye say so? Take us there, then. Get on with it!"

"Aye, sir." The steward redirected the course of the small skiff, placing it on a heading for the only other vessel located in the inlet. "They may not let ye on deck," he proclaimed. "They heard the rumors and ye might prove to be a risk to 'em. But m'self, I think it's exciting!"

The pirate took offense and his face showed it. He immediately reached inside his pocket and pulled out some hempen cord which he soaked in saltpeter and kept handy. He rolled pieces into his long, braided hair. As they approached the coaster, "Light me!" he roared to Tully.

Having seen this several times, Tully knew just what to do. He dug into his pockets until he found a book of wooden matches, pulled them out and lit the hemp in Blackbeard's hair. Now, this ominous form of a man stood. The mere figure was obtrusive, but with the fire that emanated from his head made him look even more like a monster than a man.

When the skiff got close enough to the Boston boat, Blackbeard yelled up to a crew hand walking past the rope launch. The pirate's arms were held outstretched and his eyes were swollen, looking of terror. "Ahoy, ye!" he screame. "Drop me the ropes!"

The man he spoke to fell back in horror with one glimpse of which, he felt, could only be an apparition. "What? Why, it be the devil?" He leaned over the rail of the boat. "Be ye the devil?" he asked as he stared at the glowing man.

"Aye, I be the devil himself! I've business to talk to the two captains aboard, now DROP the ladder or I'll have ye soul!"

In full-fledged fear, the man scurried along and sprung the ladder for the visitors to ascend. Blackbeard told the lad who had rowed to the boat, "Keep her here, boy. I won't be long."

"Aye, Captain."

"Now, come along, Tully," he spoke as he grabbed hold of one of the wooden rungs supported on the ropes. The two men climbed up the rope ladder and took foot on the deck above.

The sailor who dropped the rope spoke. "Ye ain't the devil, but ye be the pirate, Blackbeard! If one ain't the other! You be the one they be after!" He trembled at his presence. It had gotten dark, very dark out, and the only light came from the crescent moon and the fire from the bearded man's hair. The wind had picked up again and they could hear the little dinghy bounce off the larger vessel. Blackbeard extinguished the flames from his hair. "Aye, I be he. But don't ye fret, I ain't here to harm ye." Even though he had put out the fire in his hair, he stood extremely mysterious, mythical and quite scary. He was tall, held a belt around his chest that did not conceal the six pistols tucked within. A sword dangled from the sheath attached to the belt.

The man on deck pointed to the midsection of the boat. "They be down there, if ye want to talk."

"Come on now, Tully." He pushed the deck hand away, arrogantly strolling to the captain's quarters while Tully followed. It was a cramped walk down, and as he proceeded, he heard voices.

"I thought the reward was 200 pounds," one said to the other.

"Nay, it's only 100," the other replied, unashamedly.

Blackbeard threw the door open to the chamber, infuriated. "I heard ye! Why d'ye stop? 100 pounds it be, but *200* ain't enough to get me! Don't count ye money yet!"

Both men gazed in surprise, but then they calmed down, and the man from New York stood and spoke. "Teach, you old scallywag! It be ye! Well, well now." He patted him on the shoulder. "Now, ye have a Hollands—I been meaning to see ye on ye ship." He was visibly intoxicated and staggered as he spoke.

"Well, ye need not bother now; and I could take all ye Hollands if I feel fit to do so, Captain!"

"Now, now, Teach, there's no need of that. We have been friends for a long time. What makes ye speak harsh?" Captain Standard, the New Yorker, was a short man with some weight, wearing ragged clothing and an old, worn-out jacket. His head was wrapped in a kerchief. Captain Burley, the man from Boston, was dressed similarly, his suit soiled and a bandana covering his head—he also wore two large golden earrings, dangling loosely from his ears. He, as well as Tully, stood motionlessly while the others talked.

Blackbeard threw his right hand towards the east, pointing his index finger. "They're here!" he said.

"Oh, I see what you're talking about. You mean Maynard, of course. We've had the reports, but quite frankly, it was just a matter of time. The posters have been up on shore for a week. Won't you take a taste of Hollands, Captain?" He talked soothingly to ease the larger man's conscience, but his inebriation was predominant.

Blackbeard calmed down. "Aye, I'll have a Hollands and one for Tully, there."

"Of course, Edward. I'll fetch it m'self."

"Fore ye go, ye say ye heard the reports. What d'ye hear?"

The captain, who had begun to walk away to get the Hollands, stopped and lowered his head then sighed heavily.

"I won't lie—they mean to get ye! Spottiswood has a vendetta and ye be number one on the list! Maynard sent a scout out yesterday to look for aid in navigating the inlet, but no one would cooperate with him. The scout returned to his ship, marking the depth of the waters as he went. I hate to be so candid, but if I were ye—I'd take to sail!"

Blackbeard threw his hands to his hips. "I don't run! If they mean for a battle, it be a battle they get! I knew it was to be, but they can't maneuver through the shoals or the sandbars; they'll ground out."

Captain Standard rubbed his hand on his chin in thought. "I pray ye be right!" He turned back around. "Now, to get ye Hollands." He stopped once more. "Captain Teach?"

"Yay, what is't?"

"You came aboard this vessel for a reason, I must ask, what is it?"

Blackbeard smiled. "Tonight I go to a party. That will keep the Navy off guard. But tomorrow … tomorrow … ah, tomorrow. I want to speak with this fella from Boston. I've got a favor to ask."

Captain Burley blushed. "A favor from me?" he finally spoke. "What can I do?"

"I've got cargo aboard—*valuable* cargo! When me and Captain Standard go to the party, I'll have me lads take it upon your ship. I want ye to take it north, away from the Navy, and ye be rewarded by more than ye can think."

"Why me?" he queried.

"I know ye—ye be somewhat honest and sober; and 'cause your boat is sleek and quick. Ain't no way they're going to catch ye when they try to tangle with me, I'll hold 'em at bay. Besides, Captain Standard's ship is too slow. Ye'll get off with the wind and never look back. There's a spot I know."

Captain Burley stood still. "I am headed to Boston tomorrow and perhaps I could drop your cargo there."

Blackbeard became upset. "They'll *hang* ye in Boston if they knew ye knew me!" The recollection of the many pirates who were murdered in that city stirred warm blood inside of him. He approached the young captain. "This be important!" There was a certain fire in his eyes. "I have a spot north of Boston, east—downwind. Skip around the Cape of Cod and head to New Hampshire province, to the Isles of Shoals, off the coast. There ye find Smuttynose Island. It's just a rock, but I've got a fond following there and they'll take you in kindly."

The captain reeled. "I know of Smuttynose, near Boon Island, where it's told a ship wrecked and there was talk of cannibalism; all quite scary; and disgusting. Not to mention Smuttynose—some say that it's haunted. You want me to go there? What purpose is't? What's in this for me?"

"A fortune, you fool!" Blackbeard shouted. "I've got five chests in me fore, hidden and guarded. I'll have my men smuggle three on ye ship tonight, while we take in the party. They be watching me; the Navy will never know. Once ye get them aboard, sail with the tide and I'll meet ye at Smuttynose in one week to the day!"

"A fortune, ye say! Well, it's all very tempting. I know what's in ye chests and it ain't goods—t'aint cargo. It's plundered treasures. Again, I'll ask ye. What's in it for me?" He stood haughty now, knowing this was a last attempt from the pirate to save his 'cargo.'

"Ye get one chest when I meet ye."

"What's to say I just keep on, beyond Smuttynose, ye never see me again and that way I keep the lot?"

Blackbeard became infuriated. "Ye wouldn't dare! 'Cause I'll find ye! Then ye be one dead captain!"

The Bostonian smiled brightly. "I thought as much. What happens, though, if ye don't make it?"

"*I'll* make it! Take the cargo and I'll see ye in one week, ye hear?"

The captain pulled a napkin from his pocket. "It all sounds very attractive … and very dangerous." He wiped his chin with the napkin. "But I'll do it!"

"Aye, now, there's a good lad. I'll take that Hollands now, Standard."

"Certainly, Captain, I'm glad that's all decided." He had been standing by idly, listening. "We do have a party to attend."

"Aye, that we have." He looked over the Bostonian's shoulder, "Tully, ye be in charge of the transfer and ye'll have Peddigrew to help ye."

"Aye, sir."

Blackbeard turned back to Captain Burley. "I'll greet ye in the morn!"

"I will, Captain Teach. It's a deal! I'll take ye 'cargo'! Now let's raise a mug!"

"Aye! There be a battle tomorrow. But now I'll take a blackjack full!" He laughed. "Now, you!" He glared at the New Yorker. "Come to my boat and we'll take leave from there to that party." Then he turned to Captain Burley. "Ye stay here and watch over the transfer of the chests—and stay sober, ye'll have a long day tomorrow!"

"I'm not one much for the parties, sir," he replied.

"Good—'cause I am!" He pivoted around and left the cabin with Captain Standard shortly behind.

Chapter 2

Searsport, Maine—present day

The waves crashed off the edge of the small fishing boat owned by Kenny Buckner as it circled around the victim of his quest. He reeled at the rod leaning backwards. "Hold her steady, Rat—can't you see I got something big here?" He tugged on the end of his fishing pole while standing at the bow of the 30-foot-long vessel. The boat rocked sideways, into the waves. "And try to keep the keel running parallel to the ocean, you fool!"

The man he spoke to, Souharat Khatel; an immigrant from Calcutta, India, who was wearing a multi-colored turban and a formal suit including a tie and shoes, set the boat into neutral. He was short, slightly plump and reeked of curry. He had earned the nickname 'sewer rat,' a slight homophone of his name, in India, where he had planted insults and well-thought-out lies into other people's heads for personal gain or his own ambitions. He would talk about people behind their backs to make himself look better than they. In doing so, he was ostracized from his native country by his peers and came to America, where his shrewd and crude behavior could take advantage of others' misgivings. He was a true 'rat.' He had opened a small, flea-infested hotel outside of Belfast, Maine, and forced his family, including his two small children, to work in it for nothing. The profits were good enough for him to take vacations to India twice a year and for him to open another hotel. He had his brother come to the US to run that one, and now he was able to semi-retire. Fishing took place of work. He partnered with Kenny Buckner—a man very similar to him, deceitful and contemptuous. He was tall and of medium build and a hired thug. Money was his guide. In one instance, he was even believed to have been hired to kill for cash.

"What is it, sahib?" He tried to look in the direction of the line.

Kenny straightened up to pull with more energy and tugged, forcing the line taut. "Don't know. I can't see her, but she's a big un'." He pulled again, dropping the pole and whipping it back up into the air. He was wearing a brown cover-alls suit and an orange hunting cap. His short, shaggy beard flowed into the breeze. The 100-pound test lurched and he pulled again, reeling it in as best he could.

"I think it's a tuna, Rat!" He whirled the reel on the line again then set the base of the pole in the holder in front of the seat where he plopped down and buckled himself into the harness. "She's giving me one hell of a fight, whatever it is!" His face turned red. "Pull her to starboard, Rat—she's shifting on me."

Souharat pushed the boat forward then to the right. "What is it, sahib?"

"Can't tell yet, but it's getting closer." A form appeared on the top of the ocean, yards away from the ship. "Ain't no tuna, she ain't got no fin!"

Souharat peered over to the end of the line as Kenny tugged once more. "It's a seal!" he said. "You hooked a seal!"

"Well, I'll be damned, you're right!" He tugged at the line again and the seal pulled up to the edge of the ship. "Gaff it, Rat!"

He hesitated. "You cannot take in a seal, sahib! It is illegal!"

Kenny glared at him, "I said gaff it! There's an old saying: If *they* don't stop me, then *don't* stop it!"

Souharat set the throttle to neutral and walked to the end of the boat, pulling the gaff out from the side. "This is not legal, sahib!"

"Just gaff it, you fool!"

The seal got close enough for him to reach and Souharat jabbed at it until the gaff stuck in firmly. Kenny dropped the pole he was holding and pulled the creature into the boat. It was a small baby seal that he had inadvertently hooked into. It flopped around in the bilge of the ship as Kenny grinned. He pulled a buck knife out of his belt and quickly sliced the throat of the fish.

Souharat scanned the ocean where he could see two ships headed in their direction. "Oh, sahib, there are those who can see. This will be trouble!"

Kenny glanced around the sea. "Don't worry about it," he replied. "They can't see us from here. I'll take care of it!" He covered the seal up with a tarp he kept on board.

The first ship which approached near them held two crewmen—Todd Seekins and Bill Rowlin. They were jumping up and down inside their boat, whipping their arms in the air as they went.

The two men ran a small drag net fishing rig, used in the deeper waters of the bay and at the Maritimes. As they approached Kenny's boat, they were rejoicing. "We found it!" Todd screamed over to the other ship.

Souharat held the boat in neutral while they encroached, and Kenny covered the seal so that it could not be seen; even near its edges.

"Found what?" Kenny inquired.

"Our retirement!" Todd screamed back. Their rig, which was being steered by Rowlin, pulled up close enough to the other boat for them to speak together without yelling.

"Oh, really? How do you s'pose that?" Kenny asked.

"Lookee, see!" Todd held his hands up in the air showing off several gems, jewels and old coins, made of silver and gold. "We got our fortune!"

"Huh? What? What is that?" Kenny squinted, trying to see exactly what he was holding up.

Todd was young, maybe 20, if that. Bill, who owned the boat, was much older, but still a little naïve. Some actually thought he was a bit slow; mentally that is. Todd was tall and thin, trying to grow facial hair, and Bill was just a quiet old man of medium build, making a living off of the sea.

"Gems! Jewels! Coins!—and there are tons of it!" Todd reported. Both boats idled in the water, approximately 30 feet apart.

"Gems? Jewels? Coins? Where did you get that?"

"Found it!" Todd replied. "A sunk ship held it and when we were headed out to set our nets down, two of the nets dropped, unexpected; we don't even know how we dropped 'em. But we hauled the first net up and found this all tangled up in the string." He pointed to a large bell in the center of the boat. He threw his arms up in the air. "Woo-hoo!" he screamed, tossing the trinkets upwards and allowing them to fall inside the boat.

"So what? It's just a bell!" He stood mockingly, leaving the boat to guide itself, crossed his arms, and puffed his chest out with an uninterested expression.

Todd stalled in his movement. "Ain't just a bell. Lookee here." He held out his hand, full of the merchandise he was playing with. "It's a fortune! We couldn't raise the other net, so Bill here, he goes in the water to loose it off the rocks. When he comes back up to surface, he had this!" The man was ecstatic. "He told me he saw crates of it down there, full! He ripped the net off the rocks and now we're headed back to get the gear to haul it all up—all of it! Woo-hoo!" His hands closed around the precious belongings and he snarled at Kenny. "We're rich!" He threw the merchandise above his head once again.

Kenny became serious in a way, that he may be on to something he really didn't expect. "Found it, hey? Ain't you afraid you're going to lose it, you know, playing around like that?"

Souharat grabbed Kenny by the arm and whispered to him. "They *are* true gems, sahib, *and* jewels; *and* pieces of eight!"

Kenny turned around to him, and a strange look came over his face. "How do you know that?" he whispered. "And hold your voice down!"

He whispered back, "I have seen such coins and gems, sahib—in Surat, in India."

"In India?" They spoke low to each other.

"Yes, sahib. The monies were stolen from the merchant vessels and Muslim pilgrimage ships that traveled to the holy lands. It is a part of my history."

"Really? Then how did it get here?"

"It is pirate treasure, and one pirate may steal from another. There is no doubt of what they have found! The bell is one of a pirate ship."

Todd answered the question. "I ain't afraid of losin' it because there's too much of it to be worried! Bill took a dive and saw it. It's an old sunk ship, loaded with this stuff, just for our taking!"

Kenny lowered his head in thought then grabbed his chin. "Loaded with it, you say?"

"Loaded!" Todd replied. "We're rich! I ain't looking back at nothin'! This life's too hard. Finally I can relax and quit this lousy business and retire! Whoo-hoo!" He threw more of the coins up in the air, allowing them to land inside the boat.

Kenny contemplated with a silent stare into the water. "Who else knows about this?" he asked.

"No one—just you! We're gonna have a big party tonight!" The boat rocked sideways in the water as he spoke, a large grin on his face. "It's gonna be one hell of a party, I'll tell ya. You guys'll be invited."

Kenny licked his lips as the boat tottered in the waves. "No one else knows?" His facial expression changed to a pensive squint.

"Nope, no one.... Why?" Todd answered.

He removed his hand from his chin and relaxed. "Oh, nothing! I guess this moment deserves a picture. Let me find my camera." He looked all around the ocean and saw no boats close to them.

"Sure, sure, Kenny! That'd be nice. C'mon, stand up, Bill, and let Kenny take a shot." Bill acquiesced and stood up in a confused position, rocking with the boat as it went. "Sure ... sure," he said to Kenny. "That'd, that'd be nice!" He talked slowly, and stuttered.

"Okee-dookey, then!" Kenny reached below his seat in the front of the boat and pulled out a sawed-off shotgun. He drew it up to his shoulder and pointed it directly at Todd.

"Say *cheese*!" He fired at Todd, who held a stunned expression. The shot went true to its mark, hitting Todd squarely in the chest, and he fell backwards overboard into the water.

"That was a nice picture shoot, don't you think, Bill? Now *you* can say *cheese*." He fired again, hitting Bill firmly in the head, and he also toppled over the edge of the boat into the water.

Souharat stood up in a frenzy. "Sahib! Sahib, what do you do?!"

Kenny laughed, "Haha! Now it's MY treasure! Now *I'm* rich! To hell with them two idiots!" He placed the shotgun back below the cushion of the seat. "What's the matter with that, Rat?"

"Sahib, don't you see? They did not say where they found it. It could be anywhere! How will you find it?" He thought for a moment. "Plus, *we're* rich!" His cunning mind came to its obvious conclusion.

Kenny reeled in anguish, staring at his mate who spoke. "Damn, you're right! How stupid could I be?" He kicked the seat in front of him. "What was I thinking?"

"Sahib, your greed took away your intellect!"

"Oh, shut up!" Kenny was pacing about, disturbed.

"And there is more, sahib."

"What? What now?"

"The gun made noise that could be heard for a long distance. See, over there—that boat. It now is coming this way." He pointed in the direction of an oncoming vessel.

Kenny looked to where Souharat pointed. A small sailing vessel began to make its way towards them. A jib and mainsail boat; just a day-sailer. Its approach was slow, though.

"Quick, Rat, grab those coins out of their vessel and we'll be off."

"Yes, sahib. What about the bell?"

"The hell with the bell—it's too heavy!"

The mate did as he was told, juming over the edge of their boat and into the other, then groveled for all the loose coins inside. He hustled back over both rails and returned. "Quickly, sahib, it is getting closer."

Kenny squinted in the direction of the boat and covered his eyes. "That's Ed Crowley. He'll never catch us." He threw the engine into full throttle but still heard from the sailboat the voice echoing across the water.

"I saw that! I saw that, Kenny Buckner! I saw what you did! I'm goin' to the chief and let him know! You're a despicable man, Kenny. I saw it all and I ain't the only one, you know! I saw that even though I was a ways. No one likes you on these waters, anyways. You'll get yours, Kenny, you'll get yours!"

Kenny threw up his middle finger but never flittered. "We'll see about that, Ed!" He looked to Souharat and whispered, "Don't plan on going to sleep tonight, my friend. We have business to attend to!"

Souharat became nervous. "He spoke of others, sahib. What will we do? You know I do not want to be executed for this?"

"Like I said, I'll take care of it!"

CHAPTER 3

Ocracoke Inlet, North Carolina

Peddigrew ran down the steps to the captain's chamber and pounded on the door, violently screaming, "Captain, Captain Teach, wake up; they're coming! They're coming!" Blackbeard was a bit groggy, having spent the night with Captain Standard, drinking, dancing and carousing on shore. "'Tis too early, they can't be on us now—the tide ain't w'them yet."

"Captain, it's nearly noon!"

Blackbeard staggered out of his cot, still fully dressed, including his pistols. He picked up the sword and inserted it in the sheath on his belt. "Noon? I slept that long?"

"Ye be out most of the night, sir. Captain Burley is on deck waiting f'ye," Peddigrew spoke with a quivering voice. "The tide's high in an hour, sir. They be close to on us."

"Aye. Tell Burley I'll be right up. Get in here, boy, and fetch me my red shirt." He had worn the blue one all night long and still was wearing his shoes.

Peddigrew opened the cabin door and entered. He hesitated. "Why the red shirt, Captain?"

Teach blinked and stared at the boy. "In case I be hit, boy! So as they can't see the blood!"

"Aye, sir." He ran to the small opening at the side of the cabin and retrieved the red jersey, handing it to Blackbeard, who took it then picked up his triangular hat, holding it out to the pirate. Blackbeard received it in his right hand and placed it on his head. He removed his coat, shirt and belt then struggled into the red shirt and replaced his remaining attire.

"Let's go talk to Burley. How'd it go last night?" He walked to the cabin door and stood silently.

"It's all been done, Captain. The crates are on board his ketch, and he'll have a strong wind from the south today, but there be clouds formin!"

"Ah, the weather might be with us!" He stepped out of the door and walked the short distance to the steps leading to the top deck, Peddigrew right behind. Once he got on deck, Burley greeted him.

"Captain Teach, they be coming and I be leavin'. The weather looks too grim to stay much longer. See the horizon?" He took his hat off and held it in his hands.

"Aye, I see it. Ye be ready to travel now, then go! I'll watch ye back and hold the villains at bay."

"Aye, aye, sir. I wish ye luck."

"I'll see ye at Smuttynose in a week, and don't ye disappoint me!"

"Aye, Captain, I've got your 'cargo' on board." He looked out at the two vessels in the inlet. "Word is that they found the channel and will be on ye at high tide. I left a few of my crew on board to help ye. I saw 'em. They ain't got no cannon."

"Ah, yeah. Parker never thought of that. Ye be a good man, Captain. No cannon suits me just fine. They be at my mercy in an hour! Now, be along!" He placed his hand on the other captain's shoulder.

"Good luck," Burley said as he took leave back to his ship.

"Good luck is the skillful elimination of bad luck! Take Peddigrew with ye. He be a fine mate," Blackbeard replied with a smile.

"Aye, sir." He also smiled, and he and Peddigrew crawled down into the dinghy awaiting.

Blackbeard scanned the inlet. The schooner had her sails up and approached the first shoal. It rocked in the wind and teetered when it came to the shoal.

Tully pulled up beside the captain with his scope. "They be stalled in the sandbar, Captain," he said.

"Aye. Hand me that!" Blackbeard appeared much cooler than he had been. He pushed the scope to his right eye. "They be stalled, all right." He stared long at the ship. "There ain't nobody on her. She has no crew. I can see Maynard and his mate, but no one else is on her. Me thought is that she is a sitting duck! Fools!" The wind shifted and the boat lurched away from it. "Tully, call the crew! Have 'em set up at the cannon, the schooner be only a mile and a half away. If they reach the point, they may make the channel. Quick now, don't dally!" He had put the glass to his side while he spoke then pulled it back up to his eye. "Where's the crew?" he shouted.

Tully ran below deck and called for everyone to come to the top and take their position. The ship had a series of five cannon on the starboard side and five on port. Blackbeard paced along the deck, watching as they took place. "Crouch!" he yelled, waving his sword in the air. "The villains mean to have a fight, and if they get to me, they be the worst f'r it!" His voice was coarse and husky. "Take to it, now. I want every cannon loaded and waiting. No time now, the tide's arising." He ran back and forth, ensuring every one of his men held their post, until he came to one man who lit a pipe, staring off at the two vessels approaching. Tully stood obediently by his side. Blackbeard stopped when he saw the crewman with the pipe and looked at him directly in the face. "Ye know there ain't no smoking on this ship?"

The man slipped backwards, taking his eye off of the water and looked back at the pirate. "It's just a pipe, Captain."

Blackbeard pulled one of the flintlock pistols from his belt. "Ye Insolent dolt!" he said as he fired into the man's abdomen! The sailor reeled, then fell against the rail of the boat; quite dead!

Tully gasped and looked at the pirate. "What d'ye do that for?" he asked.

Captain Teach grinned widely. "'Cause if I don't shoot one of you now and again, ye'll forget who I am! Now reload that un'." He handed the pistol to Tully.

"Aye, sir, aye. I see," Tully responded in a mystical quandary, wondering how savage this man could be.

Blackbeard ran about, ensuring everyone was in their place. He took out the hemp from his jacket pocket and rolled it into his hair, beard and mustache. "They mean to come in, I be ready!" The mood became furious!

Lieutenant Maynard stood on the deck of his schooner as the boat hit the sandbar. His right-hand man, Baldwin, came to his side. "We've hit bottom, sir."

Maynard slouched. "Damned!" He contracted. "Are all the men below as I ordered?"

"Aye, sir. No one could see them from here," Baldwin explained. "But we be low to the water. This ship wasn't made for this battle, sir. They've means to fight, sir, and they have a strong crew. We've got no cannon!"

Maynard paused. "It'll make it, I'll make sure. The water ain't too rough but the weather comes again' us. Take time; patience is precious. They don't dare put up a fight with the Royal Navy. They'll give in. Hold her steady, boatswain!"

Baldwin grimaced. "Aye, sir." He returned to the helm while the lieutenant calculated the situation in his own fashion. He was a stately man standing short but erect. His hand fondled his own stomach, an attempt to quell a gastrological condition he suffered. His head was short of being completely bald, but he wore the garb of the Royal Navy Lieutenant he was. In some fashions he was stately, in some other way, he was obtrusive. He pondered the scene then yelled back to Baldwin. "Boatswain, come here!"

Baldwin stopped at the bow. "Yes, sir, what would ye like?" He was a young man for a second in command for the Royal Navy, but elegant and polite. He wore a commissioned cap and uniform, completely dressed in blue. "Ye asked f'r me?"

"Aye," Maynard responded. "I ain't waiting for the tide. Take everything that holds weight off the boat and toss it into the waters!"

"Sir? Toss everything, sir?" He seemed disarranged. "What be the reason?"

Maynard stood quietly, watching the pirate ship in the far distance. "Jetsam! All not worth keeping and some what is. It's weight, Mr. Baldwin. The less we have, the less we draft. Now, go!"

"What ye mean, sir? What do I have tossed?"

"The food, the crates, the rum, or the men who be disgruntled. If ye have to toss, toss it! Throw anything what weighs us down. Keep that what floats. I need to get over this bar then I can take on the pirate." Baldwin bowed his head and left knowing that what he had been ordered was true—it was the only way.

Blackbeard peered back into the telescope. "What be they be doin'?" He handed the glass to Tully, who stared into it in the direction of the schooner. He squinted once then looked again.

"They be throwing flotsam overboard. Their sail is raised and the tide is full!" He pulled the scope from his eye. "The fight is on!" He turned the scope to the inlet. The schooner had crossed the bar and was headed directly at the sloop occupied by the pirate.

"On ye guards, mates!" he bellowed to the full crew assembled on board.

"Maynard, that bastard! I knew it! He's losing weight and gaining strength. Hand me that piece and let me see where the ketch is. He should be off by now; off with me treasure." He grabbed the telescope from the crewman's hand and pointed it north to the horizon. "There he be—off, she's on her way and we be here!" The ketch had taken the strong wind well and was moving quickly north. "Well, that's done and I'm all the better for it." He looked back at the English ships. "Now, bring on the Navy!"

The weather was precarious for a ship to travel through the inlet, but Maynard had sent out a small with his boatswain to test the depths. He made his way around the shoals and the sandbars and was in a direct course for Teach's ship. The crew remained below and they had no knowledge of the activities above. Some speculated, though, knowing that their goal was the pirate vessel. The boatswain returned and gave Maynard the directions to the deepest part of the narrow channel. The ship managed through the inlet well within a couple of hundred yards of the *Queen Anne's Revenge*.

Blackbeard ran to the stern of the ship as the schooner approached, and climbed up on the aft mast ropes. He screamed in their direction, "Why d'ye be here?" He held a stern face as well as his hand on his sword. "Ye ain't got no right!"

The reply was from Maynard. "I have orders for ye to be arrested. Ain't me orders; comes from the governor of Virginia. Governor Spottiswood. It's all quite clear. I have a proclamation which has been scribed by the great governor himself. There's a reward for yer surrender and I shall generously give it to ye if ye surrender now! Ye be wanted dead or alive. It's quite a bounty been set." He embraced the collar of his vest then held out a piece of paper and waved it in the air. "It be an edict from the governor and I'm to enforce it." The ship rocked sideways in the inlet. The smaller sloop behind couldn't seem to find access to the channel.

"So what d'ye want, then?"

Maynard, never twitching or appearing out of order, calmly said, "Ye give me yer unconditional surrender."

Blackbeard paused. "For what? I have my papers, and if ye want to board, I'll show 'em to ye. I've a letter from George hisself and Spottiswood has no authority here!"

Maynard looked upward. "That won't be necessary. I've my orders. Either ye surrender or I shall be forced to take your sloop and your crew, by proclamation of the governor of Virginia!"

"The governor of Virginy? This be Caroliny."

"Fair or not, as it is, I have me orders," the lieutenant replied.

"Aye, so be it! I'll never surrender to that coward! Why don't *he* come here to arrest me?" Blackbeard climbed back off the ropes and onto the deck. "The fight is on, then! Tully! Tully!"

"Yes, Captain?" He took no time to arrive.

"Lower that friendly flag there on the mainsail and put up mine, the one with the skeleton, the hourglass, the arrow and the bleeding heart. The blood will flow! Then rotate the ship to starboard and fire cannon one!" he screamed.

"Aye, sir!" Young Tully ran throughout the deck, directing the crew. He had the flag raised and ordered the firing of the first cannon. "Fire one!" he bellowed.

The young boatswain behind the cannon pulled the chord, and the shot fired onto the oncoming threat, smoke billowing from the end of the barrel, engulfing the boatswain. The ball hit the ship near mid deck, and yellow splinters flew throughout the vessel, hitting the deck and wounding Captain Maynard.

"Cannon number two!" Blackbeard roared. The second blast left the ship, and it was enveloped in a cloud of smoke. "Number three!" His voice was coarse and hollow. "Tully!" he cried.

The man was not far away. "What it be?" he asked.

"Light me!"

Tully drew the book of matches from his jacket and lit the hemp in Teach's hair, beard and mustache. The man glowed like a jack-o-lantern on Halloween. He climbed back onto the spider ropes of the mast in the stern of the boat. "Spottiswood has no right to be here! He's a villain! Ye ain't got no crew, so how do ye s'pose ye can do it?"

Maynard stumbled with the explosions on board but was not seriously injured. He could barely see the pirate vessel through the cloud of smoke. "Perhaps he has no authority here, but I have a writ to give me the right to take you!" He held up his own script of paper. "Here, see this? It gives *me* the right!" He laughed indignantly.

Blackbeard grew ominously grim with his hair, beard and mustache aflame while he hung on to the aft rigging. "Ye be a fool, Maynard." His hair swayed in the breeze as the boat lurched with the water. "I've got thirty-five aboard and you have two. Your sloop won't make it in. Ye be mine for the taking!" He laughed a long and jocular laugh. "Hahaha!" He swung from one rope to the other until he landed back on deck. "I'll take over, Tully. Fire number three, and ye others reload!" The crew scattered about the boat, attempting to conform to their captain's orders. The cannon roared, and a blistering shot hit the *Cumberland* in her stern.

The schooner swaggered and reeled. Maynard fell against the railing, which only stood one foot up on the boat. The ship was not built for combat. After the last shock of cannon from the pirate vessel, Maynard leaned to his first mate. "Brookes, call the men up on deck!" Brookes ran below and ordered the men to surface. They came up boisterously, yelling and screaming. Blackbeard's face turned white.

"Damned rascal had 'em hid! Raise sails and head for her!" he yelled to Tully.

"Aye, sir, but now they be a crew to contend with!"

"I see 'em, ye fool, now go!" He reeled uneasily, unsure now of the enemy he confronted, then picked his hat off and scratched his head. He looked to the men raising the sails. "Full sails, gentlemen! We're gonna ram 'em!" The Navy's sails were only half full, still attempting to get through the inlet. The sloop couldn't make it and waited at the bar, bottomed out, while they sent a boat off to check the waters. The pirate ship was a bustle of activity, men running around, trying to man and reload the cannon.

"Fire all cannon when ready!" Blackbeard yelled in a frenzy. He was scrambling all around the boat, screaming at the crew. "Tully, get the bottles up here to throw—and the men to throw 'em. Quick now—we're on a collision course. Get all those with pistols on starboard and have 'em ready when I give the word! And Tully, where's ye scope?"

Tully ran wildly, back and forth, trying as best he could to arrange the crew, then he ran to Captain Teach and handed him his telescope. "I've the orders now to attend to."

"Aye!" Blackbeard said as he pulled the scope to his eye. He wasn't looking at the English Navy vessels; instead he looked in the direction of the ketch and watched it slither out of the inlet, unnoticed and oblivious to Maynard. He laughed loudly. "They made it, Tully! They made it out! Now it be our turn!"

Suddenly, puffs of smoke emerged from the English schooner, and Blackbeard staggered back, hit in the chest by one of the musket balls. He fell back, and down, immediately returning to his feet. Tully ran to him, "Are you O.K., sir?"

While he stood up again, he said, "I be fine. I'll see me treasure at Smuttynose. One shot ain't keepin' me down!" He rubbed his chest where the bullet hit, but as he had mentioned, the blood was impossible to see within his red jersey. "Send the bottles now, Tully!" he shouted.

Tully turned to the others on deck. "Now!" he screamed to the crew. They pulled up small bottles which once contained rum, but now they were filled with gunpowder and a fuse. They lit the fuse and tossed the "cocktails" at the enemy vessel. The bottles struck on the deck of the schooner, and the sound of broken glass was heard; flames emerged, causing the English Navy to panic. Shots went back and forth between the schooner and the sloop until the boats finally collided, but the English had maneuvered sideways and the wind was too much to negotiate, so the *Queen Anne's Revenge* shifted and hit the *Cumberland* broadside. A great crash ensued. The *Queen Anne's Revenge* got torn in the side and began to sink. The English boat was ripped in the mid section and it began to take on water as well. Another round of pistol fire was heard and Blackbeard was hit again, this time in the shoulder. Two wounds, and the battle had just begun. Blood flowed from both boats, but now the English sloop had made access to the inlet and was in position to aid its sister vessel.

The pirate ship and the English schooner were side by side and Blackbeard yelled to his crew, "Board her, boys! It be a fight by hand, now!" He pulled his favorite weapons, the two ancient *nimchas* (swords stolen from another pirate vessel), and flailed them around wildly. The crew, using grappling irons, hooked on to the side of the other ship, and now they had easy access to the English vessel, screaming violently as they crawled over the rails of both ships, man after man. They began fighting with swords and pistols with Teach screaming orders. Another roar of gunfire followed, and Blackbeard was hit once more, this time in the arm. He fell down against the forecastle hatch.

Tully, who had stood firmly by his side, considered him dead; instead, the grizzly pirate got back up in a whisker, dropping his swords and pulling out his pistols, firing wildly, killing many of those that had attempted to pillage his boat. He was slashed many times with sabers and eventually pulled off his jersey, making him naked to the waist, but of course, he held the two pistols, one in each hand. He was bleeding profusely from the neck, shoulders and chest. The ship was now completely on fire when Blackbeard, looking even more ominous with his shirt off and his long hair still in flame, came to face Maynard. The Englishman was quicker, and pulled the trigger of his flintlock before the pirate could react. Blackbeard was hit again, but only staggered slightly backwards, catching his balance, until another shot caught him in the back. Still, the pirate did not fall. Maynard had no time to reload. Teach raised one of his flintlocks to Maynard's head. "See ye in hell!" he screamed with a vicious grin, and an uncontrollable "Haha!" He pulled the trigger! The pistol had already been fired, and a quiet *click* was all that emerged.

At that point, he looked to the northern horizon and saw the ketch, off in the distance on her way to Smuttynose. He turned back around and whipped the weapon around to hit Maynard with the butt of the pistol.

Suddenly, one of Maynard's men came from behind, raised his broadsword high above Teach's bulky frame, and with one fell swoop cut Blackbeard's head off! Blood gushed from his neck! His head hit the deck with a *thud*. His body quivered until it, also, fell on the deck with a ghastly sound.

The rest of the pirate crew witnessed the gruesome death of their leader and decided the fight was done. They began jumping overboard, one by one, much in the same way they had come onto the boat. They swam for shore in the hopes of saving their own lives. The crew of the English Navy allowed them to escape as they called names at them and rejoiced in their victory. Soon, the other sloop had come alongside the schooner, which was sinking, and the captain called to Maynard. "We saw it, sir! Do ye need a hand?"

"Nay!" Maynard reported. "Except, we'll need a ride to shore!" He looked at Brookes, totally exhausted, then pointed to Blackbeard.

"Pick up the head and stick it below the bowsprit of the sloop!" He laughed. "We shan't have troubles with their like when they see that!" He wiped his chin. "Do what ye want with his body!"

"Aye, aye, sir." He motioned to two crewmembers. "Toss that lump overboard!" He chuckled proudly.

Chapter 4

Jonas Hale stumbled down the steps of his small cabin; the one which he called home. The steps were worn from years of neglect, and the walls showed signs of aging. It originally was only a hunting shack he had built a long time ago, until he married his wife and started a family, but since then, nothing had been done on the building, and it showed! The walls were peeling from the blistering heat of the summers and the frigid cold of the winters. The color of the wood changed due to indifference.

He held his head in his hands while he gained his balance on the railing to the stairwell. He moaned, "Elena! Elena! Fuh-kryin-out-loud! I don't feel so good! What happened to me last night?"

The aroma of freshly cooked eggs filled the kitchen at the bottom of the steps. She stood quietly in front of the woodstove, which provided heat as well as a spot to cook. She was still in her pink nightgown, standing tall over her workspace, her back to him. She stirred the scrambled eggs in a fry pan on the stove and glanced up at him with a pitied look. "Oh, Jonas, you drank all night long—don't you remember? Don't you feel it?" She was beautiful and petite, thin, very delicate, and also very tall.

His face was riddled with scars from the many fights of which he had been a part. His hair was long and uncombed, and he supported a long, shaggy beard. He pulled his hands from his head. "Oh, shut up! You never have anything good to say about me!" He shook his head around, in a vague attempt to get rid of the cobwebs from the night before, then fell onto one of the four chairs surrounding the table. His face was covered by his long, straggly beard, which was wrinkled from the salt of the many years he had spent on the sea. He grimaced at his wife. "What are ya cooking? I'm starved!"

"Breakfast!" she said. "Let me get the children up and we'll eat." She walked over to the bottom of the stairs as the eggs sizzled in the pan. "Chad! Katherine! Come on, now; breakfast is almost ready and we're going over to Uncle Steve and Aunt Julie's this morning."

She paced herself back to the stove then took a plate form the counter, in the bin by the sink where it was drying, and placed some of the eggs onto it. She picked up the spatula near the stove and scooped up the pancakes she had been cooking, putting them on the same plate. She set the breakfast in front of Jonas, who continued to rub his head. He looked down at the plate then up at her.

He ogled the contents of the plate. "What the hell is this?"

"It's pancakes, dear, and scrambled eggs." She returned to the stove. "It's breakfast, dear."

His face grimaced, and he pointed to the plate. "Breakfast? You call this breakfast? This ain't breakfast! Where's the meat? I ain't gonna eat this shit! I want meat on my plate, you useless bitch!"

She cringed. "Jonas, please, your language! You always behave this way when you've drank too much the night before. But please remember the children." She looked in the direction of the stairs. "You know we're on a budget. You know how expensive meat can be, and I didn't—"

"Shut up, *bitch*!" He picked up his plate and threw it across the kitchen, breaking the dish on the wall and allowing the food to splatter over the floor. "I'm tired of these excuses!"

She gasped, then quickly ran to the shattered mess and started to pick up the remains. "Please, Jonas, please, the children!"

"The hell with the children! I work all day while ya sit here on your lazy ass and watch soap operas. The children don't do shit!" He pushed his chair back away from him as he got to his feet. His balance was slightly off and he fell forward, catching himself against the sink, where he regurgitated violently. He held his head with one hand and with the other he turned the water on inside the sink to wash the deposit down the drain, then splashed the cold water on his face. He let out a long moan then turned to look at the meal still cooking on the stove. "No wonder why I get sick, look at this shit!" he screamed at his wife, then a wild look came over him. He spun around and swung his hand at her as she looked on in horror. The backhand landed firmly across her right cheek.

She let out a suppressed "Ouch!" then reeled against the counter. "Please, Jonas, no! Please, no! Not again!" she cried.

"Oh, shut up, woman!" He wiped the remaining vomit from his mouth and beard with the sleeve of his full-bodied long johns. He wore only the underwear and pair of jeans held up with suspenders. "What's the matter with you?"

"That's enough, Dad!" The boy stood on the bottom step of the stairwell. "I've seen enough!"

Jonas pivoted in the direction of the boy and laughed. "Well, well, well.

What are you going to do about it then, you little wimp?" He chortled in a derogatory manner.

The boy stood his ground. "You are *incorrigible!*"

"Huh? Incor ... incorrag.... What's that mean?"

"I saw you!" the boy replied. "When I see you treat mother like that, you make me want to reverse peristalsis, just like you!"

He stared at the boy. "What? What the hell did you just say? Reverse what?" He became more infuriated than he already was. "What was that comment?"

"I want to reverse peristalsis, Dad. It means that you make me want to throw up!" He spoke smugly and his father took it as an insult.

He moved towards the boy, who stood calmly, never flinching. Seeing this, he stopped. "If ya got to *throw the hell up*, then just say ya got to *throw the hell up*! What the hell is this reverse para ... para ... whatever the hell you said? Are you trying to make fun of me, boy? You think you're the genius. You and your book smarts! You don't know what it's like trying to earn a living, or keeping your kids in those fancy school clothes. You think money grows on trees?" His face turned flush as he went, becoming more irate.

Elena turned to him. "Please, Jonas, he's just a child, and he has to get ready, it's a long ride to Millinocket."

Jonas turned to face her. "Child, my ass! He thinks he's the man of the house, I reckon." He rubbed the long beard on his chin as he spoke. "If he wants to act like the man of the house, then he's gonna have to learn what it's like! Do you think I'm stupid, boy?"

The boy shrugged. "That speaks for itself, Dad."

He lunged at the boy and hit him with an open-handed slap. The lad's head spun, but he stood his ground.

Jonas leaned back. "You little maggot!"

"Jonas, please!" Elena yelled.

Katherine walked down the stairs as she said that. She was wearing a dainty new dress, completely blue, and her hair in ponytails, looking all of the fifteen years of age she was. Jonas glanced up while she descended. "What are ya looking at?" he shouted to her.

"You, Dad! Because you make me want to '*throw the hell up!*'"

He turned around and threw both arms into the air. "What a family I got! I get no respect! I work all day and ya all go about playing games and making fun of me. I'm tired of it!" He slowly turned towards the boy. "Go change your clothes." His voice was subdued.

"What?" Chad replied. "Why?"

Jonas grinned, "Because you're not going with your mother today, smarty-pants; you're going lobster fishin' with me!"

Elena took hold of his arm. "Oh, Jonas, why? They help me out there. You know how sick the two of them are. Steve is bedridden and Julie is going berserk trying to take care of him. They're both too old to take care of themselves."

"Well, why don't they hire someone? God knows they got enough money!" He pointed to Chad. "And that little brat thinks he knows it all! He needs to learn a trade, woman! All this school shit is making him a wise ass!" His disposition was tempered by his huge hangover. "You heard me, boy— now go!" He pointed his index finger in the direction of the stairs.

Chad excelled in his schooling, and this infuriated Jonas. School would be starting soon, and he thought it better to earn a living than learn nonsense that wouldn't help you later in life. He despised the whole institution, having an extremely limited education of his own. Probably because of this fact, he actually despised his own son. Perhaps it was jealousy—that Chad would make more of himself than he had.

For the first time that morning, Chad moved from his stoic stance and ran up the stairs, grabbing the rail as he went. Katherine stepped aside to allow him access.

Jonas calmed down. "There now, that's better! I'll show him how a man behaves, not like the little fairy he's turning into. He'll learn."

"Oh, Jonas!" Elena sighed, "You *are* incorrigible. Why can't you take him on the boat tomorrow, Steve and Julie both have a nursemaid coming in and they won't need us." She was at her wit's end.

"'Cause I'm meeting that fellow from Rhode Island tomorrow."

"Well, can't you take Chad along?"

"No! It's business, and we'll be talking business. I don't want that little shit fucking it up!"

"Jonas, please, your language." She had returned to the stove and fixed a plate for her daughter, then set it on the table across from where Jonas sat.

Katherine took the seat in front of the plate and began immediately eating. Elena went to the refrigerator and pulled out the carton of milk from the top tier, poured a glass for her daughter and placed it in front of her. "What are you going to do with this fella from Rhode Island?"

He placed his hands on his thighs and shook his head in mid air, bending over slightly. "This damned headache! Oh, I don't know. He wants to learn the ropes. He's one of them scholars or teachers or something. His school is paying for it. We got to talk the terms tomorrow. Ah, this damned headache! Do we have any aspirin?"

"Sure, Jonas, I'll get you some." Her expression was one of sadness. "You know, you really shouldn't drink so much."

"Oh, shut up! *You* really shouldn't *talk* so much! Just get me the aspirin." He continued to rub his head.

She went to the cupboard above the sink and located the bottle. Chad returned downstairs dressed in denim coveralls and a flannel shirt, wearing plastic boots up over his ankles. Jonas glanced over at him. "Now that's more like it. None of those sissy clothes today."

Elena shuffled to his side with the aspirin and a glass of water, handing them to him simultaneously. "Please, Jonas, try to be easy on Chad. He's not used to what you do! He is still just a boy, you know."

He set his hand out and took the aspirin then looked at the glass of water. "What's that for?" he asked.

"It's water, Jonas, to wash the aspirin down."

"Water! I don't need water. Water? Don't you know fish screw in it?" He placed the aspirin in his mouth and swallowed, using only his own saliva, setting the glass of water on the table.

"Oh, Jonas, please!" She shrank against the counter.

He turned to his son. "You better get a jacket on, it can get cool on the water. There's always a breeze." He coughed while the medicine went down his esophagus.

"Yes, sir!" the boy replied. He began to run back upstairs, but his mother grabbed him by the arm and whispered to him, "You don't have to go, if you don't want."

"But I want to go, ma!"

"You do?" She was surprised. "Why, then?" She released his arm.

"Oh, ma, I get tired of going to Uncle Steve and Aunt Julie's. It's so boring and they reek of an old, musty odor!"

She grinned with a sense of understanding that only a mother would have. "I guess so. A day with your father shouldn't hurt." She looked at him, concerned. "He'll be different in an hour or so. It's just that he's…. Well, he's…."

"I know, ma. I'll be all right."

She smiled and kissed him on the cheek. "O.K., then have a good time, but be careful!"

"I will, ma!" He smiled politely back to her.

"Where's my damned jacket?" The voice seemed to echo through the house. "I had it on last night! It's got to be around here somewhere." He poked into the furniture, hoping to find what he had misplaced the night prior.

"Oh, Jonas, I hung it up on the door to the linen closet. I didn't want you to misplace it."

He gurgled, "Yeah, that's how I lose things. You take everything away from me and put 'em where you think fit! It's all bullshit! Leave my stuff alone!" He went to the door of the closet and picked his jacket up. He had already put on a thick corduroy shirt then he turned his eyes to the boy.

"You ready?"

"Yes, sir!" Chad replied, anticipatorily.

"Well, let's go! I guess we'll just get a breakfast sandwich at the market on my way to the pier—at least *it* will have meat!"

She lowered her head. "Jonas, please!"

Chad ran out of the door as fast as he could, eager to go wherever. His father followed him out slowly, still massaging his head. The day was hot and the sun shone brightly. Chad hustled up to the passenger side of the old 1978 Ford pickup truck, placing his hand on the handle of the door. Jonas stopped near the door of the shack and cupped his hand over his eyes to block the sunlight, blinked and opened them precariously. "What are you doing, boy?"

He turned and responded, "I'm going lobstering with you, Dad."

Jonas shook his head. "There's more to lobstering than just riding in a truck and riding on a boat. There's work that has to be done!"

"Well, what do you want me to do?"

Jonas pointed to the shed. "I got bait and slickers inside there. Go fetch it. The bait is in the white buckets against the wall as you first get in, and the slickers are on those chairs near the back. You fetch those things, boy, and I'll get the truck and the boat ready." His hangover was abating, so he had become much more civil. The boy released his grip from the handle of the old truck and ran to the shed. He pulled the lock open and went inside. Although he had been in the shed countless times, he really never did know what was in those buckets. He never opened one, nor did he care to do so. He picked up two of the buckets and realized just how heavy they were. He struggled, bowing his arms away from his body as the buckets bounced off his hips; he still managed to get them to the truck.

"Man, those are heavy, Dad!" he huffed as he set them down. "What's in there?"

Jonas was adjusting the seats inside the truck when Chad approached. He laughed at the question. "You'll see, boy—it'll really make you want to go lobstering! Now, get the other two buckets and the slickers."

The lad hesitated. "Why do we need the slickers? Is it going to rain today?"

"How the hell do I know?" Jonas was visibly agitated.

"Well, don't you check the weather?"

"NO! I go out rain or shine—wind or no wind. Those assholes never get it right, anyway—I can't trust 'em. Just get the goddamn slickers and bring 'em here!" He leaned against the front of the vehicle.

"Yes, yes, sure, Dad." Chad ran back to the shed and quickly came back with the other two buckets of bait, set them by the side of the truck then returned to the shed, where he retrieved the slickers. Jonas was leaning over with his hands on his stomach. "Are you O.K., Dad?" he inquired.

He waved his hand in front of him. "Yeah, yeah, I'm fine. I've just got a little stomach ache, that's all. Here, I'll get those buckets, just get in the truck. I want to get out there early today. I want to check all my traps before tomorrow, that's gonna be a sightseeing tour." He went to where Chad had set the buckets down, picked them up and placed them in the small boat stationed in the back of the pickup while Chad threw the slickers in the back of the truck then climbed through the passenger's side door.

Jonas moaned loudly as he entered the driver's side and sat down. "Do me a favor, boy."

"Sure, Dad, what?"

"Reach behind your seat and pull me out a beer from that cooler there."

"A beer? Isn't it a little early, Dad?"

Jonas slapped his son's cheek with a quick, backhand motion. "Just do it!"

The boy sighed. "Yes, Dad." He got back out of the truck and pulled his seat forward, retrieving a can of beer from the cooler and handing it to his father, who opened it immediately and quaffed its complete contents, then threw the empty can behind him.

He looked at his son. "It's just to get the cobwebs out! A little hair of the dog, ya might say. Now, today, you're gonna learn what I do every day. 'Taint easy."

"Sure, Dad, sure."

It was nearly perfect a day to go on the bay—sunshine, a light breeze from the west and mild temperatures. The month of August was waning, and it could play havoc with the weather, but there were only scattered cumulus clouds in the sky this day.

Jonas attempted to start the pickup; an old, rusty model which most people would have junked by now, but not he. He attempted again, but the vehicle wouldn't cooperate. The third try proved just as fruitless. He pounded his fist down on the top of the dashboard. "Damned carburetor!" He got out of the truck, popped its hood, adjusted the choke on the truck manually then tried to start it once again. After a long series of near catches, the truck finally started with a loud bang as he revved the engine to keep it going, and maintained pressure on the gas pedal until the truck stayed running by itself.

Chad had sat through the whole ordeal silently. "I think you need a new truck, Dad," he finally spoke.

"Ah, shut up!" Jonas replied. Once the engine began to run peacefully on its own, he returned to the hood and closed it, ensuring it was latched down, then got back behind the wheel. "Now, let's go fishing!" He chortled to Chad.

"Sure thing, Dad."

The drive to Searsport was a relatively short one, and usually he could avoid the school buses, which could hold you up for the most of the trip. This day was no exception, and they pulled into the market within a brief period of time. Jonas got out of the truck, leaving it running, entered the store and returned with two sandwiches; one he had already opened and eaten most of, the other he handed to Chad. "Here, boy, it's better than anything your mother could make."

Chad looked at him with disdain. "Thanks, Dad."

They pulled away from the market and made their way to the Searsport pier. A cool breeze blew from the ocean when they backed onto the launch ramp, and the skies were blue above with only a distant, dark cloud formation approaching from the southwest. The old familiars stood on the dock; Samuel Edwards and Andrew Keene, leaning on the rail and gossiping together. They seemed to always be there, but they were never seen on a boat. "Mornin' Jonas," they both said in unison.

"Mornin' guys," he replied. "Anything happening out there today?"

"Nothin' much," Sam said. "But I see you brought help with you today."

Chad smiled brightly. "It's my first time out!"

The two men laughed together. "I remember my first time out. Had to be 1950, nah, nah, 1949 maybe. I was just a little squirt like you." Andrew leaned back in remembrance. "Them were the days!"

Sam tried to answer his question. "Just the regulars are out there now. I heard Kenny Buckner caught hisself a whale out there last week."

"'Twern't no whale!" Andrew interjected. "'Twas a dolphin. That boy won't let nothin' go. Kinda sad to see him kill somethin' for no reason. Just plain mean is all it is."

Jonas was lowering down the rowboat from the back of the truck, which he had backed into the water at the end of the launch. He stopped and looked at the two gentlemen. "You mean he kept it?"

"Sure did! In fact, he bragged about it," Sam responded.

"Don't ask me what he's gonna do with it. Eat it, I s'pose," Andrew added. "Or make perfume." The two men laughed together at the suggestion.

"How'd he catch that? I mean, he just lobsters like me." Jonas was a bit befuddled.

"He has a fishin' boat, too. He runs with an Indian fella, from India," Andrew explained.

"He harpooned it, I heard," Sam said.

"Shot it, I heard," Andrew argued.

Sam was a bit leaner than Andrew and had a white mustache, trimmed. He wore a red shirt and bifocal glasses. Andrew wore a blue shirt, blending into the colors of the bay. Jonas got the boat into the water and headed back up to the front of the truck. Chad had gotten out by then. "Did either one of you see it?"

Sam took the orange cap off of his head and scratched his white hair. "Well, no, didn't really see it, but that's the word!"

"When did he set that boat in?" Jonas asked.

"Oh, last week sometime. Said there ain't no money in lobsterin'," Andrew spoke.

Sam interjected. "It's the same boat, Drew, he's just fishin' off it now!"

"'Taint!"

"'Tis!"

The two men dressed alike—flannel shirts and denim overalls. They were the typical two old men from Maine.

Jonas got into the truck and shook his head. "Damned gossipers! Can't believe a word they say!" he mumbled to himself. Chad held the rowboat by the attached rope until Jonas parked the vehicle and returned.

"Get in, boy, and we'll be off," he said, stepping into the shallow water. Chad quickly jumped inside and grabbed a life jacket, placing it over him. Jonas pushed the boat into the water and looked back at the two old men on the pier. "That be about it, out there?"

"Ah-yup," Andrew responded.

Sam, who still had his hat off, spoke. "Well, no, there be more. You know them two fishermen, Todd Seekins and Bill ... Bill.... What's his name?" He looked for help from Andrew.

"Rowlin, I b'lieve."

"Ah-yup, that's it! Bill Rowlin. Well, they went out a couple a days ago and ain't never come back!"

Jonas looked at the two with suspicious eyes. "How do you know they ain't been back—you ain't here all day."

"Well, their mooring's empty, and it has been." Andrew pointed to the vacant buoy.

Jonas took the oars into his hands and began rowing to his mooring then looked over to where he knew the spot they talked of was. It was empty. For whatever reason, he rowed forward from the stern, while Chad sat in the bow, each facing the other. "That's strange, I ain't seen 'em either. I hope they're all right."

"Ah-yup!" The two spoke, again in unison. "Have a good'en out there today, Jonas."

"I'll try!" He looked to the mooring where Todd and Bill, men he knew well, kept their boat. He turned and talked to Chad. "You, know, they might be right; usually you can't believe a word those guys say, but then again, come to think of it, I haven't seen their boat in a couple of days. Maybe they went somewhere else to fish. It's getting kind of scarce around here these days."

Chad didn't know what he was talking about, he just nodded and grinned.

Seagulls soared around the pier in a swirling motion, catching the wind when possible, and landing on the land, rocks or the pier. The two old men, leaning against the rail, could be heard in the background, chattering to themselves.

"I used to lobster off a rowboat like that'n," one of them said to the other.

"Nah, you couldn't have."

"Sure, when I was a kid. Lobsters were bigger back then, y'know."

"They didn't even have lobster when you was a kid!"

Their voices faded as Jonas and Chad approached the mooring, but as they encroached, the laughter of the two old men was still audible, where only the sounds of the seabirds echoed. The ship sat low in the water and once they banked off her, Jonas signaled for Chad to get aboard. The bay was calm on this morning, and it was no effort for the boy to climb onto the deck. It was a simple vessel. It was an old wooden lobster boat.

Jonas took the rope from the bow of the rowboat and threw it up to Chad, who somehow knew what to do with it (simply hold on). He then lifted the bait buckets, one at a time to Chad. "Careful, boy, don't spill these." Even though they were heavy for him, Chad managed to get them to the deck, using both hands. His face grimaced as he placed the last one down. Jonas looked throughout the rowboat. "Where's the slickers?" he asked.

"I put them in the back of the truck."

"What the hell good are they there, now?" Jonas was perturbed. "You idiot! We ain't using them on the ride home."

"Sorry, Dad, I didn't know you wanted them in the boat."

"You don't know shit!" he stated as he climbed over the boat rail and stood up. "Ah, just as well, it don't look like we'll need them today anyway. I guess I'm to blame on that myself." He looked to the horizon and the sun, which had already painted a bright red sky in the east. His complexion had changed to one of semi compassion. "I know you don't do this every day. But you'll learn!" He patted his son on the head. "Now, let's get off this mooring and tie up the rowboat to the buoy. We can get started."

"Yes, sir, Dad. Sure, Dad!" The boy seemed enthusiastic. "Can I drive, Dad?"

Jonas grinned. "Maybe, when we get out there.... We'll see! First, ya gotta know what it's all about."

He pointed to the front of the boat. "That's the bow." He pointed to the back of the boat. "That's the stern." He pointed to the left side of the boat. "That's port." He pointed to the right side of the boat. "That's starboard."

The gestures reminded Chad of the sign of the cross. Perhaps, he thought, it was Jonas's self-administered absolution. "I know, Dad! I'm not dumb!" he replied.

They exchanged mooring lines from the lobster boat to the rowboat then he turned the key to the inboard motors, and they started without hesitation. He adjusted the throttle. "Damned boat runs better than the truck."

Chad took the seat beside him. "This is going to be fun, Dad!"

"You're going to work today. Ain't all fun!" He continuously looked over to the mooring where Todd Seekins and Bill Rowlin's boat was usually moored. "That's strange. Ain't like them, not to say nothin'."

He pulled out into the inner harbor and maneuvered around the others' lobster buoys. The sea was somewhat calm in this protected area where they were, but it could all change quickly once they got out in open water. Jonas knew this, and he took his time getting out to his traps. A strong breeze blew from the south, creating small white caps, which they could detect as they traveled along the inner part of the harbor. Clouds arose on the western horizon, providing a bleak glow of the sun there, and an ominous outlook for the afternoon. Jonas had 250 traps set, the most he was allowed by law, and there were four traps set on the boat where he had placed the bait buckets.

Chad sat in front beside his father but looked around the bay in fascination then glanced into the back of the boat.

"You gonna set these traps today, Dad?"

Jonas continued to pilot the boat towards the first set of traps he had set, near the red buoy at the entrance to the shallower water. "They're just spares, boy. I keep 'em in case one of the ones out here gets wrecked somehow. All we're gonna do today is pick up what's in the ones I got set and replace the bait if we have to." He looked south at the oncoming storm "We might just do it by hand this morning and cut the day short. It don't look good out there!" The clouds had strengthened and the sound of thunder in the far distance was audible. He watched the lightning hit off the coast of Isleboro. "It might be even shorter than I thought!" he said, watching the lightning strike the ocean. They arrived at the first buoy and he shifted the boat to neutral, grabbed the top of the buoy and pulled it up, handing it to Chad. "Pull this one up, boy." The boat began to rock as the waves slammed loudly against the edge of the boat. "I'll keep the boat steady."

Chad smiled, honored by the responsibility his father had bestowed upon him, and was anxious to see his first lobster catch. He tugged at the rope relentlessly. "It's awful heavy, Dad!"

Jonas kept his eyes on the incoming storm. "Just pull her up, she'll come up, I told ya it was work."

"Why don't we use the hauler, Dad?"

"'Cause I want ya to see what it's like to work for a living!"

Chad struggled but finally got the trap to the side of the boat and pulled it up to the washboard set on the boat and wiped his forehead in exhaustion. He looked closely while Jonas fumbled through gear under the steering wheel.

"Dad, I didn't know you put the bait on top of the traps, I thought you would put it inside."

"Of course you put it inside, what kind of a foolish question is that?" He stood, his eyes following the track of the storm, which was approaching quickly. "Now c'mon, boy, get her up here."

Chad looked again at the top of the trap. There were several crabs clinging on to whatever it was that rested on top. "The bait got out of the trap, Dad, and there's all kinds of crabs clung right on to it."

"Bait don't crawl out of the trap, you idiot!"

Suddenly, one crab crawled off and clung to the rope on the top of the trap. Chad gasped! It wasn't bait! It was a human hand, severed at the wrist! He fell backwards in horror and the trap fell into the water, instantly dropping down. He sat on the deck then crawled against the far side. "Da ... Da ... Da ... Dad!" He was in a slight shock. His voice trembled and he turned pale, his bottom lip quivering as he tried to speak.

Jonas turned around quickly and saw his son cowering. "What the hell is wrong with you? You little whimp, you can't take the smell? Then he saw the trap was not there. "You drop that? Are ya just that weak that ya couldn't hang on to it?" Damned, boy, what's your problem?"

Chad's hands trembled when he pointed to the place where he had pulled the trap up onto. "It ... it ... it ... it was a hand on top of that trap. A human hand!" He could barely talk and his whole body was shaking.

"Oh, bullshit, you pussy! It's just bait—mackerel heads, that's it! You gotta have a strong stomach and a strong back if you want to learn a trade, you little wimp! Damned, boy! I don't know why I thought you could make it out here. I shoulda known better, you ain't got the gonads!"

"But ... but ... but ... Dad, I swear, I swear. I saw it! I'm not lying, it was a hand—the veins were sticking out and there was blood. I swear I saw it!" The horror of what he saw abated and his fear began to subside while the color came back into his face. "Don't you believe me, Dad? I swear, I saw it!"

"Oh, shut up, boy!" Jonas walked to the area of the buoy while the boat idled and rocked in the waves. He leaned far out to grab the top and quickly pulled the trap up. The hand was gone! He turned to Chad, who still sat at the far rail. "Where's your hand, boy?" he said sarcastically. He opened the trap and pulled out three lobster stuck inside, throwing them on the deck.

The boy rubbed his eyes, "I swear, Dad, I saw it!"

Jonas laughed. "Yeah, sure! Go over there and open one of those buckets."

Chad shook his head in disbelief. Could he have imagined it; could it be he was seasick, or did he really see what he thought he saw? He was confused, but relieved that it was not still there. "It must have fallen off, Dad, when I dropped the trap. I swear I saw it!"

"Get up and open the damned bucket!" Jonas checked the bait in the trap, preparing to set it again. Chad got to his feet and walked to the buckets in back. He pulled and tugged at the top until he finally got it open.

"Whew! It stinks! What is this?" He gagged and stepped away from the bucket.

"It's mackerel heads. I told you, ya gotta have a strong stomach as well as a strong back out here. Now, is *that* what you saw?"

Chad leaned over to look inside the bucket with his finger pinching his nose to block the stench. "No, Dad!" he said, looking at the decaying fish heads. "It was a hand, I swear! A human hand!"

Jonas frowned. "I think you're seeing things, boy!" The rain had arrived and began to fall on them; the lightning came close to the boat. "Well, that's it, we're headed back in. Another damned day lost!" He walked back up to the wheel and spun it counterclockwise; they pulled around, headed back to shore. "A hand! God, boy! I swear you've spent too much time in school!"

CHAPTER 5

Off the coast of New Hampshire, November 24, 1718
The wind intensified, and the rain pounded down upon the deck of the small ketch which rocked mercilessly on the rolling seas of the great Atlantic. The ship shifted quickly with the ocean, and Burley fell sideways onto the starboard rail. "Peddigrew, Peddigrew, lower the mainsail!" he screamed, but the roar of the water drowned out his voice. The ship was designed for speed, setting high in the water with a square mainsail and three triangular sails still catching the wind, which had been behind them all the way from Ocracoke. The rear rig sail flapped uncontrollably with the storm; it was built to adjust to the shifting winds, but this was more than it could handle. The wind had grown too strong now, and Burley was in a frantic effort to lower them, but the men (he had only six aboard, since he left part of his crew with Blackbeard to help fight the English Navy) never heard the orders. He, himself, had trouble keeping his balance. Peddigrew tried to run up to his aid, but stumbled and fell, slipping on the water that had covered the deck at this point; his body rolled into a ball and he shifted with the rocking sea. He slid across the deck and banged his head on the side of the ketch.

"Peddigrew!" Burley yelled again, covering his face and head from the gale winds. "Where are we, Peddigrew?" His hat blew off his head and flew into the sea. The rain whipped violently upon his body as he tried to find the navigator. "Peddigrew, where be ye?"

The young mate got back to his feet with a newly found lump on his head, which he rubbed. "Captain, I be here!"

Lightning cracked near them, and with the light, the captain caught sight of him. He stumbled to greet him. "Peddigrew, where be we?"

"Can't tell ye, sir. The storm has blown us off course. I can't even tell ye where the shore is. It's time to drop sail and ride out the storm."

"Can't ye see, that's what I'm trying to do. Now, get the crew together and lower these sails. I can't see a bloody thing out there!"

"Aye, sir, I'll try." He rubbed the wound on his head and turned back to Burley. "We got over twenty foot seas if there's one. We ain't gonna make it, Captain."

Burley's jacket was flailing in the wind, his hair blowing all about. He pondered that statement. "Get those what guard the treasure and bring 'em up here. It's every man on deck, the treasure's no good to us if we don't survive and there ain't nobody gonna steal it in this weather! See to it!"

"Aye, aye, sir!" Peddigrew attempted to get to the door leading to the below deck, but a haughty zephyr whisked him back. When he tried to gain his balance, a shot of lightning hit the deck and the whole ship shifted wildly from a sharp gale wind. He fell once more, this time banging his head against the rail, knocking him unconscious.

"Peddigrew!" Burley screamed. "Get up, there's no time to dally! Quick, boy." He stepped over to where the navigator lay and saw his condition. "Damn!" he said to himself. Waves splashed over the rail and then the rail itself went under water. The shock was enough to throw Burley onto the deck.

The sails remained up. One crewmember ran to the captain; a slender man, probably in his early twenties. He fought with the wind until he reached the captain. "We're well past Smuttynose, and with this storm, God only knows where we be headed. What do we do?" His countenance was full of fear and speculation.

Burley got to his feet. "Drop the damned sails, you idiot, or we'll be awash!" He blinked in an attempt to control the pounding rain running into his eyes. "Do you know then where we be?"

"Past Rockland, way past New Hampshire territory. It be Indian land here." His jacket blew open as he spoke.

"How d'ye know?" The torrential rains tossed the two men back and forth.

The mate pulled his jacket into his chest. "I'm from Stonington—I grew up there. I know these waters. Why d'ye have that boy try to lead the way? Didn't make no sense. He's just a lad and I'm proven up here." He pointed to Peddigrew, who never got up after hitting the rail. The wind whipped again and the two men wavered. The raging sea came over the rail again, and Burley slipped on the wet deck. The ocean rumbled and shots of lightning danced around the boat.

"Can ye get us to shore?" the captain asked.

"Aye, sir, but it won't be easy. There be islands everywhere plus rocks out there and I can hardly see. But there be a harbor just north that'll take us out of the wind. We ain't got much time!"

"We've got to lower these sails, 'fore it takes us to the rocks." He watched the cumulonimbus clouds flying overhead, sending out the thunder and lightning. "Lower those sails and we'll row to shore!" His voice was strained from shouting, and he was drenched.

"Aye, aye, sir." The mate tried to walk towards the bow to get another sailor to help him lower the sails, but a large wave crashed into starboard side and the boat tipped, putting the port side into the sea. The wind kicked again and the main mast snapped in two, bringing down the mainsail. The top piece tumbled to the deck then rolled along until it went overboard, the sail with it. The boat shifted in the other direction as waves pounded its side. Burley fell down. "Well!" he screamed. "Guess ye don't have to lower the sails now!"

Suddenly a voice was heard from the bow. "Land Ho! Land Ho!" The sound was muffled by the vicious onslaught of the storm.

"Ey?" Burley screamed back. "Land? Where be it?"

There was no response but it didn't take long to find out. A bang jolted the ship and a loud crash was heard. She had hit the rocks on port side. The men began to panic and run about the deck. Even the guards who had come up from below dove into the roaring tide. The hull of the ship had split near the bow and she toppled over, listing to port.

Burley tried to stand up but was unable. "Where be we now?" He attempted to outvoice the storm.

The sailor heard him as he clung on to the cabin entrance as the ship began to sink. "We be in Penobscot Bay. I see Isleboro. It'll only take a minute or two to be lee!"

Burley screamed his last order, there, lying on the deck. "We ain't got a minute or two, lad! Every man for hisself!" Another bang was heard and the ship bounced from one rock to another.

It didn't take long for the whole crew to face the cruelty of a nor'easter and the blazing brutality of the Great Atlantic. The ship sank quickly; sideways and then capsized.

None of the men were ever heard of again. The boat took the swell and tide along with the undercurrent of the ocean close to shore where she came to rest against a rock. The break near the bow allowed the three chests, the ones that had been so carefully guarded, to fall out of the boat and land harmlessly on a small rock formation, away from the vessel. The top of one opened, and a portion of the "cargo" fell to the ocean floor. The ship, which crashed relentlessly against the rocks on the bottom of the sea, was thrashed around so viciously that it was completely destroyed.

Chapter 6

The breeze blew throughout the row of trees aligning the driveway of Charles Ritter's house while he stood on the porch and kissed his wife, Janet, goodbye. She handed him the lunch she had prepared. She was still in her nightgown; it was 6:00 a.m. He thanked her and approached his Ford minivan, then stopped by the edge of the dooryard and glanced over to where the white ash tree once stood.

The lawn was mowed and the small garden beyond the row of trees was immaculately weeded and bloomed. It was often that Janet would be seen there, weeding, watering and pruning the flower garden. Some would say that she was extremely particular and a perfectionist in her efforts.

He bowed his head in discomfort. He had planted that ash tree two years ago for his youngest daughter, who he had named Ashley; the tree was installed as her namesake. Two other trees overshadowed it, an oak and an elm. The couple had three children named Ashley, Oakley and Elmer. The two Ritters were fascinated with botany, and they planted the trees for each of their children when they were first born; to watch the trees grow as his children grew.

But Ashley fell sick with pneumonia just after her birth and she died shortly thereafter. The devastation of losing her to childhood illness enraged him so much that he cut the ash tree down. He lost himself in a form of self-pity.

He rubbed his head in remembrance. This was part of his morning ritual prior to going to his job. The guilt, for no real reason, reverberated through his body every day.

He was wearing a blue three-piece suit and a yellow tie, square glasses, and a short crew cut hairdo. He was somber as he opened the door to the minivan, his head still low. The van started immediately, as always, seeing it was nearly brand new, but as he backed out of the drive he had to stop and look at the stump which remained from the tree he had removed. His thoughts drifted back. He lowered his head once more and said to himself that he would never see a child in danger ever again in his lifetime.

He continued down the drive from his house situated just off Matunuck Beach in South Kingston, headed to his office at the University of Rhode Island in Providence. He could see Block Island from his living room and hear the roar of the ocean constantly. It helped him get to sleep at night. The weather was warm today, so he rolled the window down slightly as he went. The ride was a long one, about two hours, depending on traffic. It was a clear day and the traffic was light, thus he arrived in Providence earlier than usual. He pulled up to the parking lot at the University of Rhode Island's Chafee Social Science Building. It was a tall structure that was built in 1972 and named after the famous Rhode Island senator. It had been closed for a short time in 2000 when testing confirmed elevated levels of PCB's (Polychlorinated Biphenyls) in the soils outside the building. The ducts and surfaces were cleaned out shortly thereafter, and the building was reopened. Charles had an office on the second floor.

As he entered the parking lot he was greeted by a short, stalky young man with pimples and a thin mustache. Ben Smith was his name; a graduate student who worked in the office of the dean in the College of Arts and Science. He usually just made photocopies, answered the telephone or did little odd jobs for the office. He was working there now because the secretary wouldn't show up until the school was officially opened. It was part of a work study program established at the university to help offset tuition. It seemed a bit odd for him to greet Charles in the parking lot.

"Charlie, Charlie!" He was panting from exhaustion. In shape—he was not!

Charles rolled the window down completely as he placed the car into park and turned the engine off. "Hi, Ben, what's gotten into you?"

"Hi, Charlie. It's the dean; He wants to talk to you. Oh, man, we tried to call you all day, yesterday, but you never answered the phone."

Charles pondered the comment. "I must have been on the Internet, then. I was doing some research. What does the dean want to talk to me about?"

"I'm not sure, but ... but...."

Charles stepped out of the car, picking up his valise from the passenger seat and the lunch Janet had made for him. "But but what?" He was a bit nervous to hear the answer; the one he actually anticipated.

Ben bent his head to the side and struggled for an easy way to say what he had to say. "Well, Charlie, I really don't know, but you know how small your class is? You only had twelve students signed up for it."

He shut the door for Charles after he had gotten out. "So what?" Charles asked. "That's allowed; it's the minimum class size, still it's allowed."

Ben shook his head. "Two of your students that were signed up called and transferred their transcripts to different schools yesterday. One student just quit school. I think the dean is going to cancel your class!"

"Cancel it? They can't! I have developed a full syllabus. It was all approved." He grimaced. It was late August and classes would be starting in less than a month. He had worked relentlessly to establish a complete curriculum for a new branch of study for the university, and to cancel it would devastate him.

"That's the reason that they can. You haven't started yet and all the other students can change into a different course now. If the university continued your class, they'd have to take a beating on the low number of students and little tuition they received. They can't afford it. The other students need to be notified so they can change courses. I'm sorry, Charlie, but I heard them talking. You'd better just speak to Dean Groton. It don't look good, Charlie. I'm sorry."

Charles slammed his hand on the roof of his car. "Damn!" he exclaimed. "I was afraid of this. Damn!" He slapped his hand down once more then began to speculate about his future. He had devoted his life and education to the study of history, and when he was unable to find a good job, plus living in Rhode Island, he decided to study maritime history. He got his Ph D at the university where he believed he would be working, then soon got married, and had three children. From the acquaintances and contacts he knew, he got a job teaching there by petitioning the university board. Although classes didn't start for nearly a month, he came to the university to prepare for it. He was understandably upset. He knew Dean Groton well, being one of the men who trumped him up to get him aboard. This would be a tough, emotional meeting for him. He slammed his hand down on the top of the car once more. "Damn!" he said and looked at Ben. "Is the dean in, this early?"

Ben nodded in the affirmative and spoke, "I'm sorry, Charlie. I hope it's not what I think."

The fact that Dean Groton had shown up this early was very uncommon. Charles sensed the worst. The dean only came to the university once a week or so prior to the start of school. He felt, now, something was going on.

Charles smiled at him and patted him on the back. "It's not your fault, Ben. It was kind of crazy of me to think this class would sell." He sighed heavily. "I guess I'll go see the dean and find out exactly what he wants."

He saw the student's expression of sorrow. "It'll be all right, Ben. It's just a thing!" Ben gave him a reassuring smile back. Charlie regained his composure, and the two men walked towards the building before them in total silence. For the entire walk to the building all Charles could think of was how would he tell Janet. He was working odd jobs prior to being approved for this one, but it was exhausting on him. The wages were extremely low and forced him to work two or sometimes three jobs at a time. Due to that fact, he felt that he was neglecting his family, except for his financial responsibilities. He dreaded returning to that lifestyle. He counted on this position, but he still worked a night job. The pay was minimal. The money he would make teaching wouldn't be all that great, but it would pay the bills and they could put a little away for the future of their two remaining children. How could he make the payments on the house? The children had gotten used to their schools and he felt it would be difficult if they had to move. And move where? His parents lived in Indiana, and Janet's were in California. He struggled with his thoughts until the arrived at the door, which Ben opened for him. The dean's office wasn't far from the entrance, and they arrived at it in no time. Ben went in first to the reception room, where he worked, and politely pointed Charles to the door to the office of the dean, although it was not necessary; Charles knew it well. He walked past the secretary's desk, where Ben sat down. The regular secretary wouldn't even arrive until the start of school. Ben did all the secretarial work for the department in the meantime.

He became depressed, anticipating the worst. He knew that his idea of a course on nautical history was a shot in the dark, but he had decided to give it a try. He hesitated in the office in front of the door before knocking, the thoughts still rumbled throughout his mind. It all seemed so glum.

"Good luck!" Ben said.

He turned around. "Yeah, sure. Thanks, Ben." He adjusted his tie while he walked to the door and then knocked on the dean's door.

"Yes?" came the voice inside.

"It's me, Charlie Ritter, sir. I heard that you would like to talk to me." He waited patiently for a response.

"Oh, Charles! Please, come in."

He opened the door and stepped inside. The office was as large as they get at the university and Dean Groton was one of the nicest people he had ever met. Still, he felt down—he knew it would be as hard on the dean as it would be on him to dismiss him. "Good morning, Dean. You're in quite early today." He was at a loss for words.

The dean was an old man, approaching his eighties. His hair was completely white. He wore a smart, blue suit; it was old and wrinkled, but clean. His face was creased from the years, and dotted with brown age spots. He wore a red tie, which contrasted the suit, but he seemed pleasant this morning, not like a man ready to sack the man he spoke to. He held a broad, sincere smile.

"Come in, Charles, come in and sit, please." The dean stood up and pointed to one of the two chairs in front of his desk. Charles, holding his valise and lunch in his hands, quietly sat in the seat to the left. The dean sat back down in his upholstered chair behind his desk and adjusted the trifocal glasses on his face then glanced down to find the papers he wanted. He peered up from the papers. "Charles, I tried to get a hold of you all day yesterday."

"Yes, sir, Ben told me." He squirmed uncomfortably. "I must have been on the Internet, doing some research for the new class."

The dean grunted, "I see." He looked down at the papers on his desk. "That's what I want to talk to you about."

The atmosphere was awkward. "Ben told me that, also, sir."

"I'll be blunt, Charles. Your proposed class won't float. We have not enough interest in it. I'm afraid we must cancel the whole program." He dropped the paperwork he was holding and leaned back into his chair.

It felt as though a dagger had been jabbed into Ritter's chest. His face dropped. "I was afraid of that, sir. I thought I could give it a go. I believed it would be successful. I was wrong!" He drooped down in the chair, in shame.

"Now, now, not so glum there, Charles. I'm not finished, yet."

He straightened out. "Sir?" he said.

"Well, first of all, you know this is not my decision. It was decided by the board."

"I realize that, sir, but still...."

"Well, I can tell you I do have some pull with them. I couldn't convince them to maintain your class, but I did a little thinking."

Charles blinked and then squinted. "I'm not sure what you are getting at, sir."

"I'm fond of you, Charles. I convinced the board that it would be a waste to remove you from the university. You are too good a scholar. I've been going over some paperwork here in a survey we performed." He shuffled into the vast amounts of folders on his desk. "It seems that the students are not all that interested in nautical history. Instead, they would like to have a course in actual fishing and lobster fishing. The university has a research facility at Wood's Hole which does mainly work on the ocean, the sea life, the plant life at the bottom of the ocean floor and similar studies. It's not really part of the school, but I've talked to the people there. They seemed anxious to have students learn the history of navigation, shipbuilding and the maritime. It's all here; the university appears interested, Wood's Hole seems interested and I sincerely believe that the students will be interested. I have some letters already. I've thought it over and I and the board came up with a resolution."

"A resolution, sir?"

"That's right, a resolution."

"What are you saying, sir?" He looked befuddled.

"You could teach a class in fishing, the history of fishing and lobster fishing along with maritime history. We'll take it one step at a time. I know, personally, that you have very little experience at either fishing or lobster fishing. I've convinced the board to get you some. With your history background and a bit of practical knowledge, I think we will have a course awaiting you when you return." He placed his elbows on the desk and rubbed his hands together then smiled in a comforting way.

"Return, sir? Return from where?"

The dean remained in his position. "We have nearly fifty students who would be willing to take a course in such studies. I will need to notify them that it will be available. I also convinced the board to set it up. You will travel to a mid-coast section of Maine for two weeks to prepare your curriculum, that is, if you are interested."

Charles stared at him. "I need to pay the bills, though, sir. How could I do that in the meantime?"

A wide grin came over the face of the dean. "You'll be on a paid sabbatical. I talked them into it. We've contacted a gentleman with whom you will work with. His name is … um … um…." He opened the middle drawer of his desk and pulled out a piece of paper. "Jonas. Jonas Hale. That's it. He's a lobsterman and will show you the daily grind that's involved and teach you the ropes, so to say. After that, we'll have you hook up with a local fisherman up there and learn that trade. They agreed that we will set you and your family up for two weeks in a hotel there. In the meantime, I will have Ben send out letters to those interested students to build a new class structure. I'll need your input while you are there to 'tweak' the syllabus. If this works out, Charles, who knows? You're a bright man, Ritter, and I don't want to lose you. It's the best for all involved."

Charles relaxed to some extent, but was still confused. "Maine, sir? Why Maine?"

The dean laughed loudly. "Where else do you go to learn how to lobster? You see, at this university, our objective is to give the students the best possible *experienced* knowledge we can find. You possess an affinity for the written word, but you've never gotten your hands dirty. The hotel will be paid for and your salary will be covered so that you can still pay your bills. I know the financial difficulties you are in now. After that, we'll see what you are learning and how your class takes shape." He suddenly became very serious. "It's your only hope to remain here, Charles! I stuck my neck out for you. Now, what do you say?"

Charles leaned back in his chair. "Sir, it's something I should talk over with my family, but I have little choice." He thought for a moment. "Where in Maine is this?"

"The man you meet goes out of a town called Searsport. It's rural, but it also has a maritime museum you can visit. It is supposed to have produced the most retired sea captains in the United States—or at least something like that. It actually has quite a history."

Pausing for only a second, "Then, I have no choice, I'll go!" He smiled and stood up. The dean also stood up and stuck his hand over the desk. Charles placed his valise in the same hand as his lunch and they shook hands.

"Then it's decided! I'll have Ben set up the hotel for you today and give you the instructions on how to contact this first fellow. Before you leave, I'll give you all the details. I'm glad you agreed. I hate to see someone with your talent fall by the wayside. I will give you a day to get ready and pack, but you will be off the next. Remember, school begins in less than three weeks, so be brief and keep your ears and eyes open. Who knows, you might even have fun!"

The two gentlemen laughed together.

"Thank you, Dean Groton, for another opportunity. You really are a friend!"

Chapter 7

Charles received his itinerary from Ben just before he had cleaned out his desk with the necessary supplies he would need to build the syllabus for the new course. Once he received them, he decided to head back home and break the news to Janet. He wasn't certain how she would take it. She was not one for changes. She had her garden and the children, and she might not like the idea, he thought. What else could he possibly do? He would be getting paid, which he wasn't getting now. She couldn't argue too much, he figured.

He drove well over the speed limit, being slightly excited. His first thoughts about being terminated at the university had turned to those of anticipation. The ride took him less than an hour and a half. He pulled into the driveway at his house, and Janet was outside in the garden, weeding. He beeped to her, and she waved to him then stood up. He turned the vehicle off, exited, and motioned for her to come over. She put down the spade in her hand and walked gingerly to the van. Even while working in the garden, she still looked beautiful. Wearing a kerchief in her hair, tied in back, and a pair of jeans with a sweatshirt made no difference. She ran to him and gave him a kiss. "Oh, Charlie, the garden is coming along so well!"

He stood erect while they kissed, then he glanced over to her garden. It couldn't have been any better. There were rows of red, yellow and white petunias; lines of red and yellow cosmos; irises of blue and white; overshadowing them all were the rows of red and white rhododendrons. He glanced back to the missing ash tree. The contrast of beauty in the garden and pain from the memory of why the tree was no longer there stirred him. He then turned back to face her.

He held her by the shoulders, "Where are the children?" he asked.

She took the garden glove off her hands. "They're inside," she replied, "Oakley is sleeping and Elmer is watching television, why?" She pulled the kerchief off her head and shook her long hair, letting it fall loosely around her shoulders. She could detect that there was something on his mind. "What's the matter? You don't look yourself." His forehead wrinkled with concern. "Is it the university?" she asked.

He smiled. "Yes, yes, it is. It's nothing bad, though. We'll talk inside. I want everyone there."

She put her hands on her hips with the gloves and the kerchief. "They cancelled your class, didn't they?"

He released his grip from her shoulders. "Like I said, we'll talk inside." He walked towards the house while she stood there pondering the possibilities. Eventually, she followed him inside, anticipating the bad news. She recalled the days when Charles worked three jobs to support her and her children. She rarely saw him and it was a very difficult period of her life. She had been the one to finally convince him to go to the university, and try to set up a syllabus with Dean Groton. She met Charles at the university, where they both attended, fell in love and got married, while still in school. After getting pregnant with Elmer, she dropped out. Charles graduated and obtained his Ph D while still holding down two jobs. She didn't want to face the possibility of their having to go through never seeing him, now, to work odd jobs. They both went into the kitchen and sat at the table. The house was humble but cozy. It was simply decorated, and it was quite a struggle for her to keep the place clean, with two children to tend to, but she managed.

"Tell me now, Charles, did you lose your job?" She looked at him for comfort, but with soothing eyes.

Charles didn't hesitate to speak. "No, no, I didn't lose my job, but they did cancel my class."

"What's the difference? Without the class, you don't have a job. I felt it, Charles!"

"Wait a minute! Dean Groton has given me a chance to start a new class. It would be a mix of history, practical fishing and lobster fishing."

She shrunk backwards. "You don't do either! How are you supposed to teach a class on that? What do you know about fishing or lobster fishing? That's absurd!"

He paused. "He wants me to go to Maine and learn."

She grunted. "Oh, great! We have to move?"

"No, no. I'll be going there by myself and staying at a hotel. He gave me the connecting people to contact. If it all works out to the satisfaction of the board, I'll have a new syllabus and a job. It's worth a shot!"

"Maine? How long is this for?"

"It's only two weeks. I'll call you every day. Janet, it's my only chance to hold a position at the university."

"Two weeks!"

"Just think of it as separate vacations. It's really not that long." He smiled, begging for her acceptance.

She turned her head sideways. "What about your other job?"

"I've already quit. I let them know this morning."

"That's just great! What are we going to do until you start teaching?"

"I talked to Dean Groton. He's got me on the payroll starting tomorrow. It's more money and you know I want to teach."

She grinned and leaned on one elbow. "Well, I guess." She sighed. "I know how much this job means to you, butI don't think you can refer to it as separate vacations. I still have the kids, and I'm still here." She thought for a moment. "But I do have my garden. I guess it's O.K." She turned around to look at him. "When does this all take place?"

"I'm headed up there today. Dean Groton wanted to give me another day, but I want to get this over with. He also wanted you and the children to go with me, but I didn't think that would be a good idea. He's already made the arrangements with the hotel and with a guy I'm going to meet tomorrow morning. It's only two weeks, Janet."

She shook her head. "You're a beauty! You're a real beauty! You could have consulted me about this first." Her emotions conflicted. "Well, I suppose. All right, then, I'll get you packed and say goodbye to the kids."

He drove along quickly. It was Wednesday, closing in on rush hour, and the traffic in Providence could be brutal, but Boston would be worse. He made good time, though and with only a few minor delays—mainly construction on the Maine turnpike—he arrived in Belfast, relatively late. It was dark when he checked into the hotel on Route #1. He was tired and went to bed immediately after receiving the room key and dropping his luggage on the floor.

The morning was overcast when he awoke. He had to meet Jonas at 7:00a.m. and got the wake-up call he had requested at the front desk at 6:00a.m. He took a quick shower and fumbled through his baggage for a change of clothes and his valise. He got changed and fumbled through the valise for the directions to the Searsport landing area. He had reasoned that it should only take him 15 minutes or so to get there. He got into the minivan and headed down Route #1. The temperature was comfortable, but he still wore a sweatshirt and long johns, just in case it was cold on the ocean. He wasn't sure what to expect, except the man he would meet would be there, on the dock, awaiting his arrival. As it turned out, he got lost finding the road to the landing and it took him over half an hour to finally find it. When he approached, he could see three men on the dock. Two elderly men (Andrew and Sam) who were leaning on the rail, looking out at the ocean, talking to each other, and another man sitting on a lawn chair chewing tobacco. He pulled into the parking lot, exited the van and walked up to the man who was sitting.

Glancing at the paper in his hand which held the directions, he spoke. "I'm looking for a Jonas Hale. Would you be he?"

Jonas smiled at the way he spoke. "I be! And you must be that Ritter fellow, right?" He was wearing jeans, a corduroy shirt, rubber wading boots and his orange hunting cap. He had what appeared to be a carpenter's belt on, with an array of tools attached. His placed his right leg over his left and was whittling on a piece of wood with a buck knife. The first impression Charles had of the man was that he was arrogant and crude, sitting the way he sat and not making eye contact. He wore a long beard and scraggly hair. He was scruffy looking.

"Yes," he said, "I'm Charles Ritter. I was told to meet you here this morning." He was slightly intimidated by Jonas's appearance. Being a college man, this guy sure was not, and that brought a contrast that made him feel uncomfortable. He had been given a quick briefing from Dean Groton, giving him the authority to set a pay scale for the lobsterman and the fisherman (within limits) and to negotiate the deals.

Jonas grinned and showed his yellow teeth. "Ah-yup! Ya be late!"

"I'm sorry, but I got a little bit lost. It's my first time here."

The bearded man turned his head and looked Charles over, from top to bottom. "Ah-yup. You look the college boy type."

Charles glanced down at his own attire. He didn't feel that he overdressed in any way, shape, or manner, but that comment made him feel self-conscious. Jonas snickered. "Ya be a teacher, I was told." His attitude was one of contempt. "Never did take to teachers or schooling. Little snub-nosed bastards!"

The mood was not what Charlie expected and he breathed out heavily. "Are you still going to take me out there and show me what is involved in your business?" His concern was apparent. He had driven all this distance to meet a man who despised academia. He began to wonder if he would lose the job or if he could give the dean a call back and find another guide.

The two older men, who were leaning on the rail stopped talking and listened intently. There was nothing like some fresh gossip for those two. Jonas spit out a wad of tobacco and returned to his whittling. "I got a call from a guy named Dean Groton. Told me all about ya."

"So, you know why I'm here, right?"

"Ah-yup! To learn to lobster." He leaned back in his chair. "This fella also told me that ya ain't done no lobster fishin' before." He glanced back up to Charles.

"No, I haven't," he answered nervously. "But there is a first for everything." He struggled with a weak smile.

"Ay-yup!" He spit out another chaw of tobacco. "Ya be from Rhode Island, I was told."

"Yes, Matunuck Beach."

He spit out the remainder of the tobacco in his mouth, trying to hit the water that he faced, but he was well short.

"Ay-yup. Ya lived on a beach. Humph! They also told me ya ain't never fished."

Charles was becoming uneasy. "I have done some fishing, brook fishing—you know; inland."

Jonas laughed. "Ay-yup; brook fishin'!" He set down the piece of wood he was working on and pulled out a slab of tobacco from his pocket. "No blue water fishing?"

"Well, well, no. I never have."

He took the buck knife and cut into the slab and placed the piece directly off the knife and into his mouth. He began to chew, rolling the tobacco in his teeth. "Ay-yup! I was told ya never even did any coastal fishing."

"Well, not really."

"Ay-yup!" Jonas smiled. "I even heard ya ain't even been out on the ocean!" He spit out more tobacco as he chewed, and looked up at the teacher with a gleam in his eye. He could see this was going to be an easy target.

Charles hung his head in shame. "No, not really."

"Ain't never been on the ocean, but live on the ocean?"

"I guess you could say that."

Jonas reached down and picked up the piece of wood he had been whittling on, and began again. "Ay-yup!" His voice reeked of sarcasm, and he chuckled, a slow, methodical laugh. Charles felt awkward. This man was supposed to help him, not criticize him. "I heard ya teach about the sea."

"Well, actually, no. I teach history. But now it's maritime history." He really didn't know what to make of this man.

Jonas uncrossed his legs for the first time and leaned forward in the chair, looking directly at Charles. He shook his head, giving him the once-over. "Ah-yup! Teach about the sea. Never been on the sea!" He studied the man closely now, then crossed his legs to the original position and continued to whittle. He spit out more tobacco, tucking the remainder between his teeth and gums. "This dean guy told me that I would get paid to take you out."

"That's right."

Without moving his head, he responded, "He didn't talk money with me.

He told me that ya gonna take care of that. Ya know, it ain't gonna be cheap to learn what I know."

"I'm prepared to negotiate."

"Well, now, that's fine to my liking. Now ... let's see." He released the stick of wood and rubbed his bearded chin. "Seems to me, my time is kinda precious. I make a lot of money on my own. So, it's gotta be worth my while. It don't make no never mind to me, I can earn more in a day than them fellas are willing to pay, I reckon," he lied effectively, turning a side glance at the naïve Rhode Islander. "How much they be willin' to give me for my services?"

Charlie reflected. "Well, I don't know. What is fair then?" He was out of his league on this matter. Why didn't Dean Groton take care of the financial matters here? Because he came alone, they adjusted the financial arrangement to compensate him for what it would have cost him to bring his whole family; he had a budget, a salary and a per diem.

Jonas set the knife in his lap, leaned back into the chair and placed his hands behind his head. "Way I figure it, I could earn a good five hundred a day, the way I go about things," he lied even more. "They willin' to pay that?" He snapped his head around to view Charles. "Take it or leave it! Don't make no never mind to me!"

There was a silence. The two old men at the end of the dock whispered to each other. Charlie closed his eyes. Five hundred a day! He had been given a budget of a little over four thousand dollars for the two weeks and a per diem of fifty dollars a day for meals and the like. He rubbed his forehead. "That's a bit steep. I will be helping you fish for lobster, which will help you. I don't think the university will agree with that. Maybe I should give them a call and find out. I'd really have nothing to live on. I still have a week with another fisherman."

Jonas saw the moment slipping, and uncrossed his legs. "Well, then, Mr. Ritter, cus' I like ya. I can take four hundred a day, but that's my final offer! There's lobsters to be had out there and I'm a gonna get 'em, *with* or *without* ya!" He leaned on the arm of his chair and waited for a response.

The time stood still as Charles contemplated. This would kill his budget, but if he didn't, he might not get the job he so desperately wanted. It didn't take very long for him to decide. "O.K.," he responded. "It's a deal!"

Jonas stood up with a wide grin. "Welcome aboard, Mr. Ritter." He worked his cunning to its fullest. On a good day he might earn two hundred dollars. This was a godsend."We'll be off then, 'ey?"

They released their grips. "We'll be off!" He wondered if he had made a bad decision—he really had no idea what a lobsterman earned, he was so gullible. This would cut into his per diem. Whatever, he was still getting a salary, and had that money transferred to his account in Rhode Island.

The overcast skies began to clear while Jonas folded the chair up and stepped down the ladder to fetch the dinghy. "This way, Mr. Ritter."

The two old men gave him a thumbs up when he began to descend and giggled to each other, knowing how the deal was made.

"Watch your step comin' down here, teach, don't wanna see you fall and lose ya." Charlie looked at the dinghy and said, "*That*'s what we're gonna use?" His eyes bulged out in disbelief. "That's not made for the ocean!"

Jonas laughed. "Boy, you are green! This is what we take to the mooring—out there." He pointed to the many ships tied up at the moorings. "I got a boat tied up there."

The tide was high at this time in the morning as the two men stepped onto the boat. Charles looked around the dinghy, "You do have life jackets, don't you?" He was shaking, and holding on to anything he could as he boarded.

Jonas rolled his eyes into the back of his head. "Yes, I have life jackets, but they're on the lobster boat. If I knew ya needed one to get there, I woulda taken one with me!" His attitude turned to contempt. He never liked anybody that was more intelligent than he. He despised them. This time, though, he was in charge and knew more than the man with a doctorate. He smiled at the thought. Once inside the small rowboat, he took the oars and showed Charles where to sit; up in the front seat at the bow. He sat in the stern with his back to the shore. It was probably a habit he kept since he ran into another vessel with his back on it. Charlie sat quietly looking at the dock as they made their way to the moorings. He could still hear the two old men gossiping on the top of the pier. All of a sudden, he noticed something in the water near one of the wooden pilings which supported the dock. It was floating in the water; a strange stringy substance which stayed together in a small circle. He stared intently, attempting to identify it. "What's that?" He asked.

"What?" Jonas replied, "What's what?"

"That—over there by the pier. It's stringy and all together against one of the supports, just hanging on top of the water." He pointed in the direction where it was floating.

Jonas rolled his eyes again, stopped rowing then quickly turned around and looked. They had traveled out away far enough that he really couldn't see, then the waves would subside and he could just barely make it out.

"It's probably just seaweed. Boy, I can tell you never been to sea. I hope you're a quick learner!" He continued rowing until he reached his vessel then pulled the oars inside the dinghy and grabbed the mooring rope, tugging until the smaller boat aligned beside it. "Now, teach, I want ya to grab the rail and pull yourself up and over it. I'll hold her steady." It was a very clumsy jump onto the boat, as though he had never climbed one before. He toppled over onto the deck. Jonas untied the lobster boat from the buoy and tied up the small row boat to it, then he climbed on board.

Charlie stood up and looked back towards the pier. "That wasn't seaweed! I know what seaweed looks like."

"Ah-yup. Just take a seat, college boy, and we'll go out for a short tour, then tomorrow we'll pull traps. The life jackets are below the bow, there, if you want one. I don't like to use 'em—chokes me!" He went up front and started the engine. It was an old wooden boat, probably built in the 1980s, but it was larger than he thought. Charles was visibly shaking, being a bit nervous with the minor swaying of the boat in the small waves at the mooring.

He glanced around the harbor and said, "How peaceful this is!" The water was a little choppy when they headed out into the harbor. The sun broke in and out between the fluffy white cumulus clouds which flew rapidly through the sky. Seagulls dominated the airspace in the vicinity of the dock. Charles sat in the passenger chair on the opposite side of Jonas and locked his life jacket on. If not for the wind, it would have been a perfect day. The harbor was a broad bight open to the southward. He gripped the edge of the boat with one hand and the shelf below the windshield with the other. He wasn't accustomed to the rolling of the sea and it bothered his stomach. Jonas piloted out through the layers of moorings in the harbor at a slow pace. Charles stood up to get a good view, still holding on to the boat with both hands. "Where is that?" He pointed to the land directly in front of them.

Jonas continued to steer through the harbor. "That's Islesboro! It's an island, teacher."

Charles stared in disbelief. "That's an island?"

Jonas turned to him and laughed. "Yeah, that's an island!" The scenery was fantastic. The island was completely covered by evergreen trees with only short beaches along the edge where the waves crashed. Charles looked all around the bay. There were sailboats tacking back and forth all around the waterway.

"They be tourists!" Jonas noted his interest.

"How come there is no color on the trees? Is this all evergreen territory?" He gazed over the pilot house.

"Ain't foliage season for another month, flatlander." He pushed the throttle full open once he passed the moorings.

"Is that another island?" Charles pointed directly ahead, past the edge of Islesboro, to the left.

"No, that's Castine over there. That's part of the mainland on the opposite side of the bay." Jonas pushed his hat down onto his head and spit overboard.

"What's the name of the mountain beyond?" He squinted to see with the water splashing in his face.

"What, that? That ain't no mountain. That's Blue Hill," Jonas replied.

"That's a hill? It sure looks like a mountain to me!" He was astonished. "Wow! We don't have anything that high in the whole State of Rhode Island! You've got some pretty big islands and 'hills' around here!" he mentioned. "What is that structure?" He pointed to the stretch of towers to his left.

Jonas looked over to him. "That's the loading pier at Mack Point. They export stuff from there; oil, potatoes, general cargo and dry bulk products. Those are oil tanks there, and that's the potato conveyor tower on the railroad pier. That's the coal transporters. The water there is about 40 feet deep in some spots. They can get the big ships in. There is a lighted bell buoy on the southeast side of the ledge." He pointed to each thing as he spoke. "They still use that railroad." The wind and the waves made it difficult to hear him, as well as the noise from the engine.

They chugged up into the bay. "That's Sears Island over there." He pointed ahead of Mack Point.

Charles listened intently, with the wind blowing his hair in every direction. He wiped his glasses, removing the spray of the surf. The landscape in his view showed him the rolling hills, up and down, in serpentine arcs. There were a few bare spots in the trees on each vista, made for the power lines that carried through them. Gulls flew by everywhere and the sun beat down on the back of his neck, but the bouncing of the boat was making him nauseous.

They turned a corner around Islesboro and headed southeast. "That's Turtle Head, at the tip of the island." Jonas pointed to his right. "That's Holbrook Island there." He pointed to his left. "That'll be a part of Cape Rosier. We're gonna go as far as Vinalhaven and head back."

"Wow!" Charles stated. "The only thing this state has more of than buoys is islands! They're everywhere!"

Jonas pushed the boat forward and it bounced off the surging waves which had turned to white caps now. Charles sat back down, holding his stomach. After some time, he had to fall back into the seat and moan. He leaned overboard and watched a bird, alternating flapping and gliding with its stiff wings. It banked over the wave, just above the surface, looking like it was going to plunge into the wave, then it rose into a high arc, gliding down into the next trough.

"Ya see that, teacher?" Jonas yelled above the roar of the ocean. "That be a shearwater!" The bird took in a fish, then faced into the wind, like a pilot taking off in a plane. It ran on top of the water, unable to take off, because it held too many fish. It just ran on the top of the tide to get out of the way of the boat. "Now, ya see that bird over there?" He pointed to the south, where a different bird was hovering momentarily in the air, then tucked in its wings and plunged directly into the water, head first. "That be a gannet! It's a fine-looking bird. They can dive as deep as 30 foot to get a fish. It's a pity some o'these birds—getting trapped up in the nets and all. But at least they can fly! What's below the water don't give 'em a chance, once they're in!" He chuckled. "Oh, no!" He glanced in the other direction. "We better get back in." He pointed to another bird.

"Why?" Charles asked. His face was white and he pulled his knees up to his chest in the seat.

"Ya see that bird there? That's one'a Mother Carey's Chickens. It's a storm piper." He glanced into the sky. "It means a storm's acomin'." He spun the boat around 180 degrees very quickly.

That was enough for Charles. "Going back sounds good to me!" He reeled his torso over the railing and vomited, releasing everything in his stomach.

Once they had the lobster boat securely tied to the mooring, Jonas held the small skiff steadily, to allow Charlie to descend, and Charles was more than willing to do so. They had been out for only four hours or so. Charlie's face was flush from the ride. It did seem a bit ironic that he taught nautical and maritime history but had never really been on blue water before. It took him a while to finally get on board the dinghy, being overly cautious so as not to fall. He held on to anything, and everything he could. Jonas laughed at his awkwardness. Eventually, he made it, and Jonas jumped off his boat into the dinghy in a second.

Charles sighed heavily, and relaxed. "Phew! Well, that was different—but informative! I'm beat!" He thought for a moment. "You do this every day?" He was a bit awed at the man now.

Jonas laughed out load as he grabbed the oars inside the small boat. "You ain't done nothin' yet! Wait till we haul traps and set 'em. We'll start that tomorrow. But I can see you had enough for one day!" He rowed with one oar in a circular motion to get the boat's bow pointing to shore. This time he would face the beach while Charlie stared out to the ocean.

"I can't wait!" Charlie said sarcastically, while he glared out to where he could still see the white water. "I just *can't* wait!" He began to think that maybe this was a mistake. His thoughts returned to his family. It was essential that he complete this project; after all, it was only two weeks.

Surely, he could survive the rolling ocean that long. He smiled to Jonas, "Hey, look," he said, "I really don't know anyone here in town and I'd like to meet your family. I don't want to be garish, but I was wondering if I could stop by your house for dinner tonight. I'll bring over a bottle of wine. What do you think?" He tilted his head sideways.

"Dinner? At my house? Don't want to be garnish, 'ey?"

"Garish," he corrected.

Jonas growled at him while he rowed. "You schoolin' boys." He hesitated. "You don't know my wife's cookin'. I'm sure it ain't like your wife's."

"Oh, I'm not fussy. I like pretty much everything. It will be more social, to let me get to know them, than it will be to eat. I wouldn't even know where to go to eat out."

"Well, I s'pose it'll be all right. We eat around 7:30, if that's O.K. with you."

"That will be fine with me."

"You can follow me back in your van. It ain't far, then you'll know where it be."

"That sounds great! But you know, I really don't want to intrude."

"Ah! Ain't no fuss, it be...." He stopped rowing and pulled the oars inside the skiff. His eyes bulged out, staring at the pier. The two old men were no longer there. He squinted and stared intently at the pier. Charles could see there was something strange about his behavior.

"What's the matter?" he asked.

"Fuh-cryin-out loud! Well, teach, you remember that seaweed ya saw when we left?"

"Yes, why?"

"You were right. 'Tweren't seaweed." He grabbed his chin.

"No? I didn't think so. So, what was it?"

Jonas placed his hands on his knees and glared fixedly at Charles. "It be hair!"

Charles adjusted himself in the seat. "Hair? What do you mean, hair?"

"Ed Crowley's hair!" He gritted his teeth, staring at the pier.

"Huh?" Charlie chortled, and spun around in his seat clumsily, encumbered by the burden of the life jacket. He gasped!

There, he saw a man tied to one of the columns supporting the pier. It was low tide now, and the body was visible only just above his waist in water. His mouth had been duct-taped shut and his head hung down, but his face was still visible—it was blue and bobbed around with his body as the waves rocked him back and forth. He had rope strung around his chest to the post, but the lower part of his body didn't seem to be moving, so he guessed the man was also tied near his feet. He had long hair and a beard.

"What the hell?!" Charles screamed.

Jonas's eyes roamed the shore and then the water. He turned 360 degrees, checking to see if any one was near. "Shhh!" He placed his right forefinger to his lips and whispered. "Somebody might hear ya!"

Charles trembled but could not take his eyes from the docks. "That's so sick! Who could have done that? We've got to go help him!"

"I said shhhh! Ain't no helpin' him. He's dead!" Jonas continued to study the area. There was no one around. "We're just loadin' this boat on the back of my truck and getting' the hell outta here!"

Charles turned around to face him. "Aren't you going to do anything?"

Jonas frowned, "Ain't nothin' to do. Now, keep ya voice down, or you might be tied up beside him!"

"Well, you're going to the police, right?"

Jonas snapped his head in anger. "So I can be strapped up beside Ed? Hell, no! We just slip out of here and hope nobody sees us." For the first time since he met him, Jonas appeared to be scared.

Charles looked back at the body, rocking to and fro with the water. "You can't just leave him there!"

"Sure can!" He picked the oars back up and quickly paddled the remaining distance to the landing.

"I can't believe you're just going to leave him like that! He's a human being!" His face was enraged.

They pulled up to the ramp. Jonas pulled the oars into the dinghy and shook his forefinger at Charles. "Look, you ain't from here! You don't know what that means!" He became infuriated.

"Well then, what does it mean?" Charles responded honestly.

Jonas leaned back for a time. "That's a cruel death! Whoever did it, put him in at low tide, alive. Musta been last night. They taped his mouth shut to keep him from screaming. Then the tide rose, slow, like it is. He musta watch it come in, knowin' what it meant. The waves splash in ya face, one at a time. Then the water gets up to ya chin, but ya can't do nothin'. Then it rises up to ya mouth and still ya can't do nothin'. Then it splashes into ya nose and ya get a taste of the sea, and still ya can't do nothin', but now ya really start to struggle. The water makes the ropes tighter, and it ain't no use strugglin'. Then the tide comes up to ya eyes and over ya nose, and then it's just a matter of time. It's a slow, cruel death!" He cringed while speaking.

Charles thought. "God! Who could have done that?"

Jonas jumped out of the boat and pulled it up onto the ramp, then looked in the direction of the dead man. "Don't know! Don't know if I wanna know." He peered up the exit road to the landing. Still, no person could be detected. "But I'll tell ya one thing…."

Charles got out of the boat, listening intently.

Jonas whispered, "Whoever did it was trying to make a point!"

"A point? A point about what?"

He shrugged, "Don't know, and don't know if I wanna know! Don't make no never mind to me!"

Charles stood still on the ramp. "Is it me, or is this thing moving?" His legs buckled as he spoke.

Chapter 8

He followed Jonas to his house in Swanville and pulled onto the side of the road while Jonas turned into the driveway. He glanced at the building; it was deplorable! Only an old, beat-up Volkswagen sat in the driveway, rusting away. The structure stood one story with a large loft, but the outside was unpainted or worn from neglect. Some of the shingles were missing on the roof as well as the side of the house. The weather hadn't treated the establishment with any sort of mercy. There was a shed in the back which appeared to be in better condition. Stacks of what must have been lobster pots were piled meticulously on the lawn in front of the tree line beside the shed. He waved to Jonas, then pulled away to get ready for dinner and give his wife a call.

When he swung up to parking lot at the hotel, it was nearly 6:00 p.m. (He had gotten lost again). He rushed inside his room, took some clothes out of his suitcases and got into the shower. Perhaps he was out of line to have invited himself to dinner the way he did. It was quite possible that the fishing industry was on a seasonal basis and the man had to save money during the good times to offset the bad. Anyway, it was decided that he would go. He got out of the shower and got dressed. He tucked his shirt in while he picked up the phone to call Janet.

She picked up her receiver. "Hello."

"Hi, Janet, it's me. I'm just checking in with you." He was still shook up at what he had seen at the pier.

"Well, it's about time. I expected a call earlier."

"I was on the water all day. What a day! I'll tell you, there's more to this than I thought. I don't know what I got myself into."

She breathed out heavily. "Why? What happened?"

"Well, first things first. How are the kids?"

"Fine, just fine. I can tell by your voice that something is wrong. What's the matter?"

He adjusted his shirt and wrapped a tie around his neck. "It's different here. I met this guy named Jonas. He's the lobsterman I was told to contact."

"What about him?"

He pulled up the collar on his shirt and tied the knot in the tie while holding the phone between his ear and shoulder. "Well, he's kind of strange. I guess they're all like that up here. The other thing is...." He stalled.

She waited as long as she could. "Is what?"

He finished tying the tie, lowering the collar of his shirt around it, and grabbed the phone off his shoulder. "Well, on our way back to the pier today, we saw a man's body tied to one of the pilings. Someone murdered him."

"Murder?" she bellowed, "Are you sure?"

"Yeah, yeah, but don't worry. The thing that gets me is that when I asked this guy, Jonas, if he was going to report it, he told me to keep it quiet. Like I said, they're kind of strange up here."

Her voice strengthened. "I hope you're all right! God's sakes, Charlie, I hope you didn't get into a situation up there. Why don't you just come back? I already miss you."

"Well, I'm going to tell you, Jonas might let it go, but not me! I'm going to find out what happened and why. I'm going over to his house tonight for dinner, and I'll try to grill him for more information."

"Oh, honey! Murder!" Janet responded "You haven't even been there a whole day yet! Did you go to the police with this?"

"No. He told me not to. He said that this was done for a reason! I think it's a small clique here, and word spreads quickly. I'll find out eventually, but in the meantime, I'm going to take it slow with these guys. They're not from the city."

"Charlie, you're an outsider to them. You probably stick out like a sore thumb! Be careful!"

"I will! Look, I have to get a bottle of wine at the store and maybe some stuff for the hotel before I go over to their house. I'm still trying to figure out my way around here. I'm going to let you go, honey. Give the kids a kiss for me, and I'll give you a call tomorrow."

"Oh, Charlie, be careful! Don't make waves! I love you!"

"Don't even talk to me about waves. I've had enough of that for the day! Don't worry, I'll be careful. I love you too, dear." He hung up. He had put on his dress slacks and a dress shirt. He had come there with the expectations of being invited to some formal events. He would be disappointed.

He exited the hotel room and got into the minivan. It was cool, unseasonably cool, this night. The clouds formed along the horizon, and he turned the heat on when he started the van. He wasn't a Mainer.

"I hope ya got something to eat for this Rhode Islander! Somethin' better than the shit ya usually make!" Jonas had been drinking the entire time after getting back to his house and was becoming quite intoxicated. He began mumbling to himself, then he got loud. "And get the kids down here! I want to see what they're wearin'!" He started to get up but fell back down in the chair at the table. "I wanna impress this guy. I can make a lot of money from these flatlanders!"

"Dear, Jonas, why don't you get dressed, yourself. You haven't even cleaned up. I don't know how you can impress this man, looking the way you do. And you should stop drinking. He's not going to be impressed with you, never mind the children."

He bobbed back and forth in the chair. "Don't you tell me what to do, woman!" He stood up, holding on to the edge of the chair, then grabbed the table, knocking over the glass of rum he had. He held on to the edge of the furniture. "Now, see what ya made me do?" He staggered and reached for the glass. "Clean that up, woman!" He set the glass upright after struggling to gain his balance.

Elena, who was cooking vegetables on top of the stove at that time, grabbed a cloth from the stove and wiped up the spill. She had showered and put on a blue evening dress when her husband told her of the company they could expect. She returned to the stove to tend to the supper.

"What are ya cookin'?" Jonas screamed. He placed his hands on his hips and shook his head in an effort to sober up, then blinked his eyes several times. "And where are those kids? I told ya to call 'em!"

"Yes, Jonas, I'll call them. Why don't you sit down and I'll have the children come down." Her eyebrows bent.

"I ain't settin' down *yet*!" His voice echoed. "I'm gonna have me another drink!" He walked towards the cupboard when they heard a knock at the door. He twirled around and looked at his wife. "There he is! You wanna get it?"

"Yes, Jonas, I will. Why don't you sit down at the table? Dinner will be ready soon." She was trying to get him to act a bit more civil.

Instead of sitting, he went to the bottom of the stairs and screamed. "Chad! Katherine! Get down here, I got company I want ya to meet!" He stood there and waited until he heard their footsteps at the top of the stairs. He staggered back to the table while Elena stood, waited and watched. The knock came again. He finally sat down and leaned back, crossing his arms, motioning to her to attend to it. She turned and opened the door.

Charles stood there, holding a bottle of fine wine. He tipped his head. "Good evening, ma'am, my name is Charles Ritter. I'm working with your husband, I believe." He smiled politely.

She returned the smile, "Oh, yes. We're expecting you. My name is Elena. Please, come in." She opened the door wide, and he stepped inside.

"May I say that you look very beautiful this evening? I brought this for dinner." He held out the bottle of wine then tilted his head inside the door. "May I come in?"

She blushed and took the bottle. "Oh, of course!" She held the bottle up and looked at it. "Oh, that's awful nice of you," she said as she shut the door behind him.

"Well, well, well, Charlie!" Jonas roared, waving his arm to beckon him over. "Come on in and sit down!" He patted the seat of the chair beside him. The children had reached the dining area, which was differentiated from the kitchen area only by the table. Chad and Katherine were handsomely groomed and wore their finest clothes; the ones that were usually reserved for church.

Charles sensed the clumsy, slurred speech of Jonas, and looking at him, he could see the unsteadiness of his motions. He looked at Elena, and she turned her head in shame then called for the children. "Chad, Katherine, over here and meet our dinner guest. He's from Rhode Island."

They did as they were told, walking up to the pair near the door. Chad held his hand out. "Hi. My name is Chad."

Charles shook his hand. "Hi, Chad. My name is Charles Ritter. I've heard all about you. I was told you are very studious, and you are certainly a smart dresser."

Chad grinned, a wide grin. "And I hear that you teach in college. I'm going to go someday."

Jonas heard this and blurted out, "Over my dead body!"

Charles looked up from Chad to Jonas, and frowned then released Chad's hand. He looked to the girl.

"You must be Katherine. My, but aren't you the stunning one!"

"Thank you. It's nice to meet you, sir." She curtsied, feeling embarrassed, but quite complimented. She also shook his hand.

Charles glanced around the cabin. It was tidy, but small. There were areas along the walls and the floor that were in need of repair, but overall, the place was very clean. The interior walls were decorated with fishing and lobster fishing accessories. The table where Jonas sat was directly in front of him, the sink and counters just behind that. The stairwell was to the left, alongside of the wall, he surmised. Against the wall, to the right of the stairwell and the counters for the sink, was a large, woven fishing net used as decoration. Buoys hung to it, and there were a series of four hooks hanging at mid-wall. To the right was the living room. It held an old couch and two chairs; one that reclined, facing a television set up near the window by the door where he entered. It was very humble surroundings. Crates were used as end tables in the living room.

He blinked his eyes and flared his nostrils while tilting his head back. "Something sure smells good!" He licked his lips. "Mmm-mmm!"

Elena shied away in a humble fashion. "Oh, that's so nice to hear, but frankly, it's just chicken, potatoes and vegetables. Please, come in and sit down." She pointed to the same seat Jonas had beckoned him.

"Thank you, ma'am." He began to walk towards the table when Jonas interrupted.

"Chicken? Well, it's about time we had some meat in this house!" He could barely hold his head up.

Elena cringed. "Please, Jonas, your company! Children, you can go back upstairs and I'll call you when it's ready. Come along, now." She gently turned them around and gave a polite push in the backs to see them on their way. They followed her directions and returned to the loft.

Jonas waved his hands clumsily and spoke out of the side of his mouth. "Ah-yup. Get over here, Charlie, and we'll break that bottle of wine open and have a snort."

Charles studied the man. His eyes were barely open and they were completely red. There was no mistaking the fact that he had been drinking.

He turned to Elena. "I'm new here and don't know anybody in town. I sort of invited myself inside. If there is a better time, I can come back."

She closed her eyes after looking at Jonas. "There's no better time. There's no other time! He won't change!" Her eyes welled up. "I'd better check the dinner." The chicken had been placed in a covered pot on top of the woodstove; due to the fact that she had no oven to work with. Her demeanor was self-evident—disgusted with her husband and his behavior.

"Over here, Charlie. C'mon now, and open that bottle. Ya're in Maine now. We like our drink, y'know!"

Charles sat down beside Jonas, "I was going to save that for dinner, but then again, it's up to you." He glanced sideways at Elena, who quickly placed the wine on the table and turned around to check the vegetables.

Jonas grinned at Charles. "So, how was your first day?" he asked in a joking manner, knowing the nausea the Rhode Islander had experienced.

Charles smiled. "I'll get used to it. It's just that I haven't done it much."

"Maybe not at all, eh?" He laughed.

Charles looked back at the wall decorated with the fishing equipment. "You have fishing nets and gaffs?"

"One net and four gaffs; a four-inch, a six-inch, an eight-inch and a ten-inch."

"I didn't know you fished."

"Used to! Fished with her father, until he died." He pointed his thumb over his shoulder to Elena. "Fished in the same boat I got now. After he died, he left us that boat. It was a long time ago. Woman, fetch us a corkscrew and we'll have a taste of this grape juice."

She dropped what she was doing instantly, and fumbled through the drawers below the counter near the woodstove until she found the corkscrew, then handed it to Jonas. He never turned around, still looking at Charles. There was something about his eyes which made Charles feel uncomfortable. It was a distance, an aloofness, and what appeared to be a smugness, which may be a sign of arrogance. Jonas removed the paper from the top of the bottle, stuck the corkscrew into the cork and began twisting it in. He glanced down at the bottle. "Ah!" he said. "A Bordix! My favorite!" He pulled the cork out and poured some into a water glass for Charles, which had been set up along with the rest of the table by Elena.

The family rarely ate at the table. Usually, the kids ate upstairs, and Elena ate by herself, after everyone else had been fed. Jonas ate at the table alone. In a way, it was sad, but it was the way they all preferred. Jonas poured himself a glass-ful.

Charles picked his wine up and slowly swirled it around. "It's pronounced 'Bordeaux,'" he corrected as he checked the liquid legs on the inside of the glass.

"Whatever!" Jonas chugged the whole glass in one sip, then set the glass back on the table. "You schoolboys!" He belched loudly, and quite unashamedly.

Charles sniffed the bouquet, then took a sip from his glass. "There is something that has been on my mind that I'd like to ask you."

"Then ask. Go ahead, shoot!" This time he didn't bother to use the glass, he picked up the bottle and drank directly out of it.

Charles sighed and pointed to the bottle in shock. "That's a Chateau Lafite-Rothschild! It's a very expensive.... Oh, forget it!" He shook his head. "Anyway, what I wanted to ask you, was about that man tied to the pier. I can't comprehend why you don't want to go to the police with this. Surely, this man means something to someone."

Jonas set the bottle down. "Fuh-cry-ing-out-loud! I told ya! I don't know and I don't know if I wanna know!"

"You also told me someone was making a point! I still don't understand, what kind of point could they be making?"

Jonas placed his elbows on the table, his eyes opened wider than they had been since Charles sat down. He suddenly became serious. "'Course ya don't understand! Ya ain't from here! We live in a small community here, and the group on the water's even smaller. Everyone knows everyone." He teetered back in his chair in a weird sort of contemplation. "We work together. If one of us gets in trouble, the others will help 'im out. If someone does something that might be agin' the law, we all look the other way. That's the way it is here." He leaned forward in his chair and stared at Charles. "Understand?"

"But this is murder! A cruel, slow murder! Doesn't that mean anything to you? Doesn't anybody care about that?"

"Look, ya flatlander!" Jonas gritted his teeth, showing their stained, yellow exterior. "Whoever did that has a secret. A secret he didn't want no one else to know. Ed musta known it or figured it out. Whatever! Tyin' Ed up to that post was just a reminder to anybody else who knows that secret to keep their mouths shut!" He leaned back in his chair and placed both hands behind his head. "Another thing, Ed bein' tied up to that pole is gonna be a secret, if ya know what I mean. Else, you might taste that water!" He laughed with his teeth still clenched.

Elena turned away from the stove. "Ed? You didn't tell me about this. It wasn't Ed Crowley, was it?" She had a very concerned look on her face. She was good friends with his wife, and they often went to church together. She stepped in front of the table, between the two men, still holding a spoon in her hand. "Was it?"

Jonas turned to her. "It don't make no never mind!" he said, while he stared in his inebriated state. He spun back around to Charles. "This is my wife. Ain't she somethin'? She's got some pretty good hooters, 'ey? Hey, Elena, let's get a good look at 'em." He chuckled and attempted to grab her by the waist.

"Please, Jonas, please!" She turned red and returned to the stove.

He laughed even harder, then started clapping his hands together, and began one of his drunken repertoires:

"You take the legs from some ol' table
You take the arms from some ol' chair
You take the neck from some ol' bottle
And from a horse, you'll get some hair
And ya put 'em all together
With some paper and some glue
'Cuz I can get more lovin' from a goddamn dummy
Than I'll ever get from you!"

He finished his ditty and laughed so loudly that the chair tilted backwards, and he just barely kept it from falling over.

Charles had seen enough. He stood up and asked Elena, "May I use your restroom?"

"Certainly," she replied, "I'll show it to you." She led him through the small kitchen past the bottom of the stairwell to a room on the right. "It's right there, sir."

A loud voice echoed from the kitchen. "Ya better bring it back!" The boisterous laughter continued.

Charles stopped and turned to Elena. "How do you put up with that?" he asked with all seriousness.

She began to cry then cry even harder. He put his arms around her for comfort. "It's all right, now."

She pulled her self away from his reassuring grip but continued to cry. "I have no choice! I don't have anywhere to go! I have two children, and I've never worked. I have to stay. He's been getting worse! I just have no choice!" she blubbered uncontrollably.

What could Charles say? He nodded in acknowledgement. He had only heard of such situations. He went into the bathroom, and Elena wiped the tears from her face. She returned to the kitchen.

Jonas was standing up at the table with the bottle of wine in his hand. He drank a large portion from the bottle, while the excess dribbled off his beard. His eyes were inflamed. "I heard ya!" He screamed at Elena. "What did ya have to say that for, bitch? If ya don't appreciate me here, then there's the exit!" He pointed to the door with the hand holding the bottle, and swung around with the other, striking her in the face. "Ungrateful bitch!" he screamed.

She reeled and covered her face. "Please, Jonas, no! Please, not in front of your guest," she sobbed.

"Oh, shut up, woman! He's in the head!"

"But you're so loud, Jonas. I don't think you even know it, but you're so loud!" He swung again, hitting her in the same place. "Got eyes for 'im, don't ya?"

The children heard the commotion and came to the bottom of the stairs, watching.

"That's it, Dad!" Chad snapped. He charged at his father, while Katherine looked on in horror. Chad hit him at the waist and wrapped his arms around him. The hit took Jonas by surprise, and in his state, it caught him completely off guard. He toppled over the chair behind him with Chad still strapped to his body. The bottle of wine fell and broke. The two of them struggled on the floor together until Jonas (three times the size of Chad) grabbed his son by the scruff of the neck and stood him up. Then Jonas stood up. His mouth was agape. He didn't think the boy had it in him. His legs were weary as he stood in shock.

He began to snicker. "Hahaha. So, you think you can take the ol' man, do ya, ya little puke?" He smacked the lad in the face, but Chad never flinched. He hit him again. Still Chad stood his ground.

"Jonas!" Elena screamed. "No, Jonas, no!"

At that time, Charles came into the kitchen area, and he had seen the last slap to the boy's face. He started towards Jonas but thought against it. His wife was right—he was an outsider. He studied Jonas. He was a different man. He thought for a moment—his only choice was to leave, not to interfere, no matter how much he wanted to. He turned to Elena. "I've ... I've ... I'm sorry, but I forgot. I have dinner waiting for me at the hotel, and I promised my wife I'd give her a call before she goes to bed. I'm sorry, I'll have to cancel out on dinner tonight. Maybe another time."

She cried endlessly, "I'm so sorry. I'm just *so* sorry!"

Jonas straightened out. "Ya leavin', Chuck? Without eatin'?" His demeanor had changed once more.

"Yes, I have a dinner waiting for me at the hotel. I really just wanted to talk to you about the man tied to the pier, and I have to give my wife a call tonight." He looked at Jonas with contempt, holding back what he really wanted to say to him.

"Well, all right, then, I'll see ya bright and early tomorrow. Don't be late this time." He picked the chair up from behind him and sat down.

"Yes, yes, sure. I'll be there." He turned to Elena and whispered, "Do you have a pen I could borrow?"

"Of course!" she answered, then walked to the drawer below the cupboards that held the household trinkets and brought it back to Charles. "Here you are."

"Ya ain't gotta go there, Charlie. Ya know a woman's gotta learn her place, and so don't the children. 'Specially when they get cocky!" He got up but fell backwards against the sink. "Ah, it don't make no never mind!" He waved to Charles and held his head. Chad had done more damage than he thought.

"I'll see you out," Elena said and led Charles to the exit. He took out a piece of paper from his pocket and scratched down on it with the pen. He handed the paper to her and looked back over to Jonas, who was now sitting and holding his head with both hands, staring downward to the table.

"It's my name, the phone number for the hotel and my room number. If you ever need anything, give me a call, I'll be over in an instant!" He continued to look at Jonas, who was all but passed out at the table. "Anything!" he reiterated.

She was still crying. "Oh, I will. I'm so sorry you had to see that! He'll be fine tomorrow." Her facial expression showed confidence in those words.

Charles nodded to her. "I'm sure he will."

She opened the door and he stepped out. "Give me a call!" he stated, as she shut the door with both hands.

His thoughts wandered while he drove back to the hotel. He really didn't have anything to eat there. That was just a ruse to get away from an unsettling situation. He wondered how many other families experienced that sort of mistreatment. It was all very troublesome for him. Was this the typical behavior of all the fishermen and lobstermen in this area? Were they all alike? He pulled into the hotel and quickly entered his room to call his wife; that was one thing he hadn't lied about.

"Hi, Janet, it's me. How are you doing?"

"Oh, Charles, I'm fine, but I'm glad you called."

"Why? What's going on there?"

"Nothing, everybody's fine. Dean Groton called earlier to find out if you got in all right, and see how everything was going. I told him that you made it in, got the hotel, and met the guy that was going to teach you the lobster trade. But he asked about money. I think he wants to talk to you."

"Geeze, I forgot. I was supposed to call him. The money really doesn't matter, though. I made the deal with Jonas, and if I overrun my budget, I guess I'll have to eat it."

"Well, try to give him a call. He said he has already set up a course that he wants you to look over. He asked me for an e-mail address or a fax number where he could get in touch with you."

Charles thought for a long time, and there was silence on the line. "I'll check with the hotel. I think they have a fax, but I didn't even bring a computer so he can't e-mail me, unless you relay the message. Tell him that if he calls tomorrow. I'll be on the water all day, so it's no use for him to call me from his office. You can give him the phone number here and he can call me from home. I'm not exactly sure what time it gets dark now, but if he wants to get a hold of me here, he has to either call real early or real late. This guy has 250 traps out and it's going to be a full day tomorrow."

"O.K., I'll give him a call tomorrow and tell him that. How was your dinner?"

Charles grunted. "Oh, boy! You wouldn't believe it if I told you. He was drunk when I got there and drank my bottle of Chateau Lafite-Rothschild right out of the bottle. He's crude and worse."

"What do you mean, worse?"

"He beats his wife and children. I saw it! I can't imagine what he would have done if I wasn't there."

"Oh, Charlie! Why don't you just leave? I'll call the dean and tell him that it just didn't work out. You don't need that! You don't need to be involved in that, not to mention a murder!"

"I know, and I'm going to try to stay out of it, but if I see anything like that again, I'm going to the Department of Human Services or some other agency. She's too scared to leave on her own. There has to be an agency that can help her out. It was pretty outrageous."

"Charles, don't play the hero here! Think of yourself. I don't know why you don't just come home."

"That murder is the other thing. I'm not going to let that go unnoticed. I'm getting to the dock early tomorrow and do some poking around. Jonas claims all the fishermen are a brotherhood here and everyone is wearing blindfolds. I'll do a little bit of investigating, and if I'm not satisfied, I'm going to the police and reporting it."

"Just be careful, Charles! I love you!"

"I'll be careful and I love you too. I'll give you a call tomorrow, but right now, I've got to get something to eat. Bye."

"Bye." They hung up simultaneously.

Chapter 9

The weather was nothing more than dismal when Charles looked out through the curtains of his hotel room window. A fine mist engulfed the area, and a light drizzle fell. Charles scurried about the room to get ready so that he could get to the dock before Jonas, and see if he could get in touch with someone there who might have seen something about the murder. He had set the alarm for 4:30a.m., but hit the snooze button constantly until he finally got up at 5:30a.m. It was still dark out, and the overcast skies make it seem even darker. There were no stars, no moon and no sun visible. He jumped into the shower and quickly got dressed, thinking that he could at least talk to the two old men on the pier. He was certain they would be there this early, and with any luck, he would find other fishermen launching their boats at this time. He recalled seeing all the empty moorings when they left yesterday.

Although he still had his windshield wipers of the van operating and the headlights on, there was enough light when he pulled into the parking lot at the town pier for him to see. The two old men were there at the end of the dock, just as he anticipated, and there were two boats preparing to launch. Both of them were simple motor boats, but he could see that only one of the two was headed to a mooring, the other appeared to be going out striper fishing. Fish poles were set inside the boat, leaning against the sides. He parked and turned the engine off, then made his way to those two boats. Four men, total, were headed out; two per boat.

He hastily approached them. "Excuse me, gentlemen. Could I have a word with you?" His voice was anxious. The clouds had begun to dissipate. The drizzle stopped, and the sun cast a faint light on the sea. All four of the men twirled around and looked at him.

He walked down the launch ramp to talk directly and closely to them then he glanced at the dock support where he had seen the body tied. It was gone! He approached the four men. "Excuse me," he said. "I was out here yesterday and I saw a man tied to that post over there. He was dead. I was wondering if any of you saw anything."

"Who are you?" one man asked.

"My name is Charles Ritter. I'm from Rhode Island, I'll be here for a couple of weeks." He held his hands out. "Did you see him? I think his name was Ed Crowley—a fisherman, like you." He was hoping to get sympathy for the dead. Instead, two of the men turned around without saying a word, pushed their boat into the water and climbed inside. The other two waited for them to get out. They also ignored the question. Once their boat was comfortably out, they also turned their backs on Charles and pushed their boat out. The men in the first boat started the engine and slowly headed out to the blue water. The other two men climbed aboard their boat. They were only going to the moorings, but they didn't speak either.

"Come on, guys! Somebody must have seen him there. Somebody must have seen *something*!" His face curled, hoping to get some help from the locals. Their silence spoke volumes. He was certain that they knew something, but something, or someone was keeping them quiet. "Come on, guys, this is murder!" He held his hands out to his side.

One of the men from the second boat turned to him while the other man started the engine. "Why don't you just go back to Rhode Island and keep your nose out of here?"

Charles slapped his thighs in frustration. "That's a human being, for God's sake!" he screamed as the boat pulled away. They never looked back.

He slumped and hung his head in despair, then suddenly remembered the two old men at the end of the pier. He looked in their direction. They had watched (and heard) everything that was said at the launch. Charles stumbled up the ramp and onto the pier, eventually getting to Sam and Andrew. The two men turned away and looked out over the bay. The sun had broken through the clouds, and beamed brightly on the men. They made small talk to each other, noticing his approach.

"Guys, guys," he said as he walked up to them. They refused to turn and face him. "Guys!" He was persistent.

Finally, Sam turned around. "What do ya want, flatlander?" He smiled smugly.

"Hey, look, guys. I know you hang out here. There was a man tied to the pier right below you, yesterday. Did you see him? His name was Ed Crowley. He died a horrible, terrible death."

Sam turned back around. "I didn't see nothin'."

Andrew agreed. "Weren't nobody there when I was here. What do you care, anyway, outsider?"

Charles was becoming upset. "A man died! For God's sake, he was murdered, and you ignore it. You accept it. Why? Just tell me why!"

"Ed Crowley," Sam said. "Heard he fell overboard. Maybe got ate by sharks. Maybe just drowned. Sure didn't see him here."

"I heard he moved out of town. Left his wife, you know they weren't gettin' along," Andrew postulated.

Charles grabbed his hair. "Oh, come on, guys! I know you saw something. I *know* you know! Why not talk?" He began to calm down and took his hands out from the top of his head. "O.K., O.K.," he said. "I can see where this is going. You don't have to tell me anything. But could you do me a favor?" He was desperate.

"Favor? What do ya need?" Sam leaned on the rail of the pier.

"Can you tell me where he lived and where I could see his wife?"

"Don't know nothin'," was the reply.

"That's what I thought!" He had become totally disgusted with the locals's indifference.

At that time, Jonas pulled into the parking lot and, seeing Charles on the dock, beeped his horn for help.

Charles turned to the sound then back to the two gentlemen on the pier. "I guess that's good enough. I can't see how you guys can let this go without seeing someone being punished. He had a wife!" He spun and began to walk down the dock to the parking area.

Andrew twirled around to face Charles as he exited. "Oh, flatlander!" He hoarsely cried.

Charles stopped and looked back.

"I tell ya, we didn't see nothin', and if it be ya neck ya favor, then ya didn't see nothin' neither!"

Charles shook his head. "Of course. I see!" He continued down to greet Jonas, who had backed the truck down the ramp.

Jonas had his window rolled down while he backed up. "Hey, Charlie, why don't ya help me pull the boat off the back and I'll park this thing?" He had opened the door to the truck and stepped out, looking in the direction of the two old men on the dock. "Well, ya made it on time. What are ya talking to them about?" He tilted his head in their direction, with a snarl and look of suspicion.

"Oh, nothing," Charles responded. "I got here a little early so I decided to chat with them, since they were here. You know, about lobster fishing and deep-sea fishing."

Jonas smirked. "Lobstering and fishing, ey? With them two? They don't know shit about lobstering and fishing. Ya better watch y'self around here. Most here don't take kindly to strangers!" His attitude implied that he knew exactly what Charles and the two old men were talking about. "And keep ya opinions to y'self!" He grinned but was chewing tobacco and his yellow teeth became encased in black. He nodded his head so as Charles would get the message.

"I'll try!" he responded.

They pulled the skiff off of the back of the truck and placed it in the water at the bottom of the landing. Jonas handed Charles the bow rope and returned to the truck, moving it into a parking spot nearby. Charles waited patiently with rope in hand. They boarded and headed to the moorings. The sun had completely emerged and the clouds dissipated. It turned out to be a very nice morning.

"Did ya talk to that dean of yours this morning?"

Charles looked confused. "No, why?"

"He gave me a call, real early. He said he tried to call ya but ya weren't there. Ya must have got up pretty early this mornin'." He spit out tobacco over the side of the dinghy as he rowed to the boat. "Pokin' your nose around here, maybe?" That sideways smile emerged, the one that made Charles uncomfortable. He tried to avoid the question.

"What did the dean say he wanted? Did he tell you?"

"Nah! He just said for ya to call him when we get back. He asked me what we had done so far and I told him—I watched ya puke!" He laughed in a condescending fashion.

Charles blushed. "You really didn't have to tell him that!" Jonas laughed even louder. Charles began to wonder what the dean wanted to speak with him about. Maybe he had spoken with Janet and she told him how much money he agreed to pay Jonas and that this whole experiment was off. That would mean he would have no job when he got back. But then again, why wouldn't he tell Jonas that and save the money he was paying for this day? The hotel was paid up for two weeks already, on the school's tab. Maybe Janet was right and he should just quit and go home. This whole situation, with the murder and the people's behaviors (especially the man sitting in the boat with him), was unsettling to him anyway. He decided he would go through this day and call the dean when he got back to the hotel. He had come this far.

They reached the boat and he got aboard. Jonas handed him the bait buckets and he placed them into the stern of the boat, then Jonas climbed on. The seas were calm here, but they were in a sheltered zone. It would get worse once they got out. "What are we going to do today?" he asked.

"Ah, ya just gonna watch today. I'll show ya where the traps are and I'll pull 'em up myself. Ya ain't allowed to touch the lines until ya get a license. I think that's what that dean fella called about. He mentioned somethin' else."

Charles felt a sense of relief. Why would he get him a license to lobster if he was to be terminated? Jonas fired up the engines and switched lines on the buoy with the skiff. They headed out to where he set his traps. "You said there was something else?" He was curious now.

"Ah-yup! He wouldn't tell me though. He said he wanted to talk to you." The ship slithered out of the cove. The boat made its way around the various buoys outside of the immediate area. "Where are we headed?" Charles asked.

"We're gonna check my traps up around Mack Point first, then to the ones near Sears Island, then over to Belfast and if we have enough time, we'll head out to the deep traps."

"What do you mean, if we have time?"

"That dean of yours told me to have you in early, so as you can call him. Whatever he wants to talk to you about must be kinda important. Anyway, you'll see how to pull the traps, re-bait 'em, and reset 'em. We ain't gonna have time to do everything today."

Charles thought to himself. He had never even eaten a lobster before. He grew up in Indiana on a small farm. This life was totally different, but even when he was in school he had never even had a lobster then. He knew basically what they looked like, but that was about it. Jonas pulled up to one of the buoys with the red and black stripes. Each lobsterman had to have his own distinguishable markings, and these were the same as the buoy Jonas has displayed on top of the pilot house on the boat.

"How come you have an extra buoy mounted on the roof of the cabin?" Charles asked naïvely.

Jonas laughed. "That ain't an extra buoy. It's my color display. I got to show ever'body out here that the traps I'm hauling are mine, so ya have to display ya colors. It's the law." He shook his head and turned to Charles. "I guess we're gonna have to go over the laws of Maine so ya understand what ya can't do on board. If ya want to go on your own, ya gotta know 'em. Ya 'sposed to take a test on 'em, and pass it before ya can go out. While ya're on my boat ya can't do nothin' much but watch. Ya can't haul or handle a trap, either band or measure the lobsters, bait the bags or even take the wheel between haulin' traps."

"Then what *can* I do?"

"Just watch, that's it! Today, we'll haul some traps and I'll explain some of the other laws." He leaned overboard and grabbed the buoy, placing it up on deck, then grabbed hold of the rope, pulling it up until he got the toggle on deck. Finally the trap emerged and he lifted onto the washboard.

"How come you use two buoys for one trap?" The Rhode Islander was out of his milieu.

"That ain't a buoy. That's the toggle. Ya got two toggles on most of the traps, but this one has floating split warp instead of a bottom toggle 'cause it floats. That's to keep the warp from fouling on the bottom. Sometimes boats will run over the buoy, and I could lose it and the trap, but if I lose the buoy by someone foulin' it up, I can still see the top toggle at low tide, so I don't lose the trap."

"What's a 'warp'?" He was eager to learn more.

"That's the line. Ya see this?" He pointed to the length of warp attached to the trap.

There were several crabs inside and a single lobster. They crawled along the inside of the trap recklessly, including the lobster, which was much larger than the crabs.

"How did they get in there?" Charles was amazed that they had gotten in but couldn't get out. The trap was ovular, like the Quonset huts that were first developed near Davisville, Rhode Island, except these were made of straps of wood and nylon nets shaped like funnels.

"They crawled inside," Jonas explained. "Ya see, this is called a parlor trap. It is separated into two sections, the kitchen and the parlor. These openings here with the nylon knit heads, one on each side of the kitchen, let the lobster crawl in to get the bait which we put in the middle of the trap at the inner end of the kitchen." He pointed to the various parts of the trap as he spoke. "Once ol' 'pinchy' gets the bait, he looks for a way to escape, so he heads up the apron of this third head, which opens into the parlor, where he can't get out. Now, if the lobster is too big, it can't get in. In Maine, the maximum size is 5 inches, so the opening here is made to be 6 inches to keep the real big ones out. The minimum size is 3-1/4 inches so these openings here at the bottom of the parlor are made 1-15/16" to let the small ones escape. They are required by the law, too."

"Why are the boards on the bottom?" Charles asked. "To stabilize the trap on the bottom? It looks too high for a lobster to get inside the net."

"That's called the runners. They're required by law, too, but not for that reason. It's so the creature won't damage its claws. They been known to take their own claws off if they sense fear or danger. The claws will grow back though, sometimes bigger than before."

The whole thing looked so simple but sounded complicated. "Regeneration, wow? But the lobster in there is a lot bigger than five inches!"

"Nah! Well now, I'll show ya how to measure it." He pulled his gauge out of his back pocket. "This is what we call the measure. It's a double-sided gauge, one side shows ya the minimum size a 'keeper' can be and the other size shows ya the maximum size of a keeper."

"A keeper? What's a keeper?"

Jonas grinned and turned his head. "Dinner!" He opened the top of the trap and stuck his hand inside, pulling out the crabs, one by one, and tossing them into the water. Lastly he pulled out the lobster.

"Ya hold it like this to handle it." He placed his hand firmly on the back of the lobster from the rear with his thumb and forefinger one either side behind the "front tires" of claws. "See?"

Charles nodded in confirmation, but Jonas only showed him that for Charles's sake, because right after showing him, he used his own technique to measure it.

It was much longer than five inches, but of course, Charles was looking from the tip of the rostrum to the end of the tail. Jonas placed the gauge against the back of the lobster, holding the crustacean firmly. He explained to Charlie, "Ya place this notch of the gauge into the rear of the eye socket and measure along a line parallel to the center line of the body shell. Ya don't measure the tail! Here we are; see, she's about 4-1/2".

"I see. Then you can keep it, right?"

"That's why ya got to read the book. Can't keep this girl. She's gotta go back."

"It's a female? How can you tell?"

"Well, you look at the underbelly under the tail. There is the first set of small swimmerets. They are positioned near the base of the last pair of walking legs. On a male, they are hard, and soft on a female."

"How many legs does it have?"

"They got ten legs including the claws. This claw here is the called the crusher." He pointed to the left claw on the lobster. "And this one is the pincher." He pointed to the right claw. "The names mean exactly what they do. Ya see, a lobster is a scavenger." He hesitated then grinned widely. "And a cannibal!"

Charles stepped back at that comment. Jonas chuckled. "Heh, heh, heh. But I'll tell ya, teacher, there's an easier way to tell if they are female, sometimes."

"An easier way, how?" He looked surprised. Jonas turned the lobster over and stuck it in Charles's face with the underside towards him. He could see a series of small granules of sand or something that looked like crud all along the tail.

"What's that?"

"Eggs. Lots of eggs! Ya see, it's also illegal to keep a berried female."

"Then are you going to toss it back?"

"Not yet. Ya gonna have to read that pamphlet and take that test before ya go out. That's if ya still are here. I got to mark her—that's the law, too. But I'll show ya how."

The burly man pulled out a buck knife from inside his belt and cut two slits in one of the flippers on the tail. The cut resembled a wedge. "Ya cut a v-notch into the flipper to the right of the middle one. He placed the lobster in the water and let it go. "Ain't nobody can get her now, 'least not legally, and she can reproduce again and again." He turned to Charles while checking the trap. "Don't need to re-bait, I'll just set her back." He tossed the trap, rope and buoy back into the sea. "Getting the idea?"

Charles looked humble. He was a learned scholar, taking lessons from a man who probably never even graduated high school. "How many eggs does a female have?"

"Oh, between 6,000 and 100,000; it depends. She had quite a few." He walked back to the pilot house and they began to pull away, up to the next trap. He had several arranged in the same area here, several more in the next location, and more elsewhere.

"You mean to tell me that each female has thousands and thousands of little lobsters? There must be billions of them in the water then."

"Oh, they don't all live. In fact, they go through a long process before the female releases the young lobster. First she molts, which means she drops her shell, making her soft shelled, and then she looks for a male to fertilize the eggs. When she finds the male, they play antennae games—sorta like courtin', I guess. If he likes her, she drops over on her back and he'll come along and they have lobster sex."

He twirled his fingers about to represent the mating ritual. "Like humans, it only takes a couple of seconds for him to drop his sperm." He laughed at his own joke. "The sperm stays with the female for a long time until she's ready to spawn. Then she lays on her back and releases the eggs in a stream, the eggs pass through the sperm that she's held, like humans, for about nine months." He laughed again. "Then these fertilized eggs stick to her swimmerets and to each other. The swimmerets are those tiny little legs on her belly. She holds 'em for another nine months until they're ready to hatch then she picks up her tail and lets 'em go. Then, they're only about that big." He pinched his forefinger and thumb so they were about 1/4" apart. "Most float all the way to the top of the water and most of 'em get eaten, some by other lobsters. I told ya they were cannibals. In fact, when they molt, they're pretty vulnerable, and their own kind will crush 'em and eat 'em." He smiled broadly, watching Charles's face squint with disgust and had kept the boat idling while he explained to Charles about lobsters.

Charles thought, *It's strange how the lobster and the lobsterman are so much alike!*

Jonas turned back to the wheel to continue his vocation for the day. As he hit the throttle, they heard an extremely loud *bang!*

Charles leaned back against the starboard side. "What was that?"

Jonas placed the boat back into neutral. "That was a gunshot! It came from the other side of Sears Island. Something's going on over there!"

Without hesitation, Charlie insisted, "Well, let's go see!"

"What? Are ya crazy? I value my life, man! It's suicide to see! Why don't ya just leave it alone?"

"And see more people die? Hey, look, I'm paying you for this boat!"

"Ya gonna pay for my funeral?"

"I'm going to find out! Whoever did this is not going to hang around and let someone else identify him. Whoever doing this is too crafty for that. Let's go see!"

Jonas stalled for a moment. "Maybe ya be right. I s'pose they wouldn't hang around the scene. O.K., but I ain't stickin' around long; these shores got eyes and ears." He threw the boat into full throttle, looking at each point of land to see if there was anyone hanging out. He couldn't see anybody, and they made it around the end of the island quickly. Up ahead in the distance, they could see a boat which appeared to have no one in it. It was the only boat visible. "I've seen enough, how about you?" He glanced back to Charles, who was cupping his hand above his eyes for a better view.

"There's no body in the water! Maybe it's still in the boat where you can't see."

Jonas pulled his boat alongside the other and they both took a look. No body was inside the boat and none could be seen in the water nearby.

"That's Doug Harvey's boat. He used to run with Kenny Buckner until he got sick of him and got his own boat. The water's too rough today. If he got shot, he went under and will either go out to sea, sink or wind up on shore somewhere. There's nothing we can do here."

"Damn! Doesn't anyone wear a life jacket out here besides me?"

Jonas laughed shallowly. "No!"

Charles slumped in a sort of defeat. "All right, I guess we can't do anything here. We'll check the rest of your traps and head for shore." He paced back and forth over the length of the boat. "Who keeps a gun in their boat and why?"

"I do! Everyone does." He held up a small pistol he stored in the pilot house.

"Why? What for?" He was becoming uncomfortable with the situation he had entered.

"In case of any molesters." He grinned at Charlie.

"What's that supposed to mean, 'molesters'?"

"That's someone who fucks with your gear, pulls your traps or messes with 'em. Some guys have actually set up knives or booby traps so that if ya try to grab their buoy, ya will cut ya hands to pieces; or worse!"

Charles shrugged. "I'm not sure if I fit in here. There's something going on in these waters and I mean to find out what, even if I have to do it myself!"

The afternoon went well, and Charlie learned more in one day than he possibly could have by reading about this from any book. They had hauled in over seventy traps in a very short period of time and Jonas pulled out over sixty keepers. They hadn't gone out to the deep traps—that would wait until the next day. He was exhausted and he stunk! He drove back to the hotel with a sense of accomplishment, although he did little, still it was something new to him. He was a bit concerned about talking to the dean, and he wondered if he would even be in school this late in the day. He would postpone what he considered to be a mandatory shower to speak with the man. A true pessimist, he always expected the worst. He felt that if you anticipated the worst and it turns out to be the worst, well, then you're prepared. If you expect the best and it turns out the best, well, you expected it, but if you expect the best and it turns out to be the worst, you're totally deflated. If you expect the worst and it turns out to be the best, then you're elated. It was his mindset.

As he opened the door to the hotel room, he could hear the phone ringing inside. He nervously raced to get it before it stopped. He picked up the receiver. "Hello."

"Hello, Mr. Ritter, this is the front desk." He relaxed in a half-eased thankfulness. "Yes?"

"We have a fax for you at the desk that came in earlier today. I saw you drive in, so I knew I could get a hold of you now. You may pick it up anytime."

"A fax? About what? Who knows I'm here?"

"We're not allowed to read your mail, sir. You'll have to find that out for yourself."

"Yes, of course. Thank you." They both hung up. He threw his jacket onto the bed then he remembered that the university set him up with this room, so the fax must be from them. It might mean the end here, and at the university. He began to reach for the phone, slowly. His hand shook as he reached down to call his boss when the phone rang again. He jumped—catching him off guard. He took his time to pick up the receiver. "Hello."

"Hello, Charlie! This is Dean Groton. How's everything going up there?" His voice was upbeat, and this eased some of Charles's tensions.

"It's going well. It's a little different, though."

"Good, good, glad to hear it. Are you learning anything?" Still the voice was chipper.

"Oh, boy, am I learning. I'm learning a lot of things. Believe me, I'm learning!"

"That's just great! Hey, look, Charlie, the reason I'm calling," Charles's face cringed, "is because we have developed a syllabus for your class. It seems that there are a lot of marine biology students at Woods Hole that are eager to join a class structure which teaches lobsters, fishing and maritime history. Charlie, we've had an unprecedented response—It's unbelievable! There must be one hundred kids that want to sign up for it. Most of them want to work at Woods Hole but don't know how to handle themselves near the water, coming from a farm, or just maritime illiterates. I'll tell you, Charlie, the board is ecstatic! I've never seen them like this. I want you to hone your skills. You are learning the lobster trade, aren't you?" The sound of his voice was so bright and cheery that Charles couldn't disappoint him.

His face dropped, his heart pounded and his voice trembled as he spoke. "Ye … ye … yes, yes, sir!" He wasn't really sure if he wanted to stay. What would Janet think? What about the murders? This crept into his mind now. "Oh, yes, I'm learning! Oh, boy, am I learning!"

"Good, good, Charlie, keep it up! The board is so happy with the letters and phone calls we have received that we held a special board meeting the day before yesterday. They want you to go out on your own and lobster. We found that there will be obstacles due to the law; you are supposed to be a resident and the time to file has passed. Come to find out though, Freddy Desjardins, one of the board members, went to school with the head of the department of Marine Resources in Augusta, Maine. His name is, let's see— Curtis, Stanley Curtis. They met at U.M.O. (University of Maine at Orono) and are really good friends. They also grew up together. Freddy pulled some strings with this guy and he's willing to overlook a couple of things to get you a license. You're going have to head up to Augusta and take the test on Sunday. He said you can't lobster that day anyway, and he is willing to meet you at his house. That only gives you one more day to study. I've faxed you the materials and the study booklet and directions to get to his house. You have to pass this test, Charlie! We're really sticking our necks out for you!"

Charles was put back. This was a lot to ask of him, but he was a scholar, and to memorize a pamphlet in one night should be no problem. He shrugged. "I'll do my best. I've already learned quite a bit about the laws and what is involved. I won't let you down."

"Good, good, Charlie. Also, the board has agreed to rent a boat for you from a local fisherman. He's going to set it up for you and supply you with all the gear you need. He'll give you five buoys and traps. This Curtis guy said that's all you'll be allowed by law. The boat should be moored on Sunday and he'll meet you there on Monday morning. It's all in the fax. The results of your test will be immediate. He's going to grade you on the spot. We've taken care of everything else—the test is up to you. Learn all you possibly can on the water tomorrow and study that book. Do you think you can handle it, Charlie?" He seemed energetic.

Charles started to feel the pressure and tilted his head back, looking at the ceiling, then he closed his eyes. "I'll handle it!"

"Good, good, Charlie. Now, once you go out on your own, and if you get stuck or have any problems, we still have that Jonas fellow to fall back on. He's going to still get paid for the week. I just spoke with him and explained the situation. He agreed—actually, he was happy with it. He claims you slow him down and he hasn't even checked all his traps for the week. He seems an odd fellow. He's going to check in with you every morning before you go out. I think he likes you, Charlie."

Charlie laughed. *He likes the money,* he said to himself. "Thank you, Dean, you've really gone out of your way to help me out."

"No problem! I have big plans to expand on this 'hands-on teaching' in the future. We're going to have to send some of the students away from your course with this type of response, there's just too many. Oh, by the way, I also faxed you the syllabus for the course that we arranged. I want you to go over it and make any changes that you feel fit. After all, it is your course and you'll know more about the fishing aspects than me or anyone on the board. Fax it back as soon as you can, but you can change parts of it right up until classes start. You've got time so there's no big hurry, the most important thing is to pass this test."

Charles tilted his head upright. "There's something else about this place, Dean, I should like to tell you." He hesitated. He'd better not say anything lest the dean tell him it's too dangerous and he would lose everything, including the job which now seemed so enticing.

"Yes, Charlie, what is it?"

"Oh, nothing serious. I just don't know how to thank you, Dean!"

"Oh, no need for thanks. You may have just started a whole new branch of study at the school. Charlie, I'm so happy!"

"Me, too, Dean. Me too!" He sighed and hung up. He only had eleven more days to learn how to lobster on his own, complete a year-long syllabus and learn how to fish on his own. He had to master the boat and study the sea life around Woods Hole. To make matters worse, he had to deal with Jonas and now the unexplained murder. He pondered the difficulty of it all. All he had to do was tweak the syllabus he already had and get a little help from the university. He didn't think that the boat was all that difficult to master. How much is there to know about a lobster or a fish?

A LOT! What was he getting himself into?

Chapter 10

Charles got to the dock early again, but Jonas had already arrived. There was a commotion well off to the left of the pier. He could see that there were many people mulling around a boat on the shore. It was the boat they had approached yesterday. He walked over to Jonas, who was also watching the crowd around the boat. Jonas was cutting off a piece of chewing tobacco and standing on the pier by the steps going down to where he had tied the dinghy. "Well, good morning, Chuck, good to see ya could make it."

Charles stuck his thumb out toward the scene near the pier. "I see that they found that boat of … what was his name?" He tried to remember.

"Doug Harvey. It must have either washed up there or somebody else hauled it in. They still ain't found him."

"Are the police involved, yet?"

"What for—a stray boat? As far as any one knows, it coulda just slipped off its mooring, or Doug abandoned it. They ain't found no body yet, and ain't nobody talkin'" He chewed violently on the tobacco, and placed the knife back in his belt. "Ya talk to that dean of yours?" He smiled brightly with that question.

"Yes, I did. I guess he talked to you, too. I'm going to be on my own on Monday, if I pass this test."

"Oh, you'll pass it. Hell, I passed it—and mine was harder! You'll only be getting' a noncommercial license. Mine is commercial. If ya get anything, we'll have to have dinner, 'cause ya ain't gonna be able to sell 'em. That's another law ya gotta know."

"That sounds good to me. I'd like to see your family again, and get out of that hotel for a while. Today is going to be a full day because I need to learn everything else you can show me then I want to get back early to study. I take the test Sunday."

"That dean of yours told me. Let's go, then!"

They got into the skiff and made their way to *The Pincher*, climbed aboard and headed out to the deep water traps Jonas had set. The day was gorgeous, not too hot and not too cold, and the sunrise had given it an extra beauty with the red skies bouncing off of the thin, gray clouds. "How did ya get to take the test on a Sunday—they ain't open?"

"The university arranged it, through connections."

"Don't that figure! Politics!" They passed the various buoys, entering the channel. "That dean called me and told me ya got a boat rented with your own buoys and gear for Monday." He looked at Charles. "That's some pretty quick work. They must like ya." He spit over the side of the boat.

"Well, I guess they do. It's all happening pretty quick for me, though."

"Ah-yup!" Jonas turned back around to look in the direction they were headed. "Must be good!" He held animosity for Charles, not just because of his special treatment from the Maine D.M.R. But because he was a teacher in college, an institution he despised, but he was getting paid—well! They proceeded through the channel and off the coast to where he held his deep traps. He shifted the boat into neutral. "Look over there, Charlie." He pointed straight ahead into the bay just east of Turtle Head. Charles twirled and looked. He could see a group of animals swimming through the water, arching their backs when they surfaced from the water.

"What are they—Dolphins?"

Jonas focused on them. "You're close. That's a pod of porpoises."

Charles turned to him in confusion, "Isn't that the same thing?"

Jonas laughed. "No. There are two types of dolphins, one's a fish and the other is a mammal; a type of whale, kin to the killer whale. Either way, they both have long noses or beaks. These are porpoises, see the snubbed noses?"

Charles looked more closely and could not make out the typical dolphin nose. He thought, *They look very similar with the dorsal fins, but Jonas is correct about the nose.* "Ha! You're right! I learn something new every day."

"It'd be awful rare to see a dolphin up here. They like the real warm water." He pushed in the throttle and they approached their first trap. He hooked up the warp to the hauler and began hoisting the trap up.

Charles seemed curious. "Why do you have traps offshore like this? Everybody else seems to stay close to shore."

"Well, now, that's a good question. I'll tell ya, lobster like the rocks in usually shallow, cool water. As we get closer to winter in the fall, the shore waters are still warm and the offshore, deep waters are much cooler. I believe that the lobsters actually move to the cooler waters. It takes a lot more warp to haul 'em in, but I seem to get more here in August. Plus, everyone else in there got most of 'em already, so there ain't quite so many as there was when the season began. Nobody but me comes out here, so what's here is mine for the takin'." He grinned after he spoke. The trap came up and swung to the washboard. There were three in this trap—all keepers. "That's another thing.

You don't throw back too many out here!" He opened the trap and threw them into one of the bins beside him.

"I notice you don't band the lobsters like before, why?"

"Ah, they won't have enough room to hurt each other. That's really the only reason ya band. They'll do that at the lobster pound. I'll show ya how to do it, though." He reached into his belt and pulled out a funny-shaped tool which looked like a dentist's instrument. "I used to peg 'em here in this opening at the base of the claw, but they don't take 'em like that no more. They want the bands. I guess the pegs ruined the claw meat or something like that. This here is called the band pliers, but it opens just the opposite of a pair of pliers." He squeezed the handles together and the pliers opened up instead of closing like a regular set of pliers. He reached into the pocket in his belt and pulled out a regular rubber band, placed it on the end of the pliers then reached in the bin and took out one of the lobsters. "Ya band the crusher claw first, and really that's all ya need to band." He held the lobster out to demonstrate and squeezed the handles on the pliers again, placing the stretched out band over the lobster's claw, then released it. The band held the claw from opening. "It's that easy." He tossed the lobster back into the bin and set the pliers back into his belt.

He rebaited the trap, pulled all of the crabs from it, then dropped it back into the water. "I would usually move my traps now, but I got ya schedule to maintain. I'll prob'ly move all my traps after ya on ya own." He pushed the throttle and went over to the next trap. "Ya gotta learn where to set ya traps. It helps to know the area. When I talked to ya dean there, I told 'im that I should be with ya on your maiden voyage, so to say, to make sure ya know what ya are doin'. I'll show ya where to set 'em then. Like I said, they like the rocks and ya being new to boatin', never mind lobsterin', I think ya should stay close to shore. Ya only gonna have five traps."

Charles actually thought that was a good idea. It certainly made him feel better that he wouldn't be on his own in case something went wrong. He relaxed and leaned back. "You know," he said, "I actually wrote a paper on the history of fisheries and part of the paper had to do with the lobster industry, when I was in school."

Jonas spit out more tobacco and idled near the next trap. "Is that right, teacher? What kind of history does lobsterin' have? Is it Maine history?" He grabbed the buoy and hooked it up to the hauler. Jonas continued working while Charles talked and watched.

"Maine is the Cadillac of states for the lobster industry, but it first started in Massachusetts—that is as an industry. You know, I've never eaten a lobster! At one time they were so abundant that they would just wash up on shore. Native Americans used them for fertilizer, but not to eat. Indebted servitudes in the original colonies would be fed a diet of lobster, leaving the good food for their debtors. It was in the early 17th century that they were even considered worthy to eat, and because they were so plentiful, one Englishman saw the profit in them when he scooped out 30 with a fish net. Other people could see that there was profit in it, just from mere quantity. Then in the 1840s the canning industry boomed and canned lobster from Maine became quite popular to other states. The industry began to prosper by 'smackmen' who traveled in small boats called 'smacks.' They were sailboats that hauled the lobster from place to place. That's when a five-pound lobster was considered small and anything less wasn't worth picking through to get the meat to can. Actually, one report mentioned that there were five- and six-foot-long lobsters caught in New York Bay! But the canning industry didn't last, and fresh lobsters took over late in the 19th century. The first lobster pound was established in Vinalhaven, back then. Soon, there were 23 fisheries along the coat of Maine. I guess now they are all over the place, from what I've seen. Now lobster is pretty expensive. It's amazing how things change!"

Jonas laughed. "Sure is!" He hauled his last trap from the deep water. "I save this one for last."

"Why?" Charlie seemed interested.

"'Cause I got my special toggle on this warp!"

As the line came up, Charles could see the toggle was really a half-full quart bottle of rum. Jonas took it off the warp and smiled at Charles as he drank part of the contents. "That's why!" He laughed. This trap came up empty so he just reset it.

All in all, he had ten traps out there, but five were empty; maybe his theory wasn't accurate. "You know how to pilot the boat or do ya need me to show ya that?"

"No, I don't think so. I've watched everything you've done and I think I can handle it."

"We'll see come Monday!" He pushed the throttle in and headed to the traps he had in Belfast Bay.

The day began to wane after they finished in the bay. Jonas checked his watch. "I better get ya back. That test ya take tomorrow is real important to that dean of yours."

"It's important to me, too!" They headed back to Searsport dock.

"I'm gonna drop ya off and I'll head back to Belfast and drop these babies off so that ya can get goin' and study. I can't haul after 4:00p.m. today anyway."

Charles got back to the hotel relatively early, rested for a minute then called Janet. He had been negligent in his contacting her yesterday, and he knew she would be worried. He dialed the number.

"Hi, honey, how's everything?"

"Well, hello! It's about time you called. Everything's fine here, but I miss you."

"How are the kids?"

"They're fine, too, and they miss you! When are you coming home?"

"Well, that's what I want to talk to you about. Apparently, this class has gotten a resounding response. It does mean I'll have a job when I get back."

She sighed, "I guess so. Have you heard anything about that murder?"

"Oh, that's another thing. I think we witnessed another one. I don't know what's going on here, but everyone seems so tight lipped. I can't figure it out."

"Another one! You better go to the sheriff. This isn't funny! What kind of town is this?"

"I have to take a test tomorrow, and they still haven't found any bodies, so there's not a lot I can tell the chief of police here—and he's not a sheriff."

"Whatever, just take care of yourself and keep your eyes open. Remember, you have a family waiting for you."

"I know, and I will be careful. I have to study for that test tonight, so I'm going to let you go. I love you."

"I love you, too! Be careful!"

"I will." He hung up and opened his study material. There he sat all night in the hotel chair until eventually he fell asleep in the chair, the manual in his hands.

Chapter 11

The night grew dark and misty when Jonas finally arrived at the shack he called home. He staggered out of his truck and proceeded inside the building. Elena was sweeping the floor by the entrance, while the children were watching television in the living room. "Jonas, have you been drinking?"

He just looked at her. The question didn't need an answer, it was obvious.

"Are you drunk?"

He pushed her out of his way and headed directly for the cupboards. "I'm feelin' my oats—what's it to ya?"

"Oh, dear, I wish you didn't drink so much."

He reached inside the cupboard and pulled out a quart bottle of rum. "Ya always bitch. Bitch, bitch, bitch! Why don't ya go out and get a job?" His mood was nasty, as always. "I had a couple of pops in town, there ain't nothin' wrong with that." He took a glass off the counter and filled it up with rum then entered the living room. "Out of my chair, boy!" Chad jumped up and moved over to the couch and sat beside Katherine.

Jonas was grumpy, as he sat. "What the hell are ya watching? Damned sitcoms? Fuh-c-ryin'-out-loud! I hate these shows! Put on the news!" He took a drink from the glass. His face clenched, staring at Chad. "Well! Change the channel!"

"Dad, the news is over," he responded timidly.

"O.K., then. Well, put somethin' on but this!"

"Sure, Dad." Chad changed the channel, but it was only another sitcom. He turned to Jonas, who stared at the set in disgust.

"Ain't there anything good on TV these days?"

"We only get three channels, Dad," Chad responded.

Jonas growled, "Then turn it off! I've seen enough!" He drank the remaining rum in his glass, got up from the chair and walked to the cupboard, where he took the bottle back out and set it on the kitchen table. Elena had a cup of coffee sitting in a saucer beside his seat. He pushed it aside and poured another glass full of rum then set the bottle down on the table in front of him. He began to chant and stomp his feet:

"What do ya do with a drunken sailor;
What do ya do with a drunken sailor;
What do ya do with a drunken sailor,
Early in the mornin'?"

He laughed loudly.

Elena stopped sweeping and looked at him with pity in her eyes.

He took a gulp from the glass. "What are you lookin' at, woman?"

She bowed her head down and briskly swept all the debris she had collected into a pile.

She leaned over and picked up her cup of coffee with one hand, took a sip and set the cup back down onto the saucer, where it made a clicking sound. He put his hands over his ears and grimaced. "I HATE that sound," he screamed.

"I'm sorry, Jonas, but there's something I have to tell you." She smiled politely at him, and leaned the broom against the wall. He never looked at her. She scanned the living room. "Chad and Katherine, why don't you go upstairs and play so that I can talk to your father?" It was more of an order than a request.

The two children nodded and scurried up the stairway. She watched them ascend.

"Ya want to talk to me? Well, what is it? Come on, woman, spit it out!" He crossed his arms and leaned back.

She sat down in the chair beside him and leaned forward with her arms on the table. "Jonas," she said, "Uncle Steve passed away today. Aunt Julie just called before you came home." Tears welled up in her eyes.

He chuckled. "Is that it? Humph. It's about time. That old geezer's been clingin' on for too long."

"Jonas, please! We were close. I wish you could have a little sympathy."

"Hey, look, we all gotta go sometime, and that old man's been puttin' it off. He's been sick, ain't he?"

"Well, yes, he has been sick for quite some time. I feel bad about Aunt Julie, what is she going to do now?"

"One thing—she don't have to take care of that dead weight. She should be happy, and a bit more relaxed with that burden gone."

"But Jonas, she'll be all alone!"

"I envy her then!"

"That's the other thing I have to tell you. I'm going up to Millinocket tomorrow to help make arrangements and to comfort Aunt Julie. I want to make sure that she is all right and see if she needs anything. I'll be gone for about a week. The children are old enough to take care of themselves for that long while you're working. I'll call you and tell you how everything is going. I think the children would like to attend the funeral, so I'll let you know when everything is happening."

"Who's gonna do the cookin' and the cleanin'?" he asked, absorbed in his own self-interest.

"I've already talked to the children. Katherine will do the cooking and the two of them will share the duties on cleaning, dishes, laundry and the general chores. It will only be a week." She picked up her cup of coffee.

"I guess it can't hurt. Katherine's cookin' can't be any worse than yours." He laughed and looked at the stove, then got up and stared into the pan sitting on top. "Speakin' of that, what's for dinner? This is just water."

"Oh, I forgot. I'm making pasta tonight." She set her cup back down on the saucer and it made the clicking sound again. He threw his hands up over his ears once more.

"I told you, I *hate* that sound!" he bellowed, then picked the pot of hot water off the stove and threw the water in her face.

She screamed.

"And ya can keep ya damned pasta, too!" he yelled.

She covered her face with both hands, wailing uncontrollably. "No, Jonas, NO!" She got up and ran to the sink where she turned on the cold water and stuck her head underneath. "Oh, oh, oh, oh, oh!" She left the water running for some time, soothing the burn.

The children heard the scream and came running down the steps. Katherine stood on the bottom while Chad charged Jonas, who never moved. Instead, he stood still with the pot still in his hand. When Chad got close to him, he swung the pot around and hit the boy on the top of his head with the bottom of the pot. Chad stopped short and clutched the top of his head.

Jonas turned to Katherine, who was crying against the wall at the base of the stairs. "What's the matter with you, girl? You wanna cry? I'll give ya somethin' to cry about!" He waved the pan in the air. She immediately ran back upstairs, still crying.

Chad looked up at his father while still rubbing his head. "You'll get yours!" he said. "One day, Dad! One day, you'll get yours!"

"Get upstairs with your sister! I don't need your backtalk." He shook the pot at him, "I said GET!"

Chad reeled around and ran up the stairs behind Katherine.

Elena removed her head from below the spigot of the sink, soaked a cloth under the water and placed it over her face. "Please, Jonas, please!" She rubbed her eyes.

"Oh, get over it! Put somethin' on that I can eat, none of this pasta shit!" He grumbled then sat back down. He poured more rum in the glass in front of him and took a long swallow. He held his head in his hands. "These damned headaches!"

Elena wiped her face with the cloth, it was red but there were no blisters. "Oh, Jonas, I think we might have some luncheon meats in the fridge, I can make you some sandwiches, if that's O.K. with you."

"Yeah, that's fine. At least it's got meat."

She went to the refrigerator and took out the luncheon meats. The children had returned to the bottom of the stairs and she saw them out of the corner of her eye then turned to look at Jonas, who was rubbing his ears and staring down at the table. She walked over to the children and whispered, "What are you doing down here?" She held the meats in her hands.

"Are you O.K., ma?" Chad whispered back.

Katherine continued to weep. "I'm fine, children. I'll make the pasta after your father has gone to bed." She looked over to Jonas again. "It shouldn't be much longer! Now go upstairs and I'll call you when he's asleep. Let's go now." She flicked the meats in the direction of the stairs, signaling them to go.

Katherine went up quickly, but Chad stood still. "I'm going to get him, ma! I swear, I'm going to get him!"

Suddenly, Jonas picked his head up and twirled it in the direction of Elena. "The hell with the sandwiches woman! I need some sex!"

Chad's eyes popped open wide.

"Oh, not now, Jonas—I still have to pack and get ready. It's such a long ride and I want to leave early tomorrow." She turned back to Chad and whispered, "Quick, Chad, get upstairs." He hesitated, but finally went.

Jonas stood up in an unsteady fashion. He swayed sideways then walked up to her and grabbed her by the arm. "I said I need some sex, and if you don't give it to me, I'll take it!" He pulled her by the arm to the bedroom while she protested.

"Please, Jonas, no!"

He opened the door to the bedroom and threw her inside, tossing her onto the bed. He took his belt off at the entrance, and a wide grin encompassed his face, then he slammed the door behind them.

Chad returned down the stairs and listened outside the door. He could hear her crying, "No, Jonas, NO!" He could also hear his father laughing, and for the first time since he was very young, he began to cry.

Chapter 12

Charles woke up in the hotel chair from the alarm he had set, the booklet resting open on his chest. He picked the alarm up and looked at it closely. It was nearly 7:00 a.m. and the fax informed him to meet Stanley Curtis, the head of the Maine Department of Marine Resources at 9:00 a.m. He hurried around the room, gathering his suit and tie, took a quick shower and packed all the paperwork that was faxed to him in his valise, except for the directions to Curtis's house. He wanted to leave early enough to get there one half hour early, just in case he couldn't find it.

The morning was gorgeous as he climbed into his van. The sun shone very brightly, and he could hear the chorus of birds all around the hotel. Seagulls flocked over the water when he crossed the Passagassawakeag Bridge, more commonly referred to as the Belfast Bridge. He could see that the tide was relatively high when he peered over the edge. He had taken this route from Augusta to Belfast on the way down from Rhode Island when he first arrived in Maine, and he remembered how beautiful the scenery was then. Today was a much clearer day and he enjoyed the view for the entire trip. He didn't eat breakfast, but if he got there early enough, he would get something to eat in Augusta. As it turned out, the directions were perfect and he had no problem finding Curtis's house. He glanced at his watch. It was 8:40 a.m. He pulled into Curtis's driveway and waited in the van, until he saw a man open the door and wave for him to come inside. He picked up his valise, got out of the van and walked up to the entrance.

"Mornin'! You must be Charles Ritter. My name is Stan Curtis, I've been expecting you. You didn't have to sit out there in your cah." He spoke with a thick Maine accent.

"Well, I didn't want to bother you, I was told to be here at 9:00 a.m."

"My boy," Curtis stated, "I get up at 5:00 a.m. every day. Plus, I had to set up the test for you. Come on in and have a seat at the dining room table. My wife and kids are at church, so you won't be bothered. This shouldn't take you long at all. Would you like something to drink; coffee, tea, juice, anything?" He pulled out a chair from the table, where there were some papers arranged. He was a stately man, in his mid fifties (he guessed) and the house was immaculately clean and organized. *Obviously,* he thought, *the head of the department lives a little bit better than those that go out there to work the waters.* He sat down.

"Now, it's all pretty self-explanatory. Just tell me when you're done and I'll go over the results with you. Meanwhile, if you have any questions, I'll be in the living room reading the paper. I'm going to need some identification. Oh, by the way, I used Jonas Hale's address for you. I spoke with Jonas and he said he had no problem with that. O.K.?"

"Yes. Thank you." *Wow,* he thought, *the university* really *wants me to get this!*

"All right then, I'll have to take your valise—not that I don't trust you. You know, this process usually takes quite a bit of time. The board at the University of Rhode Island went out of their way to get this completed in one day. They actually filled out your application and e-mailed it to me yesterday. That tells me something about you, but then again, they also help us out. The university and the group at Woods Hole perform biological research that aids us in maintaining a well-balanced eco-system in the waters of Maine and we keep a direct line with them. They have also helped with our hatcheries and fisheries. I had to pull a few strings to get you in here today, but it should be mutually beneficial to both of our states."

Charles nodded his head and smiled.

"Good luck! I'll be over there if you need me."

"Thank you," he said then dug into the test.

Elena finished packing her bags early in the morning and brought out the last one to her Volkswagen, placing it in the back. She walked back into the house to wash up and brush her teeth. Jonas sat at the kitchen table watching her. The children were still asleep.

Jonas placed his hand behind his head and leaned back in the chair, nearly hitting the counter behind. "Ya think ya got everything? For Christ's sake, you might as well just pack the whole house in the car."

"It's just clothes, Jonas. I only have my toiletries to pack after I get done putting my face on and brushing my teeth." She walked into the bathroom.

"You're dressed awful fancy to meet that old bag!"

She answered from the other room, "There will be other people there, too; Friends and such. I want to look good."

"That old fart had friends? Ha!" He brought the chair back to all four legs. "Any young male friends, ey?" He held a sinister smirk. "Is that why you're all prettied up?"

"Oh, Jonas, please!" She exited the bathroom with her bag of items.

He spoke slowly, "Well, now, I suppose I have to do the shoppin'?"

"It won't kill you."

"Well, then, come over here and say bye." He stood up and held his arms out.

"Goodbye, Jonas, I'm in a hurry."

"I said get over here and say bye!" He was persistent and insisted. She stopped.

He stepped to her in an apparent loving way, then grabbed her by the arms. "I want some before ya go!"

"Oh, no, Jonas, no! I'm in a hurry!" She struggled but it was no use.

"I ain't gonna get none for a week! Ya better give me some now!" He manhandled her while she whimpered.

"No, please, Jonas, no!" Her struggling was no use. He forced her into the bedroom and slammed the door.

Chad had woken, hearing his mother's voice. That incessant "No" that he had gotten all too used to hearing. He came down the stairs and heard the struggling in the bedroom.

He pressed his ear against the door, absorbing the ordeal. "He'll get his!" he whispered. "He'll get his!"

Charles left Augusta a little after 10:30 a.m. He had sat and talked to Mr. Curtis for a while after his test while the man graded it. He had passed! He decided to stop by Jonas's house on the way back to the hotel to let him know and he had been given an alternate route that bypassed Belfast, going down Route #131. He knew there was no lobster fishing today, so he believed he would catch Jonas home. He arrived there at just after noon and pulled into the driveway. He stepped out of the van, walked up to Jonas's door and knocked. He noticed that the Volkswagen was not there as he waited at the door.

"Ah-Yup. Come in!" The voice came from inside. Charles opened the door and saw Jonas sitting at the kitchen table with a bottle of rum and a full glass in front of him. "I thought it'd be ya. Have a seat." He pointed to a chair at the table.

Charles looked around the shack. "Where is everybody?" he asked.

"Elena went to Millinocket, and the kids are over visitin' their friends."

Charles stood still for a moment, looking at Jonas, then stepped to the table, where he sat down. "I finished my test. I passed!" An awkward smile came over his face.

"Ah-yup! I knew ya would. Hell, with your connections, I'm surprised the governor himself didn't come down and sign ya license for ya." His response was not exactly enthusiastic.

"Hey, look, I had to study for that, and I got a perfect score!" He tried to get a little "Thank you" or "Congratulations" out of the lobsterman. He got no such kudos, in fact, he got just the opposite.

"Ah-yup. Figures, with all that schoolin'. I got mine without no school, and I'll be damned if my boy needs it!"

Charles looked puzzled. "What is it about education that you despise? What's wrong with school?" he asked in total sincerity and curiousness.

Jonas crossed his legs, sitting in the chair, then took a drink from the glass in front of him. His mind seemed to be wandering. "Do ya really want to know?"

"Yes, I would. It makes me feel uncomfortable."

"All right, then. It was a long time ago," he began, pointing to the bottle of rum. "Want a snort?" Charles shook his head. "Now, I told ya that I used to fish, didn't I?" Charles nodded in the affirmative.

"Well, when I was a kid, my parents fought all the time, while I was forced to sit and watch. My father drank a lot and would fight with my mother constantly. I had to quit school to work so I could help support the family. There were six of us and I was the oldest. I never got no schoolin', like most. Finally, my ma left my father and I got fed up with the whole scene. So, I left Maine to find adventure; to fish. I looked for a good place to head out from, to get onto a boat and to learn the ropes, so to say. I ended up at Quonset Point in Rhode Island. You should know where that is."

Charles nodded again.

"They took me on aboard a drag line vessel named *Edna and Flo*. I thought it was a funny name, ya know like the tides, ebb and flow." He laughed from deep within his chest.

"Anyway, I was young, probably too young to even be on the boat, but they let me go. It was before I met Elena, and I wanted the thrill of seeing what it was like being on the sea, and to get my mind off from things at home."

He smiled, and his yellow teeth showed. "The only book I ever read, Chuck, was *Moby Dick*. I worked hard on that boat, it wasn't what I had expected; there weren't the glamour I saw in movies, just backbreaking labor. My hands bled for the first week aboard.

"I was there almost a year, and we had seven men aboard her; the captain, the first mate and five hands. One of the hands was a college boy who couldn't get a job nowhere else. He worked beside me most of the time.

"We'd go out for a week or two weeks at a time, sometimes longer;

usually, until we filled the boat with fish. Well, this college boy always spoke big words, just ta piss the rest of us off, 'cause he knew we didn't understand 'im. He'd brag about his education; how much he knew and all that bullshit. Anyway, the captain and the mate ended up hookin' up with a boat headed to Alaska. They said there was more money there, so they quit.

"The owner of the boat was so impressed with that college boy—his name was Jason Randall. I'll never forget him. He was a little snotty nosed, arrogant, pig-headed fool, always kissin' ass. We were all about the same age, I guess, but he bullshitted the owner so well and kissed ass so much that he got the job. The problem was, though, he really didn't know shit!

"On our first trip out, he took us south for a week and we didn't catch hardly nothin'. We could all tell that he didn't know what he was doin', or where he was goin'. So he decided to travel into the Gulf of Maine, and up to Georges Bank. I think it's the only place he ever heard of that had fish. We got word that a storm was comin' in a couple of days. We all told him that we wouldn't have enough time to get back. He wouldn't listen, because he knew it all! Smart-assed college boy! We all talked together and wanted to toss him overboard. Instead, we went. We caught all kinds of fish on the first day, doublin' what we had. We tried to tell him that the storm was comin', but he was wild with ego. Now he could really make an impression on the owner, if he filled up the boat.

"'Just one more day,' he told us. He really wanted to make a name for himself. We pulled up one last net before the wind stopped us. When we did, there were a whole bunch of huge lobsters inside the net. I mean they must have weighed 40 pounds each and over 100 years old. Never seen 'em that big before, or after.

"The storm came overnight, so we couldn't see it, but we could feel it, and it hit hard! In the morning it was full blast, right at us. We told him it was too late to try to make shore and we should run into the storm.

"That's when he panicked. He ran around the boat in a frenzy, not knowing what to do. He ordered us to try to make it into Canada. We tried, but it was too late. The seas must have been twenty feet at that time." He snickered slowly as he spoke, then took another drink and re-poured the glass full. His eyes were blood red, and his countenance was very grave and somber, as though he was in pain from the recollection.

"I don't remember what happened next. We either capsized or split. All I know is that I was in the water, clinging on to a piece of wood from the boat and getting tossed with the sea. I held on for my life and went underwater with every other wave, or more. That bastard ignored all of us, and he didn't care, 'cause he had his prize catch.

LOBSTER TRAPPED!

"I musta been in that water for nearly an hour when I saw land in front of me. The water was freezing cold. I had no idea where I was, but the swells somehow took me right to the shore. On the way, I found the captain, floating face down. I didn't know if he was dead or alive, so I grabbed him by the arm and dragged him along with me. We crashed on a beach, just missing the rocks. I was exhausted, but I hauled him up along the shore, where I found a small cliff which served as some protection against the driving rains and hurricane winds.

"The captain was still alive, but not by much. His face was pale and I could tell he was suffering from severe hypothermia, so I huddled up to him to share body heat, and that's where we spent the day, riding out the storm. He would drop in and out of consciousness, but just tucked himself into a ball while his whole body trembled. That night the winds died down somewhat, then I turned to the captain and tried to wake him up. I poked him several times.

"His face was blue now, and he just toppled over when I poked him the last time. He had died sometime earlier that day.

"The rain stopped and it got unbearably cold." He guffawed at the thought. "I didn't care about the captain no more, and I guess he didn't care about his jacket no more either; so I took it. I hurt my leg somewhere between the storm comin' in, and getting' up on shore, but I didn't even feel it until then. I tried to stand up, but I couldn't. I wrapped his jacket around me and lay there until I passed out." He took a drink from the glass and grinned out of half of his mouth, his yellow teeth, with brown spots from the chewing tobacco showed. "The sun came out, and I finally got up and limped up to where I could see. I found out later that I was at Brandy Cove, one of the Southern Cove Islands in New Brunswick. It's hard to get off an island with no ship! I could see land, and it didn't look far off, but I was completely spent. There was no way I could swim it from there. I went back to the small shelter and passed out again. I thought I was going to die there. Funny, I also found out later that the land I saw was called Deadman's Harbor." He gave off a half-silent laugh and stared down at the table.

"Next thing I remember, I woke up in a hospital bed, all drugged up." He paused. "That's when I heard the clicking; the clicking of shoes on a tiled floor. It was the nurse who came to give me another shot. I was only awake for a few seconds, then I was out again. I don't know what those nurses wore for shoes, but every time I woke and heard that clicking sound, I received another shot. I never even had time to talk. I'll never forget that sound; that clicking sound! I cringed every time I heard it." He let out a heavy sigh.

"Finally, I got so many shots that, as I got better and stayed awake for longer periods of time, I couldn't go to sleep without that shot.

"I couldn't wait to hear that clicking sound." He smiled smugly with a look of hate for something Charles was beginning to understand. "Ya see, this doctor that prescribed these shots was right out of school, and I was his guinea pig.

"They finally released me after a month. I hung around Canada for a while, doin' odd jobs, and tryin' to get work on a fishin' boat, but I was gettin' headaches real bad. I had headaches so bad, sometimes, that I couldn't even move without my head wantin' to explode. I went back to that hospital and talked to the doctor about my headaches. Ya know what he told me?" He leaned on the table and looked Charles directly in the eyes.

"No," Charles said, "What?" He had become engrossed with the story.

Jonas leaned back in his chair. "He told me I had mental problems. He told me I was insane because of the accident and too long exposure to the freezing water. He said I was sufferin' from psychological trauma because of what happened to the rest of the crew. Huh!

"Then he gave me a whole new regimen of drugs to take and told me that he had to keep and eye on me. Hell, I didn't know, but I figured he did, with all that schoolin'. He held me in the hospital for another week to monitor me and see if I was fit to be put back into society. I took 'em drugs, but the headaches got worse. I decided he really wasn't helpin' me so I signed myself out and came back to Maine.

"That's when I met Elena and we got married, but the headaches continued so bad that last year I went to a specialist in Boston to find out what was wrong with me. I explained to him what had happened to me; with the doctor and all. He checked me out and did some tests then made some phone calls. Come to find out that all those drugs the doctor in Canada gave me were experimental. That doctor was tryin' to make a name for himself." He stopped talking and took another drink of rum.

"In Boston, there weren't no clickin' shoes and he didn't give me no drugs, but he did do some tests on me. That's when I found out." He gritted his teeth together in anger and stared at nothing in particular. The silence seemed forever to Charles.

"Found out what?"

He turned to Charles with bulged out eyes. "Those drugs that new-schooled doctor gave me in Canada somehow merged together and formed into a tumor in my brain. That *schooled* doctor gave me rat poison!" Contempt showed all over his face. "They can't operate on it now 'cause it's in the brain stem. I might have a couple of years, and I might have a couple of days, they couldn't tell me for sure. I couldn't even sue that hospital in

Canada. The doctor in Boston notified the authorities, who shut the hospital down. Their insurance company had already declared bankruptcy, and that doctor that gave me the drugs, well, nobody know where he went. Took off, I s'pose. I remembered those lobster we hauled up though, and I knew ya didn't have to go far offshore to get 'em and that's when I started lobsterin'. Keeps me close to home.

"Ya see now, it was a *schooled* captain that almost killed me, and did kill the rest of the crew! It's just a matter of time until that *schooled* doctor is gonna kill me!"

He sat up straight in the chair. "Ya asked me, teacher, why I don't like schoolin'. Well, that's why!" He startled laughing loudly then tipped his glass towards Charles. "Hey!"

Charles gulped. "Oh, my God! I'm sorry, I didn't know!" There were no words he could think of for comfort.

"Elena and the kids don't know anything about this. I never talk about it, and that's the way I want to keep it, if ya know what I mean. Hell, I told Elena I was goin' to Boston to swing a lobster deal. Haha. She has no idea. There's nothin' I can do about it now. I take aspirin for the headaches, that's it." He sighed. "And ya know, there, Charlie, sometimes I can still hear the clicking of those shoes! Heh, heh, heh. Ay-yup; sometimes!"

Charles sat mesmerized, his mouth agape. "I'll take that drink now!"

Jonas smiled at him, stretched his arm behind him and leaned over, picking up a glass off the counter without taking his eyes off of Charles.

"You have that boat scheduled for tomorrow at 10:00 a.m. so you can sleep in if you want. I know whose boat it is—it's Randy Thompson's. Your dean gave me a call and told me all about it. Randy's a tuna fisherman, but the boat is good for both tuna fishing and lobster fishing. It's a nice boat; a lot better than mine." He set the glass in front of Charlie and poured him a small shot then topped off his own glass. "He owns a 32-foot Holland with all the works. We'll go through what ya need to know about the boat tomorrow. I'll keep an eye out for ya, but since ya been here, I've been goin' out later than I usually do, that was to accommodate you. The sun rises at about 6:00 a.m. tomorrow and I'm on the water at 5:15 a.m. I'll be halfway done checkin' my traps by the time I run into ya. I'm gonna be headed out near Isleboro early, then I'll swing back to Mack Point, where I can see if Randy's boat's in. I don't think he did any lobster fishing this year at all. His boat's only been in a few times and he'll go out for a couple of days, tuna fishing or just cruisin'. He's getting' old, but he must have money. Anyway, I'll meet ya at the pier before 10:00 a.m."

They clicked their glasses together and took a drink.

Chapter 13

The sun burned through the window of the hotel room and Charles thought to himself, *I should have gotten a room on the west side of the building, if they even have one.* He groggily woke and sat on the edge of the bed; thinking. This morning, though, he had time for breakfast. He yawned and stretched, then got dressed, disregarding his usual morning shower. Jonas's story made him feel funny, and he had seen him in action, hitting his own family. He remembered from his psychology classes that the offspring will often imitate the most detested memories of their childhood. This seemed to be the case with Jonas, but the eerie part was his near death experience on the fishing boat and the revelation of his mortality. His emotions conflicted; he felt sorry for the man but was disgusted with his behavior.

He left the hotel at 8:30 a.m. and stopped to have something to eat at the diner on Route #1 between the hotel and the landing in Searsport. The sun sat fairly high in a cloudless sky. He knew he was going to be early getting to the pier, so he took his time eating. Even so, he arrived at the pier at 9:30 a.m. That was fine with him; maybe he would overhear some gossip there about the murders, which were now really bothering him. No bodies had been discovered and nobody was talking. *How strange,* he thought, *that no one wants to get involved*, but he wondered how many people would have seen anything if this was New York, or some other big city. It would most likely be the same scenario. Still, he hoped he could get a clue. He parked his van in the lot and walked the length of the pier close to where Sam and Andrew were leaning against the rail (as always). The sun reflected off the water, and the ripples, which couldn't be called waves, made fancy patterns with the light, bouncing it into irregular colors and locations. He stared at their hypnotic effects. The seagulls swarmed around the dock, looking for food. He studied the scene panoramically, keeping one ear open to the blabbering of the two old men.

Their conversation was droll:

"Ah-yup, I heard say that the ocean's rising somethin' like two inches every year," Sam spoke.

"Yup, and they had one report says that if this ozone gets any worse, them icecaps in the Artic are gonna be meltin' and comin' this way, like the ice age. When they get here they're all gonna melt and it's Armageddon!"

"Someone said that it's only a matter of time before Mt. Ephriam's gonna be almost completely under water."

"I hope it ain't in my time!" They both laughed then went silent for a minute, until Andrew said something that caught Charlie's attention.

"Ya hear they found Todd and Bill's boat?"

"Ah-yup. Over there in Long Cove, half under water."

"Yup. They still can't find either one o'them, though."

"Prob'ly fell out the boat. They weren't the two sharpest tools in the shed!" They laughed together, again. Charles snapped his head around. This was the first he had heard of this! He couldn't help but wonder if they suffered the same horrible fate as Ed Crowley. The two men turned around at the same time and looked at Charles as though they could feel his eyes upon them. They stared at him with disparagement. Sam slowly turned back around, but Andrew tilted his head the other way.

"Here comes Randy Thompson, by gory! Ain't seen him in a coon's age."

Sam turned around to look. "Yup! He must be goin' tuna fishin'; he ain't set no lobster traps this year."

"I would reckon, but I don't see his tower or his bow seat. He's settin' traps kinda late, and he's by himself!"

Charles spun to see the boat the two old men were talking about, remembering the name Randy Thompson. That was the name on the fax and the one Jonas spoke of when he mentioned the boat that he would be renting. That must be the boat. He ogled it in awe. It was a splendid craft, perfect for its intended use. The man driving the truck, trailer and boat backed the combination down the ramp until the trailer's wheels touched the edge of the water. There was a smaller boat with an outboard motor protruding from the back of the larger one. *That must be his skiff,* Charles thought.

The man got out of his truck and waved to Sam and Andrew. "Hi, guys!" he exclaimed.

The two men muttered, "Hey, Randy."

He walked up the ramp and onto the dock, studying Charles as he went, until he reached him. "You must be Charles Ritter."

"Yes, I am, and you must be Randy Thompson."

"I figured it was you; I saw the Rhode Island plates on that Ford van over there and you're the only one here I don't recognize. Nice to meet you." He was of medium build with graying hair, a thin gray mustache. He was dressed like a businessman. He looked different from the rest of the crowd he had met at the landing. He was wearing a tan cowboy hat and rectangular spectacles; for a man of his age, he was in great shape—trim and muscular. He held out his hand to Charles, who reciprocated, and they shook. His grip was powerful.

"It's nice to meet you, too," he responded. "I guess this is the boat the university rented for me. It's a beauty!"

"Well, thank you, lad. I've had some good times in it. I'm going to drop it in for you and I heard Jonas.... Well, there he is now."

Charles pivoted his head towards the water. Jonas had already moored his boat and was rowing into the loading area. "Hey, there, Randy," he shouted as the dinghy pulled up to the bottom of the ramp.

"How have you been, Jonas, you old fool?" he joked. He didn't have that typical Maine accent that Charles was getting so used to. There was a certain air about the man; a true confidence he demonstrated; a real savoir faire. He was also well tanned. *He's most likely not originally from here,* Charles thought. Jonas loosely tied the boat to the steps leading up to the pier and climbed up.

"I been doin' all right. How 'bout ya? Ain't seen ya around here in quite a while."

"Oh, I haven't been around much. I don't know. I'm getting old, you see. I think I'm going to sell my company and retire. I only took this old girl out a couple of times this year, and my wife doesn't enjoy it like she used to." He patted the side of the boat. "She wants to go to Florida earlier and earlier every year, and now she's talking as though she wants to stay there all year long. I don't know, Jonas. I still would like to go out fishing, but I can't go alone. To have any fun, I have to stay for at least a couple of days. I'm just getting too old for it." He placed his hands on his hips and tipped his head, closing his lips together. "All our neighbors have moved and sold their houses to a younger crowd. My wife doesn't have the company she once had. We know all the people around us in Florida. Of course, as you know, she's the boss!" He looked disheartened.

Jonas tapped him on the shoulder with a closed fist. "Hell, ya look in better shape than me."

"Well, I don't know about that." He appeared embarrassed, kicking the ground with his right foot and looking down.

"If ya go to Florida, are ya gonna be takin' the boat?"

He looked up from the ground to Jonas, then directed his attention to Charles. "Well, that depends on this lad."

Charles suddenly found himself in the conversation. "What do you mean by that—'it depends on me'?"

"I had a long talk with a man named Groton; Dean Groton. You know who I'm talking about."

"Yes," Charles answered, still unsure where he was going with this.

"Well, he told me that you're on some sort of test trial here in Maine and if it works out, the university might have a use for my boat. Hell, I had it up for sale anyway. In fact, that's how I think he got a hold of me; through my advertisement on the Internet. He said it was the perfect boat, because it can be used to lobster fish and to deep-sea fish. She'll last two days on the fuel I got on board right now, running all the time. This Groton guy said that you're going to be teaching a class on maritime history with a practical aspect, and you'd be going to Woods Hole all the time, not to mention day fishing and lobster fishing with your students. So, he's meeting with the board at the university sometime within this next week to see if they want to buy this one. He said that the Alumni Association has taken quite a fondness to the idea of your class, and personally, I think it's a good idea, too. Anyway, it's the Alumni Association that's going to pay for it, and quite frankly, they're not going to find any better boat at the price I'm asking. The only stipulation, he told me, is that you are the final say!" He pointed to Charles. "He's leaving it up to your discretion."

Charles was flattered by the mere suggestion that the university gave him this much power. He blushed. "How long did he say I'll have the boat before I have to decide?"

"Well, that's between you and him. Right now, they paid me to rent the boat for a week and a half." He frowned. "He said he faxed all the information to you."

Charles cringed. "He probably did, and I didn't pick it up at the hotel."

Randy turned to Jonas. "I was also told that you'd be going out with him today, so I know the boat's in good hands." He hesitated, not wanting to embarrass Charles. "How good is he?"

Jonas laughed. "He'll do fine! He's not bad for a college boy, the Great Atlantic got to him on the first day, but he's held out pretty well since then."

"Well, that's good. I left you that small boat with the 10-horsepower motor to get you to the mooring. I just tow it out if I'm going to moor the boat. I haven't used it for some time. You'll probably be happy with that, Jonas, you still row yours out, don't you?"

Jonas nodded. "I can't afford one o' them, yet."

"Well, I guess you both can use it. I'm leaving the boat, the skiff and the trailer, as well as the gear—the whole nine yards. I'm really not too concerned. The university is insuring it all, in case anything happens."

He turned to Charles. "I'll be with you starting next week to go out and do some fishing. I guess, in the meantime, you're just going to lobster fish. Well, all the gear's there. I'm going to drop the boat off and get home now. The old lady told me not to be too long. She wants to go to Bangor, shopping. I'll come back and check on the fuel and the gear. Do you want to check it out first, or can I just drop it off and get going?"

Jonas smiled. "I trust ya, Randy. It'll be fine the way it is."

"Good! Oh, by the way, the traps are all numbered and I wrote the numbers on a piece of wood and screwed it into the side by the wheel, just in case. You can see what colors your buoys are, so I don't think I need to tell you that. You know where my mooring is, don't you?"

"Sure do. We'll only be out for a little while today and he can only drop five traps, so the boat ain't gonna use that much fuel. O.K. then, let's get her in the water!

"I guess we can put the trailer on my truck for the time bein'," Jonas stated. "We'll take the skiff out together, until Charlie boy gets used to it. Is that all right with you, Chuck?" His teeth showed their disgusting color when he spoke.

"Sure, that's fine," Charles answered.

"Well, then, that's that!" Randy commented, and the three men launched the boat and tied it to the end of the long pier. They exchanged the trailer from his truck to Jonas's truck, then Randy got back into his truck. "Good luck, guys! You picked a good day to go out."

He was quite right. The weather was nothing less than perfect. It was late August but rather warm, even for this time of year. All the clouds had dispersed, and the sun beat down on their faces, taking any chill in the air out.

"Take it easy, Randy!" Jonas yelled as the truck drove off, with Randy's hand sticking out of the driver's side window, waving.

He turned to Charles, "This is your charter, mister. Might as well take the skiff to the mooring, and I pilot this boat! It's easier to do it here."

They removed the skiff from the boat, and Charles got inside. He climbed into it, from the pier, unsure of himself.

"Ya know how to handle her?" Jonas asked.

"Not really." Charles was confused, but after a quick lesson from Jonas, he got the idea. "I think I can handle it," he said. They left the ramp and headed to the mooring; Jonas in front and Charles behind him.

They tied the skiff to Randy's mooring, and Charles waited. Jonas stuck his arm out in a gesture for Charles to board, which he did, tenderly. Jonas helped him board and stood on deck. "Life jackets are over there." He pointed to the front of the boat. Charles immediately lunged forward and procured one, then placed it on, tying the straps quickly. Jonas studied the interior of the boat.

"Ya got yaself a fine vessel here, Charlie!" he said, pointing around the ship. "He set ya up with six traps, and the warp's set the way he had it. He uses wire traps made of plastic-coated wire, not like my wooden ones. I'll show ya where to set 'em today. This boat has a VHF radio, in case ya get lost." He snickered condescendingly. "Here's ya fish finder. It works like sonar; I know I ain't got one. Ya got a 12-inch stainless steel hauler with a clutch, there, and ya got radar that'll stretch for 24 miles. Ya might need that when ya go tuna fishing, but ya ain't gonna need it for lobstering. In back ya got a tuna hatch in the transom. I guess Randy will go over most of this stuff with ya when ya need to use it. Come on downstairs and we'll see what ya got inside this bad boy." He grabbed the top of the opening which went below the main deck and swung down. Charles followed but used the steps, and lowered his head.

"This is diesel, I think he's got a Cat engine." He walked to a panel board. "This here's ya breaker panels in case anything goes out. I'll show ya when we come back to the mooring this afternoon. That there is ya gear pump. Ya got a heavy-duty bilge pump in case ya take on water. Ya should already know how to run her, so let's take her out and we'll drop ya traps then come back. It shouldn't take long."

Charles looked around the bottom deck in amazement. "He's even got two beds!" He was impressed.

"Ya won't need that until ya head out to the deep water with Randy. If I know him, ya gonna go out only twice, for two full days each time, and you'll take the middle day off. When ya go out there, ya gonna find out what sea legs are!" He smiled out of the side of his mouth.

"Sea legs?"

"Ya gonna see!" Jonas went back up the steps and to the controls. "Now, Charlie, I'm gonna sit here and watch ya start her up and take her out. I'm only gonna say somethin' if ya start to really screw up or if ya need help, but tomorrow, ya gonna be on ya own, and there ain't no better way to learn than by doin'." He sat on the box at the port side of the boat. Charles seemed nervous but accepted his position behind the wheel. He looked over all the controls then to Jonas, as if asking him what to do.

"Ain't no different from my boat. 'Cept, ya just got a lot more gadgets." He crossed his arms and silently waited for Charles to act.

Charles checked the throttle and played with some of the equipment in front of him before he turned the key. The engines started, then stalled. "What do I do now?"

"Just give her a little more gas, just an easy push, then try it again." He did and the engine rumbled; the boat shifting slightly. "Now ya just steer it like a car and use the throttle like the gas pedal of your van."

The boat lurched forward then Charles pulled back on the throttle to ease the boat along. He turned the wheel to head out away from the other boats at the mooring and with a huge grin exclaimed, "Hey! This is pretty easy!" He maneuvered the boat awkwardly but effectively, being extremely cautious and slow as they went.

"Ya gotta watch the lines as well as the boats, Charlie, and when ya get out to where the lobster buoys are, ya gotta really look for the warps there." Jonas was comfortable not having to do anything, yet still getting paid. He crossed his arms and watched Charles operate the vessel. They got past the other ships and went around the large groups of lobster buoys not far from shore.

"Where should I go?" Charles asked, obviously enjoying the responsibility of being the pilot. The wind shifted slightly and the water became a little bit rougher, but still, relatively speaking, it was placid.

"Well, now, ya gonna hafta remember where ya set the buoys, so we'll make it easy on ya. Go up across the channel and ya can set three of ya traps somewhere around there. It's easy to remember and it's a good area to get 'em. Ya know, bein' a maritime historian, what the red buoy means, don't ya?"

"'Red, right return,' so I should set them on the other side of that buoy, right?"

"It'll keep ya out of the channel! Ya don't want to be too close there, 'cause the ships comin' in don't care, and ya might lose whatever ya put in there. Outside the channel, ya're pretty safe. Ya can go a bit faster, now."

Charles looked at him. "Right!" He pushed the throttle forward then back, then forward, then back. It was cumbersome, but he began to acclimate to the controls.

"Ya gonna get the hang of it!"

They completed setting the five traps, and Charles idled the boat at the last one. "That's it?" he asked.

"Ay-yup, for today! Now that we got a minute, I'll show ya how to tie the bridle half-hitch for ya warp, just in case." He picked up the extra piece of rope and demonstrated how to tie it.

Charles watched, then Jonas undid the knot and handed it to him. He tried a couple of times until he finally got it right.

Jonas smiled at him. "Good. You'll do all right. But can ya tell me somethin', Charlie?"

LOBSTER TRAPPED!

"Sure, what?"

"Well, I found out from that dean of yours that you're not even really from Rhode Island. I heard ya from Indiana. Ya went to Rhode Island to go to school. It just seems strange to me. Now, ya heard my story. What's yours? What makes a farm boy want to learn about the sea?"

Charles sat down beside Jonas and sighed. "Well, I guess we all have a story. Yes, you're right, I come from Indiana. My parents are still there and they're getting along in age. I grew up a little different from you, though. I am an only child. My parents had money that they inherited from my grandparents. I never got to meet my father's parents, and he never talked about them. They pushed me to get an education, saying it was the only way to make it in this world. Even though we weren't that far from the Great Lakes, my father never took me fishing, or even for a boat ride. I always thought that was strange, but I never asked. When I questioned him about his parents, he changed the subject. When I got into my senior year in high school, I decided I wanted to go to the University of Rhode Island to study history. My father didn't mind that. After I graduated and told him I wanted to get my master's degree in fishing and work on the water, he finally broke down and told me about his parents. That's when he convinced me to study maritime history, instead." Charles stared up into the sky. Jonas watched and listened.

"He didn't like the idea of my going out to sea and, seeing that he was paying for everything.... Well, anyway, did you ever hear of the ship called the *Eastland*?" He turned and looked at Jonas.

Jonas ran his fingers through his beard and closed his eyes, in deep thought. "Yeah, I think I have. It was a passenger ship that ran out of Chicago. I believe it sank right out of dock, a long time ago."

"That's right. The ship was built in 1903 in Port Huron, Michigan. My grandfather was born in 1894 and my grandmother a year later. They had gotten married when he was 20 and my grandmother was 19. My grandmother gave birth to my father in 1914.

"The ship was built by the Jenks Ship Building Company, commissioned by the Michigan Steamship Company. It was a passenger ship that ran between Chicago and Michigan ports on Lake Michigan. It wasn't built right, though, and in 1914 it was sold to the St. Joseph-Chicago Steamship Company. It was 269 feet long and had a beam width of 36 feet. They knew right away the ship wasn't very stable; but they were stubborn. It was built deliberately narrow to make it quick for its time, but it also made it top heavy. They called it *The Queen of the Lakes* because it could travel up to 22 miles and hour.

"They could tell there were problems with its stability when they loaded and unloaded cargo. The ship would list to one side or the other, but still they ignored it. If it started leaning one way, they would just add water to the other side to correct the list. There were some accounts of people questioning how safe it was, and so, the original owner of the boat ran a newspaper ad that basically said that those who were complaining 'know absolutely nothing about boats.' They offered a five-thousand-dollar reward for anyone who could 'bring forth' anyone 'who will say that the steamer *Eastland* is not a seaworthy ship....' Nobody came out to claim that reward. After that, they didn't get much more attention about the ship, and they even raised the passenger capacity from 2,183 to 2,500.

"My grandparents decided to celebrate their first wedding anniversary by taking a cruise aboard the *Eastland* on Saturday, July 24, 1915. They left my father with my great-aunt. They took the train to Chicago, spent some time celebrating and boarded the ship. The captain crammed all he could on it; 2,500 passengers. My grandparents got an interior cabin and were just getting settled in when the ship began to list, first to starboard, then to port. It all happened so quickly that nobody had time to react. The ship rolled onto its side right there at the dock, spilling people into the river." He looked at Jonas.

"My grandparents were trapped in their cabin below! They never made it! In all, 800 people died on that ship, and it never even made it out of dock. Not a lot of people know it, but that was the largest death toll of any single event occurring in the continental United States in the twentieth century." He stopped. "That's why my father wanted me to take maritime history instead of getting on a boat. Anyway, I met Janet in school—she's my wife, and I've lived in Rhode Island ever since. Now, I can't even call my father now to let him know what I'm doing here in Maine. He'd get rather upset!"

Jonas smiled at him. "You're right, everybody has a story. Now, that's it!" He called out. "Ya did O.K. today, college boy, now let's head for shore."

The boat slithered back to the moorings when Jonas peered off to the right as they idled up to Randy's spot. "Ya see that?" he said as Charles grabbed the mooring buoy. He was pointing to the shoreline near where the boat has washed up the day before. "That's one of my buoys! That boat must have caught her, and brought it in with it. Damned, I hope the traps with it." The two of them finished tying up the boat and got into Randy's skiff. Jonas let Charlie pilot the dinghy to shore.

Kenny Buckner and Souharat Khatel approached the designated spot along Route #1, very slowly in Kenny's old pickup truck, and Kenny checked the road. There were no cars visible. He methodically pulled to the side of the road, stopped and then eased the truck into reverse, backing off the avenue, into the woods where the trees were thinned out. He measured his entrance into the woods and continued to back up through the thicket and brush, until they were no longer visible from the roadway. It was an old path, used long ago for reasons that today were still unclear. Some say it was used by children to haul canoes down to the water and others say it had been cut out due to a forest fire that happened decades ago and had been kept clear ever since, for people who like to hike or jog along the beach. Either way, it had become overgrown with vegetation but still was not encumbered by large trees, so it was passable for the desperate. And that is what they were!

Kenny continued down the make-shift path with the scraping sounds of branches and long, newly sprouted mini-trees scratching the sides of the truck. He went as far as he could until the trail became impassable due to taller trees and overgrowth. He stopped the truck and turned it off.

"This is far as I can go, Rat," he spoke to the man beside him, "you only have about a hundred yards to walk, it shouldn't take you all that long."

They had removed Kenny's skiff from the back of the truck, just moments before at his house, and placed the enclosure over the back bed. "Let's go, Rat, come on before someone sees!"

"Sees, sahib? Who would be out here in these woods to see us?"

"Not us, you idiot, not us! IT!" Kenny growled.

"Yes, sahib, of course." He got out of the passenger's side door then stood silent for a moment. "Why can you not come with me and help?" he pleaded.

Kenny shook his head. "I told you! I have to stay here and watch your back. I'll give you warning if I see or hear anybody coming, that gives you time to get away. Otherwise, we could both be sitting ducks."

"Yes, of course, sahib." He begrudgingly shut the door then walked around to the rear of the truck. He opened the gate in the rear and pulled out a homemade litter. It consisted of two small tree limbs about 4 inches in diameter each; cleaned of all protruding branches with a piece of cloth attached between the poles. It was approximately five feet long and was easily foldable.

"Be quick, now, Rat! I want to get out of here in a hurry." Kenny was anxious.

The short Indian looked into the woods surrounding them. "Where do I go, sahib?"

Kenny pointed to a large Oak tree. "Go to that tree there and keep on going straight until you see the water. The bush isn't too bad in there, so you shouldn't have too many problems. Once you see the water, just find the path of least resistance, and get to the edge of the tree line. You know where to go after that. Just don't get out of the woods until you have to!"

"Yes, sahib." He left the back of the truck open and headed into the woods carrying the litter. It was still early and the sun was bright, but the overgrowth in the woods made it seem much darker. Light was scarce.

"And Rat!" Kenny spoke only loud enough for the other man to hear.

Souharat turned around. "Yes, sahib?"

"Snap off some small branches or bushes as you go, to make sure you can find your way back the way you came."

"Of course, sahib." He continued walking but made a mental note of the larger trees he passed, and every so often he would break a twig here or there, as he was directed to do. He struggled through some of the thicker brush and walked around anything too difficult to negotiate. After only a short walk, he could see the ocean in the distance. He looked back and could still see the truck, but just barely. He carried the make-shift stretcher in one arm and continued in a direct line to the water. It wasn't long before he came to the edge of the woods where it met the beach. He crouched down and poked his head out from behind a tree. The Searsport dock was nearly two hundred yards away to the right. There was no one on it. A situation which relieved him; and one that Kenny had guaranteed. He knew his destination, which was only about 100 feet to his right, and he slowly made his way along the edge of the woods, until suddenly he stopped.

He heard voices! Somebody was coming towards him. The voices were still quite a way off, but definitely headed in his direction. He stopped breathing and took to one knee, setting the make-shift litter on the ground beside him. His task would have to wait. He leaned up against a large Oak tree and listened.

"Do me a favor, boy," Jonas asked, as Charles was getting off Randy's skiff and climbing the ladder to the pier.

"What's that?" he asked.

"Could ya run over there and grab my buoy, then pull it up. See what's left of the warp, while I take care of the skiff. Ya might get a little wet, but it's almost up on shore. It's stuck in the kelp there, from what I can see."

"Yeah, sure," Charles said, and he walked down the length of the pier to the beach, then along the beach to the massive amounts of seaweed congested into a small area on the shore. He was thankful now that he brought those rubber boots from Rhode Island. Up until now, he very rarely had to step in water much more than over his shoes, but this buoy was a good ten feet out, tangled up in the slimy green kelp. He got to the point and stood so that the buoy was directly in front of him off shore. He daintily stepped into the water, taking big steps, thinking that the fewer steps he took in the water, the less wet he would get. He took one large step and leaned forward, barely catching the buoy in one hand. He turned around and pulled at the buoy, attempting to retrace his steps going into the water. The seaweed clung to his boots. He pulled the buoy onto shore and set it down on the beach, still holding the warp attached. He hauled the line in; it was all tangled and covered with the kelp. He pulled it in quite a ways. He thought maybe the whole thing came with it, including the trap. As he reeled in the line he looked around him at the seaweed. Then he stopped and dropped the line.

There, in front of him was a body! It was floating upside down, with only the back of the head and part of the shirt showing. He gasped and staggered backwards. His face dropped into a dazed look. "Jonas! Jonas!" he screamed, catching his breath.

Jonas was still turning the winch on the trailer attached to his truck, when he heard Charles yelling to him.

"What d'ya want?" he screamed back.

"Jonas! Get over here, quick!" He had stepped back, well onto the beach now, staring at the sight in front of him.

Jonas finished loading his skiff on his truck. He shook his head and stepped quickly towards Charles, sensing that something was wrong. "What is it, Charlie, it looks like ya seen a ghost, for Christ's sake!"

"Jonas! Quick!" He was trembling and pointing to the body he saw. Jonas shifted his gait into a trot and arrived in seconds to where Charles stood.

"What's the matter, boy?" He appeared concerned.

"Look!" Charlie answered, and he pointed to the body then looked back to Jonas. "There's your body!"

Jonas stared at it for a moment without making any facial expressions. "Ah-yup. That's Doug Harvey. I can tell by what he's wearin'"

Charles became unnerved. "Well, what are we going to do?" He was trembling, and his face turned white.

Jonas snapped his head to face him. "We're gonna pull the rest of my warp in and get the hell outta here!"

Charles looked at him in disbelief. "You're just going to let this go, like you never saw it. That's a man there! Don't you have any feelings? He was probably killed! If someone is out here killing people, there will be more! How can you just ignore it?" He was visibly upset.

"Like I said," he spoke monotonically, "don't know, and I don't know if I want to know! I told ya, boy, these shores have eyes and ears. I ain't gonna get involved!"

"Well, that's it! I'm calling the chief of police."

"If I were ya, I'd just let it go!" He was adamant. Without taking a second look, he picked up the warp from the buoy and pulled the remaining line in, wrapping it around his arm.

"I can't just let it go! I'm calling the chief, right now!" His face tightened in determination.

Jonas tilted his head in disappointment, knowing there was no sense to argue. "Do what ya gotta do, just leave me out of it!" He picked up the line and buoy and set it over his shoulder, then looked at Charles, stubbornly. "I didn't see nothin'!" He stopped and pointed a finger at Charles. "Oh, and by the way, you're on your own tomorrow!" He walked down the beach carrying his gear. Charles followed.

The Rat sat beside the tree, attentively listening to every word the two spoke. He waited patiently until they had gone down the beach to their respective vehicles and watched Jonas throw his gear into the back of his truck, start it up and leave the area. He watched Charles get into his van and also leave. He looked around the landing carefully. There was no one else in sight. He quickly scampered out of the woods and to the body in the kelp, where he laid out the litter on the beach, stepped into the water and carefully grabbed the body with both hands under its armpits. He pulled the body out of the water and onto the make-shift stretcher. He worked briskly. He got the body up onto the cloth and tied it down securely with a piece of rope attached to each of the poles on either side. He quickly pulled the unit into the woods, where he stopped to catch his breath, then he returned to the beach with a branch he snapped off a nearby tree, and brushed over the sand and gravel where the two support poles of the litter made tracks. He had toiled so methodically and with such speed that nobody saw him. He rested, again, only for a few seconds, then dragged the body on the litter through the wood along the same path in which he came. As he went he was scratched several times by thorns and small twigs, but he ignored the pain. He began to perspire heavily and had to take some breaks along the route back to Kenny's truck. There were several obstacles he had to overcome on the journey, to ensure the body made the trip.

Charles stopped at the gas store in the center of Searsport and called the chief of police, explaining what he had witnessed. The chief informed him to go back to the parking lot at the landing and he would meet him there.

No sooner did Charles put his vehicle in park than the chief showed up in his cruiser. Charles jumped out of the minivan. "Chief!" he yelled. "It's over there!" He pointed to the area on the beach where he had seen the body. He was excited and nearly jumped when he spoke.

The police officer leisurely exited the cruiser. "Just hang on now. If he's dead, he ain't goin' nowhere! I just got a few questions first." He acted nonchalantly; indifferently. "What's your name? I don't think I know ya, and I know most everybody in town here."

"Officer, please! My name is Charles Ritter. I swear there's a body over there in the kelp. I wouldn't doubt if there's more out there in the water somewhere!"

"Ritter? Oh, yeah. Ya're that fella from Rhode Island. I heard about ya. Ya're some sort of professor or somethin'." He put his hat on, which he had been holding in his hands. "All right, then, Mr. Ritter, let's go have a look at this corpse." He was a tall man, relatively in good shape, although he had a bit of a pouch around the waist. He was clean shaven and tidy. He looked to be in his mid forties. All in all, he was a sharp contrast to the average man that came to the landing. The two men walked along the beach until they came to the pool of kelp. Charles looked around, all through the kelp. The body was gone!

"He was right here! Just a few minutes ago, I swear!"

The chief studied the kelp. "Uh-huh!" he said sarcastically. "I guess he musta got bored and left."

Charles was aback. "You don't believe me. I swear I saw a body here, just a few minutes ago."

The chief turned to him with a wry grin. "Right!"

Charles slapped his hands off his thighs then walked into the seaweed and kicked it around. He poked his hands into the water, thrashing them about. "I swear!" he said.

The chief of police spoke with suspicion. "Hey, look, fella, I don't know what you guys smoke down there in Rhode Island, but I hope you don't waste the time of your local officials on your hallucinations." It was a blunt jab.

"Oh, come on! I saw him! Jonas saw him! We both saw him!" He was frustrated, and spoke hurriedly.

"Well, he ain't here now and I don't see Jonas. I heard you've been working the water for the first time in your life. It can have an effect on the mind, you know."

"Chief, I don't need to be insulted!"

He snapped back, "Neither do I! Now look, buddy, you're wasting my time. If you see this 'body' again, give me a call, but don't call me on a wild goose chase. I have other things to tend to." He turned around and headed for his cruiser.

Charles ran after him. "Chief! Chief! I swear it was right there. Maybe the undertow took it out to deeper water, I don't know, but you have to believe me before someone else gets hurt!"

The chief stopped and turned to Charles. "If you've got something you want us to investigate, then please come down to my office and fill out a report. This here is nonsense. There's no body there and there's no undertow in this water, leastways, not here." He was irritated.

"O.K.," Charles said. "I'll come down and fill out a report, but there's more. This isn't the first body I've seen. I saw a man tied to the pier support at the end of the dock over there." He pointed to the landing area.

The chief laughed out loud. "You know something? I should've guessed that! You see anything else, you know, pink elephants, or anything? You been drinking, fella?"

Charles stood silent and in a very stoic manner said, "I see! You think I'm crazy, don't you? Well, I want to fill that report out, and maybe, one day, you'll figure it all out. Right now, I know what I know. I saw what I saw. And no, I haven't been drinking, but in this town, I can see why people do!" His attitude reeked of insolence. He really didn't like the police when they were too arrogant to do their jobs properly. He had brought the matter to the attention of the authorities and they offended him. "Now, I want to fill out a report on this matter and on the other murder I witnessed."

"Look, buddy, even if you did see a body over there, what makes you think it was murder?"

He actually had caught Charles off guard. He was right. The only way to prove it was murder was to examine the body, and he didn't have one to examine. He felt humbled. "Well, the man tied to the pier didn't tie himself."

"No. Well, where's *that* body? Look, buddy, you don't really fit in here, so I think you should keep your opinions to yourself. If you want to fill out a report I'll give you my card, and you can come to my office. Another thing, there are a lot of boating accidents on these waters. If you did see something, it could be anything!" He reached in his pocket and pulled out his wallet. "Here. Here's my card, it has the address and phone number on it. If you want, just come down and I'll give you the paperwork. Right now, I've got to get going. It's my dinnertime."

"I'll be there!" He returned emphatically. "I know what I saw, and I'm not crazy."

"Just remember this: If you file a false report, we *will* press charges."

Charles nodded. "I'll remember!"

The chief turned around and got into the cruiser. While his back was turned, Charles stuck his tongue out at him.

The Rat could see Kenny's truck through the woods, just a short ways ahead of him. He pulled harder at the litter and made it to the rear of the truck, where he dropped the homemade gurney in exhaustion. He leaned against the back of the vehicle, completely out of breath. The cadaver's arms kept on flopping off the edge of the cloth and getting caught up on thickets and prickly bushes. "Sahib, sahib, you can give me a hand now."

Kenny got out of the truck. "Good man, Rat! All right, let's get him inside." He unlatched the tailgate on the bed of the truck. The top portion had been left open. The idea of placing the hood over the bed of the truck was made so that no one could see their gruesome cargo. Kenny took one end of the litter and placed it on the tailgate. The Rat took the other end, picked it up and slid the entire thing inside. Kenny shut the tailgate and the hood, locking it. "Let's get out of here, Rat!"

He didn't have to say it twice. Souharat opened the passenger door and immediately sat down, leaning back as far as he could. He wiped his forehead. Kenny got in and started the truck. They made their way back up the old path, getting near the road. Kenny stopped the vehicle and got out, walked to the edge of the highway and looked in each direction. One car went by while he waited there, but he kept himself out of sight. Once the car passed, he checked again. There was no other cars coming, and none he could hear. He jumped back into the driver's seat and gave it a powerful blast of gas, exiting the woods in seconds.

Kenny laughed. "Well, that's the last one. We're clear! Now, we can look for that treasure with no pressure. Good job, Rat!"

Souharat tried to speak, but he was still out of breath. Finally, the words came out. "Sahib!" he said, exhaling heavily. "Sahib. We have trouble!" His words came with much pain. "Sahib!" He began to catch his breath.

"What d'ya mean, trouble?" He glanced at Souharat with a curious stare.

"Sahib, when I got to the beach at the edge of the woods, there were two men there. They saw the body!"

"Shit! Who were they?"

"One was Jonas Hale."

"Oh, Jonas won't say nothin'. He knows the code! Who was the other one?"

"The new man. The one from Rhode Island."

Kenny thought. "I've seen him. I don't know him. He don't know the code of the pier, though, and that could be trouble."

"Sahib, I heard them talk. Jonas will say nothing, but this one from Rhode Island said he was going to call the chief of police!"

"Damned! I'll be damned!" He slammed his palm on the steering wheel.

"How did ya get the body out then?"

"I waited until they left. Jonas said he wanted nothing to do with the police. But the other one was determined to go and call the police. I had only moments to act."

"Oh, shit! Ya did good. Nobody saw ya?"

"No one! And I covered the tracks into the woods."

"Good. Good. They still don't have a corpse!"

"I thought about it, sahib. Even if he goes to the police, they will find no body. Who will believe him?"

Jonas laughed vigorously. "You're right, my little, shifty friend. You are right!"

"No one knows we did this, sahib."

Kenny thought for a moment. "You're right, Rat, but still I'm not gonnna take any chances. If this guy's got enough guts to go to the cops, then he's probably gonna be capable of anything. I ain't taking no chances."

"I agree, sahib!"

"Then you know what to do?"

"Yes, sahib. This one from Rhode Island will be on his own tomorrow. I heard Jonas tell him this. I saw the two of them in the boat belonging to Randy Thompson. I will take care of him, but this time, we do it MY way!"

Kenny grinned. "Whatever you say, my friend, whatever you say!"

Chapter 14

It was shortly after 4:00 p.m. when the chief of police took his leave from the parking lot at the landing. Charles watched him drive away then looked down at the card he had been given. His name was Ed McFagan. Charles decided that he might as well get something to eat and wait for the chief to return to his office. He stopped at the same diner where he ate breakfast and thought about what he had seen and witnessed. Maybe he was wrong in going to the chief of police; the man was obstinate and insolent. He couldn't blame him, though, because there was no corpse where he showed him.

But it *was* there! That was another thing; what could have happened to the corpse? All this bothered him while he ate, and he found himself completing his meal quickly. He was still determined to file a report, no matter how foolish it might make him look. He finished eating and left cash on the counter to cover the cost and a tip.

He made haste to the police station, walked through the main entrance and up to the front counter. "Excuse me," he said, "I'm here to speak with Chief McFagan." He smiled politely to the young cop behind the counter.

The officer looked up at him. "Would you happen to be that fella from Rhode Island?" A greeting that he was becoming all too familiar with.

"Yes. My *name* is Charles Ritter. I spoke with the chief earlier and he told me to meet him here."

"He's still at dinner. He should be back any minute. He told us to have you take a seat. He wants to talk to you." The man pointed to a wooden chair against the wall. Charles acquiesced and sat down to wait. The station was small, he noticed, and there wasn't much activity. There were only two officers in the building that he could see; one was typing something at a desk in back, and the other was the one he had just spoken to. It appeared his job was to answer the phones, the radio calls from any patrols and deal with people who came into the station. While Charles waited he heard the phone ring. The young officer up front answered the phone, just as he had expected.

"Searsport police department. Uh, huh … yes, Mrs. Reynolds … Uh, huh…O.K., we'll be right there." He hung up and pressed the button on the radio. "Come in, Derek."

A response transmitted over the line. "This is officer Snowe. What is it, Danny?"

"Mrs. Reynolds just called. It seems that Jake Forrester let his dog out again. She says he's running around and barking up a storm. She says she thinks it's chasing deer, but that dog ain't big enough to chase a cat. Can you go over and check it out?"

"Sure thing. Y'know, that's the third time that dog has gotten out this month. I'm done fining him, I'm gonna arrest him this time. He knows the leash laws!"

"Do whatever ya gotta do. The dog's out behind Mrs. Reynolds'."

"Ten four. I'm on my way."

No sooner did he finish than a call came over the radio from the other patrol car on duty. "Come back, Danny."

He pressed the button on the radio. "Go ahead, Red."

"Yeah, Danny, I just saw Walter Bishop driving down Mt. Ephriam Road. I think his license is suspended. You want to check that for me?"

"Sure thing. Hang on, it'll take a minute."

"Well, I'm pretty sure it is, so I'm gonna follow him anyways. Check it for me in case I have to go to court."

"Roger that!" He spun around in his chair and began typing on the computer to his right. It only took a minute before he finished staring at the screen then he called back over the radio. "Come back, Red."

"Officer Edwards. What d'ya got, Danny?"

"Well, it ain't suspended, but he's supposed to have a licensed driver sitting beside him. That was the court order."

"Ten four. He don't have anyone beside him. I'm taking him in."

"Ten four!"

Another call came over the radio. "This is Officer Snowe."

"Go ahead, Derek."

"Yeah, Danny, I got Jake Forrester in the cruiser. I'm gonna drop him off in Belfast. I get off in about an hour, so I think I'll cruise the bars in Searsport before I come in and see if I can catch some people smoking. I guarantee I will, and that should put some cash in out coffers." He laughed over the radio.

"Ten four, Derek."

Charles sat back listening in wonderment. His face was crimped in disbelief. He was here to report two murders and these guys were dealing with petty, petty crimes.

They didn't seem to care about a murder; all they wanted was to arrest somebody for something, or anybody for anything. Then he heard the front door close. He turned around and saw McFagan walk inside. He stood up.

The chief turned to Charles. "I figured you'd be here. Come into my office and we'll talk." He continued to walk past the counter, then to the left of the front desk, and opened the door to his office. He held it open, gesturing Charles to enter, then he turned to the office in front. "Danny, if anybody calls for me in the next couple o'minutes, just take a message. This won't take long."

"Yes, sir!" Danny responded.

The chief entered his office and walked behind his desk, then motioned for Charles to take a seat in the chair in front of him.

They both sat down, and the officer spoke. "Now, look, flatlander, I don't appreciate your coming to my town and starting trouble, or spreading rumors. We don't need it. *I* don't need it. You take me on some fling of yours, saying you saw a corpse that doesn't exist, and I just don't have time for such foolishness. I'd appreciate it if you just stay to yourself while you're here. I don't want you wasting my time or the time of my officers. We're busy here! Get my drift?" He spoke like a father admonishing his child for telling a lie.

Charles became quite perturbed with his attitude. "Look, Chief, I saw what I saw! This is murder I'm talking about! You're too busy to even listen? Busy? Why? What do you have to do today? Arrest a cow for mooing? Place a sting operation on a man who spits on the sidewalk? Cuff a little old blind widow for jaywalking? Busy? Busy, my ass! I'm talking murder here, and I have a witness. This is unbelievable!" He stood up during his oration.

When he finished, Chief McFagan stood also. "That's it! I've had it with ya! I didn't like you from the get-go! Why don't ya just leave, before I find a reason to arrest you? Get out of here!" He pointed to the door of his office.

"I might as well, I'm not going to get anywhere here!" Charles pivoted in front of the desk and began walking towards the door, when he saw a bell on the table near the exit. He stopped short. He leaned forward and carefully looked over the object. It stood about a 1-1/2 feet high. It was made of bronze and was deeply encrusted from age. He studied it, walking around the table slowly. He adjusted his glasses as he stared.

The chief watched him in a peculiar way. He realized that the man saw something he didn't. "I thought I told ya t'leave," he said in a much mellower tone.

Charles played with his glasses, still walking around the table in a stupor. "Where did you get this?" he asked.

The chief looked at him sideways. "What's it to ya?"

"Do you know what this is?"

"Huh? What d'ya think I am, stupid? It's a bell!" He was offended at the question, but intrigued that it was even uttered. He knew of Charles's stint here in Maine and that he was a maritime historian. Maybe this bell was more than he thought.

Charles continued to peruse the bell, studying it as closely as a jeweler studies a diamond. "I don't believe it! It can't be! It has to be!" He was dumbfounded.

"What, what is it?" The chief suddenly became very interested. "Is it worth somethin'?" He glanced at the bell but saw nothing more than that—an old bell.

"Ohhhhh, yes! It's priceless!" Charles stuttered.

"Priceless? It's just a bell!"

Charles rubbed a spot near the top on the bell. He stuck his face up towards it, nearly touching it with his nose. "It's not just a bell!" He exclaimed. "Look here!" He pointed to the spot he was staring at.

The chief got out of his seat and stepped over to where Charles stood. He had become much more civil and quiet. He fixed his eyes on Charles then drew them down to the spot on the bell where his finger lay. He squinted to see the mystery. It was difficult to see with all the rust. He got close, "QAR", he said out loud. "What's the big deal, and what's a kwar?"

"Its initials. See how crude the writing is? That means it was probably made here, in the United States. Do you see what I'm getting at? I can see the letters Q.A.R. perfectly. There's other writings on this that I can't quite make out, but I'd bet it is the name of a Saint or Saints. I'd need to do a chemical cleaning of it to be sure, but I'm sure that's what it is."

The chief was completely confused. "I still don't see what you're getting at."

"It's the initials, Q.A.R." He spoke emphatically.

"What does that stand for?"

"*Queen Anne's Revenge*!" Charles felt a tingle ride down his spine.

The chief scratched his head. "What the hell is *Queen Anne's Revenge*? Is it like Montezuma's revenge?" He wasn't joking.

Charles laughed, not at the attempt at jocularity, but at the recognition of the stupidity of the chief. "The *Queen Anne's Revenge*! It's only the flagship of the most famous pirate of all times!"

"You mean, Captain Hook?"

Charles hesitated. "No, not Captain Hook."

"Long John Silver?" He spoke in all seriousness.

Charles sighed and shook his head. "They are *fictional* pirates! I mean Edward Teach—A *real* pirate!"

"Who?"

"BLACKBEARD! Blackbeard, the pirate!" He was coming to the unsettling conclusion that this man who represented law and order in this town was a complete dunce. No wonder they arrested anybody for anything. It was clear that any type of intelligent detective work was well beyond this man's capacity.

"So, what is this all supposed to mean?" McFagan asked, still not sure who Blackbeard was.

Charles contemplated that question and rubbed his chin. "First, tell me where you got this."

The suspense was eating into the chief, until he gave in. "It came off of Bill Rowlin and Todd Seekins's boat. The boat drifted to shore close to a week ago and we can't get hold of either one of them. They ain't all that bright, so we just figured that they screwed up when they were fishin', and got tangled in one of their own nets. We still got the boat, but I drug this up here 'cause I liked the look. I was gonna have someone clean it and use it as decoration. I got no idea where they got it."

"Do they drag nets when they fish?"

"Yup. Sure do, why?"

"Hmmm. I have a theory. Yes, yes, yes, it makes sense. Do you mind if we sit down and I'll explain it to you? I believe I can tie in the corpse I saw to this bell. I can see how this bell might just lead to murder. You might be interested."

McFagan seemed hesitant. "You said this was priceless." It was more of a question than a statement.

"Oh, it is. But if my theory is correct, there's more than just this bell out there somewhere around here. If I'm right, there's a fortune in these waters!"

That did it! McFagan picked up his phone and pressed a button. "Hey, Danny, if anybody calls or wants to see me, tell them I'm busy. I'm not to be disturbed, understand? ... Good!" He hung up the phone and went back to his seat while Charles returned to where he had been sitting.

"So, what's all this about a fortune, this bell, the *Queen Anne's Revenge*, a pirate and murder?" The chief was skeptical of the connection.

"Well, first, let me tell you about the *Queen Anne's Revenge*. It was a ship built in 1710 in Great Britain, during the Queen Anne's War, which was a war fought in the American colonies for Spanish succession. At that time, the ship was called the *Concord*. In that year, the French privateers captured the vessel and modified it with a 'flute,' which means her stern was altered to carry more weapons. It went to Rio De Janeiro, where the French sacked the city and took a ransom of gold back to France. Then, I believe it was just a few years later when the ship was sailing from Africa to Martinique that Blackbeard, the pirate, captured her and sailed for the Caribbean, plundering any merchant vessels he could and taking their cargo. He also took many other ships. He built up quite a fortune there, then he sailed to the United States, to Virginia and the Carolinas. It was easy for him to take on ships there because there was no Navy, not much of a government and the people were so scattered around, they couldn't put up much of a defense. He even stole from other pirates. He was a pretty despicable man. He threw fear into people by the way he presented himself. In most of his conquests, there were no shots fired once the other ship saw his flag or, worse, him! Anyway, he had stored on board the *Queen Anne's Revenge* so much 'booty' that he had to place guards round the clock to keep an eye on it.

"As the story goes, he finally did a horrendous act in Virginia that caused the governor there to send out a proclamation for his arrest, even though he was in North Carolina at the time. A big fight ensued, where he was eventually killed, and the *Queen Anne's Revenge* sank.

"Some of the artifacts from the ship were recovered rather quickly, and some are still missing. In 1996 Intersal's director of operations found the wreck. The Archaeological Unit of the North Carolina Division of Archives and History dove to the sight and confirmed that it was the ship.

"One of the artifacts they found was a bell, like that one you have there. The thing is, it wasn't the bell that belonged to the *Queen Anne's Revenge*, it belonged to either a Spanish or Portuguese ship. They could tell this because it was engraved with the Spanish lettering "I.H.S. Maria" which means 'Iesu, Hominorum Salvator Maria'. So the actual bell for the *Queen Anne's Revenge* was never recovered. The treasure on the ship was also never recovered, even though every scholar knows it was on board before the battle near Beaufort Inlet in 1718. It is also known that at that time, Blackbeard had a group of four vessels with him or at least, under his control. Only one ship was found that they could connect with the pirate. It is greatly speculated that he hid his treasure, which in today's terms would be billions of dollars, on one or more of these ships, and the ship escaped from the battle that took Blackbeard's life.

"Now, there is some speculation about this part. Blackbeard was known to have traveled up the coast as far as Maine and maybe even to Canada. He had many hiding spots for his fortunes. I believe Castine was one. I know he had a favorite spot called Smuttynose Island off the coast of York, down south.

"It's my theory that the ship Blackbeard hid his treasure on also had his bell, though for what reason I don't know. It may be that the other ship had no bell and he had two and when the other ship took one, it was the wrong one.

"The fact of the matter is—and I could be wrong, but that's the bell; and where the bell is, I believe, the treasure is!" He waited to finish his story.

Chief McFagan's chin had dropped and his eyes bulged. "You mean to tell me that there is a billion dollars in pirate treasure somewhere around here?"

"If my theory is correct. Of course, I have another reason to believe that it is true."

The chief was in a daze—or a daydream. "Huh? What, what other reason do you have?"

"Well, doesn't it make sense that this Bill and Todd who found the bell would have also found the treasure?"

"I s'pose. That is, if what ya say is accurate."

"And now they're missing! Isn't that peculiar?" He leaned back in the chair and folded his arms together.

"So, why are they missing?" Apparently this chief of police really needed everything spelled out for him.

"Well, first of all, they drag fish. If that ship with all that treasure on it sank, it is likely they came across the wreck by accident. Then, if they aren't all that intelligent, they might have run their mouths to the wrong person. Greed sets in and they get killed."

"Yes, of course, that makes sense!" McFagan had both elbows on top of his desk as he contemplated the situation. "But then, whoever they told has the treasure now and they'd be long gone, wouldn't they?"

"That's where I think you're wrong. I don't think whoever might have killed the two knows where the treasure is."

"What makes you think that?"

"Because those two were the first to wind up missing. I know of two more. Why would whoever it is stick around killing people if they could do just that—take off with the money? I think it's still out there somewhere!"

The chief leaned back into his chair and stared at the ceiling in deep thought. "I don't know. I mean, you tell a good story, but I always thought that pirate stuff was made up and there were no real pirates. Just in movies."

Charles snickered. "Chief, pirates—I mean *real* pirates—have been around since man first built boats. There were pirates as far back as early Greece, where the Phoenicians had a thriving sea trade into what is now Lebanon. The Greeks would simply hide among the tiny islands in the Mediterranean, wait for one of the ships to pass by and attack them, taking whatever they could; tin, copper, amber and silver. That was in the seventh and sixth century B.C.! The Greeks used the term *peirates*, which was the first reference to the term 'pirate.'

"During the Roman Empire, pirates thrived on merchant ships and sold the goods to wealthy Romans who didn't care where it came from. Even Julius Caesar was kidnapped by pirates, who held him for ransom for five weeks on a small Ionic island. That was in 75 B.C.

"Pirates have been around forever, pretty much, and practiced pretty much everywhere. Even the Vikings were pirates roaming the North Sea in Scandanavia from the 8th century to the 12th century, and they traveled the open waters. As long as there have been merchant vessels there have been pirates. There were Saxon pirates in England even before the Viking pirates. These guys were pretty scary. One monk thought he could turn his ship invisible because he made a pact with the devil.

"The governments really didn't stop them, either. The one exception was the Roman pirates that Pompey put an end to when they got too close to Rome. The privateers were actually issued letters of marque by the king of England which authorized piracy. Blackbeard had one. The first king to do that was King Henry III. Of course, when he issued those letters, he expected a little something for himself, if you know what I mean.

"Then there was the Spanish Main. It was Spain's empire in America. After Columbus arrived in 1492 and brought back all kinds of goodies to Spain, the pirates went into action. The Spaniards traveled to the West Indies and killed off as many Inca and Aztec Indians as they could for gold and riches beyond Europeans' wildest dreams. This made piracy run rampant in the New World, and when the Spaniards tried to take the gold back to Spain, the pirates were waiting. It has been documented that the Indians were so put back with the Spanish thirst for gold that if they got one of them down, they would pour molten gold down their throats to quench their thirst."

"Ew!" McFagan interjected.

"Even some of the people we regard as heroes were really pirates; Sir Francis Drake and Giovanni da Verrazano both got rich as pirates. The Muslim nations had pirates, also. The Barbary coast was full of them. That's where the term 'barbarian' comes from. Some of what they stole were slaves for trading. William Kidd and Henry Avery became legends by stealing from the treasure fleets in the Indian Ocean, where the Dutch East India companies sailed. That was easy pickings, and the pirates liked to hang out in Madagascar, off the east coast of Africa. It was a big party spot. Southeast Asia was a pirate's paradise in the 17th century. One guy, Ching-Chi-Ling, had 1,000 pirate ships that would hang out in the swamps, and he was so feared that he only had to ask for ransom and he'd get it without a fight.

"Some of the pirates were pretty ruthless and nasty, like the buccaneers. One guy, I think his name was L'Ollonais, tortured his victims. One story says he cut the heart out of one Spanish prisoner and fed it to another. There were the French Corsairs that practiced piracy. The French port of St. Malo grew rich trom the profits of privateering. They got so rich that they made a statue of Rene Duguay-Trouin, who was nothing but a pirate that helped them get rich.

"But the most famous pirates were the pirates of the Caribbean, and I'm talking real people that walked and talked and breathed in the 17th and early 18th centuries. That's where Blackbeard comes in. He was the most famous of them all, probably because of how he looked and acted. He was just plain scary! Even the United States had pirates. Acutally, they played a big part in the US becoming independent from England during the Revolutionary War. The continental Navy fought the British with only 34 ships, but there were 400 privateer ships that attacked the English merchant vessels, crippling trade. And if it wasn't for Jean Lafitte, a pirate, Colonel Jackson would never have won the battle of New Orleans in 1814. So now, you can see that pirates were real! The treasures were real! This isn't Hollywood!"

The chief stopped him. "O.K., O.K. You've made your point! I guess ya know ya history like they told me. I just never heard anybody ever tell me about no pirates in Maine, and with a treasure? I think somebody woulda been lookin' for buried treasure or somethin' around here."

"Oh, it's been found. I don't really remember the story too well, but I believe a guy on Smuttynose Island was digging for a wall foundation and found two huge gold bars buried where he dug, come to find out, it was buried by Blackbeard. Other pirates have come this way; Captain Kidd for example visited Castine. It sure wasn't all that uncommon for their ships to sink either. Also, pirate treasure was just discovered off of Cape Cod, in sixteen feet of water! The pirate's name was Black Jack Bellamy, and his flagship was named *Whydah*. It capsized on a sandbar near Provincetown, Massachusetts, off of the Cape in April 1717, not long before this ship here. 143 men died. He had just returned from a run of piracy in the Carribean, where he took over 53 vessels in one year! The man who discovered it spent over 17 years searching, even though he knew where it was. That's how much sand had covered it over the three centuries of weather. He's still digging it up! It is believed there is billions and billions of treasure still submerged! The difference here, I believe, is the protection of the bay from the serious drawbacks inherent to the open sea. There are no significant underwater currents, and the tides and winds aren't quite as effective. That would suggest that the wreck is not that far below the bottom of the bay and may be much more easily extracted."

McFagan sat silent and rubbed his chin. He was well groomed and neatly attired, but the outward appearance was deceptive. "Basically, what ya are tellin' me is that there is a fortune out there that Todd and Bill found, but now they're dead and someone else knows about it, but doesn't know where it is?"

"If my theory is correct, yes."

"Well, then, I guess the next step is to find out who it is that knows. That is ... of course ... to find the murderer, of course!" His attitude had changed considerably, and Charles wondered if he really cared about the murders or rather that there might be a fortune in his jurisdiction.

"That's my intent, Chief."

McFagan fiddled with some papers on his desk and attempted to seem uninterested. "Well, I tell ya what. Why don't we just keep this to ourselves. Ya know; under our hats; our own little secret. After all, I am responsible for your safety while you're here in my town, and if word got out about this, well, you could be in danger."

"Yes, yes, of course, Chief. Now, should I fill out that paperwork?"

The manicured chief of police laughed. "What did I just say? If you fill that out, Danny's got to log it in. He'll read it, and he's got a big mouth. Then Bob White has got to type it into the computer, and he's worse than Danny. Danny tells his wife, who tells the girls at the beauty salon. Next thing ya know, it's all over town and I'll be hauling your corpse out of the kelp at the landing. So, just keep this under your hat, O.K.?"

Charles looked at the chief with suspicion. "Yeah, that's fine with me. I guess I'll be going then." He stood up and turned to face the door. "You know, Chief. That bell really should go to a museum."

The chief smiled at him. "Right now it's evidence. Oh, and by the way, if you find out who's doing this, you know, committing these murders, ya'll be sure to let me know, right?"

"Yeah, sure. Hey, Chief, isn't there anything we can do about this before something else happens? I mean, can't you go around questioning people? I'm positive that there are a lot of people out there that have seen something. The only problem is; most of the ones that have seen something are winding up dead. At least, that's my theory."

McFagan stood up. "Of course there's something that can be done and I'm gonna do it. Now, it's my job to protect the people within my jurisdiction and that's just what I'm gonna do. See, we have a police boat; it's just a small outboard and we don't use it much, but starting tomorrow, I'm gonna put it on the water and patrol the bay. If nothin' else, at least it'll be a deterrent to crime out there."

For once, the chief actually made good sense. Like he said, it might be a deterrent, but at least it would be another set of eyes and ears without the distraction of fishing. It was a good idea! Charles felt that maybe, by coming here, he had gotten something accomplished.

"Yeah, right! Good idea, Chief!" He showed himself out of the office and walked through the station to his car. He couldn't help but think that the chief, who didn't believe there even was a murder when he first talked to him, now was totally convinced there was and was eager to get involved—or was there something else on the chief's mind?

Chapter 15

It was a long ride back to the hotel and Charles was absorbed in speculation. He thought about the chief's behavior while he rambled on about pirates. It didn't seem like the man was really paying attention, but rather, it looked like he was daydreaming, and Charles knew that McFagan didn't understand who Sir Francis Drake, Pompey or Verazzano were. He was certain that the chief couldn't even pronounce Phoenicians, Madagascar (he probably thought he said 'Madawaska'), letters of marque or Ionic islands. But the chief never stopped him to ask him what he was talking about or what anything meant. This seemed strange. Or was it that McFagan was just playing dumb and really knew all about pirates but didn't want to let on while Charles talked. He wasn't even paying attention, but rather, he was in his own world.

Oh, well, it didn't matter, because Charles got what he wanted, and that was to have the police at least acknowledging his concerns. He felt a little more reassured to know they'd be out there keeping an eye on the water. He pulled into the lot at the hotel and parked his van in the spot in front of his room. He removed the keys from the ignition and slumped back in the driver's seat. This whole mission that the university had sent him on was getting out of control. He decided he'd give the dean a call in the morning and detail his accounts of the events that he had witnessed in only his fifth day in Maine. He wondered what was next. He was tired. He had gotten up late this morning and perhaps he slept too long, sort of like when you eat too much and an hour later you're hungry again; if you sleep too much, you always feel tired. Your body gets to expect it. Whatever the reason, he was going to go to bed early tonight, make an early start in morning and get back to the hotel early so that he could finish working on the syllabus. He felt he was being unduly pressured to get the class ready. School started in only ten more days, and that's not a lot of time to complete a syllabus.

It was getting dark out. He hadn't realized how much time he wasted just thinking to himself after talking to the chief. He swayed up to the door of his room and fumbled for the correct key. He opened the door, walked inside, stretched and yawned then went right to the phone to call Janet.

As he reached down to pick it up, it rang. *This seems to happen every time,* he thought. He answered it. "Hello."

"Hello, is this Charles Ritter?"

"Yes, who may I ask is calling?"

"Oh, Charles, I'm glad I got you. This is Elena Hale."

"Elena! How are you? I heard you were up in Millinocket."

"I am, Charles. My uncle died Saturday and we're going to have the funeral tomorrow. I have to stay here for a while. Have you been over to see the children?"

"I was there yesterday, but they were at their friends', why?"

"I've been trying to call the house, but no one answers."

"Oh, I'm sure they're all right. I was with Jonas this morning, and he should be just getting back from work now."

"Oh, Charles, I'm afraid he's not very good with the children. I was hoping that you could help me out just a bit."

"Sure thing, what do you want?"

"Well, now that my uncle is dead, my aunt has grown very ill. I don't know why. I have a doctor coming over tomorrow, but she's bedridden for the time being. I might have to stay even longer than I thought. The children start school tomorrow and I just can't get back. I was wondering if you could make sure that they make it to school and have a lunch to take with them. Jonas is just too unreliable."

Charles laughed. "Of course I can. I'll stop over in the morning. Don't worry, even though I'll be by myself when I go haul traps, Jonas and I are going to ride together from the landing to the moorings, so it'll be a good excuse for me to show up at your house before he goes."

"Oh, thank you so much. Tell the children to behave and I'll give them a call tomorrow night to see how their first day in school went. You've made me feel so much better."

"Don't worry about a thing. I'd like to get out soon myself so I can get back to the hotel early and work on arranging my class for the university." He thought. "Isn't this kind of early in the year to start school?"

"It's pretty much the same time every year."

"Huh, our school doesn't start for another eight days."

"This is high school, and this is Maine. Maybe it's different. This is also Chad's first day at the school in Belfast. I hope he gets along."

"He's a smart boy, I'm sure he'll do fine.'

"You will see them off for me then, Charles?"

"No problem."

"Oh, thank you. Thank you. I don't know how to thank you."

"Just consider it done."

"Could you do me one more favor, Charles?"

"Sure, what?" He felt somewhat honored that he was entrusted even more than the children's father.

"Could you give the children your phone number and address while you're here? You know, just in case."

He wondered what that meant. "Sure."

"Oh, thank you, Charles. The children have the number here and the address if you need to contact me for any reason. Any reason, whatsoever."

"O.K." He didn't know what to say.

"Thanks again, Charles, goodbye."

"We'll see you later, Elena." He hung up. That was different. He conjectured what Jonas was like when he wasn't around to see, but it didn't sound very good.

He picked the phone back up to call Janet, and she seemed chipper when she answered.

"Charlie! How's everything going there? Boy, we miss you! Oakley has a new tooth and Elmer keeps on asking about you. When are you coming home?"

"Oh, Janet! Not soon enough. What's today, Monday?"

"Yes, Charles, are you all right? You sound exhausted."

"I am. It's been a long week. I'll be home in another nine days. Put on a chicken for me, would you?" She laughed. "I passed my test to lobster on my own and tomorrow will be my first time out by myself."

He looked to the window and saw a shadow pass by, with measured steps. He always shut the drapes before he went to bed, even though they wouldn't completely shut all the way and he'd get a beam of light first thing in the morning right in his face as he lay in bed. The cleaning people had a habit of opening them when they came in to tidy up after he left and leaving them like that. There were only the thin curtains behind that kept the sun out. In the dark, he sensed the person walking by was looking in at him. The shadow passed, and he walked over to the window while still speaking with Janet to shut the drapes as best he could.

"I found a body washed up in the seaweed near the landing area today," he said nonchalantly.

She gasped. "Oh, Charlie, no! You have to go to the police with this, Charlie, you're making me nervous!" Her tone was demanding.

"Janet, slow down. I've already gone to the chief of police and they are going to have a police boat patrolling the water around the bay, so don't worry."

"Oh, Charlie! Be careful!" She took a long breath. "I was hoping that you would be having fun—you know, like a little vacation. I don't want to see you get in trouble."

"Oh, Janet, I'll be all right! I ... I...." He had been concentrating on the drapes while he spoke, and saw, through the little gap between them, the figure of a person walking by again. This time it was in the other direction. It was a short, relatively portly silhouette and again, it appeared to him that the figure turned to look inside his room. He became tense. This was not just one of the other tenants of the hotel, unless it was a sick voyeur. He hurried the conversation with Janet. "Oh, forget it, Janet, I've got to go."

"What's the matter, Charlie?" Her voice snapped.

"I don't know. I'll call you tomorrow. Tell the kids I love them and I'll be home soon. I love you!"

"Be careful, Charlie! I love you, too!"

He slammed the phone down. His eyes had never left the window. Cautiously he approached the casement. The lights from the top of the hotel, which was horseshoe shaped, beamed down over the parking area on the other side of the lot, but the lights on his side of the building weren't working properly, making it difficult to see from his room. He tiptoed up to the window to see who it could possibly be. As he advanced, his mouth grew dry, and he licked the inside; opening and shutting it, in an attempt to manufacture saliva. He reached the drapes and placed a closed fist on each side of the gap. In one swift jerk, he pulled the shades apart. There was nothing there but the parking lot. He lowered his head and breathed out. This place was getting to him, he figured, and he was making something out of nothing. He began to slowly close the drapes to where he preferred them.

In a flash the figure popped up from below the bottom sill! It was a man—as best he could tell!

His heart skipped a beat and he staggered backwards into the desk behind. His eyes bulged wide open and his chin dropped.

The shadow figure stared straight in at him then turned and ran. Charles began panting heavily. He stood silent and in shock for only a moment until he decided to see if he could get a good look at this peeping Tom. He hustled to the door and opened it. He saw the figure, quite indistinct in the poor lighting, run all the way down the sidewalk in front of the rooms and around the corner of the building. He ran after him, but as he turned the corner, the man had vanished.

He knew now that he was being watched. This was going to be a long night! He contemplated going to the main desk and complaining, but they would probably just think he was nuts. He didn't get a very good look anyway, and couldn't give them much of a description.

Was this a scare tactic because he had spoken with the police? In any case, this was the last night he was going to spend in this room.

He walked back inside the room, still somewhat shaken, and took the large comforter off his bed, draping it over the window so it was impossible to see inside. He called the front desk.

"Yes?"

"Hi, this is Charles Ritter in Room #111. I just had someone snooping around my window. I was hoping you could have somebody check the parking lot every so often for people that don't belong here."

"Oh, we're sorry, sir. Could it have been another tenant, or one of our personnel?"

"No! No, I don't know who it was, but they sure didn't want to stick around."

"We'll have our clerk take a walk around the premises every fifteen minutes or so tonight. We're so sorry about that, sir. It's probably just kids."

"Thank you." He hung up. *Just kids? Humph!*

It was dark when Charles woke with the aid of the alarm clock. It was hard to tell, because no light could penetrate into his room with the curtains, drapes and the comforter hung precariously from the supports. He had slept on the floor at the foot of the bed, just in case. He felt he was becoming a tad paranoid, but better that than dead. He quickly took a shower and got dressed then got in his car and headed for Jonas's house. It was still only 5:00 a.m. The roads in Maine were narrower than those in Rhode Island, that is, once you're off the main thoroughfare. He kept his lights on the whole way and arrived at Jonas's around 5:45 a.m. The lights were on inside. He pulled into the driveway where Elena usually parked and knocked on the door.

"Come in!" Jonas yelled from a distance.

Charles opened the door and saw no one in the house, yet. Jonas walked around the stairwell buttoning up his pants. "That was my mornin' constitutional," he proudly declared. "What are ya doing here, now?"

"Well, I don't know. I figured I could ride out with you when we go out, after you see the children off to school." He raised his eyebrows.

Jonas finished buckling his belt, pulled it out from his stomach and released it. He looked firmly at Charles. "Elena called ya, didn't she?"

"Well, as a matter of fact...."

"Ah! It don't matter. I don't care. She don't trust me, the little wench! I guess we can sit for a while and have a cup of coffee before the kids get up. I don't have to go in first thing every mornin'" He smiled and motioned for

Charles to sit.

"She said she tried to get a hold of you, but you weren't home yet."

"Nah, I went out last night and had a couple of pops and somethin' to eat. Katherine's cookin' is just as bad as Elena's!" He smiled out of the side of his mouth. "Did ya go see the cops?" he spoke as he poured hot water into a tin cup sitting on the counter. He took another cup off the shelf, set it down beside the first and poured the water into that one, also. Charles studied the coffeepot. It was a camper's pot, made of metal. He hadn't seen one of those since he was a child.

"Yes, we talked. He's going to be putting out a patrol boat this morning sometime. He's a very stubborn man."

Jonas picked up a jar of instant coffee and spooned some in both cups. "Ya can make ya own. Sugar's over there and there's cream in the fridge. I drink mine black."

"Thank you, I'll take mine black, too." He stepped over to the counter and picked up the cup, brought it to the chair Jonas pointed to and sat down.

"Well, for your sake, I hope that works. 'Cause, by goin' to the cops, ya mighta just brought on a whole heap of trouble!" He sat down at his usual chair and smiled cynically. "Once ya get to ya mooring and I get to mine this mornin', we part company until ya finish ya stuff, then I'll come back and bring ya into shore by the landin', where it's safe." He set his cup down and reached in his pocket for his chewing tobacco.

"That's fine with me." He sipped the coffee, which tasted like burnt rubber, but somehow choked it down. "You know that body we saw in the kelp?"

"Yeah, Doug Harvey. What about him?"

"Well, I went and got the chief of police and brought him back there. The body was gone!"

"Hahahaha!" Jonas slapped his palm on the table. "I figured as much! Ya got a lot to learn, flatlander!" He continued laughing as he cut off a piece of tobacco. "Now, ya have done it! Now they know you know, and they know that ya told the cops! Ya got balls, boy!" He never stopped laughing, and this began to irritate Charles.

"I also had a visitor last night!"

"Huh?" Jonas spoke as he threw the chaw into his mouth. "Whatta ya mean, a visitor?"

"Someone was peeking in my hotel window."

"Hahahaha!" Jonas's eyes were drawn shut and they began to water. "Oh, boy, ya really did it!" He stopped laughing and caught his breath. "If I were ya, I'd pack my bags now and get the hell outta Dodge!"

Charles pursed his lips. "It's not funny, and I refuse to be intimidated!" His one-time fear sprouted into a determined resolve. "I'm going to find out what's going on and who's behind it, no matter what you say!"

Jonas just nodded. "Good luck—ya'll need it!"

Chad and Katherine stepped into the room from off the steps. They were both still rubbing their eyes. "We could hear you laughing all the way upstairs, Dad," Chad said.

"Well, it's time to get up anyway. Ya gotta get ready for school. Go upstairs and get ya clothes and take a shower."

Chad looked half asleep. "There won't be enough hot water, Dad."

"'Course there will!" Jonas replied tersely, "I skipped mine this mornin'; just to save enough hot water for the two of ya to take one. See how thoughtful I am? Now, go!" He pointed to the stairwell. He really didn't take a shower very often; once a week at the most, but the ploy worked, and the children scrambled back to their rooms. Katherine came back down first with her brand-new dress, stockings, undergarments and shoes as she went into the bathroom. Chad came down with his new school clothes and sat at the table with the two men. There was a period of silence until Chad spoke.

"I heard you say that you found a body at the landing." He looked at Charles.

"Well, yes, why?"

"Did it have both hands attached?"

"Huh?" The question caught Charles off guard. "I don't know, why?"

"Because when Dad took me out for the first time last week, I pulled up a trap that had a human hand stuck on top."

"Shut up, boy!" Jonas spit out a wad of tobacco directly on the floor beside him.

"Last week? Are you sure?" This intrigued Charles.

"Dad don't believe me, but I saw it, I swear I saw it!"

"I said, shut up, boy!" Jonas's face contracted. "This is man's talk. Go back upstairs and get the rest of your shit, whatever ya take to school with ya."

"Yes, Dad. Are we going to have breakfast?"

"There's cereal in the cupboards somewhere, just get outta here. Hey, what time does your bus come?"

"6:20 a.m." Chad nearly skipped his way to the stairs and up.

Charles turned to Jonas. "Is that true?"

He scratched his head. "I don't know, maybe. I didn't see it. I guess he could be tellin' the truth, after what we've seen. Anyway, I'm gonna go load my truck and make sure that ol' Randy's motor's got gas and oil in her."

"I can make a lunch for the kids, if you don't mind."

Jonas huffed. "Elena again! Go right ahead, I was gonna have 'em make their own. The shit's in the cupboard." He got up from the table and walked outside. Charles fumbled around through the cupboards and came up with peanut butter and bread, then looked inside the refrigerator and found jam. He quickly made their lunches, took potato chips out of large bag, placing some in smaller baggies, and the sandwiches in baggies, also. He took out two paper bags and placed the lunches inside. He then reached into his pocket and removed two pieces of paper on which he had written his name and the phone number to the hotel along with a message:

If you need anything, anything at all, just call me.

He placed the notes inside the lunch bags and folded the tops of the bags neatly.

The two men drove to the pier in their separate vehicles, and arrived at nearly 7:00 a.m. The sun shone brightly now, nearly blinding Charles as he drove. There were only a few cumulus clouds on the horizon in every direction; small, white and puffy. The rest of the sky was bright blue. The sea was perfectly calm as Charles parked his vehicle, and Jonas turned around to back the trailer holding the motor boat down the ramp. "Just get in the boat, Charlie, and stand up front so as I don't hit bottom when I get her in the water, then row it over to the steps once I unhook it from the winch. Hook it up there and wait for me."

This he did, while Jonas fiddled with the winch and drove into the parking lot. Charles got out of the small boat and waited for Jonas on the pier.

Two young men were strolling by in the sand at the far end of the ramp. They stopped and walked up the pier to Charles. They were carrying clamming gear; rakes and buckets, and wearing high clamming boots and orange caps. One of them approached Charles. "You that guy from Rhode Island?"

Charles was becoming accustomed to the title. "Yes, I am. Why may I ask?"

"We heard you been asking around here about the murders. Is that true?"

"Well, yes, I suppose it is, why? Do you know anything?"

"We were out clammin' off Sears Island when we saw Doug Harvey get shot."

"You did?! Did you see who shot him?"

"Yup. It was Kenny Buckner and that Indian. They shot him, then hid over to Kidder Point."

Charles's face lit up in elation. "Well, why didn't you go to the police with this?"

Both boys laughed. "Don't you see? There's four people missing or dead that we know of, and neither one of us wants to be number five! By the way, mister, this is just between you and us. If you tell anybody else, we never even seen you before!"

"Yeah, yeah, sure! Mum's the word!" He was in a state of euphoria. Now, he could tell the chief of police, and this whole thing would be over. The boys left when they saw Jonas approaching the pier. There were a million more questions he wanted to ask the two of them, but he didn't want to call attention to Jonas. He still would keep his word to the boys, and to the chief of police. Now, all he had to do was figure out who Kenny and the Indian were.

Jonas walked up the pier then down the steps to the lower wharf, where Charles was waiting for him. "Who were those kids?" he asked.

"Oh, they just wanted to know if I knew where the good clams were. I told them I had no idea, I wasn't from here."

Jonas looked at him sideways, only believing him with a grain of salt. "Let's get in the boat," he demanded.

Sam and Andrew were leaning against the edge of the rail at the far end of the long pier. "Goin' by yeself there, Rhode Islander?" Sam asked.

"Yes, I'm going to give it a try."

"I remember the first time I went out by m'self," Andrew reflected. "Biggest storm of the year hit. I was only ten, but I handled her like I'd been doin' it f'years."

"Really?" Sam interrupted. "First time I went out, we had the only documented tidal wave in Maine history! And I was only 9."

"I never heard of no tidal wave in Maine!"

"Oh, the newspapers covered it up. Didn't want to create no panic. It were an eighty-foot wave, I reckon."

"I thought you said it was documented. Ha! The storm I was in capsized m'boat. I had to swim to shore, nearly ten miles, and that was in December!"

"Oh, yeah? Well, that tidal wave tossed me as far as Jones's farm and I was pickin' blueberries in the afternoon without them even knowin' it!"

The two voices faded, but like always, in chuckling.

Jonas dropped Charles off at Randy's boat, which had a convenient toss-over ladder for access, then he took the skiff over to his own.

Charles was a bit intimidated, being alone. He put on his life jacket and made his way to the mooring, where he loosed the line. Then, he got behind the wheel and studied the instruments again. It was more of an effort to relax than to remember. He started the engines with no problem today and proceeded out to his fist set of traps. The view was spectacular, and he absorbed as much as he could while still maintaining his objective.

Jonas waited for him and followed him away from the shore at a close distance astern. He pulled up beside him and hollered over to Charles, "I'll see ya at about 11:00 a.m., unless ya got a problem. I'll keep my eyes open after I get back from Islesboro." He smiled. "Have a good time!" He roared his engines full throttle through the channel, toward his destination.

Kenny parked his truck in the lot, then he and the Rat took his skiff out to his mooring.

The Rat pulled the binoculars from his face. "He is on his own, sahib. I know where he has put his traps. He has three near the channel buoy and two farther to the north. It is most unfortunate, but they are all close to shore."

Kenny was slumping until he stood straight up then slumped again, breathing out heavily when he did. "I heard he's been askin' questions and snoopin' around the pier."

"Yes, sahib, but they still have no corpses and now there is no one left who knows it was us!"

"Still, I ain't takin' no chances!"

"I agree, sahib, and he is alone. Today is the day. But we have been foolish in our methods."

The two men faced each other. "What? What do you mean, 'foolish'?"

"No one knows of the treasure but us and the two who found it. They are no more! Now the only reason we have eliminated the others is due to the fact that they witnessed us murder the first two. When you shot them, the sound called attention to another and we were discovered again. So, he was eliminated. When you shot him, the noise caught the attention of another and we had been exposed once more.

"As long as there are men on the water, your shotgun will attract more men until we must eliminate them all. There will be no end. We run out of luck, sahib!"

Kenny thought long and hard. "You're right, my curry eating friend. You told me that we will do this your way. Well, what do you suggest?" He tilted his head back, looking at Souharat out of the bottom of his eyes.

"There is only the one left—the one from Rhode Island. So far, he knows only of the bodies he saw. He is not from here and can not be as easily frightened as the rest. Eliminate him and we may search for the treasure without delay or worry."

"Yes, yes. What do you suggest?"

The Indian smiled sinisterly, remaining silent, until he blurted out, "A weapon with no sound, sahib!"

Kenny looked at him in puzzlement. The Rat picked up the harpoon gun with his left hand and patted the top of it with his right hand. "The quiet killer, sahib!" His grin was fiendish.

A wide smile encompassed Kenny's face and he began to laugh. "Hahaha, hummm! Of course, my conniving mate! Of course!" The two men laughed together. "Let's go!" They pulled away from their mooring, and Kenny piloted them through the maze of buoys leading out to the channel. They watched as Charles replaced the second of his traps north of the channel buoy then took into the channel for easier navigation.

"Now is the time, sahib. He is away from the shore!"

Kenny shoved his boat into full throttle, hopping over the small wind waves and smacking the hull of the boat off the pristine waters. They were aimed for an interception course for Randy's boat. Charles heard the vessel approaching and observed them in wonderment. Souharat held the harpoon gun just below the edge of the boat so that Charles could not see it as they neared.

"Hey! You! Aren't you that fella from Rhode Island?" Kenny asked as he pulled the throttle back to neutral. He wanted Charles to do the same and address him in the open, away from the windows of the housing. Charles fell for it and shifted the boat into neutral. They may have been 200 feet apart at the most.

"Yes, I am. Who are you?" he replied. Ignorantly, when the two boys told Charles that it was Kenny and an Indian, he assumed a *Native American Indian*. He never even thought about an Indian from India.

"Names ain't important!" Kenny shouted. He had Charles exactly where he wanted him; exposed and idle, an easy target. He kicked Souharat in the shin. That was the signal. The Rat hoisted the harpoon gun as quickly as he possibly could.

The moment was a flash to Charles. In a split instant he realized the reference to the 'Indian.' The Rat tucked the gun against his shoulder and at the same time Charles dropped toward the deck. The shot went off, and as he was falling, the harpoon zipped just over his head. It fell harmlessly into the water, well beyond the other side of the boat.

The hair raised on the back of Charles's neck. He lay flat on the deck, unable to move.

"Damn you, Rat! You missed!" Kenny kicked him squarely in the leg this time.

"We were too far and you should not have called him. He had time to see me raise the weapon."

"That's a piss poor excuse! I made him stop, so you didn't have a moving target to shoot at, and we were nearly sitting on top of him. Damn you! Give me my gun, I want him done in now!" Souharat had that tendency to make excuses and blame others for his mistakes: Hence the nickname 'Rat.' He fumbled for the gun, and when he finally found it, they both heard the engine of the other boat roar.

Charles never bothered to get up off the top of the deck, where he was temporarily covered by the starboard side of the boat. He simply reached up above to the throttle and pushed it as far as it would go—to full power. The boat raced along at top speed with a ghost pilot. His heart pounded and his breathing became erratic. He couldn't see where he was going!

Kenny just received the gun from the Rat and be shot aimlessly at the boat to no avail. "C'mon, Rat, let's go get him!" He ran to the wheel and pushed the throttle in full. His boat was much faster than Randy's, and it wouldn't be long before they would be within gun range, that is if they left at the same time, but Charles had a good headstart.

Charles began to panic, knowing he was bound to crash into something if he didn't get up and look. He slowly lifted his head, just enough to see over the stern and Kenny's boat behind him. He was far enough out of gun range, he felt, that he could stand now. Once he did and looked forward to where he was going, he realized that he was only seconds away from the large red channel buoy and headed directly at it! He spun the wheel to starboard, dropping the side of the boat into the water and nearly capsizing. A tremendous wave was produced, covering the buoy with white foam. He still kept the throttle full, avoiding lobster buoys throughout the water. He had slid sideways out of the channel and into a mass of lobster traps. Luck had been with him so far, then he remembered that there were almost no buoys inside the channel. He corrected his course to remain inside the channel, but Kenny's boat was closing in on him swiftly. He heard shots emanating from the boat at his stern, but the bullets seemed to drop harmlessly into the bay. He looked around again. Kenny was getting much closer!

He tried to think of what to do and where to go. Another shot was heard then another. His boat was bouncing so violently from the speed and the waves that he nearly lost control several times. He banked the boat, first to starboard then to port, hoping to create a moving target, making it harder for them to get a clear shot at him. He was headed out into the deep part of Penobscot Bay. The breeze held his hair running parallel to the waters, and he had lost his glasses sometime during the melee. His head burned from the spray of the water and the uncertainty of his fate. His vision was obstructed from the spray over the bow. He was overthinking. He glanced behind once more and saw that Kenny and the Indian were now within firing range. That's when he recalled the lobster pound in Belfast Bay. They wouldn't dare follow him in there; it was just too crowded. He was at the delta near the mouth of the bay when he cut the wheel to enter. Kenny let out one last shot, which sailed just past Charles and lodged into the panel board. He jumped sideways when he heard the shot hit. He noticed Kenny nearly upon him when, suddenly, Kenny's boat stopped! He had made it far enough into the bay that Kenny didn't dare maintain chase without the horde taking notice. Charles slowed down but not to an idle. The lobster pound was only seconds away. He eventually idled the boat and spun his head around to watch the two men in the other boat yelling at each other. He found a dry towel on the steps leading down to the bottom deck and wiped his face and most of his body. He was soaking wet. He bent down and picked his glasses up off from the deck, then placed them on his face. He trembled uncontrollably as he brought the vessel to the lobster unloading area at the pound.

One man stood there watching what was going on. "You know there are speed limits around here, mister? I don't know what game you were playing, but you're lucky the game warden didn't see you."

"Hey look, I have a problem. I can't tell you the whole story, but that guy back there was trying to kill me. I'm in danger if I try to go back to Searsport today. Do you think there is any way I could leave my boat here?" He acted desperate. He *was* desperate!

"Oh, no! No way. This is only a commercial lobster drop-off and we've got a business to run."

"I'll pay you! I'm really in a spot. I'm telling you, my life is in jeopardy. Please?"

"Come on, guy. I can't, but ... wait a minute. Art L'enfant pulled his boat off his mooring for repairs. He said he's not even putting it back in this year. He just might let you use his spot. He's eating inside now. Let me go ask him." The man turned and walked inside.

"Tell him I'll pay him!" Charles bellowed to make sure that he heard.

After a minute or so, the same man came out with another man. He was short and thin and very old. He spoke with a thick French accent. "You, ah, want, ah, da rent da spot."

"Please, I'm in a real mess. I'll pay you."

"Don't worry about da moneee. My mooring is, ah, over dere. Help yourself, ey!" He pointed to the closest mooring to the pound.

"Oh, sir, thank you very much. You don't know how much this means to me!"

"No problem, ey!" Art began to walk back inside. "Oh, sir!"
Art turned back around. "Ey?"
"Do you think someone could give me a ride back to shore?"
The Frenchman laughed. "Dat be a good idea, ey! You just stay in da boat, we come get ya, ey!" He continued chuckling to himself as he went back into the pound. For once, Charles had found an uninhibited individual in Maine. A real good man. He swung the boat over to the mooring Art had shown him, tied it up and waited. It wasn't long before Art L'enfant and another gentleman pulled up in a small outboard. "Get in dere, ey," Art spoke to Charles. "We give you, ah, a ride back to da pound. You can, ah, use da phone dere, ey." He patted Charles on the back while he boarded their boat, somewhat for stability but mostly for comfort. Charles didn't realize it, but he was as white as a ghost and looked more like a demon; his hair unfurled, his clothes drenched and his eyes completely red.

"Thank you, Art, I'll be calling a cab."

"Ahh, tough day, ey?" The man was jubilant. Charles began to relax and feel much better, but completely spent from exhaustion.

"It was a *very* tough day!"

They alit from the boat at the pound and entered. The sounds were melodious—water running and the chatter of people purchasing seafood. He asked one of the employees if they could place a call to the local cab company for him. They did, and while he waited he took his own little mini-tour of the market. It was the first time he had ever been in a lobster pound, or even a fish market. It was ironic that he should be teaching a class in which the students might know more about it than he. There were lobsters in bins everywhere! No wonder Maine is considered the lobster capital of the world. This place accentuated the point.

The cab arrived and rode him back to the hotel front desk, only seconds from the pound. He went inside and asked them if he could change rooms—he felt uncomfortable in the one he had. The hotel politely accommodated. He returned to his original room, collected all his items and brought them to the new room.

He called the police station, where Danny answered.

"May I speak with Chief McFagan?"

"Sorry, he's patrolling the bay all day today. Can I take a message?"

"I was on the water today and I didn't see him."

"He had to get our patrol boat this morning. After that, he's been out all day. May I ask who's calling?"

"Yes. Just tell him that Charles Ritter called and I'll try to get a hold of him later."

"Yes, sir." They both hung up. It really didn't matter when he spoke to the chief. They still didn't have a corpse, and his escapade today was simply his word against a well-known local's word. The only other witnesses that existed simply would not talk to the police. It all appeared so useless.

The rest of the day he decided he would work on his syllabus and take sporadic naps.

Chapter 16

The chattering of the children on the school bus echoed down the road as the bus pulled up in front of Belfast High School, forcing traffic to wait. The unprepared commuters always hated this day—the oncoming of bus traffic ensured traveling delays every morning from now until May. The choices were few; either reschedule the ride into work in an attempt to 'time it right' or find a route where there was minimal to no bus traffic. Either way, it was a necessary annoyance.

The din emitting from the bus only became more vociferous upon the opening of the door outside the school. The rekindling of friendships and rivalries after a long hiatus makes for a ruckus. Chad and Katherine exited the bus for their first day of school. They were dressed in the same garments they wore when they first met Charles. Katherine, who was fifteen, was accustomed to the ride and the environment. Chad, who was only thirteen, was experiencing this trip to his new school for the first time. Chad sat with his friend, Colin, near the back of the bus, playing and fooling with each other and those around them for the whole trip. Katherine sat alone.

Kids yelled and screamed as they ran from the door of the bus to the entrance door of the building. It was a brick structure, accommodating the many students within the several grades for this school district. Katherine did not join in the revelry, instead she walked despondently into the building, her head held low. Chad ran inside, excited to start a new school year. The bell rang and the stragglers who decided to tour the outside grounds hustled inside and the revelry came to an end, but the chattering did not. There was some confusion as to where to go and who to speak to. Chad's friend Colin was in the grade ahead of him, and he directed Chad on which room to first report. Katherine knew where to go, and by the time the second bell rang, everyone was in their correct location and the school day began.

After a brief indoctrination, it was time for the first period of the morning. In Katherine's case, she had English class with Mrs. Morrill. Chad had social studies with Mr. Fletcher. The bell rang again and the students went to their respective classes. When Chad walked into the room with his book bag and class schedule, he recognized about one-third of the kids from his previous school. He sat beside Sean Quinn, one of the students who he had gone to school with all his life. The two boys liked to play the fool. No sooner were they all seated than Mr. Fletcher entered the room carrying an armful of paperwork. A hush fell over the area except for Chad and Sean, who continued to play jokingly.

Mr. Fletcher cast his eyes upon the two boys and gazed sharply at them over his cup-shaped spectacles. "Ahem! Gentlemen, the bell has rung." He spoke calmly and waited for the two to settle down. He was a tall, slender man, wearing a sports jacket and dress slacks, a white shirt and red tie. His hair was trim and his facial expression was serious. He spoke deliberately, nearly rehearsed, and his voice was stuffy as though he was straining to act more intelligent than he really was. He pressed his hands down over his chest.

The two regrouped and sat silently in the back of the room. The teacher grimaced, then glanced through the paperwork he had set on the desk. "Now, class, I suppose the first thing we shall do is get to know each other." He turned around and faced the blackboard, picked up a piece of chalk and wrote 'Mr. Fletcher' on the slate. He set the chalk back down on the sill at the bottom of the board then pivoted to face the student body. "My name is Mr. Fletcher. Now, starting at my left in the front column and continuing down that column, then back to the top, I would like each of you to stand and state your name, so that we may become acquainted."

The students obeyed the request without error. When the last one sat down, Mr. Fletcher again stood up and gathered a stack of papers from his desk, walking it to the first student to the far left and, after carefully counting out the correct number of copies, handed her a partial stack. "Please, take one and pass the rest to the student behind you. This is the overview of what I expect of you to learn over—"

Chad had leaned in his chair, raising his behind in the air, pointing it at Sean. Then he audibly passed gas. Sean twisted his head in the direction of Chad, and the two children began to laugh, lowly at first, then loudly. Mr. Fletcher, who had now approached the second column of students, stopped and stared to the back at the two boys. "Is there something amusing you two would like to share with us?"

They burst out laughing. Sean tried to speak but kept on choking on his own snickering. "He ... hahaha ... he ... ha ... he farted!" The entire class broke up at that exchange.

Mr. Fletched became upset. "Children! Children, that's enough!" The class calmed down. He looked at Chad and Sean. "If you two continue to be a disruptive force in my class, you will be separated. Do you understand?"

"Yes, sir." They spoke in unison, lowering their heads, and Mr. Fletcher continued to pass out the papers. Sean and Chad would look at each other from time to time and suppress their laughter as best they could. Mr. Fletcher completed his task and returned to his desk with the extra outlines he did not need. He sat down, glancing at the blotter on his desk, then picked his head up and, with the index finger of his right hand, counted the students in the classroom.

"Well," he said, "it appears that everyone is here. Now, you may take that outline home and look it over. Today, we are waiting on the books for the class to be delivered sometime this afternoon, so in the meantime, I will quickly go over some fundamentals to see how well you have met the prerequisites I demand for this course of study. I will ask a few questions you should have learned in the seventh grade. Let's try a geography question. If I call on you, please stand and give me your answer. Could anybody tell me what is the highest peak in North America?"

Mary Coombs, who sat up front, raised her hand.

Mr. Fletcher nodded at her. "Yes, Mary."

"Mount McKinley!" Mary responded with a bright smile on her face.

Chad cupped his mouth and whispered to Sean, "Once you've seen one mountain, you've seen them all." Sean snickered and Mr. Fletcher glanced over at the two but said nothing to them.

"Very good, Mary. Now let's try a history question. Does anybody know who our 27th president was?"

No one in the class raised their hand, even though Chad actually knew the answer. He hated playing these types of games and refused to participate.

"Very well, then, I'll give you a clue. He succeeded Theodore Roosevelt."

Still, there was no response. "He was our last president to have facial hair." The students remained still. "He was the only president who also served as a Supreme Court Justice." Finally, Will Avery raised his hand. "Yes, Will." Mr. Fletcher recognized him.

"William Howard Taft!" Will spoke with elation, thinking he was the only one in the class to know that.

"Very good, Will!" Mr. Fletched praised.

For no reason, and out of the blue, Chad blurted out "He was also fat!" Mr. Fletcher heard him. "Chad Hale, do you have something to add?"

Chad stood and smiled, "Yes, I said he was also our fattest president!" Some of the students chuckled at the way Chad seemed so arrogant and humorous when he spoke.

Mr. Fletcher smiled. "You're right! He was the largest president of the

United States. I suppose that's all you know, and God knows why you would know that!"

Chad continued to stand. "Because Taft is an anagram for fat!" The children now laughed out loud for a short period of time.

Mr. Fletcher was irritated. "Fat has only one 't,' Mr. Hale."

"Not for him. He was so fat he needed two!" The class roared again and Mr. Fletcher waved his hands to quiet them.

"You seem intelligent, Mr. Hale. I don't suppose you would like to teach this class?"

"Sure!"

Mr. Fletcher leaned back in his chair. "Oh, by all means, Mr. Hale. Go right ahead and I'll just observe." He had become impatient with Chad and now wanted to see him make a fool of himself in front of the class.

"O.K.," he agreed. "Now, class, let's try a question in zoology, more specifically, vertebrates." He was speaking in the same tone of voice as the teacher, obviously imitating him. Mr. Fletched turned red at the intentional mimicking. Chad placed his open palms on his chest and brushed his clothes downward, then stuck his nose in the air. "Ahem, ahem, ahem."

Sean giggled at the silly emulation of Mr. Fletcher's behaviors and mannerisms.

"Ahem. Could anyone tell me what is long and green and smells like a pig?" The class sat quietly. He looked around the room and pursed his lips in a sign of his teacher's vanity. "Hmmm? Hmmm? Nobody. The answer is *Kermit's finger*!"

The class fell about in hysterics. The laughter was deafening. Sean had to hold one hand on his stomach and one hand over his mouth while his cheeks hurt from his cramped facial expression.

Mr. Fletcher stood up in anger, "Mr. Hale, that's it! Class, class, stop it! Mr. Hale, get up here to my desk right now!"

The roaring of the students began to dissipate. Chad walked from his desk to the teacher's desk. Mr. Fletcher stood up and grabbed a new group of papers from his desk, handing them over to Mary in the front row. "Mary, would you please distribute these to everyone in this class while Mr. Hale and I take a walk to the principal's office. Now, class, you will read this while I'm gone and when I return you will be quizzed on the content. It will count on your grades, so I suggest you heed my word and read this. You may thank Chad Hale for your first quiz." He turned to Chad. "You, sir, have just earned a zero on your first test, since you have an unexcused absence from it. Now come along, and you shall greet Principal Thibodeau. I think you and he shall become quite familiar." He snapped his head back to Mary. "Mary, see that order is maintained. I will know who read this and who didn't when I return." He grabbed Chad's ear and tugged at him through the door and down the hall.

The students in the room shuffled and mumbled quietly when the two exited. Sean leaned over in his chair and very loudly passed gas, a subdued amount of laughing resulted amidst the shuffling of papers.

Jonas returned to the pier and moored his boat early seeing Randy's boat had been moored to Belfast Bay at Art's mooring. He asked at the pound about the boat and they explained what they knew of the situation then they told him that Charles had taken a cab back to his hotel. This bothered Jonas, so he decided to call it a day and go to the hotel to see what the circumstances were. He had a feeling it wasn't good. He arrived at the hotel about two hours after Charles. He had to go to the front desk and ask which room Charles was staying in. The woman at the desk looked at him suspiciously then realized she knew him from around town.

"Jonas. Jonas Hale. I didn't recognize you. Charles Ritter just changed rooms today. He looked a mess when he came in here. He was pale and wet, looked like he saw a ghost."

"He might have. His own!" Jonas replied.

"He's down here, not far from the office. The second room on the left."

"Thanks, girl!" Jonas said while he walked out of the office. It took him no time to find the room, and he knocked on the door.

Charles carefully pulled the curtains aside. It was still very light out, but his nerves were on edge. When he saw Jonas he immediately opened the door, let him in and shut the door and locked it behind him. "Jonas, am I glad it's you! How did you find me?"

"I'm glad I went to check my traps in Belfast this early. I saw Randy's boat moored there and I knew somethin' was wrong. What happened?"

Charles sighed and rubbed his head. "Well, part of this I can't tell you, but now I know who the murderer is!"

"Who?" he asked.

"A guy named Kenny Buckner and some Indian fellow. An Indian from India."

"His name's the Rat! That figures! What happened today?" He was anxious to hear the details.

"Who is this Kenny? Hey, Jonas, he tried to kill me today!"

"I knew it! I told ya to take off. That it was a bad idea to go to the cops! I warned ya! But ya wouldn't listen. Nooo! Ya had to be stubborn! What am I gonna do with ya?"

"I still have a problem. There still isn't a corpse that can be identified, autopsied or show any evidence of murder. No matter how much I know, who's going to believe me? You have to come to the chief of police with me!"

Jonas held up his hands in front of Charles. "Oh, no! Not me. I still got a while to go before I meet ol' St. Pete." He thought. "So, what are ya gonna do?"

"Well, I changed rooms so they can't find me and my van is still in Searsport. They won't be able to track me down, I don't think. Tomorrow, I'm staying put and making some phone calls. This is getting very scary for me."

Jonas paced back and forth. "Ya know, if ya ain't goin' out tomorrow, I think I'll stay in, too, and think about this. I wonder what the hell Kenny's doing and what he wants. He's an asshole, but all them murders? It's gotta be somethin' big." He rubbed his beard then looked at Charles. "Ya know more about this than you're saying, don't ya?"

Charles was caught off guard. "No," he said in a very low voice. "I just want to lie down right now and take a nap. It's really been a long day."

"Yeah, ya do!" Jonas grinned. "Ya will tell me when they try to kill ya again!" He laughed. "Give me a call tomorrow if ya want to talk."

"O.K., sure," Charles said. Jonas walked out, got into his truck and drove to the tavern down the street before returning home.

"You idiot, Rat!" Kenny screamed. "Great idea—use a harpoon! Where did you learn how to shoot?" The two men had moored their boat and loaded the skiff onto the back of Kennny's truck then moved the truck out of sight. They waited for Charles to return to the pier, but he never did. "This guy musta stayed in Belfast!' Kenny said. "He's only got five traps and he ain't even come back to haul those. Damn!" He stared down to the short, pudgy immigrant. Well, ya know where he's stayin' don't ya? I want him tonight!"

"But sahib. Why do you pinch the penny?"

"What?"

"You have a revolver. It makes noise. The hotel in which he stays has many ears. But if you buy a silencer, to muffle the sound, I will get him for you tonight!"

The larger man crossed his arms. "Hmm. That might be a good idea. I know where I can get one. All right, Rat, I'll get ya a silencer and ya can make up for ya stupid idea of the harpoon, if ya get me a Rhode Islander!"

"Yes, sahib. Tonight!" The two men laughed together.

Jonas sat at the kitchen table in his usual spot when Katherine walked through the door after school. It was only 3:30 p.m. He had a quart of rum in front of him on the table, and was drinking from a cup. "Katherine," he said in a mellow voice. "Where's Chad?"

"He's coming in now, Dad. He's right behind me."

"Good. Good. Now, why don't ya go upstairs like a good girl and change ya clothes."

"Yes, Dad." She ran up the stairs, still carrying her books and school supplies.

Chad took his time coming inside. He eased the door open and peered into the house. He knew his father was home early because his truck and the skiff were parked in the dooryard. He was hoping to get in unnoticed. It was an awkward entrance. His head was bowed to see only the floor as though if he couldn't see his father, then maybe his father couldn't see him. He wanted more than anything to turn invisible at that very moment. He tiptoed inside. Jonas sat at the table with one arm draped over the back of the chair and one hand holding the cup of rum. Chad stealthily walked towards the stairs without saying a word.

Jonas spoke softly, slowly and systematically. "Chad."

Chad stopped walking, with his back to his father. He turned his head to the side, but made no eye contact.

"Yes, Dad?"

"Why don't ya come over here and we can have a little talk."

"Sure, Dad, sure." It was a moment he dreaded. He turned back towards the table, never picking his head up, but rather he stared at the floor like a puppy with his tail between his legs. He was carrying no school books in his hands, just the backpack hoisted over his shoulders and two pens clipped onto his shirt pocket. He made it to the edge of the table.

"How was school today, Chad?" Jonas spoke acerbically, his green, brownish teeth pressed together and exposed on one side of his mouth. It was a gnarled expression, one Chad feared.

"It was O.K., Dad," Chad lied.

"Oh, really? I coulda guessed. Ya know I got a call from a Principal Thibodeau?"

"I didn't know that, Dad." Again he lied.

"It seems he had a teacher come to him first thing in the morning with a student. He said the student had a disciplinary problem. You wouldn't know anything about that, would ya, Chad?" He gulped his rum down.

Chad began to shiver. "Ah, umm, maybe." He squirmed in place where he stood.

"This Thibodeau fella said that a Mr. Fletcher brought an unruly student to his office. He said that student's name was Chad Hale." His expression changed as he leaned forward, placing both arms on the table. "Apparently, this Chad Hale, ya know, was makin' fun of this Fletcher. He imitated him and embarrassed the poor guy, who was only tryin' to do his job. Does any of this sound familiar, Chad?"

Chad scratched his nose. "You know, it's starting to come back to me. I was sitting—"

Jonas slammed his fist on the table. "Shut up! You little insubordinate asshole! Who do ya think ya are? They said they barely had time to clear their throats this mornin' when ya started actin' up! Then ya get hauled to the principal, and ya act up in his office. Makin' little fart calls from under ya armpit. This Thibodeau said ya were suspended from school for two weeks until ya realized who's in charge there. You little wise ass! Suspended! Ha! If I did somethin' that stupid when I was in school they'd a put the wooden ruler across my back. Suspended! What am I gonna tell ya mother? She'll blame me! Ya act so goddamn smart, then ya go to school and act so goddamn stupid! Well, ya know somethin', maybe they can't punish ya the right way in school now, but I sure as hell can! Ya go up and change ya clothes and come back down in five minutes, and ya gonna get a little ol' Jonas discipline! Now go!" he screamed at Chad and Chad backed up, expecting a fist to come flying at him at any given time.

Without one coming, a sudden burst of courage engulfed Chad. "You're no better! You tell me how much you hate school and yet when I perform a small act of rebellion, you're all of a sudden on their side. I don't know what you want me to do. You're just a loser, Dad! I hate you!"

Jonas jumped up and backhanded his son across the face. "Don't ya disrespect me! Ya can get away with it in school, but ya ain't getting' away with it here! To hell with getting' changed!" He pushed the table away from him with one hand then drew back and hit Chad with an open palm directly on his cheek, which turned instantly red. "I'll show ya who's boss under this roof!" He lunged at Chad, who spun and ran up the stairs. Jonas chased him, but Chad had the headstart and was much more agile (and sober). Chad slammed his bedroom door and locked it from the inside. Jonas made it there just behind him. He slammed his fist against the door. "Open this, boy, or you're really gonna get it."

"Go away, Dad. I hate you! You're just a drunk!" In a nervous state, Chad pulled one of the pens out of his shirt and began pressing the bottom in and out, allowing the tip of the pen to protrude then retract. The motion made a repetitive clicking sound.

Jonas grabbed his ears with both hands. "Stop that! Stop that, Chad!"

At first, Chad wasn't sure what he was talking about. Then he realized it was the clicking of the pen. He had found a weakness to his father's gruff exterior. He clicked the pen in and out in spite. "Go away, Dad, or I'll keep on doing it." He continued to click the pen and waited for a response.

Jonas pressed his hands tightly over his ears, and his face tightened up until the veins stuck out of his neck and forehead. His head pounded, his eyes closed and his teeth were clenched in pain.

Finally, when he could hear no more noise outside, Chad released his grip on the pen.

Jonas pulled his hands off from his head. He was full of fury. Without saying a word, he dropped his shoulder, leaned back and charged Chad's door, hitting it with all his weight. The door shattered, splinters of wood flew everywhere.

Chad's face dropped. He could see the madness in his father's face, and before he could move, Jonas had hold of him by the neck. He whipped him against the near wall then grabbed him again. "You little asshole!" he hollered as he nearly lifted him off the ground and tossed him into the upstairs hall against the closet. "Ya think ya...." He grabbed him once more and with one motion he whipped him off of the wall at the top of the steps with such force that Chad bounced off the wall and toppled down the stairs. He banged his head off the rail, bounced back down, did a flip then when trying to catch his balance, slammed his forearm on one of the posts supporting the handrail to the steps. The post broke and he partially went through the opening. His head snapped backward then forwards hitting the top, square post top on the bottom structural support for the rail. His head hit sideways on the sharp object near his eye. Blood gushed everywhere from his head to his torso. His cheek was cut. He eventually fell, unconscious at the bottom of the steps. Blood flowed freely.

Jonas watched Chad lie on the floor, unmoving. He slowly walked down the steps and checked Chad's pulse. He was still alive and that's all that mattered. He stepped over the boy and returned to the kitchen table, where he poured another shot of rum.

Katherine watched in horror at the scene. She never dared to move, or be heard. Once she knew Jonas was comfortable behind his bottle, she ran down the stairs to check on Chad. He was in need of medical treatment. His body was in disarray. She began to cry. She ran to the sink and grabbed a cloth, wet it with cold water then brought it back to Chad and wiped his blood-soaked face with it.

The cool water must have made a difference, because Chad started to open his eyes and speak. "Ah, ouch, that hurts! What happened?"

She whispered to him, "Just lie still, I'll take care of you." She wiped the tears from her own face. Chad regained consciousness and tried to open his eyes completely, but the one which made contact with the handrail was fused shut, and he could only attempt to open it. Katherine placed the cloth over that eye and then checked the rest of Chad's body. It wasn't quite as bad as it looked. It appeared he was bruised everywhere, and his right arm may have been broken. His eye took the worst of the fall.

Chad sat up and held his head. "Oh! Ouch! Katherine, what happened?"

"Here, Chad, lean up against the wall and hold this to your eye." She handed him the cloth. He tried to use his right arm but couldn't move it. He picked up his left arm and held it across his body to the cloth over his right eye. Katherine pulled his shirt apart and checked his chest and abdomen. There were just bruises. "Just stay here, Chad. I'm going to call Charles to come down and take you to the hospital."

"Yeah, yeah, O.K." He was slightly incoherent.

Katherine ran to the phone and started dialing. Jonas looked up. "Who are ya callin'?" He screamed.

"Just a friend," she said.

"Make it quick, I'm expectin' ya mother to call."

She looked back at him in disgust. She got a hold of Charles at the hotel, and he was on his way.

Souharat walked from where he had parked his vehicle in the parking lot behind the hotel and crept along the sidewalk with the revolver stuck inside his jacket. He crept up to Room #111 and cautiously looked inside. All the lights were out! He began to think to himself. *It is very early to be asleep, but perhaps.* His van wasn't out front, but he knew that, because it was still at the landing. He looked inside the window and could see there was no one in the bed. *Perhaps he has changed hotels.* That would appear unlikely, since he knew that the accommodations for the hotel were arranged by others. *Ah, yes! He must have changed rooms! Now, how to find out which room?* His cunning, devious mind shifted through several possible means to achieve his murderous ends. *An emergency phone call from the university!* He looked in all directions before heading to the nearest pay phone, for which he would have to drive to use. He couldn't just go up to the desk and ask. They would surely remember that when they pulled Charles's body out of the room. He had to do this in a way in which they would never suspect him. He drove down to the store about a mile away and got onto the payphone outside. He dialed the number to the hotel and asked for Charles Ritter. He had done his research, and that was why Kenny put up with him Kenny wasn't much of a thinker. Both of them were cutthroats, murderers, liars, thieves and worse. But Kenny acted on the spur of the moment; hastily and usually unwisely. Souharat thought things out in a much more planned, crafty manner. The two worked well together in such a convenient arrangement. The phone rang.

"Hello."

"Good evening, madam, my name is Sandip Singh. I believe we have one of our professors residing in your establishment for the evening, Dr. Charles Ritter."

"Yes, sir, he's staying here."

"Very good. Could you patch me through to his room, I believe it is number 111?"

"Sir, he's no longer there. He changed rooms today for some reason. He's no longer in room #111."

"Oh, dear! That does pose a problem. You see, in order for our books to be arranged properly, we must have the correct room number."

She paused for a second. "Well, let me see. Oh, yes, he's been moved to #102. Do you want me to patch you through?"

"Oh, that won't be necessary. I will call him directly on his cell phone. Thank you so much, madam."

"Anytime." He hung up.

"Damn," he said out loud. "That room is very close to the front desk. I must park in back and approach from the other side. This means walking all around the facility."

He decided he would try it. The walk to the room wouldn't be as long as the walk back. He got back in his car.

Charles arrived in a cab at Jonas's in less than one half hour. He had to pay the cab driver $30.00 to take the cab out of its normal circulation and get him there as soon as possible. The driver didn't seem to mind traveling in excess of the speed limit the whole way. He told the cab driver to wait outside, and he would be right back. As an incentive, he threw him a fifty-dollar bill and said there would be more if he could produce the same timely transport to the hospital. The driver smiled and agreed. Charles entered the house without knocking and saw the horrific scene. Jonas was passed out with his head on the table, and the empty bottle of rum beside it. Chad and Katherine were huddled against the wall, where Katherine was performing minor first aid to Chad, who was now fully awake and aware of what had happened.

Charles rushed up to them and quickly checked Chad over. He checked for broken bones, but the only problem he encountered was his elbow. "He'll be all right, it's just a bit scary to see at first. Come on, Katherine, let's get him into the cab and we'll be off."

The two of them helped Chad to his feet and basically carried him out to the waiting vehicle. Katherine continued to press the cloth over Chad's eye.

The driver earned his pay that night. He got them to the hospital in less than a half hour. Considered the distance to the establishment, that was remarkable. They instantly admitted Chad, while Charles and Katherine filled out the paperwork then sat down in the waiting room. Katherine began to cry again. Charles held her hand. "It'll be all right. It's just a couple of cuts and maybe a broken bone. You guys can stay at the hotel with me tonight and leave for school from there tomorrow."

"Chad's been suspended!" she wailed. "That's how this whole thing happened."

"What do you mean, that's how this happened? He fell down the stairs, right?" She cried louder and did not answer. "Well, let's not worry about it tonight. I'm not going anywhere tomorrow and we'll figure things out then. It's all right! Really, everything will work out, you'll see."

Souharat parked the vehicle in the back where he wanted; out of sight. He crept along the sidewalk of the hotel from its beginning away from the front desk to room #102, near the front desk. The lights were on inside! He checked the area. There were only a few people staying at the hotel. He could tell by the vehicles outlining the parking lot. Those that were there had their drapes drawn shut. He crouched down when he got to the window and slowly picked his head up to peek inside. The drapes were open and it was a clear view. The bed was made, but he saw no signs of anyone inside. He waited patiently. Perhaps he was in the bathroom. He was becoming unsettled. The hotel stood within sight of the road, if by chance anyone glanced over they could see he was up to no good. He couldn't chance waiting there much longer. He placed his ear against the window and could hear nothing. No running water—nothing! He pulled the revolver from within his shirt and peered inside once more before he gave up. He was taking too much of a chance sitting out here. He stayed squatting for only a minute or two when his own nerves won out in a battle of patience and will.

He crept backwards a few paces then stood up and walked casually the way he had come. He returned to his car and sped off. Why couldn't Kenny be the one who took such chances? He felt that he was being used by a bully. *Perhaps, things will change!* he thought.

In the meantime, this would have to wait!

Chapter 17

The three awoke simultaneously. Charles had given Chad the bed, being in the condition he was in. The diagnosis was somewhat better than he had expected. All the blood covering Chad's body when he first set eyes on him was a very ugly sight, but there were only the two lacerations on his body, and both were on his face. He had been given 32 stitches to his right eye and 8 stitches to his right cheek. His arm was not broken as he had originally thought, he had a minor fracture of his right elbow in his ulna. This injury was not serious and would require that Chad wear his arm in a sling for less than a week or until he felt comfortable to stretch his arm. His body was bruised from top to bottom, but that was just a matter of time and some discomfort. There were no internal injuries. The diagnosis was bed rest.

Charles had spoken with the hotel and they allowed him to borrow two cots for him and Katherine to sleep on for the night. He pulled his body to the edge of his cot while the two children rolled over in an attempt to fall back asleep.

"Katherine," Charles said. "You have school today."

She rolled back over and looked at him. "Do I have to go?" She didn't want to leave Chad.

"I'm afraid so. I know you don't have any clothes here, so you can just take a shower and wear the same clothes you wore yesterday. I'm sorry, dear. I don't think your mother would approve of your playing hooky this early in the school year."

She sat up on the edge of her cot. "How am I going to get there?"

"I'm going to call a taxi for you. I asked at the desk last night, the school's not that far from here." He opened his wallet, which he set on the desk behind him, and poked through it. He was quickly running out of money. He regretted not bringing the credit cards that he had left with Janet to make sure she had enough to get through without him. He certainly didn't expect to be going through what he was at this juncture. He pulled out a ten-dollar bill. "Here," he said. "You can pay for the taxi and buy some lunch." She stood up, still fully dressed, and accepted the cash.

"Should I come back here after school?" She was hoping that she could. Her father was now acting in a behavior that she had never witnessed before, and it gave her the chills to be home alone with him.

"No, you can't. Look, I'm going to call your mother today and talk with her. You'll go back home tonight. Your father should still be on the water when you get home, and if your mom tells me that she wants you to stay here, well, then that's fine with me. But I don't want to be presumptuous. I think you're old enough." He smiled at her reassuringly. "Remember, you have my number here if you need to get in touch with me. O.K.?"

She nodded and bowed. "I guess so."

Chad sat up in bed. "Am I going to stay here today?" He grimaced in pain the pushed up on the bottom of the sling attached to his arm.

"Yes. I don't want you to move around much, so I'll take care of you for the day and we'll see how you are feeling tonight. I'm going to call your father, also, to see if he wants you to come back to take care of you or, if he's too busy, we'll have to make some sort of arrangements." He leaned over and fluffed up the pillows behind Chad's back, then he studied his face. The stitches encircled his right eye from the top of his nose, all the way around the edge of his eye then below it to the tip of the cartilage in the center of his nose. His cheek was sewn with all the stitches covering only a small area, to minimize the scar that would undoubtedly emerge. The stitches were still red with dried blood, and his eye was swelled up so badly that it opened only slightly. His eyebrow was virtually missing. There were several cuts on the inside of his mouth from where he must have banged it on the rail and his teeth cut into his cheeks. He wore his arm sling to bed and slept on his back. His body was covered with bruises, and he kept the hospital gown he received when they took him for his preliminary evaluation. Putting his regular clothes back on might have been too painful, so the hospital allowed him to keep the gown. Even with this horrific form, he acted jubilant.

"Cool!" he exclaimed. "Do they have cable TV here?" His pain appeared to abate with the prospects of a mini-vacation.

"I don't know," Charles answered. "I really don't watch much television."

Chad was excited. "Can we get Chinese food for lunch?"

Charles laughed. "We'll see," he responded. "Now, let's go, Katherine. You've got to get ready. Do you need anything that maybe I can get here at the hotel?"

"Well, do you think I could get a toothbrush?"

"Of course. You jump in the shower and I'll call the front desk. How about you, Chad?"

"Yes, a toothbrush, also." He had already turned the television on and was checking the channels. "Hey, Mr. Ritter, you do have cable!" He beamed through his stitches.

"I suppose you can watch whatever you want. I've got to make several phone calls this morning. I've got to let your father know where you are so he doesn't worry. I hope you guys don't mind missing breakfast this morning." They both shook their heads.

Katherine went into the shower, turned the water on and shut the door. Charles turned to Chad, who was watching cartoons on television. Charles took the chair from the desk with the television on it and set it beside the bed. "So, Chad, do you want to tell me what happened?"

Chad adjusted himself in the bed to a more comfortable position, not only physically but socially. "Not really." He then turned his head towards Charles and realized that this man was only trying to help. He had already helped. "Oh, I got suspended from school!" He was embarrassed.

"Suspended? Why?"

"Sean and I were fooling around in the back of the room and I guess I went a little too far. I made fun of the teacher and I guess he didn't appreciate my sense of humor."

"Chad!" Charles spoke in an authoritative tone. "This was only your first day! Boy, what got into you?"

"I don't know. I was just so happy to be in school and out of the house. I felt so free!"

Charles considered the comment. He leaned back in the chair and crossed his legs then placed his hand to his chin and mulled over the situation. Was Chad rebelling? Was he imitating his father's outlandish behavior? Was he trying to get back at his father for years of abuse? It wasn't for him to decide. Once he talked to Elena, he would make his suggestion—counseling should be considered; perhaps family counseling. That is, if the situation hadn't gone too far. No, that wouldn't work. Jonas would never agree.

Charles stopped. "Chad, how did you fall down the stairs?" He leaned forward and stared Chad in the face.

Chad looked at him with a distant stare. "I was thrown down the stairs!" he said bitterly.

Charles fell back in the chair. "Katherine didn't tell me that! She said you fell down the stairs." He paused. "Did your father do this?" Chad nodded.

"Don't worry, he'll get his!" There was a hollow resolve in his words; a strange, bitter pitch that made Charles shudder. No wonder they didn't wake their father up when this happened. They didn't dare.

Now Charles had to make a decision. This was flagrant child abuse. He was in a quandary. Why was he even involved? This whole assignment was out of control. He decided he would talk to Elena first to see what she thought.

Katherine emerged from the shower. Her clothes still had spots of dried blood here and there. Charles called a taxi for her and attempted to wipe the stains off her clothes. For the most part it worked, and she was presentable. "I don't have my books and paperwork," she mentioned.

"I think you can go one day without it." He suddenly become conscious of the fact that she would be going back to the house after school. "You know, if you really want to come back here after school, I don't see why—"

She interjected, "It's O.K., Dad would be upset if I stayed here, plus all my schoolwork is there. I don't mind going back home. I have to cook dinner for Dad, anyway." She was so tender and gentle.

Charles smiled. "You might be right. Chad told me what happened, so you don't have to cover for your father. But it was between him and your brother, not you. You shouldn't have anything to worry about. He should be out hauling traps all day today. You do have my number if you need to get in touch with me—for anything!" He tapped her on the shoulder. A horn was heard outside the door. "Well, that's your cab. Have a good day in school."

She leaned over and kissed him on the cheek. "Thank you!" she said, with tears welling up in her eyes.

"For what?" He spoke sincerely.

"Everything!" she returned. She opened the door and got into the cab. Charles shut the door behind her and picked up the chair, placing it to the edge of the desk so as not to interrupt Chad's watching television. He pulled the phone over in front of him then pulled out his wallet for his list of phone numbers. The first call went to Jonas, who answered it promptly.

"Hello, Jonas?"

"Charlie, whatta ya doin'? Do ya know where my kids are? I fell asleep last night and now they're gone." His voice was gruff and hoarse.

"Don't worry, Jonas. I have Chad here, and Katherine went to school this morning. They both stayed here with me last night."

"What for?" He was contemptuous.

"Well, I thought Chad needed to have a few stitches so I brought him to the hospital for a quick fix. I think he should stay here for the day and rest. He's still in some pain and I don't think he should move for the day."

"Yeah? That little wimp! He can't take a spankin'!"

Charles held back his words. *Spanking?* he thought. It was just possible that Jonas didn't ever remember what he did the night before, so he didn't dare mention it, figuring it would only irritate him more. "I'll see how he feels tonight. If he can move around, I'll send him back home."

"Ya can keep 'im for all I care!"

"I can't do that. He should be a lot better tonight. Are you going lobster fishing this morning?"

"I already told ya, if ya ain't goin' out then I ain't goin' out. I'm still getting' paid—even though this'll be my last day. I might just as well stay put. I'm gonna try to figure out what Kenny's up to. He's a slimy character."

Charles forgot that Jonas had told him he was not going out today. He panicked slightly. The thought passed his mind that Jonas might start drinking early, before Katherine got home, and do something he couldn't even contemplate. He should have had Katherine come back to the hotel. "I wonder if I should tell the police about what happened to me yesterday. The other thing is; I'd like to pick up my van and bring it back here. I can't afford to be taking cabs everywhere. I don't need it today, I don't think."

Jonas laughed. "We'll do it tomorrow. I might take a ride to the pier this morning and check around to see if anyone knows what Kenny's doing. When I go there, I'll check on your van. I wouldn't go to that chief of police if I were ya. That boy is about as bright as a two-watt lightbulb, and the rest of them there are worse!"

The fact that Jonas was going to the pier made Charles feel better. It would get Jonas out of the house and, with hope, it would keep him from drinking himself into oblivion. "Thanks, Jonas, I appreciate that. I'll see you tomorrow."

"O.K. We'll pick it up at night, when no one's around. That way they won't wait for ya or follow ya and they won't see me helpin' ya!"

"O.K.," he repeated. "I'll call you tomorrow." The two parties hung up.

Chad wriggled in the bed. "Can I watch a movie?" he asked with trepidation.

Charles thought that might keep him quiet for a couple of hours, so he could make his phone calls in peace. "Just keep the volume down and you can rent a movie. Keep the subject matter clean!"

Chad smiled, holding the remote control for the television in his hand. "It is clean. It's called *First Blood.*"

Charles squinted at Chad. He had seen the movie. It was good—the first of the *Rambo* movies, but he wondered about the selection. He hoped Chad didn't have a reason to chose that movie in particular. "I guess that's fine," he said, and he picked the phone back up and dialed a number.

"Hello, is Chief McFagan in yet?"

"Is this that fella from Rhode Island?"

"Yes, why?"

"The chief's in the patrol boat. He'll be out all day. He told me that he wants to talk to you. He claims he didn't see anything yesterday, whatever you guys talked about, and he needs more information from ya. He said he tried to call you but you weren't in your room and he couldn't find your boat."

"I moored it in Belfast. I have Randy Thompson's boat now. I don't know if I told him that or not."

"Neither do I. He said he'll be in early tomorrow morning and he wants you to call him then."

"Will do!" Charles hung up.

"You see, sahib, he does not return. He is frightened! Our exhibition with the harpoon has served its purpose. His boat is not here, but his van is." He pointed to Charles's vehicle, still parked in the same spot as the day before. "We now have all day to search for the treasure." The two men stood on the top edge of the landing, looking around the moorings. Kenny had rested his truck with the skiff beside the pier, while backing it into the water.

He reflected and mulled about in frustration. "I don't know how he got away without us seein'. I want him today! If he's gone to the police once, he'll do it again. He ain't very bright! But after watchin' him pilot that boat the way he did, I think he's gettin' better."

"His van remains here. He will not be here today, and the daytime holds too many eyes about. It is best if it is done at night. If he does not come to the pier today, he will be eliminated tonight. I, too, become frustrated!"

"Ya haven't done nothin' yet! Ya coulda got him with the harpoon, then at the hotel twice."

"Only once did I bring a weapon to the hotel, sahib. It is not as easy as it seems. I know now where he stays. He has changed rooms. I shall be quick and powerful, like the tiger. He will not get away again!"

"Ya'd better come through this time! I got ya that silencer and that weren't easy. Now, do ya job!"

"Yes, sahib, but we have new trouble!"

"Man, what are you talkin' about now?"

Souharat pointed out to the bay near the far edge of Sears Island. A small outboard motor could barely be seen, skimming along the top of the water. "Who's that?" Kenny asked.

The Rat leaned into the skiff and drew out the set of binoculars he stored there. "Look, sahib!"

Kenny took the instrument from his aide and pressed it to his eyes. He focused in the direction of the boat. "Damn!" he exclaimed. "It's the cops' patrol boat! I ain't seen that out here in a long time." He continued to gaze.

"And if that don't beat all! That's the chief, himself, runnin' it! That Rhode Islander's been talkin' to the cops!"

"So it appears, sahib. Still, no one knows of the treasure but us. He must be investigating the missing people. There is no evidence of a body. We have disposed of all! The only evidence is purely circumstantial."

"Yeah? What about shootin' at that Ritter fella? What if he told the cops about that?"

"I do not believe so, sahib. The Rhode Islander has not shown up after our chase. The patrol boat was out here before that."

Kenny pulled the binoculars from his face and looked down at the Indian. "How do you know? I didn't see him."

"He was out early, but not near us. He traveled up the route which the fishermen travel, asking questions about the two who found the treasure. He saw nothing yesterday!"

"Like I asked, how do ya know?" He often became irritated by his mate. The Rat always knew more about what was going on in the bay than he did. It infuriated him sometimes, but it also aided him. The Rat was a fiend's fiend; a necessary evil which he couldn't do without. Sometimes the methods were suspect, but his information was vital to Kenny's operations.

"I ask many questions, sahib. I keep my eyes open. He went as far yesterday as to the coast of the Isle Au Haut. He was asking to see where they dropped their nets."

"I wonder why."

"It has been some time since we disposed of them, sahib. One of their relatives surely must wonder what happened to them. The boat was found, but not them. It would be wise to believe that they were lost at sea."

"Yes, of course."

"It is most likely that the chief is only investigating their disappearance. He has no knowledge of their deaths, or of the treasure. There is no tie-in with us."

"Yeah, I guess ya're right. We'd better find that treasure fast and get the hell out of town. If he's startin' with them two, it won't be long before he starts looking for the other two. If he asks too many questions, we might get involved."

"Yes, sahib. Not only do we run short of luck, we also run short on time!"

"If he's out to where they actually fish, then we're safe. Those two didn't go out that day. They dropped a net by accident just after they left. Isn't that what Todd mentioned? He said they were just headed out, so the treasure's close to shore; here!"

"Yes, sahib, that makes sense."

"Good! Only *we* know that. Let the chief go searchin' for bodies where those boys fish. It'll keep him out of our hair." His face twisted into a malevolent, wry grin. "That idiot is doin' us a favor! Heh, heh, heh! Let's go do some treasure hunting, my dark-skinned chum!"

"Yes, sahib! And we will have not a worry after tonight!" He chuckled.

"Hello, Janet."

"Well, is this my estranged husband?"

"Janet, I just talked to you yesterday and I've been busy."

"You didn't talk to me yesterday, mister. You called me the day before. At least *I* remember."

He thought for a second. "That's right. Sorry, but yesterday was really a forgetful day for me!"

"What happened now?" She was tired of hearing these horror stories about Maine. She wanted her husband home where he belonged, and not in some sort of cult proceedings. "Don't tell me another murder?"

"No. But I think someone's out to get me here."

"Oh, Charles, that's it! If you don't come home, I'm coming up there to see what's going on with you. I'm worried, Charlie!"

"You can't come up here. What are you going to do with the kids?" He certainly didn't want her near him, with all that he was going through.

"I can leave them with Mrs. Hauser, she doesn't have anything else to do and she adores the kids," she pleaded.

"That old hag! She spoils them rotten. Oh, Janet, please don't come up here. It's really too dangerous right now." The words fell on deaf ears.

"I'm coming there, Charles! I'm coming there, whether you want me to or not. Actually, it will be good to get out of the house for a day or two."

"But ... but—"

"No buts! I'll talk to Mrs. Hauser today, and I can be there sometime tomorrow."

"Wait! Wait, Janet. All right, you can come up here, but give me a couple of days to straighten things out, O.K.?"

She said nothing for a brief moment. "O.K., but you have to promise me that you'll call me every day before I leave or I'll be up there sooner."

"I agree. I love you, and tell the kids I love them, too."

"I will. I love you too, Charles." They hung up. He still held his hand on the receiver.

"Can I watch another movie, Mr. Ritter?" Chad was recovering nicely. "And I'm getting hungry."

Charles had arranged his paperwork while the movie played, and he had lost all track of time. He glanced at his watch. It was nearly noon time. "Yes, sir. But please, call me Charles or Charlie—not Mr. Ritter. O.K.?"

"Sure, Charles. Can I watch another movie?"

"Yes, you can. I'll order a pizza now if that's all right with you. I still have to make some more phone calls."

He played with the remote, seemingly quite content with his surroundings. "A pizza sounds good, Charles, with pepperoni!" His smile said it all. "You know, Charles, this is the first time I've ever stayed in a hotel room."

I can believe that, he thought. He looked up a pizza restaurant in the area that delivered and placed the order. "Now, you have to keep it down while I make the rest of these calls."

"Sure thing, Charles!" He found his movie and relaxed against the pillows on the bed.

Charles picked the receiver up again and dialed.

Jonas arrived at the pier early and unloaded Randy's skiff from the trailer. Sam and Andrew were leaning against the railing on the long wharf, gossiping with each other.

"Morning, Jonas." They spoke as one. "Kinda late for you to be headed out, ain't it?" Sam asked.

"Mornin', guys. I ain't goin' out. Just takin' a ride to see who's out and about in the bay. Have ya seen Kenny and the Rat today?"

"Ah-yup," Andrew responded. "They headed out kinda early. Don't know what they're doin'. Fishin', I guess."

"Ya know that whale Kenny pulled in t'other day?" Sam looked at Andrew.

"'T'weren't a whale, I told ya."

"No, 't'weren't. I heard it was a hybrid beast. A mix betwixt a whale and a sea monster."

"Is that right? I seen one o'them before. It was down by Rockland. It musta been fifty foot long. Had scales and arms. A big web skin stretched from its hands to its hip for swimmin'."

"I seen a beast that had twelve arms it used for crawlin' on the ocean floor. Had a big nose that stuck out about six feet from its head and could suck a large tuna in with one breath. Heard it killed a man."

"Well, this one I see...." Their conversation went on as Jonas motored out beyond their gibberish. As always, their nonsensical tales ended in a chorus of laughter.

He took the boat into the channel, looking for Kenny and the Rat. He saw the police patrol boat returning from the Islesboro area. "Damned Charlie got them out here!" he muttered to himself. The police boat went in to the pier. *Must be headed to lunch,* Jonas thought. He continued down the channel when he finally caught sight of Kenny's boat. He looked around and decided to get closer to shore and out of sight. He was determined to follow Kenny for the day to see his motives for the murders, if, in fact, it was he that was doing it. He pulled past the red buoy that outlined the channel. There were a few boats puttering around the bay, and if no one was looking for him, he would most likely go unnoticed. He idled the boat and watched. It was strange. Kenny and the Rat were looking over the side of their boat into the water. They weren't fishing. They were looking for something!

Maybe they were looking for one of the missing bodies before the police found it. He decided to wait and watch for a while to see where they went next.

The phone rang at Randy's house and he answered it. "Hello." He was wearing his smoking jacket and reading the paper. He had a lit pipe in his hand.

"Hi, Randy, this is Charles Ritter. How are you doing today?"

"Charles, I've been meaning to call you. I'm fine, just fine. How are you doing?"

"Oh, I'm O.K. Look, the reason I called is that I don't think I'm going to be ready to go fishing tomorrow. I haven't even pulled the traps yet."

"That's what I wanted to talk to you about. I went down to the pier yesterday and I couldn't find my boat. Jonas had already moored his, so I figured you'd be out, too. I got a bit worried, so I went back again this morning and it still wasn't there. I started getting real nervous, but just as I was pulling out, Jonas showed up and told me you had moored it in Belfast. What for, he didn't say. Anyway, I went to Belfast and saw it moored way up by the pound. I knew that was old Art's spot and he hangs out at the pound, so I went over there and sure enough, Art was there. I asked him what happened and he really couldn't tell me anything. Then I asked him for a ride to check it out and he got one of the other guys there to give us trip out. Well, this guy did after a while and I got to see it."

"I had to moor it there and that guy, Art, was real nice. He let me use his mooring."

"Well, I saw that, but what disturbed me is, when I checked the boat out, I saw gunshots embedded in the panel board."

"Ah, yeah." Charles spoke hesitantly. "Well, I can try to explain that, but it is a long story."

"Now, Art told me that you weren't in the best of shape when he saw you.

Are you all right?"

"I'm fine, don't worry about that."

"Are you in any kind of trouble?"

"Like I said, it is a long story."

"Well, hell. I don't care, but I can't have my boat being shot at. I don't know what's going on with you, but I think you'd better get in touch with your dean. I called him and voiced my concerns. Of course, it is up to you. If you're going to buy the boat, I don't care if you blow it up, but if you're not, I might have a problem with picking pellets out of the wood!"

"I understand. I'm going to give the dean a call right after I get off the phone with you and tell him that it is perfect for what we need. He said it was up to me, so I say we're going to buy it."

"Well, I'm glad to hear that. You talk to the dean and I'll give him a call tomorrow. If you don't want to go out fishing tomorrow, I can understand that. Boy, I hope you're not in some kind of trouble!"

"It's nothing I can't take care of. I'll have your boat back in Searsport tomorrow, also."

"Good. Now, I checked the fuel and the lines and everything I could. You've got plenty for a couple of more days. Let me know when you want to go out fishing. I'm looking forward to it, really. Oh, and by the way—be careful! Remember, I was full of piss and vinegar, too!"

"I'll be careful and I'll probably give you a call tomorrow if everything goes right."

"Good luck!" He hung up.

Kenny and the Rat peered deep into the water along the shore off of Coombs Point on Islesboro. "Why do we look here, sahib?"

"'Cause this is the way those two used to go out for their fishin'. They always went the long way. Neither one of them knew what they were doin'."

"What are we looking for?"

"Their net, you idiot! They ripped part of it off when they pulled it up. I saw it on their boat when we killed them."

"*You* killed them, sahib! There are many, many places here where it could be. It is of no use! I cannot see the bottom, there is too much salt and foam."

"Just keep lookin', you pimple of a man."

"Could they not have dropped the net anywhere?" The question was legitimate.

Kenny stood up and scratched his head. "Yeah, you're right. There's got to be a better way to find it. Right now, though, hand me that chart and we'll mark off the places we've checked already. At least we'll no where it ain't.

We might have to find it by the process of elimination. Hurry up and grab me that chart and a marker."

Souharat handed him what he asked for then glanced all around the bay. "It grows late, sahib. Perhaps we can sit down on land and try to think of a better way. Perhaps I can find those who saw them in the morning that day. I do have my ways. But to poke around on a wild goose chase, looking for the needle in the haystack, is very much time consuming. We can go over their route on the chart and do much thinking. After all, sometimes it is better to think for the two hours to save the ten hours of the search."

Kenny was marking up the chart and could see that they had barely scratched the surface. "Ah! You're right, again. O.K., you win. We'll go back to my house and go through this little by little. Your cunning and my knowledge of the area should give us a better picture of where to look tomorrow. It might just save time."

"I agree, sahib! I also have a duty to perform tonight!"

"Yes, that's right. Let's get back in."

Jonas watched as the boat the two men were in took off and headed back to their mooring. He waited, wondering what they were looking for and why they stopped. Once they got out of sight, he headed back in to his mooring. He would follow them again tomorrow.

There was a knock on the door of the hotel room. Charles got up from the desk and opened the door just a crack to peer through. It was the pizza man. He grabbed the box and handed it to Chad then reached in his wallet to pay the man. He shut the door and returned to the phone. Chad opened the box and dug out a piece of pizza for himself.

Charles dialed. "Hello, may I speak to Elena Hale, please?"

"This is Elena, is this Charles?"

"Yes, it is."

"Oh, I'm glad you called. I've been so busy here. We've buried my uncle, but now my aunt is deadly sick. It's been quite hectic. Is everything going all right there?"

"Well, Chad had an accident."

"Oh, no! Is he O.K.?"

"Yes, yes, he's O.K. He's here with me now in my hotel. He's received a couple of cuts and a small fracture. It looks a lot worse than it is. I figured he could stay with me today and tomorrow to rest up somewhat and then I'll take him back to your house."

"What happened?" She sounded frail.

"I'll tell you when I see you again. Right now, don't worry about it."

"Where's Katherine?"

"She's in school now. She's headed home when she gets out."

"Oh, I knew I shouldn't have left. Did Jonas hit Chad?"

It was hard to fool a mother. He didn't want to upset her now while she was going through her uncle's death and her aunt's convalescence. She surely had enough on her mind. "Well, Chad acted up in school and got suspended. I guess Jonas didn't approve." He didn't want to lie either.

"Oh, my! Suspended? He's such a good student. He's trying to take after his father, I swear! Oh, I wish I could come back tonight, but I can't. The doctor said he didn't think my aunt will make it through the night. Oh, my. It's all so depressing!" She sounded all choked up and on the verge of tears.

"You stay put with your aunt, and I'll see things are taken care of here. Don't worry about anything. I'll let you know if anything happens."

He could hear a voice in the background of the phone. "*Elena! Elena! Elena!*" It must have been her aunt calling for her.

"Oh, Charles. I have to go. Please keep an eye on things for me, and I'll be back as soon as I can."

"I'll do that."

She muffled her voice. "I'll be right there, Auntie!" She put the speaker back to her mouth. "Charles, I have to go. I'll give you a call tomorrow." She hung up. Charles did the same.

Chad looked over at Charles. "Boy, you sure do spend a long time on the phone!"

Charles nodded. "One more phone call, and I will be done. Then I can relax and watch a movie with you." Chad smiled.

He picked the receiver back up and dialed once more.

"Hello, Dean Groton?"

"Yes, Charlie, how have you been?"

"Well, it's getting a bit thick up here, Dean."

"Thick? What is that supposed to mean? I talked to that guy with the boat today. Umm … Thompson, I think, yes, here it is. Randy Thompson. He seemed a bit worried about you, Charles. He said he found gunshot in his boat. Is that true?"

"Well … yes, it's true. You see—"

"What's going on there, Charlie? I'm getting a little worried myself. Are you all right?"

"I'm fine. Look, it's a long story, but I think I've come across something which could be of great importance." His words were thought out systematically. "First of all, I think we should buy his boat. It's great and fully equipped for both lobster fishing, deep-sea fishing or just cruising. I highly recommend it!"

"Great, Charlie. That's great. Now, what was this about something important?"

Charles sighed. "When I went to the office of the chief of police, I saw—"

"You went to the police? Something is wrong. There's gunshot on your boat and you went to the police? What did you get involved with there?"

"Please, Dean, let me finish. I went to the police station and saw a ship's bell. I inspected it, and I believe it is the real bell that came off the *Queen Anne's Revenge*. Not only that, I believe that the wreck of one of the boats that was with that boat was sunk here, somewhere."

"The *Queen Anne's Revenge*. I've heard of it, but I can't place it right now. What about it?"

"Well, to make a long story short. It was the flagship of the pirate Blackbeard. He had a volume of treasure which has never been recovered. If the bell is here, I believe that the rest is here, also."

"Now I remember! They're digging it up now off the coast of the Carolinas. I read about it in a magazine. You really think that one of the ships that sailed with it is up there somewhere?"

"I'm sure of it!" He spoke loudly and with conviction.

"Then weather the storm, Charles. This could be a significant find for archeology and, more importantly, the university. I give you complete authority to stay as long as it takes to find this ship. It means prestige for the school! I'll bring it up to the board, but keep poking around and, for God's sake, keep me in touch!"

"I will, Dean!"

"Good luck, Charlie. God, this could be great news!"

"Thank you, Dean, but I—" The dean had hung up.

Charles leaned back in his chair. What a bizarre conversation that was! The dean seemed interested in the fact that he believed he might have found one of the most significant archeology discoveries of the century, but he offered him no help. If he really believed there was a chance that what he told him was true, wouldn't he send up a crew of archeologists or experts from the university to perform the search properly? Charles stretched his neck. It had grown sore from talking on the phone all day. Everyone was acting so strangely. He wondered as to his own sanity. Was he the one that was really losing it? Even though he didn't think it was a good idea, he couldn't wait to see his wife. A small breath of reality would surely help him out right now.

"Shove over there, Chad. Let's watch a movie!" Chad shuffled his pillows to one side of the bed, and Charles sat against the bed's headboard on top of the covers.

Katherine had dinner almost ready when Jonas walked into the house. He had stopped at the pub before returning home and it showed. He leaned against the door sill for a couple of seconds before continuing to the cupboard and reached up to secure his quart bottle of rum. He took a glass from the counter and placed it and the bottle on the table in front of his favorite spot to sit. He never said a word as he poured a drink into the glass then recapped the bottle.

"Ma called," Katherine broke the silence.

"Yup! What'd she want?"

"Nothing. She was just checking in. She knows about Chad."

"Ah-yup. Charlie musta talked to her." He took a long drink from the glass.

"She said Uncle Steve got buried and now Aunt Julie is real sick. They don't think she's going to make it through tonight."

"Humph! She say when she's comin' back?"

"She said it might be a couple of days. It depends on how Aunt Julie does."

"Humph! What's for dinner?"

"Franks and beans. It's all we got."

"Humph! It sure smells good. Maybe ya can teach ya ma to cook." He chuckled and burped.

"Yes, Dad."

"Is Chad still with Charlie?"

"Yes, he's going to stay there tonight, and Charlie said he'd bring him over here tomorrow."

"Humph! That's good." He was subdued. His demeanor had changed from the rough and gruff personality he usually demonstrated to one of kindness and humility.

"Why don't ya just take that off the stove and come over here and sit beside me and we'll talk."

She looked up from the pan then pushed it off of the heat. "Talk about what, Dad?"

"Oh, I dunno. Whatever ya want, I guess."

"O.K." She moved towards the chair beside him.

"Now, now, Katherine. Why don't ya come over here and sit on ya father's lap."

She pulled her head back with apprehension. "I'm kind of big for that, Dad."

He patted the top of his right thigh. "Now, now, you're still my little girl. C'mon now, have a seat."

Her face recoiled. This was a novel request. She slowly stepped towards her father and sat down on his leg in apprehension. He put his arm around her. "There, there, now. It's been a long time since we got to talk together." He rubbed her back. She became more and more uncomfortable. Then he placed his left hand on her left knee.

"Dad, what are you doing?"

He pulled his right hand up to her head and brushed her hair with his callused hand. "I always thought you had beautiful hair. It's so soft and pretty." He pulled the hand out of her hair and brushed her cheek with the back of his hand. "And your skin is so smooth, like your mother's used to be." His left hand began to ride up her leg while he gently rubbed her thigh as it went.

"Dad, what are you doing?"

"I think you're more beautiful than your mother ever was!" He kissed her on the cheek.

In a fit of angst, she stood up posthaste. "Dad, what do you think you're doing?"

He stood up and grabbed her by the shoulders. "Your mother's gone and you're the woman of the house now. You'll take on all the woman's chores. Cookin' ain't the only one, ya know." He pulled her to his chest and threw his lips onto hers.

She turned her head, but he was too strong. "Don't fight it! Enjoy it! Ya ain't never had a man before, have ya? Well, it's about time."

"No, Dad, NO!" She struggled in his arms, but he overpowered her and dragged her into the bedroom.

"Ain't no use screamin', ain't no one gonna hear ya!" He threw her on the bed and drooled over her. She wriggled around in an attempt to get back up and off the bed. He removed his belt in a second. Blood was in his eyes. "Just relax and enjoy it! Daddy's gonna get his tonight!"

She screamed and he fell on her, the mere weight of his body pinned her to the mattress. She fell to his mercilessness, disgusting brutality. Her screaming proved to be in vain.

Souharat parked his vehicle in the same spot as he had earlier. He made sure no one saw him exit the car as he tiptoed along the far edge of the hotel. He was determined to attain his goal for the night. He peered around the corner. The main desk was directly in front of him, and he had to cross the entire complex to reach room #102. He walked casually so as not to draw attention.

There were only two vehicles in the lot, which gave him more courage to continue. He held the revolver with the silencer under his jacket, tucked into his belt. He got to the far side of the hotel with no problems. He began to perspire. It was warm but overcast this night, and the clouds made it difficult to see. This also gave him the fortitude to finish the task he was set out to perform.

He got to room #103 and stopped. He looked at the window to room #102. It had been raised about two inches. This was perfect! He didn't have to shoot through glass. Everything so far was ideal. The weather, the poor guest list and the window all worked to his advantage.

He saw that the lights were on in the room, and he could hear the television. He crouched down and picked his legs up one at a time from the knee, slowly stepping in the direction of the open window.

Chad looked at Charlie when the movie ended. "I've got to go to the bathroom," he divulged. "I've had to go for a while, but I wanted to watch the end of that."

Charles laughed. "Go ahead then, it is over there." He pointed to the wall to the left in the room. There was a mirror and a small basin beyond the wall, and to the left of that was the bathroom. Chad got up and walked to where Charles pointed. Charles reset the remote control on the television then leaned back in the bed. He was tired. Even this day, where he never left the hotel, seemed like a long day. There were just too many questions, and the fatigue he felt was most likely psychological. He placed his hands behind his head and stared at the ceiling. How crazy everything was.

Chad had only been in the bathroom for a minute when Charles heard him yell from behind the door. "Charles, there is no toilet paper in here."

Usually, the chamber maid would set up the room for the day, but when she showed up this morning, he sent her away because Chad was laid up. He remembered that they stored it in the small cabinet below the basin in front of the bathroom. "Sorry, I forgot. I'll get it for you." He got up from the bed and walked to the cabinet, opened the door and pulled out a roll.

The Rat stuck his head up into the window. There he saw Charles standing in the small room in front of the bathroom. He pulled the gun up into the narrow opening between the bottom of the window and the sill. He pointed directly at Charles's head and pulled the trigger.

Charles fell to the ground. Souharat saw this and dropped below the level of the window and quickly shifted around then stood. The shot made very little noise, yet he was paranoid. He stepped with a long gait, attempting to act normally. He paced himself this way the entire length of the hotel without turning around. Once he got to the opposite side, he began to run. He had accomplished his mission! He jumped into his car and sped away, elated that not one person came out of their room to check on the noise. He breathed a long, hard sigh of relief.

The bullet bounced off the edge of the wall near Charles's head. He had only dropped from the noise of the blast. It was silenced, but he had been on edge for some time now, and the least noise made him react in defense. He stayed on his stomach on the floor.

"What was that?" Chad asked from within the confines of the restroom.

"Just stay in there!" Charles demanded. He crawled to the wall at the corner of the room, where he could not be seen from the window. He still had the roll of toilet paper with him. He opened the bathroom door ajar and tossed the roll inside. "It was a gunshot!" he explained. "Stay where you are and I'll check it out."

"A gunshot?" Chad queried.

"Yes, a gunshot. Just stay in there and I'll let you know when it's safe to come out." He slipped back down to his chest on the floor and slithered, like a snake, to the footboard of the bed. He never picked his head up completely but barely showed it to look at the window. He wasn't sure, but he didn't think he could see anything outside. He glanced back up to the wall where the bullet hit. A large chunk had been broken off, exactly at where the level of his head had been.

He shuddered in fear. He lay there and waited. Nothing! Finally, he built up enough courage to slide across the floor to the opposite wall, then along that wall to the wall with the door. He began to feel safe. If he was going to get shot at again, it most likely would have been when he went across the floor unprotected. His courage came to its head, and with his back pressed up against the wall, he grabbed the doorknob. As quickly as he could, he turned the knob and swung the door wide open and jumped outside. Nothing! Nobody! His heart beat so loudly that he could hear it pound into his head. His hands were clammy, and a firm layer of perspiration covered his face. He sighed out many times, then tucked his head down and placed his hands on his thighs.

"You can come out now, Chad." He shut the door behind him and leaned against it.

"What was that all about?" Chad asked as he walked into the room.

"I don't know, Chad. All I do know is that it is not safe for you to stay with me. You see, I seem to be quite a popular man with madmen!"

"But I want to stay!"

"I'm afraid that's not possible. Look!" He pointed to the chunk of wall that had broken out from the bullet. He then looked over to the wall to the left of the bathroom. The bullet had ricocheted off the edge of the first wall and wedged itself into that wall. Charles studied the trajectory. How could that have possibly missed him? Now, he too, felt his luck was running out. "That's a bullet, Chad. Someone's trying to kill me!"

"Wow!" Chad's chin dropped. "Neat! They won't believe me when I tell them about this in school! That is, if I go back to school."

"Right now, you're going home! I'm calling you a taxi!"

"Why? I don't want to go. I like it here. I like you!"

Charles spun his head to face Chad. "Then you'll do as I say. It's just too dangerous here!"

"Sahib, it is done! I have eliminated the Rhode Islander!" Souharat opened the door to Kenny's house without knocking. He was proud of himself.

"Are ya sure?" Kenny was sitting at the table going over the nautical charts.

"I shot, he fell. Do you need more?"

"As a matter of fact, yes! Did anybody see you?"

"Not a soul. The silencer worked like a charm."

"Good, good. How did ya get rid of the body?"

"Get rid of the body? You said nothing of that, sahib." All of a sudden, his jubilation turned to dread. "I did not even think of that!"

"You idiot! They don't have a body yet. Don't give them one now! Damn, Rat, ya the one that's supposed to do the thinkin'!"

"My folly, sahib. It is too dangerous to drag the body across the complex of the hotel. That would be noticed for sure."

"Well, now they got a housemaid or cleanin' lady goes in there in the morning. She's gonna notice a dead body on the floor, don't ya think?"

"Of course, sahib." He thought. "Perhaps I have an idea."

"Bring it on. I wanna hear it."

"We have tonight. We go there—both of us. We pick the body up, one under each arm, and carry him to the vehicle. No one will expect anything but a wild, drunken party, where one had too much to drink. It is very common. That is, if anyone even notices us."

"That's a good idea, Rat. I knew ya had it in ya."

They arrived at the hotel almost immediately in Kenny's truck. They pulled up to the same area where the Rat had hidden his vehicle. They casually stepped around the corner to the hotel as if they were guests there, or just looking for a room. There was nothing to fear at this point. They carried no weapons, and Souharat had removed himself from the area without being seen. As they turned the corner they saw a taxi positioned outside of the room that Charles occupied. Chad exited the door and got into the cab.

Kenny held his arm in front of the Rat's chest. "Who's that?" he asked while holding both of them immobile.

"I know not, sahib. It looks like a child."

Suddenly, Charles walked through the door and handed the driver some money, waved to Chad and stepped back into the room, shutting the door behind him.

Kenny looked at Souharat with his teeth clenched and his body stiff. "I thought you said you got him!"

The Rat stared at Charles's door. "I swear I did! This man has many lives, like the cat, sahib!"

"I'm real tired of your excuses. C'mon, let's get out of here. He's gonna be on his toes tonight. Maybe, it's my turn to finish off what ya can't seem to! Ya can't do anything right, can ya?"

"But my shot was true! I saw him fall, sahib!"

Chapter 18

It was Thursday. The weather maintained it gloomy, overcast manifestation in the skies above Belfast, Maine, casting shadows of depression across the darkened land. It was well documented that dismal weather spawned dismal attitudes. It could be that is where the term 'there's something in the air' came from. A bright, cheery day brought out bright, cheery people. Today was the opposite. It didn't matter much inside the hotel room where Charles was staying. He couldn't even see outside when he awoke. He had closed the window he inadvertently left open the night before, draped the bedspread over the window to preserve his privacy and deter the all-too-common practice of someone "peeping in" on him. He hoped it would also prevent his getting shot at, which also was getting to be all too common. He had slept, fully dressed at the foot of the bed on the floor, not that he slept very well. He yawned and sat up on the floor pulling back at the sheets he had stripped from the bed. He felt that if someone was going to shoot randomly inside the room at him, the obvious shot would be where the bed was. Sleeping below the mattress would at least soften the blast. He curled his legs up to his chest and rested his head between his knees with his arms encircling his legs. He rotated his head to relieve the neck pain from sleeping in an uncomfortable position. He stood and threw the sheets back onto the bed. He stretched his entire body and yawned deeply then placed his hands on his hips. "Well, I survived another day!" He walked to the window and pulled off the bedspread. It wasn't much brighter outside. He contemplated what he would do now that he told Randy he wasn't going fishing. The first thing he was going to do was get hold of the chief of police and tell him what he knew. Maybe he could help resolve the situation. It was just before 7:00 a.m. and the chief should be at the station. He went to the phone and called.

"Searsport Police Department."

"Yes, this is Charles Ritter. I was wondering if the chief of police was still there."

"Hang on, he's been expecting your call."

"I'll wait."

It didn't take very long. "Charles. I've been waiting for you to call. You just caught me before I headed out to the bay. It's a bit overcast out there, so I don't think I'll see too much traffic, so it's not such a hurry for me to hit the water."

"Chief, I need to talk to you. I've been trying to get a hold of you for the last couple of days."

"Well, I'm doin' what ya wanted me to do. I'm researchin' the disappearance of Bill Rowlin and Todd Seekins. I'm learnin' a little, but I could use your help. I just don't have enough information."

There was something about the way the chief talked that made Charles leery. It sounded phony, but he had nowhere else to turn and this man was the law. "Chief, I've had two encounters where someone is trying to kill me."

"What? Kill ya? Who wants to kill ya?"

"I think it is the same ones that killed the two missing men you're looking for."

"Who is it then?"

He was overly anxious, Charles thought. "I think we'd better talk face to face and I'll tell you what's been going on."

"O.K., Charles. That sounds fair. Do you know where the diner is just outside of town on Route #1?"

"Yes, I've eaten there a couple of times."

"Why don't ya meet me there in about, oh, a half hour and we'll talk there and get a little breakfast in. Does that sound like a good idea to you?"

"Could you make it an hour so I can jump in the shower and call a cab, I still don't have my van back, yet."

"An hour it is. If ya have information like that, I can sure wait!" They both hung up.

Charles sat down in the chair beside the desk in deep concentration. There were just too many secrets here. He thought about the conversation with the dean. There were too many secrets there, also. Why didn't the dean call Woods Hole and organize their resources? *They have a myriad of sophisticated underwater equipments and trained personnel that can operate it to perform exactly the functions he expects of me. This is most strange!* For some reason it bugged Charles, but he tried not to think about it. Right now, he just wanted to save his own skin. He took a quick shower and called a cab.

Souharat pulled into Kenny's driveway at nearly 6:45 a.m., parked and exited his 1985 Subaru. The car was in extremely good shape for its age, and he didn't drive very much, which helped keep it that way. He lugged with him several books and more charts to Kenny's door and knocked. Kenny answered it. "C'mon in, Rat. What's the books for?"

"I have a plan, sahib, to find where the treasure is!"

"What are ya gonna do, read about it?" he said sarcastically while walking towards the counter in the corner of the kitchen. "Coffee, Rat?"

He shook his head. "I only drink tea, and yes, in a manner of speaking, I am going to try to see where this treasure came from to see if it gives us a clue." He dropped the books on the dining room table and laid the charts down beside the books.

Kenny poured a cup of coffee for himself out of the ten-cup coffeemaker in the very corner of the counter then placed the pot back to its base.

His house was much bigger than Jonas's. There was a large living room to the right of the entrance, with several windows adorned with curtains and drapes all neatly hung and meticulously clean. The dining room was situated at the entrance to the house, and the kitchen sat beyond with only an opening in the wall, complete with door sills but no door, between the dining area and the kitchen. The kitchen sink was within view of the entrance and the dining room, and it was completely encircled with counters. Above the sink was a small vent window. The living room to the right was very large, well decorated and spacious. Kenny's wife had died a few years before due to complications with what would have been their first-born. Neither she nor the baby survived. He had kept the house up as best he could, but not being accustomed to domestic issues, he paid his niece to come in once a week and clean. The house itself was given to him by his parents when they retired to Florida. It was situated in Searsport on the Mt. Ephriam Road.

Kenny stepped out of the kitchen area holding his cup of coffee. "Ya talked about a plan?"

"Yes, sahib. I think we approach finding the treasure in three different directions. First, I need to look at the coins we retrieved from the two men's boat. I will examine them to check their authenticity and the dates they may contain. This might tell me where they came from. I then will check the history of the coins to see if I can determine from what ship they came. Then I will see if I can find the history of that ship and perhaps a description of when and where it sank. This would be most helpful if such records exist. That will be my step one." He waited for a response from Kenny.

"So far, that sounds about right."

"Yes, but I do not think we will find such a record. If one existed, surely the ship would have been found by now."

"Yeah, you're right. What's your step two?"

"Ah! Most important, sahib!" He tried to twirl his thin, sparse mustache. "We recreate the morning that the treasure was found. I have done some poking around. I know that this Todd Seekins lived alone and had no girlfriend at the time. But this Bill Rowlin, who was older, has a wife. She lives on the Back Belmont Road in Belfast—I have checked. She would know his habits; where he went and more important, *when* he went to go fishing that day. We can then determine how far he could have gone before we ran into him. If we know exactly what time he went and the difference in time to when we saw him then where he found the treasure would take us one-half the time to reach it from where we met him!"

Kenny stood up. "Brilliant! Brilliant! My educated, contemptible friend. I think I know his route. If we know exactly how long it takes and follow the same route then, by gory, we're there!" He partially jumped and skipped at the thought. "Ya one smart cookie, Rat!" The grin nearly overpowered his face. "Yes!" He clutched his fist and pumped it into the air.

"I checked at the pier with the regulars. Nobody saw them leave that day. Right now, we can only narrow it down to a few hours. This is too much. I think we should pay a visit to his widow … ah … er … ah, that is to say, his anxious wife. She would know of his departure time from the house, and we may reconstruct the timing of the rest."

"Ya are thorough!" He shook his head in awe. "Ya're one hell of a rat, Rat!"

Souharat considered that a big compliment, and his glowing countenance acknowledged it as such.

Kenny took a sip off his coffee. "Ya said there were three parts to ya plan, didn't ya?"

"Yes, if all else fails, sahib. The third part is what we have started; the process of elimination, but we may start that here at this table."

"At this table? How?"

"The boat that was recovered is stored in the public yard. It is quite accessible; I have checked. They found the treasure using nets that scrape the bottom of the bay and ocean. These nets are only of a certain length. If we measure that length; the farthest they can go down in the water, we can eliminate any depths greater. This may be quite a bit of work we avoid."

"Good! By gory, Rat, we're almost there! With your brains and my guns, we'll be rich in a couple of days. If them two dolts fell across the treasure without thinkin', then we should be able to find it *by* thinkin'."

The two men laughed in a deliberate gloating until their faces strained in their greed.

"First, Rat, to the widow … ah … er … ah, that is, grieving Mrs. Rowlin. How do we approach her? We can't tell her what we're looking for."

"I have thought of that also. We will tell her that we are from the Missing

Persons Bureau of the F.B.I. and we hope to find her husband. We work in consort with the chief of police. She will never check, and even if she does, it will be too late."

"You're right, Rat; 'A minute of thinkin' saves an hour of work'. We'll look into this thing about the ship and the nets after that, but she might be all we need!"

"Very well, sahib. I will leave everything here."

Katherine went off to school on time while Jonas sat at the table watching her get ready then leave through the door. She avoided eye contact with him the entire morning, and she never spoke one word. A shadow crossed her face. She felt guilty and ashamed. Mostly, she felt contempt and disgust at her father, who also said nothing that morning. Once she left, he got up and went out to the truck.

The water was engulfed in fog when Jonas arrived at the landing in the morning. The thick, smoky surface reminded him of an old English movie. He pulled in facing forward, up to the fence separating the parking lot from the rocks at the beach. He could not distinguish a single boat out of its mooring. The only vehicle in the parking lot was Charles's van. The pier was empty, and nobody walked the beach. It was virtually deserted. He put the truck into park and waited to see if the fog would burn off when it started to sprinkle. He began to regret not checking the forecast before he left, but he never did. He could still go out in this. He decided to just sit and wait. He had a six-pack in the cooler behind the seat and the radio worked; plus there wasn't anything to do at the house. If nobody showed up in an hour or so, he'd either head back to the house or go out and check his traps. He turned the radio on and reached behind him for a beer, opened it then sat and waited, watching the tide roll into the shore.

The taxi dropped Charles off at the diner earlier than he had assumed. It seemed the cab company was getting to know him, not only as a frequent customer, but also as a big tipper. He exited the cab and walked inside, where he saw the chief was already sitting in a booth, drinking a cup of coffee.

"Over here, Charles!" The chief watched him walk inside, but he didn't need to call him over, Charles was walking in that direction already. He sat down facing McFagan. "Oh, Stella! Another cup of coffee over here, please."

The waitress had been walking by the booth, scribbling down on her order pad, when he stopped her.

"Sure thing, Chief." She was a pretty girl, very young and extremely busy. The weather had kept everyone who normally spent the morning outside inside today. The place was crowded, and she was the only one manning the tables and booths. She hurried away, ripped the top page off the pad, stuck in on the skewer at the ordering counter, grabbed one of the coffeepots nearby along with a cup and returned. She set the cup in front of Charles and filled it up with coffee from the pot. "Menus?" she asked.

"Yes, please," the two men answered, and she scampered off to another table.

Chief McFagan leaned forward and placed his elbows on the table, looking directly at Charles. "Now, ya told me that someone's tryin' to kill ya. Ya said it might be the same ones that mighta killed Bill and Tom, even though we don't even know if they are even dead yet. So, I gotta ask ya again'. Who is it?" He sipped his coffee without removing his eyes from Charles.

"Well, first of all, there's no way I can say it is the same people that tried to kill me, who might have either killed or committed foul play with the two fishermen. That's just an educated guess. What I can tell you is who the two are that tried to kill me." Stella returned and hastily threw two menus on the table then hurried off with the pot of coffee still perched in her other hand.

"Go on." The chief was all ears.

"Well, I have been stalked at the hotel. One night, I saw a figure at my window. Last night, I was shot at through my window, but the bullet missed me, and not by much! The other day, I went to haul traps on my own, and I was confronted by two men who tried to shoot me with a harpoon then a shotgun. I have evidence of all of this."

McFagan listened attentively but showed signs of impatience. "Who? Tell me who this was."

Charles picked his hands out from on top of his lap and placed his elbows on the table in the same manner as the chief. "They were Kenny Buckner and an Indian man that they call 'The Rat.'" He was relieved now that someone else knew the whole story of the treasure and the murders. He could only hope that something would be done to prevent another murder—more specifically, his own!

The chief of police leaned back against the cushion of the booth. "Kenny and the Rat! Ha! I shoulda guessed that! The two o'them are lower than whale shit!" He placed his hands behind his head in contemplation. "Well, ya done the right thing comin' to me!"

Stella stepped up to the booth. "You guys ready?"

The chief didn't hesitate. "Number 1, Stella; sunny side up, bacon, white and a large orange juice." She scratched her shorthand onto the pad then turned to Charles.

"Just the pancakes, please."

"That it?" she said as she picked up the menus, which hadn't been touched by either man.

"Yeah, that's it," the chief replied, and she spun around, still jotting things down on the pad.

Charles was a bit more relaxed. "What do you think you can do about this?"

"Well, now I know what I needed to know. It's a good thing ya came to me, y'know. I mean, ya could be dead right now. Let me think on it. Now, let me see. Ya say that these two fellas, Bill Rowlin and Todd Seekins, found that bell there in my office. Ya think there's a treasure what goes with that bell? Ya think someone killed 'em to get the treasure for themselves? Now, ya tellin' me it mighta been Kenny and the Rat, who are tying' to kill ya. What makes ya think that they'd be tryin' to kill ya?"

"I saw them! I know who shot at me! For God's sake, don't you believe me?" His lips quivered incredulously.

"That's not what I meant. I meant, *why* do ya think they'd be tryin' to kill ya?"

"Well, I suppose, because I know they did it."

"Right! Ya're an outsider. Hell, they prob'ly got half the bay scared to death, but not ya! Ya the only one, they figure, foolish enough to go to the police. They don't trust ya, boy, and if they mean to get ya, they're gonna get ya!"

Charles fell back onto the cushion behind him.

Stella arrived with two plates and the glass of juice and set them down in front of the two men then scurried off.

The chief sat up straight and began to eat. Charles picked up his fork and the syrup that was on the table. He squirted some on the pancakes and cut one of them with the fork, holding it in the air as he spoke.

"So, can't you question them? Can't you do some sort of investigation? I mean, this is at least attempted murder. I still have the evidence lodged into the control panel of Randy Thompson's boat. Can't you check to see if this came from a shotgun owned by Kenny Buckner? Can't you do anything?" He placed the piece of pancake in his mouth and began to chew.

"Oh, I'll have a talk with them boys. But it's your word against theirs, and if nobody else saw anything, it's gonna be pretty hard to accuse the two of them of a crime. But there is something else I can do."

Charles chewed and began to swallow. "What's that?"

"Have ya arrested!"

Charles coughed and gagged on the morsel he was attempting to swallow.

He held his clenched hand over his mouth and intentionally coughed to force the food down his esophagus. He tried to breathe normally, but it took a second.

"Me? Have me arrested? I'm the victim here!"

"That ain't the point. Ya life might be in danger. Now that I know about this situation, I think it might be better if ya stay where we can protect ya. Ya know, keep an eye on ya!" There was a fiendish glow in the chief's eyes that Charles recognized. This wasn't a sign of concern or a show of compassion. He realized it now. It was greed! The chief of police had all the information he needed to work his authority in the name of profit. No wonder why he was so anxious to find out who the murderers were. It wasn't for the victims, it was to find out who might know where the treasure actually was.

Charles dropped his fork. He mused on the term 'keep an eye on ya.' That's exactly what he wanted to do; keep him under surveillance so that he wasn't allowed to get involved. He knew too much! The chief of police had worked the situation into his advantage. This town reeked of corruption.

"You can't arrest me! That is, not without my consent. There are laws preventing just such actions." Charles was completely at a loss for an educated argument. He suddenly lost his appetite.

"It's all for the best, y'know. Ya already been shot at and someone's stalkin' ya. I gotta look out for your best interests, ya know. I'm gonna have to bring ya to the station when we get done eatin' and put ya into protective custody. It'll only be for a couple of days, until we get to the bottom of this and see somebody behind bars that's out there to hurt ya. Understand?"

Charles's ideas swirled around in his mind. This is just what the chief wanted. Oh, how easy he made it for him. How foolish he felt now. He had sensed something about this man, but this was beyond his comprehension. He had to think, and to think quickly—this man was sure to have him arrested and cut off from contact with the outside world.

Oh! he pined. *What have I gotten myself into?* The chief sat immobile and continued eating. *He's not very bright!* Charles thought. He had an idea.

Kenny and the Rat arrived at Bill Rowlin's trailer within a half hour of leaving Kenny's place. The weather slowed them down a little. They parked the truck and approached the door.

"Sahib, allow me to do the talking."

"Go for it. Ya have ya silver tongue."

Souharat knocked and listened.

"Come in!" a voice echoed from inside. "The door's open!"

They opened the door and stepped inside to an overwhelming stench of cat feces, and cat in general. Two cats were curled up, lying passively on the couch. A lady emerged from down the long hallway to the side of the trailer.

The structure was old but well maintained. It was narrow, with a kitchenette to the left, a bedroom to the far right and the living room where they stood. A large cabinet and a series of shelves separated the living room from the kitchen, and it was impossible for them to see what lay beyond the corridor from where the lady came. She was short and plump, wearing a bright pink stretched-out spandex top and bright green tights. Her hair was long and greasy, and she had no top teeth in her mouth, with only a few on the bottom. She shook her head to remove the hair from in front of her face, with her bottom teeth sticking into her upper lip.

"Yeah?" she said. "Whatya want?"

Souharat cleverly pulled his wallet out from his back pocket and flashed it open to her. She was so far away it was quite impossible for her to see its contents. "Good morning, ma'am. My name is Niro Haswami and this is my colleague, Tom Banks. We are from the F.B.I.'s Bureau of Missing Persons and we have traveled this distance from Washington, DC, last night, and we would like to talk to you, if you have a moment."

She put her hands on her hips. "Is this about Bill?"

"Yes, ma'am. We only have a few questions. It will not take long."

"I already told everything I know to that Searsport cop, McFagan. I don't know how he got involved, seein' how this is Belfast."

"Yes, ma'am. That is why we are here. You see, it must be a combined effort with all your local officials." Souharat was a natural liar.

Kenny simply stood there with his arms crossed. He didn't realize that the chief had already spoken with her.

"You see, we have the chief of the Searsport police searching the waters for signs of your husband. We have also recruited the aid of the sheriff in Belfast to also look. We will exhaust all efforts to find your husband, but we would like some more information to help us in our search."

She seemed put out. "I was right in the middle of laundry and I.... Ah ... all right. Have a seat." She pointed to the table in the kitchen. It was pressed up against the wall on the far side of the appliances. There were four chairs surrounding it, but one was pinned between the wall and the table. She sat down on the chair furthest away from the two men. Kenny sat at the opposite end of the table, and Souharat sat on the middle chair.

"We will try to be brief," Souharat said. "Now, so that we may adjust our records. Could you tell us, when did you notice your husband was missing?" Rat pulled out a small notebook from the top pocket of his shirt along with a pen, folded over a few pages and wrote when she spoke.

"Ha!" she blurted out. "Missin'? That man would leave here to go fishin' and come back sometimes two weeks later—and broke! Missin'? He was *always* missin'!"

"Then, if this is so, why did you report him as being missing?" Even the Rat didn't quite understand this one.

"I didn't! That chief of police called me up askin' a whole bunch of questions. I guess they found his boat driftin' in the bay and they couldn't get a hold of him. I guess they got that boat held up on some sorta public land and they want it outta there. So they called me. I told 'em, I ain't seen 'im, but that ain't nothin' new. One thing though. It's the first time I remember that he went off on one of his toots without tying the boat up." She giggled and Kenny laughed, picturing in his mind, the fat lady at the circus. The laughs were similar and the physical characteristics were the same.

Souharat squinted. "'Toots?'" he asked without having to pretend. He had absolutely no idea what she was talking about.

"Oh, yeah. The two of them used to go out for a couple of days on the water and get a whole bunch of fish, go sell 'em then come back here and party. They'd end up spending almost everything they earned before they realized they had to go back out so they could afford the next party. I got pretty sick of it. Their friends knew when they were here, that they had money, and next thing I know the whole damned neighborhood is over. I got to clean and cook. It weren't too bad at first, at least I knew where he was. But then that Todd Seekins started bringin' over drugs and it got outta hand."

"Drugs?" Souharat began to forget why they came. He was getting interested in her story.

"Yeah. Cocaine. He'd bring it in and they'd hide it from me so I wouldn't know. Still, then, I didn't mind too much. It all seemed pretty harmless until that Todd started bringin' over crack. Then they went overboard."

"Crack? What is crack?"

"That's cocaine, too. But they cook it and it's a different kinda high they get. They really tried to hide that from me, but they couldn't 'cause I could tell by the way they acted."

"How did they act that you could tell?"

"Ha! I put it into six steps. I could even tell ya how much money they made by tellin' ya what step they were in."

"I do not understand, these 'steps.'" The conversation had strayed, but the Rat felt as though this might have some bearing on what the two men did the morning they found the treasure. Regardless, they were there, and the way he looked at it, you could never have too much information.

"Yeah, that's the way I sum it up. The fist step is when they first get high.

They start talking a lot—about nothin' really, but they think they're so smart, and can solve all the problems of the world. They would do more and go to step two, where they thought they could hear noises or that someone was watchin' them or whatever. Then they'd do more and they'd become quiet, that's step three. They'd hide the drugs for whatever reason and think that they lost somethin', always lookin' on the floor. Then there's step four, where they'd start lookin' out the windows thinkin' somebody's watchin' them, and they'd get real paranoid. Then there's step five, when I seen 'em start to sweat real bad and grab weapons thinkin' they're bein' followed or cased. I even seen Bill hide behind the door, he was so paranoid, and one time he hid under the bed. It was all so strange! I couldn't take it anymore. I told them that they can do what they wanted to, just don't do it here!" She giggled again.

"You did not mention step six."

"Oh, yeah. I ain't seen that yet. But that's when they kill themselves. I wouldn't be surprised if that's what happened to 'em." She didn't appear overly upset at the thought.

"You do not worry?" Souharat leaned back.

"Hell, I don't care. If ya put up with what I put up with, ya'd feel the same. Anyway, I told 'em they couldn't come back here if they was on a toot, so they started goin' to other people's houses and, like I said, sometimes I wouldn't see 'em for weeks at a time. I think they get it before they go fishin', and do it on the boat."

That is very unsettling, Souharat thought. "They pick up this drug before they go fishing?"

"Yeah, they got a spot over at Head of the Cape at Cape Rosier, where they meet a guy in the mornin'. Bill calls him at night and the guy's waitin' for him on some beach by some rocks or somethin'. He just hands it to 'em, they hand 'im the money and they go out fishin'. Hell, I don't know how they function out there. All I know is they usually come back broke. I had to go out and get a job just to pay the bills."

A cat jumped up on the table between them and purred. She politely pushed the feline to the floor. "Get off the table, Muffin!"

Rat smiled. Now they had a starting point. "Now, ma'am, this is very important. When was the last time you saw your husband? What day and what time?"

"Well, let's see. It was two Mondays ago. I can't remember the date, but I remember it was a Monday because that's when I get my hair done." Kenny dropped his head into his hand. He wanted to laugh but held it back.

"Todd met him here in the mornin', and they left to go out together."

"It is very important, ma'am. What time was it when they left?"

"Six o'clock sharp. I remember 'cause I was cooking breakfast, but they were in too much of a hurry. That's why I figure they were stoppin' to pick up their drugs. I told all this to that Searsport cop. He was a bit rude, too."

"Of course. Thank you, ma'am. You have been very helpful. I believe we have the information we need. I apologize for inconveniencing you." He flipped the pages of the notebook over to expose the cover and placed it and the pen back into his top shirt pocket. He stood.

Kenny grabbed his arm. "Wait!" he snapped. "Ya forgot one thing." The Rat frowned at Kenny.

"Ma'am, just one more thing. This guy they buy the drugs from. Ya got his name or number?" For once, the Rat was glad Kenny was there. That information could prove to be invaluable. "We don't want to arrest him or cause him any need for worry. We just want to find your husband. He might be our only witness."

She hemmed and hawed. "Ya are from Maine, I can tell by the way ya talk. This other fella here ain't."

"That's why the Bureau sent me here. I fit in better in the local community than my immigrant colleague." He had made that one up in an instant.

She shook her head. "I don't know. Those folk have a way of findin' things out. I'd better not."

"It could be a matter of life and death, ma'am. We fear the worst." Kenny could lie just as well as Souharat.

She scratched her greasy hair. "Ya ain't gonna play games with this fella, just ask him about Bill?"

"We're not even gonna see him. We just want to talk to him. It' very important." This was the truth.

She reached to the shelf on the stand by the table where the phone rested and pulled out a piece of paper. "O.K. then. Bill calls him Ron. I never met him. Don't ya tell him where ya got that!"

"Oh, we won't, ma'am. We won't!" He shoved the paper in his pocket, and they left the trailer.

She stopped them at the door. "Oh, guys! I am kinda concerned now, with all the people gettin' involved. Let me know anythin' when ya find out, would ya?" Her eyes were narrow, round and moist, showing evidence of emotion.

"Of course, ma'am."

Charles looked all around the restaurant and decided he would attempt his plan. The setting was in his favor, he believed. The chief continued to eat, and while he was occupied, Charles could make his move. He leaned back in his chair and placed his hands behind his head. He acted very cool and calmly. "You know, Chief, you're right!"

The chief was gobbling up a piece of toast in one hand and then took a drink of orange juice from the glass he held in the other. "Good, I'm glad ya think so. I really don't want to do this, but I can't just let ya go out there and get killed. It's my duty, ya understand."

"Oh yes!" Charles said. "I'll be so much more at ease, knowing no one is going to kill me tonight! I'll tell you, I've had a real hard time sleeping. I might finally get a full night of rest!"

"See! I'm doin' ya a favor." He wiped his mouth with a napkin.

"Only thing, though, is that I've got to call Janet, my wife and let her know. She wanted me to do exactly what you're asking me to do. She'll be so relieved! I appreciate your helping, Chief McFagan. It takes a load off my mind! Do they have a payphone here?"

The chief looked up by the counter, where they placed the orders to be picked up. "Over there, but make it quick, I'm almost done.'

"Yes, sure. It'll only take a second." He eased his way away from the booth and walked over to the phone. He knew where it was. He had checked everything out while the chief slopped up his meal. It was directly next to the entrance to the kitchen. He had also noticed that there was no other door inside the establishment except for the one that they had entered. If he remembered the codes, and how restaurants operated, he knew there was a backdoor inside the kitchen. He walked to the phone and placed change into the receptacle. He slowly turned around and looked at the chief, who looked back at him and smiled.

Then the chief stuck his face back down into his plate. Charles could waste no time. He hung the phone up and dashed through the swing door into the kitchen.

The cook pivoted with his eyes wide open. "Hey! You can't come in here!" He couldn't have been much older than nineteen, a tall, skinny kid with a pimply face. Charles drew into his pocket and quickly pulled out a twenty-dollar bill then threw it at the kid.

"This is for my meal and the rest is yours, if you keep your mouth shut!"

The boy grabbed the bill before it hit the floor. "Hey! I never even seen you, mister!" He wore a wide grin.

The backdoor was right in front of him, and it was open! The heat from the kitchen must have been unbearable for the cooks. He darted outside and stopped to look around. There were thick woods directly in front of him, the parking lot on either side of the restaurant with woods on the outer edges of each lot. He knew if he went straight ahead through the woods he would eventually come to the bay. He didn't know how far it was, but once he hit water, he could find the landing. He ran into the mass of trees and thickets, disregarding the thorns and entanglements. He fought his way through.

He had eaten at that restaurant more than once and knew it wasn't far from the piers. As he went he stumbled several times and fell as many times. Then after only a minute or two he could see water. This inspired him to push harder, and soon he was on sand.

The chief of police took his last piece of toast and wiped his plated clean. He then glanced up at the pay phone. Charles was gone! He jumped up, spinning his head back and forth, looking for his new prisoner. Stella was walking by and he grabbed her arm. "Stella, where's the guy that came in here with me?"

"Beats me. I've been busy, why?"

"He's a prisoner! He's escaped!"

"Didn't look like a prisoner to me. Maybe you should have handcuffed him." She pulled her arm away from his grip. "I've got work to do!"

"Bitch!" he whispered. He ran to the front door and pushed it open, then stood in the parking lot, looking around. Charles was nowhere to be seen. He slapped his thigh with his hand. "Damn!" he shouted.

Charles ran along the beach as fast as he could. It wasn't long before he could see the piers. He stopped and caught his breath. He was all scratched up from the branches and bushes in the woods. Once he gathered himself, he continued to the landing. There he saw Jonas's truck sitting near the fence on the opposite side of the dock area. He ran up to the truck. "Jonas! You wouldn't believe it. I told the chief of police about Kenny and the Rat and he wanted to arrest me. He said it was for my own best interest. We were eating at the diner down the road and I escaped out through the kitchen. I've got to hide!"

Jonas had a beer in his hand and the radio was blasting. He leaned over and turned it off. "What? Why does the chief want to arrest ya?"

"'Cause I know too much! He knows everything. About Kenny and the Rat and about the treasure."

Jonas reeled back. "Treasure? What treasure?"

Charles forgot. He never did tell Jonas about it. "Hey, look, Jonas, just help me get out of here and I'll tell you all about it. Right now, I think McFagan's going to come looking for me!"

LOBSTER TRAPPED!

"I tried to tell ya not to go to the police. They're stupid and corrupt. All right, let me think. He knows ya van is here. He will come here lookin' for ya." He grabbed his beard and closed his eyes, gently fondling his whiskers.

"There's an old path that runs up from the beach over there." He pointed to the edge of the tree line and the shoreline. "It ain't gonna be easy travelin', but it's ya only choice. Ya gonna hafta enter the woods with ya van any way ya can then hit the path. There might be some small trees in the way, but I done it with my truck. Ya get her into the woods to the path and ya ain't gonna have no problem getting' her out to the road. I'll watch and help until I hear a car comin', then I'll get back in my truck and stall 'im here. C'mon now. Ain't no time to waste." He jumped out of his truck and walked behind Charles, who ran to his van.

Charles unlocked the driver's side door to his van and climbed inside. He placed the key in the ignition without shutting the door. He turned it over. The rain, which now had turned into a light mist, must have affected the engine.

Rrrr, rrr, rrr. "Damn!" He tried it again. *Rrrr, rrr.* "Come on!" *Rrr, rrr, pop, pop, vrrrrrmmmmm!* The engine turned over. He hastily shut the door and spun around. He had to take the van up toward the exit of the landing to the edge of the woods to gain access to the beach area. He traveled along the tree line looking for a place to enter. He drove slowly, trying to make sure he could at the very least get off the beach. There! Just up ahead was a spot he felt he could make it in. He took the van directly for it.

Jonas screamed from the parking lot, "Car coming! Get that thing off the beach!" He ran back to his truck and got inside. The approaching car was only seconds away.

Charles looked into the woods where he wanted to enter. A small sapling, about two inches in diameter, stood directly in the path. He wouldn't be able to get over that! He turned his head and saw the nose of the chief of police's vehicle coming into the parking lot.

He hit the gas with all he had, turned his head sideways and closing his eyes. The tree bent over but did not break. He had gotten halfway up on it then hit the gas again. The chief of police's car pulled up beside Jonas's truck. Charles gassed it again, and the sapling snapped back up into the air behind his vehicle. The remaining way was relatively clear. He continued along the rough path until he finally came to the much more open trail. He managed to get on the trail and head up to the roadway before McFagan got out of his car. He had done it! He continued along the trail, scraping trees and bushes as he went.

The chief walked up to Jonas in his truck with his hands tucked into his holster belt. "Hello, Jonas. What are ya doin' here?"

Jonas smiled. "I go lobster fishin' from here, Chief."

McFagan heard Charles's van cutting through the woods. He stuck his head up in the air and held his hand to his ear. "Do ya hear a boat?" He asked.

Jonas breathed out. "Oh, yeah. That's some kids out there playing on an outboard. They just left before ya got here."

The chief looked around the parking lot. "Where's their vehicle?"

"Didn't bring one. There were four of 'em and they carried along the beach from over there." He pointed to the shore in the opposite direction from where Charles exited.

The chief stuck his head into Jonas's truck window. "I smell beer."

Jonas held up the beer he was drinking. "I ain't drivin'. I'm just waitin' for the fog to break to go out."

McFagan pointed to where Charles's van had been parked. "Ya see that Rhode Island fella take his van outta here?"

"Nope! It was gone when I got here."

"Yeah, right!" He acted haughty. "Tell that flatlander that I wanna talk to him when ya see 'im."

"Sure, Chief. Sure."

He walked back to his cruiser, shaking his head.

Jonas watched him and snickered out of the side of his mouth.

Chapter 19

"We will first look at the coins, sahib. Just to see if they are authentic." Souharat opened one of the books he had set up on Kenny's table. Kenny went into the kitchen area, disappeared then returned with a tin box. He handed it to the Indian, who was deeply engrossed in his text. Souharat set the volume in front of him, opened to a page he had selected. He took the tin and opened it, removing all of the coins and a few of the gems. He picked up some of the chunks of gold and studied them, then set them back into the box. He gently raised each coin, one at a time, into the air against the background light, and twirled it back and forth then set it down on the table in some particular order he had ascertained. Once he completed this task with all the coins, he pulled the opened book towards himself and passed his index finger across the page and back to the array of coins. As he did this, he would grunt, "Um hum," over and over. He then placed his hand in his jacket pocket and withdrew a small jeweler's magnifying eyepiece. He gingerly placed the instrument in his right eye, closing the left, and examined the gems he had removed from the tin. The entire process took several minutes. He eventually removed the glass from his eye, set it on the table and leaned back in the chair.

Kenny had watched in silence. "Well?"

"It is all very real, sahib. And very, very valuable!" His facial expression never changed. "From what I can tell, this sample hails from several places. That would suggest to me that it is an accumulation of various ships' cargo. That would indicate that it had been seized over a period of time and stored into one mass location. This could only have been pilfered, in other words, it is from a pirate vessel."

"I thought you knew that?"

"I needed to be sure. Whoever the pirate was that accumulated such a cache was very good. These items come from all over the world."

"How much do you think it's all worth?" The true gist of the matter on Kenny's mind.

"What you see on this table is worth close to half a million dollars, but collectors would buy it for more. The historical significance makes this priceless!"

"And there's more of it down there!"

"It must never be shown to anyone. The government would surely confiscate it. We must be savvy in the disposition of the goods."

"What do you suggest?"

"I know of several people who know others who can afford such memorabilia for their own vanity. A meeting could be arranged with each individual and the entire collection could be disposed of in less than one year. We would be rich beyond all means if we find the remaining treasure!"

"We'll find it! Don't you worry about that! We'll find it!" Kenny was nearly drooling at the possibilities.

"These coins, sahib. They are all very old; most are over 300 years old. The gold itself can be sold separately. If this is all that those men could carry in a couple of handfuls, the worth of the remaining treasure must be astronomical!"

"Yes!" Kenny clutched his fist. "Now, to find it. Did your books tell you anything about that?"

"I searched, sahib. It is my guess that a ship wrecked here somewhere with this cargo stashed aboard. There are no records of such a wreck. It may have been a secret operation and that would make sense. I have narrowed the time of the crash to be between 1675 a.d. and 1725 a.d., but this is of little use to finding its whereabouts. If a ship did crash in this bay at that time, it went unnoticed, as I feared. The location must be ascertained by our second method. We must know the exact time that the two found it and retrace their steps. This task I afford to you. You must speak with this man who sells drugs and find the exact time the two encountered him. Discover the time they left, if indeed they ever made contact with him. If they did not meet this man and they left Mrs. Rowlin's house at 6:00 a.m., our search is easy. It would be somewhere on the way from the landing to this 'Head of the Cape.' I am, however, not very good in dealing with such people, sahib."

"Yes, Rat. That's my job all right!" He walked over to a small table against the wall and picked up the phone while he removed the sheet of paper from his pocket that held the man's phone number on it. He dialed in a hurry. His hands were shaking in anticipation. They were so close!

"Hello. Hello, Ron?"

"Yeah, who's this?"

"Ron, this is a friend of Bill Rowlin and Todd Seekins. They asked me to call you."

"Ha! What for?"

"Well, they wanted to get something from you, but they didn't want to call."

"Who is this?"

"My name is Kenny, I'm a lobster fisherman. Me and Bill and Todd like to party together sometimes. They want to party today, so they asked me to call you."

There was a long pause. "I don't know what you're talking about. I only know them two as friends. They take me out on their boat sometimes."

"Look, you don't have to pretend. I know all about everything. If you don't want to meet me, that's fine. I'd just like to know where I can find those boys. They were supposed to meet me at my house and I ain't seen them." He quickly changed from an attempt to make physical contact to simply getting the information he really wanted.

"I ain't seen them in a long time. Usually, they're here every day. Tell that Todd, if he ever wants to do business with me again, he'd better pay me what he owes me first!"

Kenny sensed the weakness in his words, but he had to play it right. "Sure, sure. He said he's got the money, but he's embarrassed, that's why he wanted me to call."

Another long pause.

"All right, I guess. But just Todd and Bill can meet me, I don't take any chances. He's got to pay me for last time, too."

"That's another thing there, Ron. When was the last time? Todd said he don't remember, and he don't remember what he got."

"He'd better remember! It was two Mondays ago. He said he spent all his money that weekend, but they expected a big catch that day and he'd meet me the next day. I went down to the regular spot and they never showed up. I wasted my whole morning."

"Yeah, he said he met you on a Monday. He just doesn't remember what time it was."

"Hey, look, I don't like talking on the phone like this. Anybody could be listening."

"No, no. Ain't nobody listening, I got all the electronics that detects that shit. I cover myself, too. You see, my man's real paranoid, so he bought all the equipment to keep ears off the line."

"Why don't you go to *him*?"

"He's outta town. Todd wants to make good. Now, do you remember what time in the morning you met him?"

"Same time as always. Eight o'clock sharp." He stopped talking for a moment. "Why do you need to know that?"

"Well, Todd says he don't remember leaving ya. He says that he was kinda under the weather that day. He just wanted to make sure that he really owes you money before he sees ya again."

"Oh, he owes me money!"

"Did ya see where he went when he left ya?"

"I took off before they left, but they head towards Eagle Light almost always, out to go fishin'."

"And they left ya at 8:00 a.m.?"

"Yeah, why? What's this all about? You ain't a cop, are ya?"

He rushed through the rest of the conversation. "Oh, no, no, no! Like I said, I'm a lobsterman. Thanks, Ron, I'll let Todd know ya wanna talk to him." He hung up quickly.

"Ha!" He slapped his hands together. "I got it, Rat! I got it! They were at the Head of the Cape at 8:00 a.m. then they headed south towards Eagle Light." His face glowed with an egotistical sense of accomplishment, but his gloating lasted only as long as it took for him to recall the reason for his temporary delight. His face folded to the shape of a reveling sailor on shore, whose time at sea made him try to whistle at the women, but his mouth, parched from the salt, wind and heat, could not. "What time was it that we ran into them?"

"I do not know. All I remember is that we were in your truck at around 9:30 a.m. To gain such information, I had to ask the two old men at the pier."

"Damn, Rat! Ya can't trust them two!" His lips were still pursed, contemptuously.

"I believe they are right at this. They mentioned the seal you caught; despite the fact they thought it was a walrus. For once, we must accept their version as correct." Buckner scoffed. The Rat spoke like a robot; deliberate and meditated, showing very little emotion. As such, his measured responses were well thought out, and it would be very difficult for him not to trust those few words of Rat's for they spoke volumes. He nodded.

Souharat leaned back into the chair, placing his palms down onto his thighs, and his mind drifted back to the altercation with the two fishermen. "Our vessel had just passed Dice Head Light when we encountered the two. At the time of their disposal, they were quite excited on what they had found. The only two other vessels within range of ours or theirs was from the men they call Ed Crowley, and well past him, to the south, was Doug Harvey." One hand came up to his mouth and he cupped it, bouncing it off his thin mustache and thinner beard in a deep trance. "This Ed Crowley mentioned nothing of the treasure. Doug Harvey must have been too far away to understand their euphoric display. They would be the only other two who could possibly know of the treasure."

Kenny's face bubbled. "And they're both dead!"

"Yes, sahib, they are."

"So there's no way anybody else could know about the treasure, is there?" He puffed his chest.

Souharat, still poking at his whiskers, glanced up; his complexion had changed to that of parents just now discovering their child is missing. "One other, perhaps!"

A look of disbelief broke on Kenny's brow. "Who? How?" It didn't make sense to him.

"We were folly in our judgment, sahib."

"Folly? How were we 'folly'? If nobody else saw them, then how could we be 'folly'?" he pressed.

"When I jumped to their vessel and scooped all the treasures, I left one—you claimed it was too heavy to bother."

The moment was relived in Kenny's mind. He drew back to the meeting of the boats. "You mean that bell?"

The Rat crossed his arms. "It is unfortunate that we did not also take it with us. It provides a clue, especially to one who might determine its origin." The words worked like needles into Buckner's torso, still he did not understand.

"This man from Rhode Island is a professor of Marine History—a noble yet insignificant course of study, unless your fate brings you to a discovery such as this. He is a scholar, and if he has seen this bell, I am sure he will place the pieces of the puzzle together. I am convinced he will realize that this bell did not travel alone. I believe *he* knows of the treasure!"

Kenny jumped back, turned pale, and the expression of the thin, pursed lips that held the look of that sailor trying to whistle, but not being able to returned to his face. "I knew it! I knew it! I knew we shoulda got rid of him a long time ago. No wonder why he's askin' questions all over." He slammed his fist into his palm. "Rat, he's got to go, before he blows it for us. We're so close!"

In meticulous fashion and no visible signs of fret, Souharat replied, "Tonight, for sure!" His confidence, once again, won out Kenny's heart and blocked his mentality. The previous attempts were forgotten for the moment.

"Let's sit down today and figure out exactly where we'll look for this treasure tomorrow and I leave everything up to you tonight!"

Souharat grinned. "I will not fail!"

The rain and mist played intermittent roles in the afternoon's forecast; once one stopped, the other would begin and so on. When Charles pulled into Jonas's driveway, it had turned into only an overcast day with the dark clouds traveling at breakneck speeds above. Flashes of white clouds would mix in with the dark, sending an ominous hue throughout the firmament. The winds were aloft, and only a slight breeze stuck close to the ground. Charles got out of his van and instantly looked it over to assess the damage. The sapling he first hit made its mark on the fender, leaving a small dent and several clumps of leaves jammed into the undercarriage. He walked all around the vehicle, looking at the scratches and gouges along the sides and even in the back. In his haste, he didn't realize, nor did he care, how much injury the van suffered. The tolling of the bell was at hand in his mind. He could trust no one, except—he shuddered in the realization—except Jonas— the man whose repugnant actions had Charles regretting ever coming to Maine! Now, he had no choice. He returned to the driver's side of the car, where he had left the door open, and sat down on the seat with his feet propped up on the sill of the door. He pressed his hands to his head and brushed back his hair, staring down to the ground. He waited patiently until, after perhaps a half hour, he heard a vehicle approach. Looking up, he saw Jonas pull into the driveway alongside of him. He stood and peered at the large man who exited his truck, holding on to the roof, shaking his head.

"Hey, Charlie! Don't ya beat all! Now ya got the chief of police on ya ass. Don't ya beat all! Well, let's go inside. No sense sitting out here and getting wet." His attitude was upbeat, nearly radiant.

Oh, boy! Charles thought, *here comes the 'I told you so.'* He followed Jonas into his house. "I'll be all right parked here?" he asked, thinking the chief might come out there to arrest him 'for his own good.'

"Ya're in Swanville now. If McFagan wants ya arrested here, he's gonna have to call somebody else. I hate the guy m'self, and I'll shoot the bastard if he thinks he's gonna get in my house without a warrant." His gruffness in some way comforted Charles. Perhaps that's what he needed, a no-nonsense approach to the whole situation; an I'll-die-before-they-take-me! disposition. Unknowingly, he already possessed it. He was just too scared to realize it.

The inside of the house seemed much the same, except that the small amount of rain they had received had seeped in along the walls, creating stains. By close inspection, dried-up stains could be seen running even further down the walls from earlier, more vicious rains. The wooden floors even had small, standing pools of water at various low spots. Jonas immediately went to the cupboard and drew out a fresh quart of rum, took a dirty glass from the counter, wiped it clean with his shirt and sat down at his spot at the table. He motioned for Charles to sit. "Take a load off ya mind there, Charlie, we got some talkin' to do." He poured his glass full. "Would ya like somethin' to drink?"

"Thank you, no." He sighed. "You know, Jonas, I think that you might be the only one I should have confided in, but I trusted that Chief McFagan. I think I made a mistake." He took his seat, speaking with a trembling voice.

"Ha! I coulda told ya that! He came here one time, tellin' me I was runnin' moonshine. Moonshine, my ass! He said he was gonna clean up Swanville and get rid of the filth like me. What he didn't say was how his brother is the biggest dope dealer in Waldo County, but ya don't see him before Judge Dyer too often. He said he weren't gonna move until I showed him where it was. He was talkin' my still. I showed him where it was all right. I sent buckshot into the cruiser door and he run like a scar't rabbit. Heh, heh. That's when he first joined the force. He ain't never been back since. Heh, heh!" He took a drink of rum, sitting sideways in his chair, and held the glass to his chest. He crossed his legs, then leaned onto the table, staring directly at Charles. "Now, what's this about a treasure?" It was a thirsty stare from a face which had seen the ravages of life at sea. The wrinkles were deeply embedded into what could not be seen and mistaken as flesh; the salt encrusted deep within each crevice made them look deeper than they were. The rosy complexion from the wind and water on his cheeks, all surrounded by the brown glaze that the day sun, and the sweltering heat confined within the pilot house of the boat, burnt upon it. He didn't look human.

It was a far sight from the mild, tender, spoiled skin of a professor of history who spent as much time in the library as the man before him spent on a boat. The contrast was distinct, and Charles was out of his milieu. Not so much when it came to the knowledge of the history he possessed, but to the actual meeting of those who made such history. As he looked at Jonas, he could see the pirates; he could see the history before him. He froze in the fixation.

He snapped from the vision and spoke. "I was sworn to silence by the chief. He said it was for my own safety that I didn't reveal what I thought. When I went to his office to report the body we found in the kelp, I saw the bell to the pirate ship *Queen Anne's Revenge*. It was the flagship for Blackbeard, the pirate. Anyway, I believe that, just before he died, he stowed all his treasure onto one of the smaller vessels of his fleet and sent it northward, possibly to Smuttynose Island. I also believe that the ship never made it. It is documented that shortly after the battle in North Carolina, where Blackbeard was killed, a strong storm emerged—a nor'easter—and that this storm threw the vessel with the treasure off course. The bell I saw is the evidence I used to figure out that ship was here, or somewhere around here. I think that the two who found the bell also found the treasure but couldn't get it out of the water. Anyway, they never made it back to shore without someone else finding out about their discovery and, in greed, killing them. That was the beginning of all the killings; of all we've seen."

Jonas never moved until Charles stopped talking. He leaned back in his chair, set sideways to the table, and fondled his beard in contemplation. "Umm, hmm!" He blinked his eyes several times. "Sure makes sense! That's what Kenny was lookin' for. Sure makes sense! It's got to be big. Bill and Todd musta been headed back to shore to get more gear and Bill's suit."

"Suit?"

"Yeah, his frog suit. What ya'd call scuba gear. I got it, too, but I don't carry it on the boat 'cause I don't really use it much, but it sure might come in handy now." He casually rubbed his nose and whiskers as he spoke. "Kenny must not know where it is, I saw him searchin' all over the place. He musta killed those two before they told him. He won't figure it out, either. He's too dumb. But that Rat with him—he's a sly creature and just as rotten, if not worse. He'll figure it out." He gulped at his drink. "Hmmm. Hmmm. Now the chief knows about it, I believe?" He turned to Charles, who nodded and bowed his head. "Well, this is gonna be interestin'!" He picked up the quart and poured another glassful. "Ya say this ship wrecked, and that's an easy enough thing to do, but with a seasoned captain around here, ya'd think the crew woulda made it to shore and then come back for the treasure."

The air turned on Charles and this husky man of brawn had made an interesting postulate; one that Charles hadn't even considered. He had checked to see if there were any witnesses to the wreck and no such record existed, but he didn't check on the possibility of survivors, though it seemed unlikely, being the end of November when the *Queen Anne's Revenge* was sunk. The Gulf stream, which kept much of the eastern United States coastal waters warm, even in winter, shot away from the coast at Cape Cod and the water temperature along the coast of Maine had to be so frigid that survival for any period of time would take nothing less than a miracle. He spun his head sideways and tugged at his ear. "To be honest, I don't know how they could have made it this far into this bay."

"There's guides; day markers and bells and all kindsa lighthouses comin' into the bay. Dependin' on which way they came in past Vinalhaven, they shoulda been able to see a lighthouse every step of the way. First, ya got Matinicus Rock Light, the Cape Elizabeth Lights, Cape Neddick Light, Cuckholds Light, Vinalhaven Browns Head Light, Owls Head and Rockland

Breakwater Lights, Curtis Island Light in Camden and Grindel Point Light on Islesboro."

Charles tried to interrupt, but Jonas went on:

"Headed east past Vinalhaven, they'd pass Matinicus still then Stimpsons Island, Stonington light, Eagle Light and if they got far enough, Dice Head Light. Either way, if they came this far up, they shoulda been able to see Fort Point Light way up ahead.

"They shoulda been able to guide themselves in and get to cover in one of the coves, eh?" He spoke hoarsely, never moving. "Leastways, ain't far to shore no matter which way they went." He turned back to combing his whiskers with his hands and staring straight ahead at the wall.

Charles shrugged, his body raised up in the chair as though, now, he knew more about the area than Jonas. "First of all, almost all of the lighthouses you mentioned were built in the mid or late nineteenth century. The earliest was Matinicus, built in 1827, and the last one was the Isle of Haut, built in 1907. You must realize that this ship I mentioned sank in 1718, over one hundred years earlier. In fact, the first lighthouse in the United States was built in Boston on Brewster Island, just two years before this boat went down. It wasn't until 1771 when there were only a total of eleven lighthouses on the coast of the United States from Portsmouth to Georgia, and none were in Maine! Once the United States got their independence, the government set up the US Lighthouse Service, which was ultimately taken over by the Coast Guard in 1939, and that's where it is today."

The burly man seemed insulted. Some of those lights he had seen looked very old; extremely old! He attempted to dodge his erroneous statements. "Without any lighthouses, that's a real bad stretch of water, dodgin' all them islands. It hadda have been a bear. They musta got real lucky."

"No doubt!" Charles reiterated. "The captain was probably new and didn't know the area. My guess is that they took water and got dragged along until they hit rocks or a shoal and sank. The thing is, the bottom of the bay around here is soft, so the ship might be completely buried underwater by sand right now. It was a long time ago, a lot of things could have happened in the interim. The only saving points that we have to go on is the bell and all these murdered or missing people. Someone must know something!"

The mood shifted to one of speculation with the large, gruff, ominous Jonas and the small, meek, thin, scholarly Charles; side by side, both fixed in conjecture.

"Ya know, Charlie, I don't recall any ships sinking in Penobscot Bay. I can't even think of one sinking anywhere in Maine at all."

The professor of history wasted no time in relaying a small portion of the shipwrecks he knew which took place off the coast of Maine that he had learned of from his studies. "There have been many such wrecks. In 1836, *The Royal Tar*, one of the first steamers to transport along the coast of Maine, carrying ninety-three people and an entire circus entourage including all the animals—horses, lions, a leopard, a tiger, a gnu and an elephant called 'Mogul'—caught fire off the coast of Vinalhaven right here in Penobscot Bay. Thirty-two people perished in the conflagration, not to mention all of the animals. *TheBohemian*, a steam ship which brought mail, dry goods and immigrants from Europe to Canada or, in the winter; Portland, run aground off of Cape Elizabeth in Maine in February 1849. Forty-two people died or vanished, at least, that was the best estimate that could be made in that disaster. There were many others; *The Australia* near Cape Elizabeth in January 1885 sank on the rocks but killed only the captain. Others include *The Bay State* in 1916, *The Polias* in 1920 and the *Oakley L. Alexander* in 1947.

"The ugliest and most horrific of all, though, was on Boon Island, just off the coast of York, within sight of the mainland and only eight years before this one we have now. The name of the ship was the *Nottingham Galley*, which hit rock in December of 1710, coming from Ireland and headed to Boston on trade. The fourteen men on board climbed onto barren Boon Island in the worst of the winter. They stayed there for nearly four weeks with no food—it was just a rock in the water. They ate mussels and seaweed to survive and actually fought over the intestines of a seagull one of them caught. They had no refuge, just some scraps which floated to shore from the wreck, so they huddled together at night to exchange body heat. After two weeks, they grew boils over their entire bodies and their skin peeled off with ease. In desperation, two men built a make-shift raft but died trying to make shore.

"A third man died from the unbearable conditions. The rest of them, starving and slowly dying, had him cut up for food. They closed their eyes and thought of chicken as they consumed his human flesh!

"They were finally rescued and brought to shore. All but the captain lost all use of their fingers and toes due to frostbite, and one had his foot amputated." He hesitated. "God knows, this is a dangerous life. In a way, I understand how my father feels, hearing stories like that, and occurring in your own backyard. That's only a few of them, and they happened right here in Maine, usually in November or December." His tone had become hollow and his voice weak. Poseidon had become Hades and the ocean became hell. He turned to Jonas for a response.

The magnanimous figure of a man chortled in indifference. "No one ever

LOBSTER TRAPPED!

said it was safe ... or *pretty*!" He considered his stubbornness a manly trait. "None of that is gonna find that treasure for us. My guess is that Kenny's hot on the trail and that chief of police, I know he's got somethin' up his sleeve. Like I said, it ain't gonna be easy." He topped off his glass, took a drink then set the bottle back down on the table. "We've got to think there, flatlander, we've got to think!"

Charles did just that. He remembered Jonas telling him that lobsters were scavengers and cannibals. After recounting the story of Boon Island, he realized how closely the lobster was to the lobsterman; a scavenger and, in some cases, a cannibal. The pursuer was much like the pursued. "I'm much more interested in ending these murders and staying alive! The shipwreck should be brought to the attention of the Coast Guard or some other government agency to handle, and the wreckage, including the treasure, should be given to a museum. The point that I get stuck on is that we're not positive the treasure exists. If we find it and notify the authorities, allowing them access to the bay, I believe the murders will end."

"Maybe, flatlander, maybe."

The charts were arranged in order on the table when Souharat pulled some tools from a pouch he had brought. He produced a scale, a protractor, some pens, pencils, hi-lighters and a compass kit. He neatly set them on the table in front of the first chart and took off his watch, setting it beside the assembly. His head darted in the direction of Kenny, who stood nearly leaning over his shoulder, absorbing the Indian's techniques. "Where do we start?" Kenny asked.

The short, scraggly man pulled the chair he was sitting in closer toward the table then stuck his index finger on the chart. "First, we examine what we know. They left Bill's trailer at 6:00 a.m. and drove into Searsport. The entire trip is only 10 miles or so. Depending on traffic, lights and if they stopped for breakfast, which would have consisted of just picking up a sandwich, if Bill's wife is correct, they would have arrived at the landing at around 6:40 a.m. It would take them time to set up before leaving. This, I believe, could be done in twenty minutes. That would put them on course at 7:00 a.m." He picked up the scale near the chart and measured along the parchment. "The distance from Searsport Harbor to Head of the Cape is approximately 15 miles, depending on their course. Their vessel travels between 10 knots and 20 knots. Let us say they moved at 15 nautical miles per hour. The arrival time would be exactly 8:00 a.m., just as we now know."

The map was big enough for Kenny to peruse the theoretical path described by Souharat. "So, everything fits!" he exclaimed.

"Yes, sahib. We arrived at the landing at 9:30 a.m. after mooring. The distance from where we met the gentlemen is approximately...." He once again scaled from the chart. "...8-1/8 miles, give or take. We traveled at maximum velocity for part of the distance until we reached the harbor. I will estimate our overall speed to be 20 nautical miles per hour on average. For 8-1/8 miles, the time consumed works out to be...." He began scribbling numbers down on one of the charts they did not use. "...approximately 28 minutes, let us say a half hour. It took us nearly twenty minutes to get the truck off the pier. That would be 50 minutes total. This means we met the two at 8:40 a.m." He scratched his head in disbelief at his own figures, staring intently at the chart, then recalculating over and over again.

The air filled with an uneasy trepidation while Kenny tried to make sense of what Souharat had done. "What does this all mean, Rat?"

"There can be no mistake! I will go over this with you several more times before I am certain, but I believe I am correct; I believe there can be no mistake!"

"What? What? What are ya getting' at?"

The careful, systematic, logical, disciplined mind of the Indian spun to the unnerving yet welcomed conclusion. He batted his eyes and leaned back in the chair. "The two men said that this Bill Rowlin 'took a dive and found it.'"

"Yeah, so?" Kenny was not sure where this was headed.

"If, sahib, he took a dive. Either he placed on scuba gear and dove deep, or the treasure is within shallow waters."

"Yeah! That's right. I don't think they keep diving gear on the boat. It musta be shallow where it is. By gory, Rat, you're right!"

"And now, sahib, the most intriguing part!"

Kenny fixed his eyes on him, absorbedly. "What?"

The Rat never flinched. "According to my calculations, and assuming it took them a total of 30 minutes to raise the portion of treasure and the bell which they did, then they would just have enough time to reach us from 8:00 a.m. when they met the drug man until 8:40 when we met them."

"Which means...?"

"That they went nowhere after they picked up their drugs. The net must have fallen as they left that spot. It means the treasure is just off shore near the Head of the Cape!"

Kenny reeled backwards. "Damn! That's pretty soft bottom over there except for a couple of spots. I think there's an island just off shore that ain't even on the maps. If you're right, my turban head amigo, then this is gonna be a piece of cake! Let's go get it!"

Souharat held his arm up in the air. "Patience, my friend! We do not know the exact location yet. This may take time. First, we must rid ourselves of any obstacles that come between us and our futures!"

The two men looked at each other until extensive ear-to-ear grins encompassed their faces. They began to laugh, slowly at first, then energetically. The hunt was on!

The shack was quiet as the two men sat at the table, neither one initiating any conversation until Chad walked down the stairs, stopping at the bottom. He was wearing pajamas and the scars from two nights before. He rubbed his eyes, tenderly so as not to tear any stitches, and tried to focus in the light. Both men turned when they noticed his presence. "Chad, I thought ya were in bed," Jonas said in a degrading tone. "Come here and let me see those bruises."

Chad had returned to the house while he was sleeping, and this was the first time he had seen his son since the 'accident.' Chad groped along to where he sat. He twisted and turned Chad's head, attempting to get a look at the damage from every direction. Chad still wore the sling.

"Now, that ain't so bad! I told ya that ya gotta be careful walkin' up and down them steps; it can be dangerous." Chad glanced over to Charles, who said nothing.

"Now, why don't ya get somethin' to eat and get back upstairs."

This reminded Charles. "Oh, by the way. These are yours, Chad. I forgot to give them to you when you left the hotel." He reached into his pocket and produced a vial of pills. "This is for the pain and discomfort," he explained. "You should take one when you want to get to sleep." Chad smiled at him and accepted the container.

Jonas picked up the glass from the table and swallowed down the remainder of its contents. He then picked up the bottle and poured another glassful. At that time, Katherine walked through the door. "Well, if it ain't my little girl comin' home from school." She said nothing and walked directly to the stairs then up them. "Well, she's actin' awful anti-social!" Jonas said.

Charles felt uncomfortable. "I'll think about it, Jonas. We'll come up with something, I'm sure. Right now, though, I want to check out of that hotel before something else happens." He laughed. "I didn't know I was such a popular man! I'm going to have to find another room."

Jonas laughed with him. "I'll tell ya what I'm gonna do. I'm gonna call that chief up and tell 'im that I know where ya went. I'll tell 'im that ya gettin' a hotel in Bucksport, that'll give ya time to go back to the hotel and pick ya stuff up and get checked out. Now, I know of this place that's off the road, not far from where ya are now. It has a long driveway and some cottages near the water on the bay. Ya can park ya van there and they can't see it from the road. I know the guy that owns it and he don't get out much, so I don't think he knows anythin' about the missing people or anythin' about ya. He also don't care. Ya don't have to give 'im ya real name; he won't check. That way, no one will know ya're even still in town. It's a little bit more expensive, but a hell of a lot safer. Whatta ya say?"

"That sounds good. Just give me the directions and I'll go over there right after I check out of this other place."

"Consider it done! When I tell McFagan that you're headed to Bucksport, that'll keep the Belfast cops off your ass, too. He's such an idiot!"

Charles stood up. "O.K. then, as long as I make it out of this other hotel, I should be good to go." He turned and went to the door.

"I'd still keep my eyes open if I were ya!"

"I will!" He exited.

Chad and Katherine watched television for the rest of the afternoon while Jonas sat at the table, quaffing down rum after rum. The time grew late. "Chad!" he screamed. "You hungry?"

The sharpness of the stillness broken startled Chad. "No, Dad, I couldn't eat a thing. I'm still pretty sore, I think I'm going to go to bed."

"Take one o' those pills like Charlie said, before ya go." His words were slurred and his actions were erratic. "Did ya hear me?"

"Yes, Dad, I heard you." He got up from the couch and walked over to the counter, picked up the vial of pills, took one out and placed it in his mouth. He then took a glass from the counter, poured water into it from the spigot and swallowed the pill. He turned to Katherine, who was still sitting on the couch, then he pivoted and went upstairs.

Jonas bobbed his head up and down until finally, he spun around to Katherine. "Ya gonna cook some supper, girl?"

She hopped off the couch without much enthusiasm. "What would you like, Dad?"

Jonas barely kept his eyes opened, with his head teetering. One side of his mouth turned upward in a grin revealing his dirty, stained teeth. "Come here, girl." He threw his arm into the air aimlessly.

Katherine shunned away. "I said, come here, girl!" There was voracity in his hoarse banter. The invitation was not received well. Katherine turned to head up the stairs when Jonas stood up, leaned over and grabbed her by the arms. "I want you, now!" he mumbled.

"No, Dad, please, no! I still hurt!"

"Oh? Yeah? Don't worry, it'll be just like the first time. Give your daddy a hug." The raunchy stench of stale alcohol danced from his mouth, and his body reeked of salt and that disgusting fish odor. He was unsteady on his feet, but she was too petite and weak to struggle again. He pressed her body up to his while she tried to push him away; he reached around her torso and picked her up off the floor, guiding her into the bedroom. "It'll be just like the first time! Just like the first time, honey!" he continued to mumble.

"Please, Dad, no … no … no…!" Her voice failed her. She could struggle no more. Something inside her had given up, not only with her father but with herself. She didn't want to live anymore.

Souharat pulled up behind the hotel, as was his normal modus operandi. He crouched down low and turned the corner at the building. He wore the same suit every day, including the same turban. This evening, he was carrying a black satchel, like a nineteenth-century physician. He carefully surveyed the neighborhood. There was Charles's van, in front of his room at the hotel. All the lights were on in his room. Surely, this time, he could not fail. He was carrying enough explosives in that bag to take out the entire room and the adjacent ones. There were no people loitering about, and the traffic on Route #1 was minimal. He needed only a second to drop the bag off, walk back across the compound and enter his car before he was off. He casually strolled directly through the parking lot, as though he belonged there. Even if someone did happen to see him, they would not think too much of it; he was just a traveling businessman staying at the hotel for the night. Then he realized the turban would give him away. He ripped it off as he approached Charles's room. Not one person could be seen, and this put him at ease. He nonchalantly opened the bag he held and threw the turban inside. It was time he got rid of it anyway. The night had drawn quite dark now, and only some of the outside lights at the hotel worked. He felt invisible. He didn't dare get close to the window of Charles's room. He curled around to the next room, where there were no lights on, no vehicle in the pre-arranged parking spot, and it looked deserted. Gently, he set the bag down in front of Charles's hotel room, then he briskly retraced his steps across the parking lot, around the end of the hotel and into his vehicle. He started it up and drove away from the area as fast as he could. He hadn't gone more than 100 yards along the road when he heard the ear-shattering blast. It shook his car on the road, but he didn't stop. Horns could be heard making a ruckus behind him, and the sky was alight with flames. He looked into his rearview mirror and watched a plume of smoke ascend from the building from whence he came. He laughed loudly. Now, Kenny could not be disappointed in him, he had done his job!

Charles arrived at the hotel shortly after leaving Jonas's and getting something to eat. He parked his van outside of his room, exited, opened the door of the room and walked inside. The maid had been there, everything was changed; the bed, the towels, the soap, everything. He scrambled around the place to find all of his belongings and threw them in his suitcases, just as he found them. Jonas had made this part of an uncomfortable return much easier, knowing that the chief of police wouldn't show up and attempt to arrest him again. He philosophized as he packed. The mere thought of this treasure had brought out the worst in every man he dealt with. The chief was no exception. Was it human nature to allow greed to control your emotions and intellectual processes? It seemed so. Was he so different? Was there a bit of greed in him that he just didn't see? It was possible, but in a much less obtrusive manner. These people were willing to kill to sate their quest for wealth! It certainly wasn't a new revelation; this sort of thing had been going on since the beginning of time. Men killing men for greed; small parcels of land, a few dollars at a poker table, anything that somebody else had that they wanted. It all seemed so futile; so useless.

Was it greed or jealousy? He theorized that the two went hand in hand. What good does a masterpiece painting do for you? You look at it once and absorb the pleasure of seeing it. But to have it! Moreover, not to let anyone else have it! That meant it was either jealousy or vanity. He gave up trying to figure out the dealings within the mind.

He finished packing everything he could and closed his baggage up, then brought it out to the van and loaded it. The night had grown dark early. The weather was dismal all day, and the night was a true reflection of it. He shut the back of the van and walked the two doors down to the main desk at the office. A young girl sat behind the desk watching television.

"Excuse me, ma'am," he said as he approached.

She jumped up, "Oh, I'm sorry, I was watching this and I started to get into it. I didn't even hear you come in." She was a tiny girl with long blond hair draping across her shoulders and bright blue eyes. Her complexion was fair, but she seemed awfully young to work here. She was wearing a thin, cut halter top with no bra, a pair of faded jeans and sneakers. "What can I do for you?" She acted eager, placing both hands on the counter before her.

"I'll be checking out, I'm afraid," he answered.

"Now? It's awful late to be checking out now! I can't check you out now unless I charge you for tomorrow. Checkout time is noon for the day."

"That's fine, just charge me for another day." Charles was in a hurry to get to the new place Jonas told him about and this process could take time, he noticed.

"Well, let's see. What room?"

"102."

"Oh, yeah, here we are. Mr. Ritter, right?"

"Yes, that's me."

"Wait a minute. This bill has already been paid up until Sunday. It's a corporate account, I think." She gawked at the books with a bewildered stare.

"I was sent up here by the University of Rhode Island. They made the arrangements, but I have reason to change them. I can't stay any longer." He was sympathetic to her naïveté, but also in a rush to get out of there.

"I don't know how to do this. Oh, God. They just put me behind the desk tonight. They said it would be slow and that there wouldn't be anyone coming in or going out tonight, and this checkout is not what they taught me. I'm sorry, this might take me a while."

"Could you please hurry it up just a tad, I really need to be on my way."

"I'd better call the owner, he'll straighten this out. I don't know how to give a credit, which is what I think I'll have to do. Do you mind waiting just a second while I call him."

Charles sighed heavily and shrugged his shoulders, like the doomed Christian awaiting the entrance of the lion. "Please, could you be as brief as possible."

"Oh, yes, sir. I'm so sorry. This should only take a minute." She walked back behind the wall to the left, down a small corridor to a phone hanging from the wall then picked it up.

She dialed a number when…. *Ba BOOM!* The wall behind the desk gave way, throwing plaster and wood directly at Charles, who was swung backwards into the glass window at the front of the building. Glass shattered everywhere and the front door blew first inside, then outside, heaving heavily, as it was torn from its hinges. The ceiling plaster fell mercilessly to the floor. The girl at the phone was tossed against the wall to her side, she hit firmly then dropped in a second. The desk behind the counter flipped over and the counter itself snapped at the blast. Charles, who had only slightly penetrated through the wall in front, was cut from the broken glass over his entire back and parts of his side. Debris flew wildly about the office. When the initial blast of the explosion subsided, Charles hustled to his feet to check on the girl. She lay on the floor, not moving. He ran through what was left of a gate at the desk, up to her side, and rolled her over. She was completely covered in drywall and dust. He face was black from soot or material that had burnt. She opened her eyes. "Wha … what happened?" she forced out.

"Are you all right?" He was in a quandary.

She stretched the muscles on her face, opening and shutting her jaw several times, then shook her head. "Oh, I'm fine. What happened?"

"I don't know," Charles said, and in saying, he noticed that the wall between the first apartment adjacent to the office was on fire. "Does the phone still work?" The two could hear the humming on the receiver which she somehow still hung on to.

She regained her feet. The shock of the explosion was more damaging to her than the explosion alone. She stood and placed the receiver of the phone back into its cradle then picked it off again and put it to her ear.

"It still works!" she exclaimed in amazement.

"Call 9-1-1," Charles said. "The hotel is on fire!"

Without hesitation, she did so, and Charles ran out of the front door, which now hung by only its bottom hinge. The explosion was centered at his room, which was engulfed in flames. The smoke billowed out of the broken windows and the devastated door. His van was thrown nearly 150 feet across the parking lot, and the hood had flames emerging from the grill area. He ran back inside the office, spinning back and forth; searching. He saw what he wanted behind the desk; a small fire extinguisher. He grabbed it off its stand and ran out to his van, manipulating the locks and plastic guards on the tool as he went. He sprayed it before reaching his vehicle and held it on, dousing the hood of the vehicle until the flames went out. He glanced back around to the hotel. His room was totally demolished, and the two rooms abutting his suffered immense damage, blackened by the burning cinders. The office and the room two doors down from his also experienced damage, but not as bad as the three in the center of the holocaust. His thoughts ran amok, wildly, and he came up with only one conclusion. That bomb was meant for him! Surely now, the police would want to talk to him, a situation he wished to avoid. He turned back to his van. Most of the windows were cracked and covered with cinders. Debris had hit the body in several places, but overall it still looked operable. Not wanting to wait around and answer questions, he jumped inside and prayed the thing would start. He stuck the key in the ignition and turned it. The van started on the first try.

"Whew! I'm out of here!" He didn't even have to back up, because the van had traveled so far through the lot that he could pull directly out. He squealed his tires as he went. The new hotel was only about a mile up the road and that was a good thing, due to the fact that he had two flat tires up front. He rode the rims the whole way. A fire engine was heard well ahead of him as he pulled onto the narrow street which served as an entrance to the hotel. He never looked back again until he got the van out of sight well down off the road. He pulled in behind a building, so that even if they looked for him, they would never see the van from the road. He shifted into park and removed the key from the ignition. He breathed in deeply and released it then slumped over the top of the steering wheel and lay there for several minutes.

The sound of the rescue operations at the hotel down the street could be heard for several minutes. He crawled out of the van and approached the cabin which read 'Office' and knocked at the door. An elderly, balding man opened it. "Yessa, what can I do fer ya?" He had a strange appearance, wearing a corduroy shirt and jeans with suspenders.

"I'd like to rent a cabin." Charles looked exhausted.

"Y'all right, mista?" A concerned look came over the old man. "Did ya just come from that hotel up there?"

Charles leaned against the sill of the door and nodded in the affirmative. "I guess I can't stay there!"

The man laughed in a low tone. "I should say not! I heard the damned thing. I stepped outside, and I could see flames as high as Blue Hill. That was one hell of a blast. I wonder what happened. Did somethin' blow up?"

"I don't know," Charles lied. "Maybe a boiler or something. I was just going to check in when it happened."

"Well, well, now it looks like ya took quite a bit of the blast y'self. C'mon in and I'll find a place fer ya. That musta been quite the scare."

Charles walked inside after the old man. They sat down and talked for a short period of time, rehashing what had happened to the hotel. Charles was careful not to say too much; not to draw attention to himself. He told the man his name was John Twimbell, and he had come down from Boston for a week to arrange some business deals with the local fisheries.

The man ate the story, hook, line and sinker. "I only got two places left and I'm closing up the whole operation here, for the winter. I can give ya one till then, but if ya can stay until ya business is done.

"Well, I ain't gonna keep ya. I can see ya might wanna take a shower and a long nap. That blast had to be somethin'. Humph! We'll read about it in the paper tomorrow, Mr. Twimbell."

"I was afraid of that!" Charles whispered.

Chapter 20

Light broke within the skies before 6:00 a.m., even though the weatherman had placed sunrise at 6:08 a.m. Souharat awoke early to arrive at Kenny's before heading out to look for the treasure, eager to watch the morning news in hopes of seeing the zenith of his efforts. He rushed there and caught Kenny unexpectedly, still not dressed. He was wearing a long bathrobe tied at the waist, and his hair was tangled up from the tossing and turning he experienced in his sporadic attempts at sleep that night. "Hey, Rat! No turban?"

It was a clumsy salutation. "Please, sahib. We will have time for the small talk later. I wish to have you watch the morning news. It is important to our efforts." He was carrying a valise and a large instrument in his hands, which Kenny took note of, but he didn't ask.

Kenny walked to the television in the living room and turned it on, then disappeared to his bedroom around the corner. "This'd better be good," he said while exiting.

The weather report took precedence, then the local Bangor news and sports. The station was aired from Bangor and, apparently, Belfast took a backseat. Then the fire was mentioned and a quick photo shown. The story would follow a commercial. "Hurry, sahib, it is coming on now!"

Kenny emerged from his room fully dressed, and he fixed his eyes on the television. The fire was shown, citing it as 'suspicious' and that it was 'under investigation.' There was no mention of casualties. They showed pictures of the aftermath of the explosion, which the two studied closely. The room Charles was staying in was completely consumed; no one could have possibly survived that! Still, there was no mention of any deaths. Then, the news jumped to a separate, unrelated story. "Well?" Kenny looked at Souharat. "No mention of the Rhode Islander."

"It is still early in the shifting through the rubble, and they may not have found his body yet. We should wait for an update tonight."

"It looks like ya did a pretty good job. The place was a mess. Are ya sure that was his room?"

This brought a strange suspicion to the Rat's mind. Where was the van? He did not relay his concern to Kenny. "He must be dead, and buried inside!"

"I sure hope so, Rat." He was adjusting his apparel as he spoke and examined the equipment that Souharat brought with him. "What's all this for?"

Still in a dazed state from the lack of information outlined in the news, the Rat only heard the question peripherally. His head snapped up once the words set in. "Ah, sahib. I spent time yesterday after leaving you to acquire what we will need to find the fortune on the bottom of the bay." The two men stepped back into the dining area and he threw the valise on the table, opened it and pulled out a large chart. "I have blown up the map of the area which we shall explore. I broke it up into sections, basing each section on an anticipated day. I believe we can check an area of a quarter square mile per day. The search will be tedious. We have not done such a thing before, and we are unsure of the exact depths of the waters. From our work yesterday, I do not think it will take us longer than a week to find something. Once we find a spot where we may determine the treasure exists, it will be up to you to go below the water and examine it yourself. If it goes as I expect, we will be rich in a week!"

Kenny grinned, a wide, evil grin. "Good, Rat. What's this thing ya brought with ya? It looks like a metal detector." He pointed to the instrument in Souharat's hand.

"It is! But it is an underwater metal detector. I bought it yesterday in Northport. It is specially designed to search for metals and gold in salt water. It is waterproof for depths up to 200 feet. The arm only extends perhaps three feet from the handhold here." He grabbed the handle in demonstration. "I worked with the retailer, and we added an arm and an additional cable to run alongside. This will increase the reach to approximately ten feet. I also purchased another arm to use, when necessary. We will have at our disposal a total depth of over sixteen feet from the surface of the water. The instrument becomes too flimsy after that, so if we encounter deeper portions in the areas I have designated, we must dive. I think, if Bill Rowlin was able to dive with no equipment, then we will not need the second extension to locate what we seek."

Kenny rubbed his chin. "Hmm. This is made for salt water?"

"Yes, sahib. Once we receive a signal, we should scan the entire area to see if we can find a stronger signal until we pinpoint the greatest mass of metals of gold as is possible. I will mark the chart, and when we find such a spot, we may stop and dive. It is the easiest method I could think of—and the fastest!"

"That's a great idea, Rat! It's almost impossible to see below the foam and waves to the bottom." He stepped over to a cabinet in the living room and drew out his scuba gear. "Let's load up now; we might find it today!"

"I suggest we use the skiff with the detector, it drafts lower to the surface, extending our reach, and it is more mobile. I will pilot the skiff and the instrument while you remain in the boat. I will relay what I find and you can mark it on the chart."

"This is it!" Kenny bellowed.

Charles woke from the sun beating on his face. He was sore, and covered with cuts and bruises from the explosion the night before. It hurt to move. He eased his way out of bed and glanced out the window towards his van. It would take all morning to have it fixed, he felt. This made the trivial physical pain worse. He would have to call Dean Groton before he found out about the hotel melee. He groped about the room, with all the amenities within reach. This day was going to be spent everywhere but on the water. This trip was proving quite an experience for him, and a large strain on his patience and beliefs. Was there such a thing as Nihilism?

He picked up the phone and dialed. Ben answered at the other end. "Hello, Office of the Dean, College of Arts and Science."

"Ben, this is Charles Ritter."

"Charlie! How's it going up there? Having fun, I bet."

"Well, don't bet on it, Ben. Is Dean Groton in yet?"

"Yeah, sure. Hang on a second and I'll patch you." He waited patiently.

"Dean Groton here. How is everything, Charles?"

"Well, Dean, I have a little problem with my vehicle. I'm going to call Randy Thompson and tell him that I can't make it again today. I'm in the middle of something here."

"I understand. I haven't told anyone about your revelation about the ship, but I sincerely want you to pursue it. This could be just what the university needs now. Don't worry about Randy. I've already talked to him and he doesn't expect to go out at all, even though I didn't tell him why. By the way, we bought his boat, so he doesn't even care anymore. He said if you do want him to go out, just give him a day's notice and he'll be glad to help. Also, Charles, I would like you to get to the bottom of this pirate ship thing; enough so that I am willing to have a substitute fill in for you until you have everything worked out. I've been given the authority by the board. As far as the class goes, we're going to use the syllabus and schedule that you edited and we'll just have the substitute perform the academia portion until you return."

"That's all very comforting, Dean, but I was hoping that Woods Hole could—"

"No need to thank me, Charles. Just keep up the effort and we'll get back hold of you."

"Dean, there's another thing. I've changed hotels—you'll find out when the bill comes. I put the costs on the same credit line, I hope you…"

"Fine, fine. That's fine, Charles. Whatever you need, just jot it down to that account. Take as long as you need. Look, I've got to get going now; I have an appointment with one of the board members. Good luck, Charles, and we'll stay in touch. Quickly, I'm going to switch you to Ben and he'll get your new phone number and straighten out the account. Bye, Charles." He hung up hastily.

Charles took the receiver from his ear and held it out in his arm at length, staring blankly at it. The dean was too much in a hurry to hear him out, for no apparent reason. There was a strange, eerie intonation in his voice, and this vexed him. Was the dean withholding something? Ben took the line, and he relayed the required information to him.

Charles hung up and called Jonas's house. Chad answered the phone, and Charles gave him the new hotel number just in case he needed it for anything.

Then he thumbed through the phone book on the table by the phone and called AAA. He spent the rest of the day cleaning up his vehicle and watching them work.

The morning was as usual for Jonas. He waited at the table in his favorite chair until Katherine caught the bus, then he headed down to the landing. He glanced over the mooring area when he arrived and saw that Kenny's boat was already out. As he looked to the water, he noticed that Chief McFagan was patrolling the bay in the police boat. Sam and Andrew stood in their regular spots at the end of the pier. "Mornin', Jonas, ya getting here late. Wife ain't home yet?"

"No, Sam, she's still in Millinocket." He scratched the back of his neck, never taking his eyes from the police boat. "What the hell is the chief doin' out there?"

"Heard he's lookin' for an escaped felon." Andrew removed his orange cap and scratching the white outcropping of what remained of his hair.

"I heard that they been lookin' for illegal immigrants headed here, in on the ships comin' back from Europe," Sam suggested.

"Y'know they found a bunch of immigrants floatin' up here from Cuba on a rubber raft. Made it as far as Stonington last year. Might be lookin' for more."

"Could be. Might be lookin' for drugs comin' up from there too. I heard that's getting' to be an epidemic in Penobscot Bay."

"I just hope it's Viagra!" Andrew said, and the two of them began to laugh in their own mundane way.

"Jesus, those two go on!" he whispered as he rolled Randy's skiff off the trailer on the back of the truck, still watching the police boat heading towards Castine. "What the hell is he lookin' for?" He turned to the two old men once more. "Did ya fellas see Kenny leave?"

"Ah-yup. He left early. Earliest one out here, I reckon," Sam said.

"Did ya see where he went?"

"That's a funny thing, there, Jonas. Him and that Indian fella, who lost his bandana hat, went out together, but Kenny took the boat and the other guy took the skiff." Jonas peered out to the mooring area. Their skiff was gone!

"Turban!" Andrew interjected.

"What?" Sam asked.

"'Twern't no bandana, it's called a turban, ya fool."

"Whatever. Ya know that chief might be lookin' for rats. I heard they been findin' 'em in the bilges of the ships comin' in from overseas. Getting to be a problem in town."

Jonas set the dinghy in the water, tied it to the pier and returned to his truck, parking it in the lot. He pulled the skiff to himself and climbed inside.

The television blared loudly, too loud for Chad to hear a car pull into the driveway. The afternoon had passed him by in the monotony of being alone, and having nothing to do but watch old re-runs on TV. He never got dressed out of his pajamas. He sat in a lackluster position, daydreaming of nothing in particular and regretting being suspended from school, an oasis to the humdrum he was now experiencing. He was so caught up in the melancholy that when he heard a banging at the door, he merely thought it was the wandering of his mind, bringing him a make-believe playmate to pass the time. He then looked at the clock and noticed that the time which had passed in boredom, must have signaled Katherine retuning from school. He lowered the volume on the television. The bang came again, and suddenly the door was forced open by a large wooden object; the bottom of which entered first, followed by a human leg, then the body of the entity emerged above the leg, owned by no other than Elena.

He jumped to his feet in celebration. "Ma!" he cried in a squeaky voice. "You're home! Boy, did I miss you!" His rejoicing brought him up to her before she could entirely traverse the entranceway. "Let me give you a hand, Ma!"

She turned to him brusquely. "You just sit down, young man, I want to look at you and check you over. I also want to talk to you. Now, go along, sit back down." The object she carried was a medium size grandfather clock, made of solid oak, beautifully finished in a brown glaze, but quite heavy and cumbersome. She managed to wrestle the whole thing through the door and set it up against the wall below the stairwell. "Phew!" she said. "That thing's a bear!" She stood upright, glancing at the clock, and straightened out her clothing, ruffled from her excursion with the timepiece. She turned to Chad, who, contrary to her request, never moved. Her lips tightened when she looked at his face and the sling over his arm. Without words, the two embraced as though she had been gone for months. Chad's face glowed brilliantly as though the wasted day had been atoned for by her presence. After the long hug, she pushed him away to arm's length to get a better look at his injuries.

"My God!" she spoke with a passion. "Look at you!" She dropped to one knee, and beginning at the eyes, she methodically inspected his entire body scrupulously, making brief comments in a disapproving fashion; words like "dear" and "my" and "ah." Her face was crippled with concern. "You're a mess, Chad. I want you to tell me exactly what happened."

"Oh, Ma!" he said calmly. "It looks a lot worse than it is."

"Well, it *can't* be any worse than it looks! When do these stitches come out?" She had gone over each bruise, the fracture and every cut on his body, then began again at the eyes and re-inspected him.

"I go back in a couple of days, but some of the stitches get absorbed and don't need to be removed. Only the ones on the outside have to be taken out," he answered staunchly.

She sighed heavily. "Oh, Chad, what happened?"

"It was nothing really. Sean and I were fooling around in class on the first day, and I got caught. The teacher tried to embarrass me, but instead, I embarrassed him, and I ended up getting suspended. That's about it."

"*This* didn't happen in school!" She stood and waved her arms over his entire body. "How did *this* happen?"

At that time, the door opened once more, and Katherine stepped inside. "Ma! Ma, I'm so happy to see you! Oh, Ma!" She dropped her books and school accessories on the floor at the sill of the door and jaunted to her mother, nearly jumping the whole distance in one motion. Her mother spun around and held her arms out. They, too, embraced. This time, Katherine took her mother in a power clutch, swinging her back and forth in slow, jerky movements. "Oh, Ma, I've missed you so much!" Her face lit up.

Elena broke the hold. "My!" she said. "I didn't expect this type of reception. I missed you guys, too." She stood back up and put her arms on her hips in an authoritative fashion. "I'll talk to you when I come back inside, Chad. Right now, I've brought some groceries I need carried inside. I also have some of Aunt Julie's...." She stopped short on what she was about to say and reflected.

"Why don't the two of you sit on the couch for a minute, I've got something to tell you." She gently pushed Katherine in the back, and the two children walked to the couch and took a seat. Elena paced around the room, arranging her words. The children sat silently, waiting.

"I suppose there's no easy way to put it," she admitted gently. "I'm afraid Aunt Julie passed away last night."

The two sat on the couch and remained silent. This was not big news to them; in fact, it was just a matter of time; they also knew how much Aunt Julie and Uncle Steve meant to their mother, being the last of her remaining kin, and they lowered their heads in an expression of sorrow.

"You're all I have now," she said condolingly. "Before Aunt Julie went, she asked me to take a few things with me. That clock is one." She tilted her head in the direction of the piece of furniture against the wall. "There's some more stuff in the car. I'm going to have to go back up there tomorrow; the wake will take place just before the funeral. Everything had been arranged before I left." She puttered around, at a loss of words. "They'll have the wake in the morning, seeing that everyone is already in town, then a graveside service in the afternoon; we rushed to minimize everyone's inconvenience; it being so soon after poor Uncle Steve." She paused and looked directly at the children. "I'll be doing my second eulogy in a week!" A tear welled up in her eye, but she smiled tenderly. "Humph! In a way, it works out best; everything happening at once instead of dragging on for days, months or even years. I don't know what I would have done. Aunt Julie couldn't have stayed by herself in the condition she was in. I suppose...." The recollection and the memories churned up inside her as she glanced around the house. "Their house is so beautiful. They have brand-new curtains, a gorgeous living room with new furniture everywhere, pictures on the walls, expensive appliances, a handsome bathroom with mirrors on every wall, and polished floors." She looked up at the ceiling and saw the water stain from the rain. "They ain't got no leaks, and everything was so clean. When I come back here, I see...." She shook her head without finishing.

Regaining her composure, she turned to Katherine. "Now, girl, you help me carry some of this stuff inside, and Chad, you just stay here and rest up. I'm not done talking to you, yet." He nodded, and Katherine took to her feet.

The car was full, but they managed to get all of the things inside in only a few trips. Elena began putting the groceries away. "What have you been eating?" Elena asked when she opened the refrigerator. "There's nothing here."

"I made due, ma," Katherine spoke proudly. "Dad never did go shopping."

"Oh, dear!" Elena sighed. "Well, go upstairs, Katherine, and get dressed, you don't want to ruin that pretty gown you're wearing." Even though she didn't have much to choose from in her boudoir for apparel, she always looked stunningly charming. She hustled up the stairs at the request.

When Elena had finished putting all the groceries away, it seemed they had more now than ever before. She then went back out to the car and opened the trunk, removing her luggage and bringing it inside the house. "I have to do all this laundry," she moaned. "I suppose you kids have a bunch, also."

Chad, who was still sitting on the couch watching television, nodded in the affirmative. Katherine had now returned downstairs. "I've done some in the sink and let it dry outside, but we sure could use a washer and dryer for the rest of it."

Elena wiped her head in fatigue. "Get it together and I'll go in town tonight and wash and dry it there. Well, I think I'm going to take a break. While I do, Chad, you can tell me exactly what happened to you, to get this banged up." She took one of the bottles of juice out of the refrigerator and poured herself a glass. Katherine walked over to the couch and sat on the outside beside Chad. Elena took a sip of juice from the glass. "Well?" she asked curiously. "What happened?"

Chad stuttered in a very low tone, not making sense.

"I can't hear you, Chad. Speak up!"

"Oh, Ma! Dad was drunk when I got home from school that day, and he threw a fit. I ran upstairs and he chased me. Then he broke into my room and started throwing me around. The last throw was down the stairs, and I banged my head on the edge of the bottom post. It was really a freak thing! Don't worry, he'll get his!"

Elena froze. "He did this intentionally?" Her hand started to shake. "This is no accident, Chad. He could have killed you! That's it, I can't take this anymore!" Her demeanor changed to one of disgust. "I'm only gone a short time and this happens! What's next?" She began to pace around the room in deep reflection. "This has got to end! It's bad enough he hits m...." She stopped and glanced at the children who were sticking on her every word.

"Look, I've been thinking about this. I want the two of you to know. I've been contemplating leaving your father." She lowered her head. "I've tried to be patient, God knows! We won't have much to get started on, but I can find a job. Right now, I don't have anyone to turn to. I just don't know!" She was in a quandary. On one hand she knew she must leave, not for herself, but the safety of the children. On the other hand, this was all she knew. It was the only security she had. The prospect of going on her own was a scary endeavor; one she had never done and only thought of doing. Then a strange thought came over her. An uncomfortable, disturbing thought!

She turned to Katherine, who sat silently with her hands between her knees. She had those puppy dog eyes, sympathetic and shy; naïve. There was something about the way she sat, the way she didn't speak, and her withdrawnness.

Elena's lips pursed and her face wrinkled. "Katherine," she said calmly. "Did your father hit you?"

Katherine turned her head, her hair flying across her cheek. "No, Ma, he hasn't hit me," she spoke softly.

A feeling came over Elena. A feeling only a mother could have. She blurted out without thinking, "Katherine, I want you to be honest with me. Has he touched you?!" Her eyes darted out of her head.

Katherine couldn't look at her directly. She faced the wall on the opposite side of the room and began to weep.

"Katherine! I asked you a question! Has he touched you?!" Her voice was raised to a yell and vibrated with each syllable.

Katherine placed her elbows on her knees and dropped her head into her hands. She cried. The tears streaked down her face and exploded into a pouring gush onto her lap. "Ma! It hurts when I go to the bathroom!"

The question didn't need to be answered.

Elena dropped her glass of juice on the floor. "OH, MY GOD!" She, too wailed uncontrollably then rushed to her daughter and fell to both knees, placing her arms around her in a mighty bear hug. "Oh, my God!" The two cried for what seemed to be an eternity.

Chad, who had risen to his feet, cried with them. "He'll get his, ma! He'll get his!" He understood the implications and had to brush back the tears from his own eyes. "He'll get his! Oh! I promise! He'll get his!"

Elena rocked Katherine back and forth like a little girl. "Oh, my baby. My poor baby!" She clutched her head and drew it to her breast. "My poor, poor baby!" Her eyes had reddened, to match the hue of a matador's cape, and they had shut to mere slits.

Katherine's breathing became erratic in her attempts to stop crying and return to normal. Each effort resulted in another burst of tears and wails. Her body trembled all over.

Elena tried to comfort her. "It's all right, baby. It's O.K., honey! We'll leave here and start over. It's all right." She brushed her hair with her hand and looked her directly in the face.

Her tears began to diminish. "Are you O.K.?" She placed her thumb under Katherine's eyes and wiped away the tears. Katherine nodded, still choking and gasping for air. "It's my fault, honey, I should never have left."

"No ... no ... Ma. It's not ... (sob) ... your ... (sniff) ... fault. Ah, ah, ah—" She tried to catch her breath but could not.

"Easy, easy, now," Elena said, then ran to the kitchen and removed a brown paper bag from the drawer below the sink and returned to Katherine's side, opening the bag. "Here, breathe into this, slowly until your calm down." She stood up and let Katherine cough and cry it out of herself.

"Oh, God!" she repeated and walked over to the phone table, pulling out the drawer below and reaching inside, where she took out her copy of the Bible, pressing it to her chest with both hands. "Why?" She stared up at the ceiling. "Why? Why us?" she begged, her eyes blinking open and shut in rapid succession, then closing completely with water tricking down her cheeks.

Chad stumbled across the room until he came to the sink area and kicked the cabinet below, denting in the thin metal door. "He'll get his!" he reiterated.

Elena came to grips with the situation. "We've got to get out of here! We've got to get out of here, today! I just don't know where to go!" She spoke erratically, still confused, her voice was packed with emotion.

Chad had the look of the devil on him, then he remembered. "Ma!" he said in a euphoric tone. "Charlie called this morning. He could help us!" His remembrance of the gunshot in the previous hotel tousled in his mind, but he reassessed the situation and spoke with an assuring tone, "He said he's staying in a different hotel now where nobody knows where he is. He left the number."

The idea of imposition never crossed her mind. "Yes, of course! Charles! He'll help, and he's all we've got. Give me the number, Chad, and I'll call right now. He'll help us, I'm sure of it."

Chad ran over near the table where he left the paper with the phone number on it. "Here it is, Ma. He said he'd be home all day."

She hastily glanced at the sheet, wiped her eyes once more to remove the residual tears and dialed.

"Charles?" she asked.

"Yes?" was the reply.

"Hello, this is Elena, I'm back in town."

"Elena! It's good to hear from you, what's going on?"

"Charles, I need a big favor!"

"Anything, what can I do for you?"

"I need a place to stay for the night. For me and the children. It's a long story, Charles, but we all have to get out of here. It's very important."

There was a brief pause. "I can't let you stay here, it's just not big enough. There is another cottage next to me that's empty, I guess you could stay there. I'll ask the owner. What's going on? Is everything all right?"

"No, it's not. Please ask him and call me back."

"Sure. Give me a minute." They hung up. Elena never moved from the phone for several minutes, until Charles called back.

"He said that's fine. Come over any time you want. I gave Chad the directions this morning."

"Thank you. Thank you so much. We'll be right there. Oh, you don't know how much this means to me." She paused. "Oh, Charles, I have no money! I can't—" She began to cry again.

He sighed. "Oh, boy! I guess I can take care of it." He saw all his money going out the window. He would have to spend everything he had, except for his per diem. This sounded as though it was an emergency. He couldn't refuse.

"Oh, Charles! Thank you!"

"You're welcome. I don't know what's going on, but I guess we can talk when you get here."

"Sure, Charles, sure." She hung up again. "Children, go pack what you need for clothes and hurry before your father gets home. I want to get out of here now!"

Chapter 21

The chief of police had followed Kenny's boat out into the bay, remaining a long distance away and keeping out of sight as much as possible, only wanting to know the direction in which the other boats traveled. He kept a keen eye on them as they worked their way around Islesboro and south of Castine. He remained about a mile away, just enough to hold the boats within his vision, and he would occasionally lose sight of them, grab his binoculars, pick up their track again and move closer, to within scope of the naked eye.

Souharat maneuvered in the skiff beside Kenny. They approached the Head of the Cape, which would be the beginning zone for their search. Maintaining a vicinity of vocal contact between the two vessels, he spoke to Kenny as they idled near the spot of his choice. "On the chart, sahib," he spoke as he struggled with the underwater metal detector, attempting to set it up, "I have broken down the search into grids that I designated as 1, 2, 3, and so forth. Each of these grids is further broken down into boat lengths. I will signal you as I work the instrument back and forth, scanning in three-foot widths, to the length of each sub-grid, approximately ten feet long. If I hear no sound from the machine in a pass of one sub-grid, I will hold up a clenched fist. You will use the blue marker on such a reading, to color this grid on the chart; this tells us there is nothing to record. I will repeat this for each ten-foot length. If I hold up one finger, color that block with the yellow marker; two fingers, the orange marker; three fingers the green marker and four fingers the red marker. Each color represents a higher signal reading from the instrument. This signifies a larger amount of metal, or element detected. When I have completed fifty such readings, you should be at the end of the first column on the chart. I then will work backwards from that spot and pass down the next column. This process will continue until we fill in all the grids with colors. This may take us several days. When we finish, if we do not hit something very big early, then we will know from the groupings of colors where to dive in the most lucrative spots. Do you understand?" He cupped his hands and placed them over his eyes, to block the sun, while looking up at Kenny.

"I think so. Blue means nothing. Yellow is one finger; orange is two fingers, and for three fingers.... Oh, I forgot!"

"Sahib, I have written it all down on the chart in the corner, in case you get confused. Do you see it?" He waited.

"Oh, yeah. O.K., no problem. You want to start now?" He studied the chart for some time.

"Remember, sahib, I will be wearing the headset and I will not be able to hear you. You must signal me that you have marked the chart after each hand signal of mine is completed. Do you understand?"

Kenny nodded.

"We begin here at the shoreline and work out; as you see, the number one is this location."

Kenny looked the chart over, noting that the Rat had done his homework well. "I'm ready!" he yelled back.

Souharat held the boat calmly in the unwavering water. The bay was perfectly still on this fine New England morning; an opportune time to perform their task at hand. He placed the headphones over his ears and tested the machine, then, once he was satisfied as to its workability, he placed the coil end into the water and lowered it by hand to the bottom of the bay. He swept the arm around the bottom perpendicular to the boat once, then shifted his position in the boat and performed the same motions from that new location. He continued until he reached the other end of the boat and then he held up his hand fully clutched tight. He looked up at Kenny and removed the headphones.

Kenny turned his vision from Rat to the chart and picked up the blue marker from the group. "Blue in grid one!" he exclaimed. "I get the idea."

The Rat smiled and nodded his head briskly with a wry grin, then shifted the boat forward, setting in place the stern, to where he had held the bow previously. He reset the receiver on his head, and they proceeded down the column of grid rectangles. As they went, their system caught into a groove, and they moved much more expediently as the time passed. It seemed a tedious procedure for Kenny, but he maintained his poise for most of the time, only occasionally becoming bored.

The chief of police turned off the engine to the patrol boat and watched the activities of the two degenerates for a long period of time. He cast his eye across the bay slovenly, espying other boats in the vicinity, but he wasn't interested in knowing if anyone could see him. That is, anyone except Kenny. Who should care that he was in the bay performing his job? After all, he was the law! No one could tell him what to do, even though he might be stretching his authority well beyond the statutes; he shouldn't be second-guessed. He was in pursuit of a murderer, and the average citizen must understand the significance of his actions. For the time being, he simply watched, contemplating his method of approach. He had positioned the patrol boat near the middle of the channel, almost a mile from the two boats off the Head of the Cape.

Jonas pushed off from the landing as the two old men rambled on in their nonsensical manner:

"That's how them diseases get here, y'know, like AIDS and SARS and that new one.... What's it called? Ah, it don't matter. They get loaded up right onto the merchant vessels from them Third World nations, then dropped off right here on our doorstep!" Sam lamented.

"Damned foreigners bring it with 'em," Andrew agreed. "They ought to spray them ships down over there before they let 'em come into our harbors!"

"It's the government tryin' to save a buck!" Sam watched Jonas getting ready to start the small engine. "Hey, Jonas!" he yelled abruptly.

Jonas's neck flicked to the side, directing his vision to the two old men. "Yeah, what?" he screamed back.

"Ya hear about that explosion last night?"

Jonas paused from what he was doing. "Explosion?"

"Ah-yup. A big one! It was at one o'them hotels in Belfast. Kenny said that fella from Rhode Island was in it!"

Jonas stood up firmly in the boat, his eyes fixed on the pier, and his lips pursed, as though he had just eaten a lemon. The wrinkled face reflected the sun with a flash of white. "Kenny said this?" His arms fell limp to the side of his body.

"It's true!" Andrew echoed. "It was on the early news this mornin'. They said they found his body, just acinder. Musta disintegrated in the heat like my ex-wife's cookies!"

The two old men giggled and coughed then each one looked downward and gently kicked the end of the pier.

"I didn't hear about it!" He sat back down and tugged at his earlobe, then scratched his bearded chin. "Hmph!"

He didn't need the lobster boat today, just the skiff. That was all he anticipated to use for the time being, until he found out what was developing. He slipped out of Searsport Harbor quietly and quickly, entering the open channel within a short period of time. In the distance, he lost sight of McFagan, then he could barely make him out. There was a secret aura surrounding the chief's conduct—he was up to no good—he felt it! He idled his craft, reached down inside the netted pocket attached to the inside of the boat and removed a pair of binoculars. He drifted in the calm water, allowing the boat to maneuver itself, as he placed the binoculars to his eyes, pointing them in the direction of the chief, and to his amazement, the chief was also using binoculars; gazing to the east. Jonas decided that it would be best if he hid. He spotted a deep inlet at the west bank of Cape Rosier, north of Orr Cove and south of Harborside. When he approached the point, jetting out into the bay, he glanced in the direction that the chief had been perusing. He now saw what McFagan was looking at—Kenny's boat; miniscule in the distance, it seemed to be anchored, but that could be just from the mere separation between him and the other boat. He squinted in an attempt to judge movement, but he could not detect any. He pulled the skiff up to the shore by Orr Cove, turned off the engine after building up enough momentum to coast the vessel onto the beach, where he picked up the outboard and slid onto the gravelly sand. He jumped off the boat and pulled it on the beach as far as he could so as not to be affected by the tide or any waves that might pop up. He walked south along the shoreline, keeping an eye on the chief of police and one on Kenny, switching his vision between the two. All three boats were motionless in the water. He stealthily hustled along the shore, staying close to the tree line to remain unnoticed, watching the three vessels as he went. He had traveled far enough now to see Kenny standing upright in his boat, his head bowed, staring into a chart, making notes. He could not see what the chief was doing, however, but neither one was paying attention to anything other than what was in front of them. He stopped and got comfortable against a spruce tree, manipulating his binoculars from a much nearer distance than he held previously. He saw the small skiff of Kenny's moving slowly around the larger boat, with the Rat at the helm, holding the metal detector in his hands. Now, he realized what was going on. This was the location of the treasure! In his heart of hearts, he knew the Rat would figure it out. The chief must be on an arrest mode of some sort. He watched humbly, sitting statuesque, unmoving, so as not to be discovered.

The small skiff, guided by the Rat, shifted once more, and the plotting of Kenny's went on, until McFagan dropped his binoculars and started the engine of the patrol boat, heading directly to the Cape and the two. He moved pensively, at half throttle, watching the two men work in their languid fashion. Kenny and the Rat were so absorbed in their efforts that they never even noticed him approaching. He shifted into audible range, and even the sound of the engine did not distract the two. It was too simple, the chief thought. He reached into his holster and removed his pistol, holding it in his right hand while he steered the boat with his left.

So caught up with the dreams of riches and faraway places, the two journeymen paid no heed to the oncoming threat. They diligently charted the area for later use, until the chief cleared his throat in an effort to gain their attention.

"Ahem!" He was close enough for both of them to hear.

Kenny's head spun around like an owl's in the search of prey, when the slightest noise might represent dinner. The Rat, who just peered up to signal Kenny, snapped his head upward upon seeing the lawman, like a dolphin signaling the keeper in a water show.

"Ahem! How ya doin', boys?" McFagan cried in a reedy voice. "Souharat. Anythin' bitin' on the end of that fishin' pole?" They had been caught red-handed, and the chief proudly showed the gun to the two, letting them know who held the upper hand.

Kenny's lips pursed and Souharat's mouth dropped open, startled by the intrusion. He ripped off the headphones and tossed them down to the bilge of the boat. Kenny dropped the chart while the chief waved the pistol carelessly in the air and puffed his chest out arrogantly. "Now, the way I see it, boys, ya ain't really doin' much fishing today, are ya?"

Kenny stammered, "We ain't hurtin' no one, Chet, we're just out playin' a little." His voice was faint and abstract. "Ain't no harm in that, is there?"

McFagan grinned and laughed silently, inhaling as he did. "No. No, ain't no harm in that. But there is harm in murderin' people, y'know."

"What d'ya mean, Chet? We ain't murderin' nobody. We're just out playin', y'know, havin' fun."

"I didn't say ya was out murderin'—that ya already did, and I got proof!" His demeanor was staunch and overpowering; both men crumbled at the words.

"Proof? What kinda proof?"

"Well, ya know ol' Miss Bradbury—the lady that never got married, and lives over in Stockton?"

"Yeah, I think so. What about her?" This was all very confusing to Kenny, and he couldn't imagine where it was leading.

"Well, it seems that she owns more than that little house she lives in. She's got property over by Sandy Point near the water. Not only that, she's quite the tree lover. She likes 'em so much that she goes out all year long plantin' trees. A couple of days ago, she went to dig a spot up out there on Sandy Point and ended up diggin' up a body!" He snickered ingratiatingly, with the knowledge of having the two of them under his thumb. "The Stockton police gave us a call. They identified the body as that of one Todd Seekins, seems he had a hand bit off by some kinda fish after he was shot!"

The chief's complexion was grave, and his face became vivaciously serious. "Looks like he caught it in the chest from a shotgun, y'know, Kenny, like the one ya own!" He pointed his gun directly at Kenny.

"Now, wait a minute, Chief!" The words reformed themselves, and he choked, coughing violently. He turned to Souharat and growled, shaking his head. The Rat raised his shoulders up to his ears and gritted his teeth.

"Oh, don't worry, I got more evidence than that. Seems ya boys been pretty busy—ya been rackin' up bodies all over the place."

"Now, ya can't prove it was us, Chet. Ya know us, we're the salt of the community, upstanding citizens."

"Ya the scum of the Earth! Now, I'm gonna ask ya politely, Kenny; Hold ya right hand in the air and reach real slow like, below ya and take hold of that shotgun with ya left hand, then hold it up in the air for me to see. Remember, I can pick off a flea's nose at fifty yards with this." He shook the pistol doggedly, bestowing a fit of irritation.

"Sure, sure, Chet! Just be easy with that; no need for anybody to get hurt. We ain't doin' no harm here, and we'll cooperate. Anything for you, Chief." Perspiration broke on the edge of his brow as he leaned forward, holding his right hand above him, and produced the shotgun with the other. He eased the weapon above his head. "Here ya go, Chief, I don't want no trouble."

The chief shifted to the bow of his boat and reached over to Kenny's. "Now, hand it to me!" His voice was gruff.

Kenny tenderly leaned forward in his boat and only stepped slightly, in order to reach the Chief's outstretched hand. The transfer of the weapon went smoothly, and McFagan set it down inside his boat. "Now, there. That was simple enough!"

Kenny lowered his hands. "What do ya want, Chief? We ain't doin' nothin'." He was begging.

"Well, boys, I ain't here to arrest ya. No, no, no. I'm here to make a deal with ya!"

Kenny shifted his weight to the balls of his feet, and he stood on his toes. His head tipped sideways as if he didn't really hear the man properly. "A deal?" he murmured from the side of his mouth. "What kinda deal ya talkin' about?"

McFagan relaxed and in a low, hoarse voice said, "Ya don't have to pretend. I know all about the treasure and why ya killed those people. Seems to me, there's got to be quite a bit of it there for you to go to such extreme measures. But the way I figure it, there's more than enough for just the Rat and ya and I can't see how ya gonna get away with it—without some help!" He laughed harshly.

"Treasure, Chief?" He acted dumb.

"Oh, don't bother playin' games! I know all about it. As much as ya do, maybe even more, I reckon." The smile disappeared from his countenance. "Don't get me wrong, Mr. Buckner; I've got enough on ya and ya little turban-headed goon, to put the two of ya away till the bay dries up! Then I'll have the whole damned treasure to myself! But like I said, I'm willin' to make a deal." He leaned forward, propping one foot up on the edge of the boat and resting both forearms on his heightened knee.

Kenny struggled for words, and a loophole. "Ya ain't even in Waldo County anymore. This here bein' Hancock County. Ya ain't got no authority out here, or on the water either."

"Ha!" He pointed the weapon in his hand directly at Kenny's head. "This is my authority! I carry weight in these parts—everybody knows who I am, and if the Coast Guard gets involved, I know how to work 'em. There ain't nobody else knows about these murders, except them in Stockton. I told 'em I'd take care of the matter, seein' that Todd hails from Searsport. I told 'em that I'm still lookin' for his next of kin, and I don't want nothin' leaked out to the press just yet. Ya see, I'm taking care of the public, and I'll let the two of ya take care of finding this treasure and getting' rid of it. We'll split the whole damn thing, three ways. That's the deal, and if I were ya, I'd be thinkin' it's a pretty good deal—one ya can't hardly resist! We'll both benefit from it." He turned to Souharat. "How long before ya think ya locate the mother lode?" His behavior was all business now.

The Rat, so far content with simply listening, snapped to attention. "Ah … ah … I can not tell for sure, but if it is where I believe it is, we may find it today, or at the most, one week from today. If it is not in the area I have designated, we would have to reassess the possibilities. I am confident, however, that it is here, near where we are."

"Let's see; a week at the most. I can hold off the public until then. How big an area have ya designated, Rat?"

He scratched his head. "Based on all of the evidence with very little speculation, I have narrowed it down to a quarter-mile diameter to where we should definitely find something. This arrangement of yours sounds very helpful. I think, Kenny, we should agree with this proposal." He turned to his right to look at Kenny, who never moved.

Kenny was studying the chief, from top to bottom. *The corrupt bastard wants to hone in on what is mine.* His thoughts became contorted, and his mind slipped back to the basic elements which drove his being and placed him in this position. "Yeah, Rat, it does sound good. Why don't ya point out the area here that ya think we'll find it, to the chief. Ya know, to give 'im an idea of what we're lookin' at, for time and all."

McFagan shifted his attention to the Rat, who pointed to their beginning of their search and announced the remaining search area, slowly pointing over the scene. The chief watched his arm navigate over the water at full length while the Rat described the time scale. He was relaxed, still resting his arms on his knee while he followed the motions of the Indian; the gun rested limply in his hand, pointed down at the water.

Kenny saw the opportunity! He instantly reached down to the shelf in the boat below him, raised the revolver with the silencer on it, aimed at the chief of police and fired the gun three times in succession. The first bullet struck McFagan in the right shoulder, twisting his body backwards; the second landed firmly in his chest, and the third caught him somewhere above his clavicle, toppling him backwards and overboard into the bay below. Kenny stood motionless, the hot weapon tightly gripped in his hand.

Souharat jumped at the sound of the *pfffts* emitting from the gun then turned quickly to watch the chief flop into the water. Kenny waited for what seemed forever, then he began to chortle, lowly, harshly, building up to an indolent guffaw. It was a knee-slapping, belly-aching guffaw.

The Rat watched in silence, until the laughter pierced through him, and the realization of the act performed was thoroughly comprehended. Then he, too, laughed boisterously. Kenny wiped his forehead with the sleeve of his shirt, "Whew! That was close! The damned fool, wantin' me to split the treasure with him! Damned fool! He had too much on us, Rat, to trust 'im. Ya think we'd have split that three ways? The damned fool—he don't know who he's dealin' with!"

Souharat ceased his laughter. "It would have been nice to have the protection, though. It will be difficult for us to get out of town now. We must find this treasure as quickly as possible before more such meetings occur."

Kenny's laughter turned into a few heavy breaths and some final laughs. He looked over to the Rat. "Sandy Point? How stupid can ya get? I told ya, don't bury 'em near the water. Damn, Rat, ya screw up everythin'!"

He pulled his shoulders up to his ears again. "It looked deserted, sahib. The digging was easy and I did not know of this tree lady."

"'Course the diggin' was easy! Why d'ya think that's where she wanted to plant her damn tree? The tree-huggin' bitch! Curse her!" He glanced back over to the police patrol boat. "O.K. now, Rat, let's think. We've got to get rid of this boat, and the chief's body. This time I want 'im weighed down and sunk—and the boat with 'im. That'll give us time. They won't even know he's missin' for a week or so. We should be sippin' margaritas by then. C'mon and give me a hand. I'm a little edgy right now. That was too close for comfort. We'll sink him in the deep part of the channel and call it a day, then get an early start tomorrow."

"Yes, sahib. We have done much for one day as it is. If we keep this pace, the area will be complete within three days. How does the chart look?"

Kenny reached down and picked it up. "We got a lot of blue around the edges; some yellow around the blue; and orange here and there. Then we got a group of green, all together, surrounded by three grids of red, right where ya are. We must be getting' close!"

"Yes, sahib, we may see what I want to see tomorrow. I will mark this spot with a small buoy which can not be seen from shore. Look, see how close this is to shore? Retracting the treasure should not be a problem!" The two men laughed silently, and smiles cracked through their sun-baked faces. "Let us dispose of the body and boat. The closer we get, the more my nerves affect me."

"Me, too!" Kenny confirmed.

Jonas watched the entire incident involving the chief in a minor state of shock. He had returned to his feet and pressed his back against the spruce, whose protruding roots he had used as a seat, espying the incident. McFagan had been eliminated! This boded well with him, but he realized that Kenny and the Rat would soon depart the area for the day. He didn't want to take the chance of their seeing him there, so he shot off back north, the way he came, except this time he held the tree line closer than before, to remain hidden as much as possible. Now that their attention had been swung from treasure hunting to covering up murder, the two men he was watching would surely be more aware of who else was anywhere nearby. He fell into a gaping trot and reached Randy's skiff quickly. He pushed off shore and started the engine, returning to the landing unnoticed and well ahead of the others.

Chapter 22

Jonas panted heavily as he threw open the door to his house, thumping it loudly against the interior wall. The doorknob struck the already shattered circle of dry-wall; the hole being only slightly larger than the knob, from many such previous collisions. Clinging on to the portion of knob connected to the opposite side of the door, he stopped abruptly and gawked throughout the dwelling. No sounds could be heard, nor could any activity be seen. His chest swelled and then contracted; a brief sigh released. He gently shut the door behind him and walked to the bottom of the stairwell. "Chad? Katherine? Is anybody home?"

There was no response. "Hmph!" He brushed back the tangled outcroppings of hair on his head with both hands then tugged at his whiskers with his right. His face clamped tightly, emphasizing the forlorn crevices, dominant on his visage. As he stood silently, mulling over the scenario, he noticed the small grandfather clock positioned against the wall. "Elena?" he whispered, and his facial wrinkles disappeared. "She's back?"

He shuffled his feet without picking them up, to the refrigerator, and looked inside at the new assortment of foodstuffs. "Hmph!" he growled and shut the door, spun and meandered over to access the cabinet where he kept his libations. He reached the end of the table when the phone rang. He halted in mid-stride, snapping his head towards the clattering of the phone which broke the dead silence then paced himself over and picked up the receiver.

"Yeah?" he answered.

"Hello, Jonas. This is Charles. How did your day go?" he annunciated in an upbeat, elf-like voice.

"Charlie? I heard ya were dead!" he said doggedly. "What happened to ya last night?"

"Oh, I'm all right! That's all that counts. I'm getting used to being the target in Maine's version of 'The Running Man!' I was targeted for some midnight fireworks, but I avoided the *grand finale*! If you know what I mean! I read that they found an incendiary device near my door."

Jonas tittered under his breath. "Kenny and the Rat, no doubt! That reminds me; I know what Kenny's up to—he's on the mark for that treasure ya mentioned. Damned if it don't look like he knows where it is."

Charles's ears bounced upward, and his entire body stretched. "Really? Where's that?" His tone changed.

"Ah ... um ... ah ... well, I can't be sure, I'm gonna see where he goes tomorrow." He bit his lip and squinted, unable, for whatever reason, to release that information—even to Charles!

"That's fine." He spoke indifferently. "I wanted to let you know that, well, I'm sorry, but I'm afraid that Elena's aunt passed away last night." He waited for some sort of empathetic response and was prepared to deliver words of condolence.

His wait was in vain, so he continued. "She came back from Millinocket to get the kids and asked me to call you and tell you that she has to return to Millinocket tomorrow. She and the children will be the only ones there representing the family." There was an unrehearsed sincerity to his words.

"She's back? I knew it! Where is she now?" His wide shoulders reared backwards, stretching his chest outward and his torso propped up. He fondled his whiskers with his right hand, rolling his extended fingers through his beard, one finger at a time.

"She's got a room for the night—to rest. She's had a long week and wants to get a good night's sleep before returning to greet the mourners. I'm sorry about your loss, Jonas; it must be difficult having them both go at the same time like that." He spoke passionately.

"Yeah, yeah, yeah! It's too bad," he said hurridly. "Why can't she talk to me? Why did she have to have ya do the callin'?"

"She tried to call all day, and now she's taking a nap. She's been at quite a pace. She took the kids so they can leave directly from her room, early in the morning."

"Hmph! So, that's the way it is! I see. I s'pose I gotta fix my own dinner!" He grunted loudly then paused. "Oh, I forgot to tell ya. Ya ain't gotta worry about Chief McFagan harassing ya anymore—he's dead!"

"Huh?" The response sounded like the air brake on a locomotive, nestling to an abrupt stop. "Dead?"

"Yeah, dead! Kenny got 'im. I saw it. I'd say that ya better watch yaself around him and the Rat, but they think ya're dead. I heard it at the pier, but I'd still watch my back if I were ya. I'll be usin' Randy's skiff tomorrow, if that's all right with ya, unless, of course, ya got a plan to use it."

The phone was sharply quiet. "I don't think I'll need it tomorrow; I've got some things to take care of on shore. My van took quite a beating in the blast, and I'm going to need more work done on it before I head back home to

Rhode Island."

"Ah-yup. Good, then. When d'ya think ya gonna need that boat back?" He cringed, figuring out his timetable.

"Ah, let's see; today's Friday. School starts on Tuesday. I've got to get those pots out of the bay. I'll tell you what—you keep it tomorrow, I'll talk to the dean and work out a plan. I figure I'll need it by Sunday."

"Yeah, O.K., call me tomorrow night."

"That's for sure. Bye."

Early is a relative term; to a banker, 9:00a.m. is early and to a lobsterman, 9:00a.m. is late. Jonas woke early to the datum of both; at 4:30a.m. This morning, he went to the large storage closet situated below the stairwell and picked up his gear and an underwater flashlight. After running these items out to the truck, he returned inside and hurried through his morning rituals, grabbing clothes and a quick snack from inside the refrigerator, which he ate before heading out the door. A light breeze blew across his face, making a chilly morning rather cold. He drew the collar of his shirt tightly around his neck. The two seasons of spring and autumn had a way of keeping a Mainer guessing on what to wear. It might be cold in the morning and blistering hot in the afternoon, producing such clichés as "If you don't like the weather here, just wait a minute." Jonas knew that the breeze on the water was usually more intense than the sheltered land breeze, but he wore clothing that could be easily removed when necessary. He jumped into his truck and headed to the Searsport landing as fast as the truck would go.

The piers were empty and the area deserted as he pulled into the parking lot off Cottage Street and backed down the landing into the shallow water. He got out of the truck and set the boat into the harbor, tying it up along the edge of the wharf. He drove his truck along Cottage Street and parked around the corner on the side of the road out of sight from the landing, but far enough off the road that no one would complain. He walked back and boarded the boat, pushed off the pier and started the engine after lowering it into the deeper waters. The sun wouldn't rise for another hour or so, and there was a light covering of clouds which made the bay look gloomy—mysterious and black! He eased the boat out of the harbor, using the flashlight to guide him past the moorings and the buoys until he reached the outer portion of the harbor and, eventually, the channel. He proceeded cautiously, keeping an eye open for stray, randomly placed traps as he traveled towards Castine. He passed Turtle Head on Islesboro and turned southward in the direction of Cape Rosier. His mode was slow and deliberate, being in no great hurry; it took him longer than usual to pass

Coombs Point when the sky illuminated nearly instantly. This was the prelude to sunrise, which didn't occur until after 6:00a.m. officially. As his eyesight increased, so did his velocity through the lower channel of the Penobscot River. He passed Harborside, motored around the Head of the Cape then pulled into Redman Beach, where he coasted up to shore and vaulted over the bow into the short, breaking waves. Only his feet got wet as he jerked the length of the boat onto the sandy shore; bow, hull and stern, then rotated the small craft parallel to the shore line. It sat inoffensively in that harmless state, beyond the view from any stray eyes anchored off the Head of the Cape and its surrounding waters, unless the region being searched extended south of the Cape.

He walked due north until he reached Ames Cove Road and followed the street, west to Point Road, all the way to a row of evergreens, just shy of the western shore of the Cape. Here he could see the beach, the bay and the region which Kenny and the Rat so carefully examined the day before. He made himself comfortable in a minor clearing that did not block his panoramic vista but disallowed any type of reciprocating view. He sat between the dried bark roots of a tall pine tree. He plucked the slab of chewing tobacco from within his pocket, sliced off a piece, stuck it in his mouth, chomped on it noiselessly, and waited.

The sun had overpowered what remained of the chill in the air, and the trace amounts of dew clinging on the surrounding ground disappeared, except in the shadows, below the trees. It didn't take long for Jonas to see what he expected. Kennys's boat and the skiff pulled up together, side by side, near the exact same location of their latest crime, and Kenny dropped some sort of anchor to hold the larger boat in place. They both cut their engines off. From where he had perched, Jonas could hear the conversation from the two, in part due to the thinness of the surrounding atmosphere, and also the lack of any other noises within audible range.

"Here is the buoy, sahib." Souharat pointed to the small, capped bottle floating in the short waves. His voice was just a whisper, battling the *whoosh* of the light breezes that drifted through the foliage.

"Ah, good, Rat!" Kenny's words were much louder. "Do I dive now?" His complexion was slightly pale, and it grew red when he spoke. He was standing on the deck of his boat, poised and erect, awaiting the small Indian to respond.

Souharat grunted. "First, we check the immediate area around yesterday's readings. I wish to be sure that our discovery was not just a freakish hunk of metal from the ship's wreckage like a cannon, a swivel gun, and some other sort of armament or anything else made of metal which would be useless to us." He played with the underwater metal detector as he spoke, connecting the shaft to the coil, snapping together the wire connections then adding the second, supplemental pole and connecting it. "From the charts, sahib, you will find our final reading from yesterday, before the ... um ... accident. It should be colored red."

Kenny bent over and picked up the chart, reviewed it. "Yeah, I got it. We were working our way out away from the shore on a forward pass with sweeps." His self-derived locutions for their method of search contained the words 'forward pass,' meaning traveling away from shore; 'backward pass' entailed heading towards shore; and 'sweep,' the three foot search parallel to shore at each of Souharat's stalled positions in the skiff. Like all true fishermen, the nomenclature changed with every new function he performed. "Y'know," he said, "we covered quite a chunk of area in one day!"

"Not even a full day, sahib!" Souharat reminded him. "But also remember, this treasure may be spread out over a large distance due to the centuries of tides and currents which have passed since its unfortunate fate abandoned it here."

Kenny covered his right ear with the palm of his right hand. "If ya take stock in what Bill Rowlin said, then the treasure's all in the same spot, that is, if he saw lots of it like they mentioned."

"Perhaps! We do not know yet." He completed the assembly of the detector and dropped the coil edge into the water. "It is the same procedure as yesterday." Kenny nodded, and the Rat adjusted the headphones over his ears. He performed his first 'sweep' of the day at the base of the buoy he set the day before, then worked his way along the boat until he reached the next setup. They plodded along in this same, monotonous manner for hours on end; but time flew by.

Jonas shifted his position several times on the uneven ground where he sat, in an attempt to get comfortable. He snorted and grumbled to himself, "At least they're doin' somethin'! Well, I ain't gonna wait forever." He stood up and stretched, yawning broadly, then he wiped his eyes. "And I'm getting hungry!"

"Whoa!" Souharat screamed, above any other sound on the water. "Sahib, I have something!" He pulled the underwater metal detector out of the water and onto the boat, setting it down horizontally inside the vessel. The instrument banged loudly as he let it fall. He rubbed his hands together and stood upright, lifting his feet off the flooring of the dinghy in a type of dance. His eyes bulged out—wide open!

Kenny dropped the chart to the deck and inclined forward, resting his hands on the rear shelf of his boat, his arms outstretched. "What? What is it, Rat? What have ya got?"

Souharat placed his hands on his knees, panting spasmodically, and coughing every so often. He held his hand up over his head with the palm extended flatly to Kenny. He cleared his throat and placed his hands on his hips. "Excuse me, sahib."

"C'mon with it, Rat! What d'ya find?" He shook his upper body with impatience.

Souharat cleared his throat again and shook his head. He pointed to specific areas in the water as he spoke, "Over there, sahib, is a large depression in the bottom of the bay. It drops sharply to a much greater depth, but I could not tell how deep; the pole will not reach the very bottom. The abyss stretches over thirty feet and is very narrow. On the sides of the trench are a series of rocks which crop up in an irregular pattern. I can tell they are rocks when I hit them with the detector, I receive no reading and yet they are solid, for the end of the machine gives way to their bulk. I moved the detector over these rocks, and found another underwater depression between them. It is here, sahib, that my detector goes wild with noise. I thought my head would explode. My ears still ring!" He placed his pinky fingers in his ears, twisted them in a circular motion, closed his eyes and gritted his teeth. Returning to his normal pose, he continued: "My guess, sahib, is that this ship that sank, lies over much of the floor of the bay. Not just here does it lie, but all over. It must have been damaged severely before it came this far, and only the hull of the vessel came to rest in this spot. We are lucky for this, I think. You see, this must be the treasure, held within the hull, wedged between these rocks below the water surface! It must be so! From what I have detected thus far, these rocks form a huge protective circle where the hull of the ship got stuck, and where the treasure has been wedged for such a long time."

Kenny lurched sideways, his whole body quivering. His head whipped back, and his eyes turned towards the heavens. He held his arms away from his body with the palms of his hands turned upward. "Yes!" he hollered. "Yes!" He drew his right hand into a fist and punched the naked air. "Yes!"

The light breeze tossed Kenny's hair into his face, and that brief distraction brought him to the moment at hand. "Rat, did ya bring my divin' gear?"

"It is in the lower deck, hanging up where you placed it, sahib." He motioned towards the front of the boat.

"Yeah, that's right." He shifted from his position near the starboard side of the boat and traversed to the small opening inside the pilot house. The scuba gear hung on the wall, complete except for the tank, which lay on the floor. Kenny studied the arrangement. "Hey!" he barked. "Somebody's been into my gear! The tank's separated."

"Yes, sahib, I took the precaution of ensuring that your tank was full, but observing that it was not, and to expedite matters, I took the prerogative to replace it last night. I hope I did not overstep my bounds, sahib." He rubbed his hands together and grinned with a pitiful smirk.

"It was out? Well, then, I'm glad ya changed it. Hell, I didn't think it was even low on air. It's all good. Now, c'mon up here and help me get suited." His solid façade radiated with anticipation. "Ya did ya job, Rat, but now it's my turn. No more notebooks, no more charts; now it's fins and a mask. Ya done good, my little turban-headed pimple!"

"Yes, sahib. I have done my job well. You will see, I have done my job very well!" His arms had returned to his side, and he threw out one of the oars to hook onto the larger vessel, then pulled the skiff towards it. The two boats bounced together, making a soft bang. Kenny produced the diving gear onto the main deck and lifted the suit in the air to examine it. Souharat climbed into the larger boat, tying the smaller skiff to one of the cleats on the starboard shelf.

Jonas could not hear the entire conversation but could surmise the outcome. He pounced towards the beach, in plain sight of the two in the boats. Their attention had been drawn by an unknown force; a cause for elation and celebration. He summarily determined that was the only reason for the change in their behavior; they must have found the treasure! He had no time to waste, so he pivoted back to the forest behind and ran through the flora at breakneck speed. Kenny brought out his suit, which meant he would be entering the water alone. Jonas calculated that this would allow him time to approach the two vessels, with only one man to confront. The greed drove him forward to his own boat, and the possible scenarios obstructed his train of thought. It didn't matter to him at this juncture, he simply needed to get there before Kenny surfaced, if, indeed, he would dive now.

He arrived at Randy's small boat expeditiously, pushed it into the water in haste, and jumped inside. The boat was still floating backwards when he lowered the outboard and started the engine. It hummed gracefully as he revved the throttle. He twisted the hand grip and propelled forward, around the Head of the Cape, and headed towards the two other boats.

Kenny had slipped into the wet suit and was adjusting it, along with the gloves and the flippers. Souharat placed the tank on him, with the regulator and the connecting hoses, and checked them to ensure that they weren't tangled. He lifted up Kenny's regulator and set it back down on his chest.

Kenny pushed his arm away. "I know how to suit up, ya stupid little cull!" He gave Souharat a nefarious, long stare. His eyes burned into the Indian's face, then he turned back to inspect his instrumentation; the pressure gauge, depth gauge, the dive watch and compass. All components checked satisfactorily. He slid the mask over his head and climbed into the water, over the starboard side, holding on to the edge of the skiff. He removed the mask, spit into it to seal it and adjusted it over his eyes. He held his underwater flashlight in his hand and a diving knife tied onto his suit. He gave a thumbs up to Souharat, then placed the mouthpiece in and dove down into the stagnant blue water, disappearing from sight.

Souharat leaned back and crossed his arms, cuddling his own body, and rubbing triceps. He began a hoarse, shallow, gurgling snigger. "Who is the fool, now?!" he blurted out loud. "Hahaha! Who is the idiot now?!" His snickering turned into an exuberant laugh, and his chest puffed in and out, the air emitting through his nasal passage.

Kenny descended through the water nearly vertically, with only a short shift to the large rock area he could see as he went. The formation was exactly what the Rat had described; sharp, ragged outcroppings of rock formed a circular pattern stretching for as far as he could see, heading away from the shore. Various other crags, isolated boulders and stones dotted the top of the landscape of the bottom of the bay. He swam to the moon-like rock grouping. He began to get dizzy as he went, and his head throbbed with a fierce pounding that made him stop several times. He looked to his left and saw the deep depression the Rat had spoken of. It contained the ribs of a wooden craft, despoiled by years below the water, but uncovered for some strange reason. The bottom of the bay was mostly sand, and he deduced that most of the sunken boat was buried. It was odd that this piece had remained uncovered for so long. He continued to swim past the wreckage; then, he saw it! As he reached the first range of rocks, he made out the edge of a large chest, and the cover was slightly ajar. Looking inside, he saw the treasure, just as Bill and Todd said; there was tons of it! To the opposite side of the first chest, there was another, and another! The height of the rock group prevented the sand at the bottom of the bay to cover these up, though they did have some sand jammed between the crates and the rocks. The inside of the rock circle was totally filled with sand.

His heart beat randomly, and his eyes blurred. He became confused, and felt nauseous. He grabbed his head in pain. Something was wrong! He lost the ability to breathe. He gagged and coughed inside the mouthpiece then vomited. Then, he fell into an unconscious state.

Souharat watched the last of the bubbles float to the surface where Kenny had dove. He sustained the low, heinous laughter, until the last of the bubbles vanished, then he broke into an unrestrained, boisterous, all-out laugh. He fell into a chaotic euphoria and began to ramble out loud, staring at the top of the water.

"*Who* is the fool?! Hey? Who is the idiot?! Ha! I do all the thinking! I do all the work! What do I get in return? I get laughed at, and insulted! Ha! There will be no more, 'Rat, do this,' and 'Rat, do that.' Rat, bury this body. Rat, kill this one!

"Now, who has the treasure? Now, who is the boss? Haha! 'Rat cannot do anything right'? Ha! This! This, I have done right! Hahaha! I knew I could win your trust, Kenny Buckner! Is this the act of a fool? Now, who is the fool? Enjoy your last breaths, dear Kenny. Carbon monoxide works very quickly. Ha! I know how to mix the gases just right, so you could not tell. Is this the mind of a fool? I do not think so, Kenny Buckner! You! You are the fool, and the treasure is all mine! Hahaha!" He had stretched his hands outward and spoke to the water, as though he was talking to his victim.

Unexpectedly, he heard a bang, and the boat shifted. He staggered at the sudden movement of the vessel, attempting to retain his balance. He turned around and saw Jonas standing up in Randy's skiff, abutting the fishing boat he was in. His eyebrows rose in shock, and his chin lowered. "Jonas! What … why…. What are you doing here?" His words were shaky, and his body trembled.

Jonas stood calmly with one foot propped up on edge of the boat, and his sunburned face radiated in a pleasant visage. He was holding a pistol in his hand, staring at the Rat scornfully. "Hello, Rat! It appears I don't have to worry about Kenny no more." He looked over the Indian's shoulder and snapped his head up and down, signaling him to look in that direction.

Souharat turned around.

Kenny had floated up to the surface on his back, with his arms stretched out over the water. The mouthpiece had dislodged from his suit, or was ripped out, and vomit was stuck to the rubber portion, as well as a pool of puke floating beside his head. They checked into his face through the mask. It was bright red and held the gruesome signs of death; poison or drowning, it didn't matter; it was an ugly sight. Souharat coughed and gagged at the spectacle, then spun his attention back to Jonas.

"My only regret, Rat, is that ya couldn't take care of that fella from Rhode Island. That would leave me as the only one who knows about this treasure."

"The one from Rhode Island lives?" He leaned against the rail; his back to it. His hands gripped the edge.

LOBSTER TRAPPED!

"I talked to him this mornin'. Ha! Ya blew it, again!" He turned his eye back to the floating carcass of Kenny. "Ya did a good job on that one, though, Rat. It was nice and quiet, and I bet he didn't even suspect a thing. Ya are a cool customer! And a very dangerous one! Where did ya get the carbon monoxide?"

The Rat glanced towards Sears Island and the loading cranes. "The piers hold many things, sahib; useful to those who know how to manipulate their strength." His chest bloated outward in pride. "I am a man of resources. I could be a very valuable partner with you, my friend."

"Who cares?" He pointed the gun at him.

"No, no, wait, please, sahib. A moment of your time, and I believe we can work out a compromise. We can share the treasure! I know you know what I have found. I am reasonable. You are a smart man, and I have great faith in you. Like I said, I am a man of many resources. I can help you, and you can help me. You also will need help, as would I. I have meant to ask for your help for some time, but you see, I had to dispose of Kenny first. I was caught up in...." The usual verbal manipulation of the immigrant didn't work on the crafty, street-smart lobsterman.

Jonas didn't bother to hear the rest. He pulled the trigger on the revolver and the Rat tumbled overboard, floating beside the corpse of Kenny Buckner. The bullet from the weapon hit him in the forehead, directly above his nose. Jonas laughed to see the small hole spurt out red blood in so tiny a spot.

He tied his skiff up to a cleat on the larboard side of Kenny's craft, climbed over into Kenny's boat, then into the smaller skiff, already tied to the side. He reached out and pulled both bodies to him, picking them up one at a time and tumbling them over into the skiff. He then manned Kenny's controls and headed out to the open waters, dragging the skiffs with him, and the bodies inside.

Chapter 23

"Chad, Chad! Come on, get up. We've got to get ready and get going." Elena poked him as he lay, rolled up comfortably under the covers of the single bed. Katherine had already risen and was resetting the linens and bedspread on the bed she had slept in the previous night. Elena's bed was already completely made. The cabin was exactly what she wanted; it consisted of three rooms and a bathroom. The first room was large; used as a small kitchen, living and dining area. A stove, a refrigerator, counters and a sink outlined the far left wall as one entered through the front door, making up the kitchen area. An eating table had been set up to the right of there, used as a dining area. A long couch and two cushioned chairs surrounding a coffee table and the television in the corner completed the living area. There were no walls differentiating the areas. Windows overlooking the bay were stationed on the far right wall, giving a spectacular view of Belfast Bay. Smaller windows were positioned at various locations; the scenery through those, however, was just a view of the cottages within the complex. Nautical decorations and pictures hung on the walls to give the average tourist the taste of Maine that they expected. Two bedrooms were separated by the bathroom in between. Elena slept in the large double-wide bed in the master bedroom, and the children took the two smaller beds in the second, smaller bedroom.

Chad moaned, "In a minute, Ma." He turned over to his other side.

Elena stood over him, without moving. "Come on, Chad. The wake is at 10:00 a.m. and I told Mrs. Blake I would be there early to make sure everything was all right. Let's go! I'm not going to tell you again!"

"Good!" he yelled, and he rustled through the sheets to find a more tranquil position. He set the pillow over his exposed ear, blocking out the rude interruption to his slumber.

Elena had enough! She grabbed hold of the bedspread and the sheets in one hand and gave a tremendous yank, pulling everything off Chad, who now sat up in bed.

"Hey! What are you doing?" He rubbed his eyes.

"I told you—we have to get going." She was visibly perturbed. "I want the two of you to bring your church clothes, today. Oh, dear, I hope they're clean. Don't put them on until we get there." She paced through the room, gathering up her own apparel. "Now, come on, Chad, you have to make your bed, too."

He yawned and stretched, "What time is it?"

"It's nearly 4:00a.m., almost time to leave." She had arranged her own attire and was now picking up miscellaneous trash and debris, tidying up, prior to leaving. "I have made coffee, I guess you guys can have some. It'll help you wake up a little."

Katherine picked her nose up in the air. "Mmmm, it sure smells good, ma." The aromatic blend filled the small structure and even got Chad to stand up.

"It does smell good. We never get to have coffee." He was more eager to rise now.

"Who's Mrs. Blake, Ma?" Katherine tried to recall.

"Oh, you've met her. She's the nurse who was taking care of Uncle Steve for so long when I couldn't be there and then she stayed with Aunt Julie up until the end. The two of us made all the arrangements for today, so I don't want her to take the burden of making sure everything is ready before the guests arrive. Flowers and the caterer will arrive early; around 7:00 a.m., and I'd like to be there before that, to help set up the chairs and the tables. I want to leave in a few minutes, so let's hustle up, the two of you."

"Where are you having the wake, Ma?" Katherine inquired.

"Aunt Julie wanted it right in the house. She stayed so calm just before...." Her actions became temperate. "Well, that's where she asked that it take place, and frankly, I think it's a good idea. The funeral director had taken her body to his establishment and was going to prepare her yesterday to bring her back last night. I hope that's all been done. We'll see once we get up there. Have a cup of coffee and we're going to have to leave soon." She paused and looked around the cabin. There was nothing left for her to do except get dressed; the cabin was spotless. "We're all going to take showers and get properly dressed when we get there. It will be a long day. It takes two and a half hours to get there, and we'll be coming back today. If you want, you can sleep on the ride there, but I'd like to get on the road as soon as possible."

Chad tossed on the clothes he had worn the day before over his briefs. "What about breakfast?" he wearily asked, still blinking to gain his bearings.

"We can stop in Bangor and grab something." She poured three cups of coffee. "In the meantime, you can survive on this." She handed a cup to

Chad, who accepted it enthusiastically and drew it close to his nose, sniffing in the fragrance before taking a sip. Katherine did the same. Elena picked up the bags she had packed with sundries she had arranged for their trip and stepped outside, loading them into the car. Katherine went into the bathroom and got dressed. She packed certain toiletries and brought them out. Elena returned from outside. They all finished their drinks. The children took their belongings, and they exited the cottage, gathering inside the vehicle. It was now 4:20 a.m.

Charles woke at 5:00 a.m., unusually early, since he had not been on the boat since he had brought it to Belfast on Tuesday, nearly a week ago. He had only used Randy's boat once by himself, and that was when he was shot at from Kenny and the Rat. He still had the traps in the water and hadn't been able to check them since that boat chase. He decided to call Jonas to have him return the skiff. He might not use it, if he felt it would present a danger to himself, but it would be good to take it off from Art's mooring.

He dialed, hoping to catch Jonas home.

"Yeah?" he answered.

"Jonas, this is Charles, how are you doing this morning?"

"Ah! Not bad, I guess. Are Elena and the kids still there?" he said taxingly. "I have to do everything here by myself, and I don't like it!"

Charles shifted the curtains on the window above his sink, peering into the darkness across the yard to the cabin he had arranged for Elena and the children. The car was gone. "I think they're on their way to Millinocket; it's a long drive, and she wanted to get there early."

"Ah-yup. Are they comin' back today, do ya know?" The concern was for himself.

"Elena said they were, but it might be late. They're going to have the wake and the funeral, all today."

"Ah-yup. That's just great! Oh, well!" He sighed heavily. "But I got some good news for ya."

"Good news? What?" He was intrigued.

"Ya don't have to worry about Kenny and the Rat no more. It seems that they didn't get along after all!" He chuckled softly. "They're both dead!"

"You have to be kidding me! That should be it then, and this whole damned thing is over now! It's all over! That's great! This means I don't have any more problems on the water, and I can go retrieve the traps that I've ignored for almost a week." He rubbed his mouth. "It's finally over! Hey, Jonas, do you think you could do me a favor then?"

"What kinda favor?" he drawled, suspiciously.

"I'd like to get the skiff back, so I can go out and check the traps. Do you think you could drop it off for me?"

Jonas eased his tension, "Oh, of course, sure. Let's see, you're still moored in Belfast. I can bring the dinghy over on the trailer and lock it onto the back of ya van, then head back Searsport and go out to do what I gotta do today, from there."

Charles considered the idea, then wondered what he meant by saying he could 'go out to do what I gotta do. "By the way, Jonas, when you saw Kenny yesterday, did you find out anything about the shipwreck's location?"

"Ah ... um ... well ... um ... I didn't see anything, if that's what ya mean. I ... ah ... saw Kenny and the Rat. That was it. I'll tell ya what, though, if I do find out anything about it, I'll let ya know—first thing. The way I figure it, we can be partners, if one of us finds the treasure. Y'know, split it fifty-fifty!"

Charles choked. "I don't want the treasure! I think the whole thing is a priceless artifact and belongs in a museum somewhere. The treasure is just a small part of it. This ship represents history; something like this comes around once in a lifetime. I just wish that the university would help me find the remains and send up an archeological team to surface the whole thing. They have the equipment and the knowledge on how to do this right. I don't!"

"Well, that's all well and fine, but we have to make sure it's actually there. I'm gonna check today, O.K.?"

Charles was hesitant. "That's fine, Jonas. If you find anything, please let me know."

"Yeah, yeah, sure! Hey, I'll have your skiff over to ya in a couple of hours. I'll just leave it on the beach in front of ya spot, O.K.?" He hurried himself.

"Sure. Bye, Jonas." Charles hung up the phone and tried to digest the way Jonas talked. He was hiding something; the feeling was there. He knew that Jonas didn't like the idea of the university getting involved. The reason why was bothering him. The hanging climate of heavy greed filled his being with disgust, and it gave him a bitter taste.

The vehicle pulled into the stately home of the late Stephen and Julie Pendergast, just before seven o'clock in the morning. Two other cars had arrived before it; one was Mrs. Blake's and the other was new to Elena. It was one she did not recognize. The kids had slept most of the ride, and after they reached Bangor to have a fast-food breakfast, the sun came up. The rest of the ride to Millinocket was a very scenic one.

The house was situated outside of the Little Italy district, near the center of town. It was an old building, probably one of the first built around this area, and the Pendergasts had owned it for over 150 years. It had been remodeled once in the past, and very little else had been done to it over the interim. The structure itself was a colonial frame dwelling, built on gently sloping property in the early nineteenth century, possibly earlier; no one knew for certain. The building stood erect between several solitary trees outlining the front lawn. The façade gave a warm, rustic and yet elegant ambiance. Elena placed the vehicle in park and woke the children. They grumbled in disapproval but sat up in their seats, poking their heads around to observe their surroundings. Chad smacked his lips, relieving his cotton mouth, developed during his nap, and Katherine stared through the rear window. "Where is everybody?" she asked, drowsily.

"We're here early, dear," Elena explained. "The rest of the guests won't be arriving for a few hours yet." She gazed at the building and allowed her thoughts to wander into the beauty of such a simple piece of architecture. It simply belonged there! It had a hooded entrance porch and stood two stories tall; a sharp sloping roof added to the feeling of roominess. A large, well-constructed brick chimney crawled up the right side of the building, dividing the dwelling potion of the structure from a large patio (a room in itself) which was surrounded by ten wooden columns, supporting the equally sized terrace above, with access to the second floor. The terrace was enclosed by a wooden railing system and was used in the summer as a gathering spot. The front of the building, facing the street, contained five large open two-tiered windows with fancy shutters. The colors of the outside of the house melted into a wonderful aura.

The three got out of the car, walked up to the entrance porch, and Elena knocked on the door. Mrs. Blake arrived in a short period of time, wearing blue jeans, a solid black-colored sweatshirt and a kerchief tied into her hair. She had yellow plastic gloves on her hands and slippers on her feet. She was an elderly lady but didn't look it, with a stern face and a fair complexion; she was also in very good shape for a woman of her age. She held the door open. She saw who it was and stepped out of the way. "Elena, I'm glad you're here. It must have been an early morning for you, coming from the coast. Please, come in."

Elena stepped through the entrance to a small vestibule, which was provided with a clothes closet. The children followed her inside.

Mrs. Blake had worked as a personal maid for Elena's father and mother, as well as her aunt and uncle. If anybody knew the house better, they were no longer alive. She had babysat Elena when she was just a child, and the two were good friends. It was as if she was a part of her family.

The Pendergasts had developed a fortune in the early nineteenth century on local mercantile and exporting goods. Her relatives were strong supporters of Harry Truman until one of her distant cousins got into some sort of political trouble, and the family drew apart. Her father became a fisherman and lived a rowdy sailor's life. He never quite maintained the fortune that his brother—her uncle—Steve did. He worked his way up from the dirges of the scrutiny which surrounded the family and was able, under his father's guide, to inherit this house, instead of her father, who preferred the adventurous lifestyle. It was often thought that her Uncle Steve would enter politics, but he never did, and in his latter days, he drew into a sedentary existence. His death may have been just the final statement.

Mrs. Blake held out her hand as Chad attempted to pass and pushed it against his shoulder, holding him still at arm's length. She lifted her head, examining his body with her eyes, up and down. "What on earth happened to you, young man?" She swiveled her head from side to side in an attempt to see into his bruises.

"I had an accident," he replied, "I fell down the stairs." He flicked a quick smile.

"Uh, huh!" she countered cynically, and folded her arms. "Your *father* wouldn't have anything to do with this, by any chance, would he?" She tilted her head, anticipating his response.

He hesitated, "It was really just an accident."

Mrs. Blake turned abruptly to Elena. "I told you to get away from that man. I've been nursing for all my life and I've never seen this family without some type of mark on them; either you, or the children. I'll tell you, Elena, if you stay with him, one of you is going to wind up dead. I don't know why you put up with this sort of behavior. Chad doesn't have to tell me, I know how he got these bruises, and that eye needs attention." Her ravings humbled Elena, and she shrunk in shame. "Why did you even marry the man?" Her voice rose.

Elena shrugged, "It was my father's idea. You know I had a beau before I met Jonas. But Jonas fished with my father, and they grew quite close. Dad always pitied him for some reason and wanted him to do good. I never understood it, but I married him because he was my father's choice." She shook her head. "I don't know if I can take it anymore!"

"Well, it's about time you woke up! Look at that boy!" She pointed to Chad. "If I see anything like this again, I'm going to the authorities—there's just no reason!" She had become irritated, and loud. "That beau of yours, what was his name?"

"Peter. Peter Arnold."

"Yes, that's it, Peter Arnold. He still lives here locally, you know. I heard he was quite successful. He's an engineer, and designs bridges, I believe, and he's still single! If I were you, I'd keep him in mind and get rid of that beast you've got!"

Elena shriveled. "Please, not in front of the children! I'll do what I have to do. I'm so confused right now. Please, let me handle it, and please don't go to the State."

Mrs. Blake huffed, then looked back at Chad. "It's such a shame. There's just no reason for it!" She eased up, "We can talk later. I guess we can see what has to be done here, for now. The funeral director will arrive at eight o'clock. I've made arrangements for everyone to park along the side of the road except, of course, for you and the hearse. I have set up the caterer's tables the way I want them, but I'd like you to go through it with me to see what you think." She led them through the vestibule into the huge central hall, where at the rear was a staircase lighted by a window. The hall was abutted by two other rooms, divided by wide inter-room openings, providing access to each; one being a living room and the other a dining room. The living room contained a large brick and tile fireplace. The dining room opened to an ell of the building, which contained a large spare room, the bathroom and another stairwell leading to the second floor. The entire place was more of a mansion than an old, rustic house. Chairs had been set up in the living room, where the casket had been brought and set up. The furniture was arranged all through the room for the mourners, and that was where Elena assumed she would deliver the eulogy. The cushioned chairs and couches had been pushed against the walls to make room for the fold-out chairs which filled the heart of the room. The dining area had already been arranged with tables, but no caterings had been delivered as of yet. "I've done most of the rearranging already, but I want to dust off the tables and wipe down the furniture. I bought some table cloths to place over the dining room tables. The caterers will be here at about nine o'clock, and they're going to bring the food, napkins, plates, sodas and the like. We put the regular dining room furniture onto the top deck. I've set it up so that any smokers can go outside on the porch to satisfy their habit.

"The way we decided it, is once the eulogy is over, we have a small gathering in the dining area, then proceed to the graveyard. After that, everyone goes home. It's the simplest way to do it, and unless you have objections, it's the way it's going to go."

"No, no, that sounds fine. I'd like to get back home today and put this all behind me." She ogled the mansion panoramically, with her eyes. It was exquisite. The nautical decorations, from eons past, hung on the walls in the living room; her uncle's pride and joy. Flowers had poured in and were arranged by the casket. She looked the casket over and saw her aunt for the first time after she had been embalmed. The undertakers had done a remarkable job! Her aunt's appearance was so serene and peaceful. She thought to herself, *She's finally at peace.* Without a reason, she became curious. "Oh, Mrs. Blake?" She turned to face the elderly lady.

The elderly lady spun around, "Yes?"

"There's a car I don't recognize in the dooryard. Whose car is that?" She lowered her right eyebrow.

"Oh, dear, that's Nathaniel King. He's a lawyer. He's picked a rather inauspicious hour upon which to perform his duties, but he's performing a preliminary assessment of the property of the estate. There is some sort of rush clause that your Aunt Julie placed in her will. He said he would be brief this morning and be gone once the mourning party arrived. He's been no trouble so far, but I daresay he's rather a ghoulish presence. His timing could have been better. No matter, he'll be on his way shortly." Her words faltered.

"I hope you have some time after the funereal, and hour or so, to stay here for a while. Once the services are complete, and we return here, I'm going to talk to you."

"Talk to me? About what?"

"I have a couple of surprises for you! You'll see! That's for after the ceremonies. Right now, get the children a shower and into some decent clothes, and the two of us will get to work straightening this place out. Is that O.K. with you?"

"Yes, that's fine." She cupped her hands together. *A couple of surprises?* she thought. *I wonder what that could be.*

The phone rang at the cottage before Charles could exit through the door. He had seen that Jonas left the skiff and trailer where he mentioned, secured to the back of his van. The phone rang again. He closed the door and hurried his way to it before the other party hung up then picked up the receiver. "Hello," he said.

"Hello, Charles. This is Dean Groton, how is everything today?"

"Oh, hello, dean. It's getting better here and I'm not in danger anymore. Apparently, things have worked out for the best so far."

"Good! Good! Good, Charlie. Have you gotten anywhere on that sunken ship? You know how important this could be to the status of this university, don't you?"

"Well, yes, I guess so, but Dean...." He stopped, unsure of what to say.

His life had been in danger, and the prospects of learning any more about lobster fishing or deep-sea fishing seemed remote, yet the dean was pressing him about the ship.

"Yes, Charlie, what is it?"

He moaned low with a whiny voice, "Dean, don't you think that this is something for the people who know what they're doing? I mean, like the marine archeologists or the crews from Woods Hole. I'm just one man, what can I do?"

"Charlie, don't panic. We're going to arrange all that. The only thing I'd like you to do, is to acquire as much knowledge about it as you can, while I get together the right people and talk to the right organizations. It might take time, but since you're already there, I thought you could keep us abreast of the circumstances, and keep me informed. Now, do you have any new information about the ship?"

Charles, even now, remained perturbed at the whole circumstance. He arched his back in fatigue and sighed. "Well, I might know something about it. I'll find out more in a couple of days, I think. There is a lot of things going on in this town that are just beginning to make sense. I hope I can tell you more the next time we talk."

"Good, good, Charlie. I knew I could count on you!"

"Huh? Count on me? Oh, by the way, Dean, do you have my class set up with a substitute?"

"Oh, yes, Charlie. I hired a new man to take your place. We can keep him for a couple of weeks, if it takes you that long to get back here. By that time, I'll have an exploratory division sent up to you, to take over there. In the meantime, I hope you can get as much information as possible."

"A new man? What's his name?"

"Ah ... um ... let me see, here ... ah ... ah, oh yes, here it is. His name is Professor Pearlman. He's a Ph D in marine biology and knows his nautical history. He's perfect to set the class up for your return. We're going to have him follow your basic syllabus for two weeks; if you're not back by then. He'll lecture on the beginnings of the various maritime cultures, chronologically, taking you up to the modern-day era. We will wait for you to come back before any of the students will be going out for boat trips. Again, we'll follow your syllabus and split the class from that point on, with one-half classroom time and one-half time on the water. That will be completed in two different class periods. We've made contact with Woods Hole for day trips there for some of their lectures. It's all going to go quite smoothly, I believe. Don't worry about anything on this end of the spectrum, Charlie, just finish what you are doing there, and we'll stay in touch. Give me a call back in a couple of days and we'll talk some more. School starts tomorrow, and I'm as busy as a bee right now, so I've got to let you go."

"I guess so, Dean. I'll talk to you tomorrow."

"Bye, Charlie, good luck!" He hung up.

The room reeked of stale silence. Charles held the receiver in his hand, until it began to beep that annoying sound, then he set the unit down on its base. His face was contorted in a series of newly acquired wrinkles. He walked to the door, and out of the cottage. He had the skiff now and could go back out into the bay and pick his traps up.

Katherine stepped into the dining area, still dressed in her beautiful backless blue gown, with a low front, that she had worn to the ceremony at the graveyard. The dress accented her features voluminously, and even though she had only worn it once before, it still fit. She had placed her hair up, swirling it in layers on her head. For a young, petite woman, she was a dazzling work of beauty. Her fair skin shone in the lighting from overhead, and her perfume filled the air with a sensuous, aromatic delight. Chad also looked his best—apart from the bruises, which stuck out on his young skin like leprosy. He wore a formal black suit and tie; it also was only the second time he wore it. The other occasion on which the children had worn this clothing was at their grandfather's funeral, over a year prior.

The day had been rather grueling to them, greeting people they didn't even know, but who kept telling them how they remembered when they were just 'that high.' They had been pushed from person to person to the point of mental fatigue, trying to remember names. That exercise in futility was short lived. Now, they were just happy that the whole thing was over. The remaining guests were gathering the last of their belongings from the vestibule, with Mrs. Blake seeing each had the correct items. Elena stood on the opposite side of the vestibule, rendering final words of comfort as the two women saw the last of the crowd out to the parked cars. The guests had departed, and the two ladies returned inside.

The children were devouring the remaining catered foods that had been left over. The smell of the various sundries, each with its own particular aroma, overwhelmed their olfactory sense, triggering a hectic eating spree.

Elena, more beautiful than ever, observed their glut. "Children, please. You've had enough. You're going to get sick! That's it, Chad, no more!" She pulled a croissant out of Chad's hand and set it back down onto its tray. He wrenched his head in her direction with a stare of confusion, still chewing on one of the finger sandwiches. Once she turned away from him, he grabbed as much as he could from the table and filled his pockets. "*Chad!* I know what you're doing!" She wasn't even looking in his direction. *It's that mother instinct,* he reasoned, holding two cookies in midair.

Mrs. Blake stepped inside and giggled. "Oh, it's quite all right; I need to get rid of it anyway."

Chad smiled triumphantly and continued filling his pockets.

She stepped quietly behind Elena, still dressed in her black mourning gown with the veil removed. Her golden hair had been pulled back and tied; her scant portions of make-up drew out the natural beauty in her features.

Elena stopped, sensing her encroachment. She turned and faced Mrs. Blake. "Yes?" she asked. Her dress had been tailor fit, altered for her dimensions, and was a sharp contrast to the apparel she wore back in Swanville. It consisted of the joining of two separate colors; pink and sky blue, which blended into a dazzling summer-like display; as did the yellow of the honeybee complement the pink and white blossoms of the Paulownia plant. The objective is to make honey, sweet honey; so, too, her garments made sweet honey, to the observer's eye. Her hat was sky blue, with a pink ribbon tied in the back. Her demeanor was elegant and sophisticated. She had applied just enough make-up to hide her worry lines, grown thick in the last few weeks. She wore an imported perfume; the fragrance could only captivate one's senses.

"Dear, Elena. I told you that I had a couple of surprises for you." She blinked and drew a forced smile.

"Yes, you did, but I can't imagine what." She half-bowed her head, then, from the living room a figure emerged; a man, dressed in a three-piece blue suit with a red tie. He stood tall and sturdy, sure of himself. His chin stuck out slightly off his face when he stalled his movements and placed his hands behind his back. His eyes were dark and strong, and his face was smooth, like a child's. His hair was cut short and neatly groomed, combed from front to back. He stood motionless.

"Elena?" he asked in a soft, polite and educated annunciation. "It's been such a long time."

She stared at him for a moment "Peter? Is that you, Peter?" She held her hand over her mouth then turned to Mrs. Blake, who stood watching her, then winked. Elena pivoted back to the man.

"I knew you would be here today, so I asked Mrs. Blake if it would be all right for me to show up and say hello." He shrugged. "I hope that's all right with you."

There was no response.

"You look very stunning today!" His eyes wandered over her entire body, and he grinned with approval. "It's been such a long time, Elena. May we talk ... alone?" He was handsome beyond her recollection from school, where they met many years ago. He was wearing a white lilac corsage on his suit, a very strange adornment, she thought. Then she remembered her prom night, when he gave her the same corsage, explaining to her that the white represented purity and the white lilac represented 'first love.' She blushed at the sight of it and of her memory.

"You turn red, Elena. Have I insulted or embarrassed you in any way?" he quipped, unabashedly.

"Oh, no, Peter! I feel quite complimented, actually. It has been a long time, and so much has transpired since we last met." She froze in place, unsure of what else to say. "I would be delighted to speak with you, alone. There's so much to catch up on. Shall we repair to the living room?" She acted giddy and twisted her body sideways, sticking out her right knee, raising her right shoulder in shyness, like a young schoolgirl.

He swept his arm downward, pointing it to the living room, "After you, Elena." She giggled at the politeness, then turned to the children, "Would the two of you please help Mrs. Blake clean up and get dressed, we must leave shortly." Her head twisted when she spoke those words, but as she looked at her former beau, she could see the words also disappointed him.

Mrs. Blake walked up to the children and began to bark out orders to them in a low tone, then she turned to the stylish couple. "The two of you go and talk, we'll take care of everything out here. Now, go, go!" Her lips pursed, showing thin age lines along the edges.

Elena tipped her head to her and walked in the direction that Peter indicated. He followed her into the other room and stood, waiting for her to take a seat on one of the couches which were still set up against the far wall of the house. She cupped her dress at the knee and sat. He sat on the far end of the couch, beside her.

"Peter," she said, "it's very nice to see you again. It looks like you're taking care of yourself."

He smiled. "Thank you, and I must say, you are more beautiful than I remember! Either that, or the years have been very kind to you, and you have simply grown more gorgeous with the passing of time." His speech flowed like a bard's.

"Oh, Peter, you always had a way with words."

"I've never forgotten about you, Elena. I've tried.... That is, I made the effort.... What I mean to say, is ... I wanted to call you many times. I loved you, Elena!"

She gasped, "Please, Peter, you know, I'm married. Those are my children in there."

He fidgeted in the chair. "Yes, I know. I've been told. I've heard that they are very studious. I do love children. But Elena...." He shuffled in his seat. "I also know that you've had a hard time, and, I was—"

She jumped out of her chair. "Don't tell me! This has all been arranged by Mrs. Blake! I knew it!" She waved her finger in the air. "I knew that she set this up!" She paced about the room. "I'm so embarrassed!"

He stood up, and gently placed his hands on her shoulders. "Calm down, now. Mrs. Blake is not to blame."

She stopped and welcomed his touch, giving her a comfort she had not felt for quite some time. Then, she rocked her body sideways, inviting more. He pulled her back to him and embraced her from behind.

"I will admit she mentioned something to me, but it was my idea to come here. I wanted to see you, even if you didn't want to see me. She told me about your life. I was concerned. That's all."

She spun and looked at him, eye to eye. "Oh, Peter! It's been so long!" She melted within his grip, begging for his attention. He did not disappoint her.

He pulled her up against his body and they passionately kissed; a long, seductive kiss. Their tongues rolling together with zeal, enjoying their hearts' desires, until she spun away from him and glared down at the floor. "Peter, please! I want to ... I want so much ... I ... I—"

"No, Elena, stop. That wasn't you. It was I. I'm sorry to push myself like that, it's just, well ... it's just.... Oh, Elena, I still love you!"

"That's enough!" she blurted out. "I told you I was married!" She stomped her foot firmly on the floor and drew away from him. "Peter, can't you see, I have a family!" She was adamant.

He grinned, "You're right. I've overstepped my bounds. Please, forgive me." He reached inside his pocket and took out his wallet, shuffled through it, and finally pulling out a business card. "Here, Elena," he said as he handed it to her, "this is how you can reach me. I don't have much time right now, but if you ever need someone to talk to, please, give me a call."

She accepted the card and held it out. "Oh, Peter! You know I would like that, if I could. But I have the family and I just can't ... well, I just can't.... Oh, you know!"

He smiled and gave her a peck on her cheek. "Yes, I know, but please ... don't lose the card!"

She hugged him. "Thank you, Peter. I won't!" She sighed heavily. "Well, I must get the children and go home. It's an awful long ride back."

He gripped her hands. "I know it is, Elena. Be careful driving. I'll see you out."

"Thank you, Peter," she said, and she twisted to exit the living room with him directly behind. Their hands never separated as they walked into the central hall and met the children. Chad ran up to her and grabbed her around the waist. Katherine stayed back with her hand stuck in between her knees.

Elena released the grip with Peter. "Chad, Katherine, I would like you to meet Peter Arnold, an old friend." She courteously pointed to him.

"Hi, Peter, I'm Chad." He backed up and held his hand out.

"Chad, it's nice to meet you," Peter acknowledged.

Katherine bowed her head and said, "Hi."

He tipped his head back in her direction. "Hi, Katherine, it's nice to meet you." She nodded. "Well, Elena, I'm glad I had a chance to see you again, and maybe we can get together sometime. I'm really not that far away."

"Yes, Peter, it was a pleasure to see you, and, well, well, maybe!" She curtsied to him, and he bowed to her. He walked back through the greeting room, and into the vestibule, where Mrs. Blake stood, waiting with his hat.

She whispered, "How'd it go?" She leaned into the greeting room, lest Elena may hear.

He grinned and looked at his watch. "It went fine, I suppose. I do have to be going, though. I have an appointment with one of my clients in Bangor; it's sort of a dinner meeting. I would like to thank you for your hospitality." He turned to Elena, "It was great seeing you again, Elena. I just wish it was at a more auspicious occasion. I'm sorry about your aunt and uncle."

"Thank you, Peter," she said, waving as he left the building. The children both waved to him.

Mrs. Blake held the door open for him and shut it after he left, then turned to Elena. "Well, now, that went fine," she stated.

Elena jerked back and placed her hands on her hips. "Mrs. Blake, how could you?" She stirred angrily. "How could you be so blatantly intrusive? You know I have Jonas and the kids. Why would you set me up like you did? Don't lie to me, I know you did!" She waited for her response.

Mrs. Blake fluffed her hands in the air. "Oh, girl! You'll thank me in the end! Heavens! I'm just trying to help you out, that's all!" She stepped into the greeting room and placed her hand to her chin. "Oh, by the way, that's only the first surprise I had for you."

Elena looked stunned. "Huh? There's more? What is your other little tidbit? Another man?" she huffed.

"As a matter of fact, yes!" She pointed to the area beyond the greeting room. "Yes, it is. Elena, I would like you to meet Mr. King. His name is Nathaniel King; the lawyer I mentioned."

A gentleman stepped out from the room behind the greeting room, wearing a finely groomed tuxedo and carrying a folder with papers. He was of medium stature and his hair was pressed back, complementing his sturdy looks. He was clean shaven and wore a set of glasses that made him appear sophisticated. He shifted the paperwork to his left hand and held his right hand out to her. "Mrs. Hale, it's my pleasure to meet you."

She winced and gripped his hand, unsure of the intention. The two children went inside the vestibule to watch. She turned to Mrs. Blake and let go of his hand. "May I ask what this is all about?" she inquired.

Mrs. Blake raised her eyebrows and shrugged, like a child caught with their hand in a cookie jar. "I don't know." She avoided the question.

He recognized the trepidation in her response and returned, "I'll answer that, Mrs. Hale."

"Well, thank you. I should hope so!" She peered over to Mrs. Blake, who had turned her back to them. "I would like someone to be outright!"

He chuckled. "I'll try!" He shuffled sideways in a humble gesture. "You see, I've been appointed here."

She rolled her eyes at him. "Appointed? About what?" She looked concerned.

"Oh, no, no, no. It's nothing bad, I assure you!" He made a fist with his right hand and held it to his mouth then coughed. "May I explain?"

She stared at Mrs. Blake, who still held her back to the two of them, and folded her arms. "I certainly wish somebody would!"

"Well, Mrs. Hale, I've been appointed by the law offices of Reed, Reed and Durgin, to assess the value of this house. I've also been appointed as executor to the will of your late aunt and uncle. I would like to give my sincere apologies for your loss!"

She flicked her head to the side in curiosity. "Yes, thank you. What does that have to do with me?"

He glanced down at the paperwork in his hands and rubbed his chin. "Well, quite frankly—everything!"

"Everything?" She tilted her head to the other side.

"Well, yes, everything! It is all here!" He tapped his forefinger on the paperwork in his hand. "It's all very clear!"

"What are you talking about?"

"The will of your aunt and uncle. I'm here today to assess the value of the house; your house."

"Huh? *My* house? What do you mean?"

"That's right, *your* house. It seems that, as the only living relative of your aunt and uncle, they left everything to you! It's that simple!" He lowered the papers to his hip then slapped it off his body. "It's all here! I could show it to you, but this is just the preliminary documents. Don't worry, you'll be notified." He batted his eyes.

"*My* house?" she stumbled. "My house! Oh, my God!" She clutched her breast and swaggered slowly to one of the chairs at the table, then sat down. "My house?" she asked again in disbelief.

Chad and Katherine jumped out from the vestibule after hearing the announcement. "Ma!" Chad screamed. "We get to live here? We get away from Dad?" He was jubilant. Katherine roamed aimlessly through the room, gazing at everything as if it were her first time there.

"Chad! Katherine! That's very impolite!" Elena cautioned them. "Now, now, children, don't get too exited. We don't know yet."

King held the papers out to her. "Oh, it's all here. It might take some time, but it is yours. Not only that, but there is a substantial amount of money involved." He was chipper.

She poked her head up from her daze. "Money?"

"Oh, yes! A substantial amount. Your relatives were quite wealthy when they departed. I would like to express my condolences once more, I was told you were very close." He held his head down in reverence.

"Money?" She slumped in the chair. "How much money?"

"Well, that's hard to say, right now, but don't fret, you'll be taken care of for the rest of your life." He spun around to Mrs. Blake, who now was devouring the conversation. "My dear lady, I must be going, my efforts here are complete."

She nodded and looked at Elena. "Any other concerns will be answered shortly." He reached inside his suit pocket and drew out a card, then handed it to Elena. "This is my number, if you have any questions. Regardless, you will be contacted very soon. I do have to remind you that this takes time. It was a pleasure to meet you!" He tipped his head to her and proceeded to the vestibule, where he picked up his hat and exited the house.

"The ... the ... the pleasure was mine!" Elena blurted out as he left. She then turned to Mrs. Blake and moaned, "Well! Do you have any more surprises for me, old woman?"

Mrs. Blake smiled at her. "No, that's it!"

Chapter 24

Jonas left Belfast Harbor early and spun through the arrangement of buoys, stationed dangerously close to one another, in a clumsy maze. He managed his way along, having dropped the skiff off at Charles's, and loading his skiff onto the back of his boat. The sun was still shining brightly as he went, but the bay was reckless today. As protected as it was in its position, it was still subject to the wind. He tooled along, unconscious of the waves, heading directly east. The further he traveled, the worse the sea took hold of his boat, until he got to Turtlehead, and the ocean calmed. He glided peacefully in the still water and tried to think where he had met Kenny's boat. The general location was no problem; that was Cape Rosier, but the exact location was fuzzy to him. He struggled to recall the spot as he turned into the East Penobscot Bay. *Fool!* he thought. *I should have written it down. Ah, well, it can't be that hard to find.* His rationale made him feel more at ease. The ride to the peninsula was brisk and tedious, but he made it.

He eased the boat into neutral and looked around in the water, hoping for a revelation. The problem was—he had no idea! Everything happened so quickly, he never got a good look at the place where he killed Souharat. He trolled the coast looking for a sign; a tree, a rock, some sort of line on shore, anything to let him know where they had been. He found no help. The sun beat down mercilessly on his neck, and he felt it. He stalled the boat and leaned over the side of the vessel in the hope of seeing something—the treasure; anything! The water was too deep in the area he had chosen, so he lifted his head up to check again. He reached into his pocket and pulled out a handkerchief, then wiped his brow. There were no signs he could recognize.

A small boat hummed in the distance, with two young men on board. They espied Jonas and headed over to him, yelling and screaming in a jocular way. He cringed as they approached. "Hey, Jonas!" the younger one cried. "What are you doing?" He had a drink in his hand and held it up in some sort of celebration. "Whatcha lookin' for?"

Jonas put on a straight face and turned to the two. "Uh, ain't lookin' fer nothin', boys. You be on your way, now. I lost at trap here, and I was hoping it wound up on shore by here. That's all!"

"Hell, Jonas, it looks like you're checking it out pretty good! Ain't looking for no bodies here, are ya?"

"What? What is that supposed to mean?" He shriveled into a ball. "Now, the two of you go about your business, and I'll tend to mine, understand?"

The older of the two took his comments as an insult. "What are you so upset about? Steve didn't mean nothing."

"Yeah, good! Can't you just leave me alone?" He leaned back. "I know you boys, but I just don't need to see ya. Now, I gotta get back to Searsport!" He stepped back up behind the wheel of his boat and hit the throttle.

"Good day, boys!" He tipped his head and traveled away from the point as fast as he could. *Damn!* he thought. *Can't make this a sport! This is a job better done very early or very late; in the cloak of dark. I run my gambit during the day!* The wake of his boat rocked the other boat, and the buoy that Souharat had set, rolled it, within the foam.

The weather wasn't going to get any better, she decided, so she packed the small amount of supplies and the kids into the car. After a short goodbye with Mrs. Blake, she got in the car and headed back to the coast. The day was very warm and she grew tired from the sun pelting through the windshield, but she continued, still dreaming of Peter and the house. The money was not yet realized, but it was there; in some form. She knew it! The kids didn't take long to fall asleep on the ride back. This would be the day she would finally tell Jonas goodbye! Chad's injuries and the memory of her being mauled by the drunken man stirred inside her, but the thought of her daughter being subjected to the same treatment ground fiercely at her insides. She started to hate the man. No, she didn't start—she did hate him! She fantasized about revenge but shirked the idea.

The ride only took a little over two hours when she pulled off of Route #1 into the cabin area. She noticed that Charles's van was there, and she was hoping to have him watch the children while she retrieved some of her belongings back at the house. She wanted to do this while Jonas was gone. There was still enough time to the day that the odds were he was out checking traps. He should have a long day on the water, since he had ignored the traps for so long. She parked the car and woke the kids, who got up relatively easily. They got out of the vehicle and went into the cabin.

She went directly to the phone and called her house, but there was no answer, even though she let it ring several times. *That's good!* she thought. *He's not home!* Feeling more relaxed with that, she walked over to Charles's cabin and knocked on his door. He opened it and asked her inside.

"Well, Elena, how did your day go?" he asked.

"Oh, it went well. It was sad, but we got through it, and I had a couple of surprises." She was gleaming.

"Oh, is that so? What?"

"Right now, I'd rather not say. I came over here to ask you a favor, if you don't mind."

"Anything. I just got back from Searsport. I took the boat back over to the mooring. What do you need?"

"Oh, Charles, you've been so good to us! I was wondering if you could watch the children for a little while so I can run some errands. That is, if it's not too much trouble."

"No trouble, no trouble at all. Sure!" He smiled. "What kind of errands?"

She hesitated and gripped her chin. "I want to pick up some things at the house. I just called, and there was no answer. I'd like to do this while Jonas is gone."

"Are you sure? I wouldn't like to see you go back over there, unless you really have to!" He was concerned. "But I didn't see his boat at the mooring when I got there." He paused. "I guess you'll be all right. He was here earlier, and I know he has a lot of work to do in the bay. So, yeah, sure, I can't see the harm."

"Oh, thank you, Charles. You are a gem!"

"Do me a favor, though?"

"Huh?" She didn't understand. "What?"

"If you see his truck out front, get out of there! Please, do that for me. I have this funny feeling about him."

She paused. "Of course!" A grin of understanding came over her. "You're not the first one to tell me that today! It's just that I left a clock over there that is very special to me—especially today. I'll explain it to you later. But thank you, Charles!"

"O.K., then, bring the kids over."

She hustled out of his cabin to hers and returned with the children, who ran directly over to the television. There was cable at the cabin, which was something they were not very accustomed to, and it kept them busy. "Thanks again, Charles, I should only be a few minutes."

"You're welcome," he replied.

She left and he went to the phone, while the children were consumed with the television.

The ideas in his head swarmed with different theories about the university and Dean Groton. The man had been too abstract in their last conversation.

School was still open, so he dialed the number to his office.

A strange voice answered. "Dean Groton's office." It was a woman speaking, and that threw him back.

"Hello. Yes, this is Charles Ritter. May I inquire as to whom I am speaking?" He expected Ben to answer.

"This is the dean's secretary, Susan Lassiter. How may I direct your call?"

"Susan Lassiter? I don't believe that we've met. Isn't Ben Smith there anymore?"

"Yes, sir, but he's on vacation for the week, and I'm taking his spot. How may I help you?" She spoke with trepidation. The day was getting late, and she sounded eager to be over with this conversation.

"Well, I didn't mean to call so late, but I am a professor there and I have a substitute at my office. I was wondering if I could speak with him, to see how my class was progressing. Could you patch me through?"

He could hear the sounds of ruffling papers, then silence. "Hello? Hello?"

"Yes, sir, I'm sorry. What's your name again?"

"I'm Charles Ritter. I have an office on the second floor. I'm a teacher there!" He was becoming irritated. He hated dealing with new people that didn't know what was going on.

"Charles Ritter?" she asked. "I had a Charles Ritter here, once, but he quit a couple of weeks ago."

"Quit?! No, no! *I'm* Charles Ritter! I was sent up here for two weeks to research lobster fishing and deep-sea fishing. I have a course there that Dean Groton set up! Check again, I know I'm not there now, but I should still have my office!"

His blood boiled. *Incompetence!* he thought.

"Look, sir, I have the list in front of me, and Charles Ritter is not on it! Trust me!"

"O.K., O.K., I guess that could be. I have a substitute there who is taking my class while I'm away. Could you patch me through to him?"

"Who?"

"My office, damn it! Room 201!" he shouted.

"Who are you trying to get in touch with?" She was trying to be polite but did not need the yelling.

"Wait a minute." He checked his wallet and found the note he had scratched down when he talked to the dean. "Here it is," he said. "Professor Pearlman. Would you let me speak with him, and find out what's going on?"

There was a long silence. She finally responded. "I'm sorry, sir, but there's no Professor Pearlman here, either! I'd like to help you, but that's the only information I have."

"Huh? Well, can you do me another favor, please? Could you check that paperwork you have in front of you, and tell me if my class is still there?"

"What class is that, sir?"

"Oh, God! It's 'The Practical Aspects of Maritime History.'"

"You are kidding me, sir, aren't you?"

"What kind of a comment is that? I've done the complete syllabus myself and sent it here, through this office to the dean, and the whole damned board approved it! They bought me a boat. It should all be there, in front of you!"

"I'm very sorry, sir, but you're mistaken. I do have everything right here in front of me, and that's not there! Not only that, it's NEVER been here!" She spoke sarcastically.

"What?" He pulled the phone away from his ear and breathed in and out several times. "Something's wrong, then!" He calmed down. "I'll tell you what. Can you just let me speak with Dean Groton, please?"

"Oh, I'm sorry, sir. He's on vacation also."

"What?" His anger returned. "School just started and he's on vacation? What's going on there?" He was furious. "I better not have wasted my time here!"

"Sir, please, there's nothing more I can do for you. The office is closing, sir. If you would like to call back tomorrow, maybe someone else can help you. I'm new and I've told you everything I possibly can. Goodbye!" She hung up the phone in anger.

He pulled the receiver away from his ear. "Yeah, *goodbye*!" he said, absolutely stymied, then hung up the phone. "Huh! That's very, very strange!"

Chad turned around on the couch. "Did you say something? What's strange?" he asked.

Charles slumped down. "No, I'm sorry, Chad. I need to call my wife, that's all."

The golden foliage began to show in the trees on the side of the road as she went, and the purple lilacs were in full bloom. She rolled the window down to get a good autumn blast of their fragrance. It was soothing! When she arrived at the house, Jonas's truck was not there, so she quickly parked and ran inside.

The place was completely trashed. Bottles and food were scattered about. She spun and immediately turned to the clock to inspect it. There was no apparent damage. There was no rush at all! She placed her hands behind her back and wandered through the house, glancing at the furniture and the walls.

What a difference from the house she was about to inherit. *To hell with Jonas,* she bragged in her mind. *Yes, of course,* Jonas*!* The whole idea scared her.

She ran up to the children's rooms and took what she could, then shuffled all their belongings to the car. She came back for the clock. She didn't know why, but that piece of furniture had a special place in her heart. She had to see it work, to see it function. She strolled over and turned the knob. It began to tick in its charming melody.

She absorbed it and totally enjoyed the melody. How beautiful! It was so peaceful to her in her state, and she began to dance with herself. She placed one hand over her heart and the other in the air. A walk here; a turn there; she was in her glory! Peter rolled back in her memory. Oh, how graceful the two could be together! She saw his shadow on the wall and pretended to dance with him. First, she asked him, and he nodded, taking her hand. How romantic! She glowed with the infatuation of him; her new prince. The pieces of furniture became the entourage, and the lamps became chandeliers. It was a glorious thought! The ticking played on, perhaps Brahms, perhaps Beethoven. She didn't know, but it was so intoxicating she couldn't stop romancing.

Then, as she fantasized, she glanced at the clock. In the background, just above the clock, she saw her husband standing at the door of the bedroom! He leaned against the sill.

This startled her, and she pulled all her extremities into her body. "Jonas!" she said. "I didn't expect you!"

He stood at the door, enormous, and perturbed. "Ah-yup! And I didn't expect ya, either! What the hell ya doin' here?" His face was grizzled, and he wasn't wearing a friendly smile.

"Oh, Jonas, I came back to get the clock. Let me explain—"

"Oh, shut up, bitch! I heard enough of ya damned explanations! What d'ya want?" He was bitter, waving his finger in the air. "I asked ya, what are ya doin' here, bitch?"

"Please, let me explain," she said.

He pressed his hands over his ears. "What's that sound?"

The clock continued ticking. He closed his eyes, and his cheeks inflated. "What's that damned sound?" He spun around and gritted his teeth in agony.

She noticed his uneasiness, then looked over at the clock. "Oh, that? It's a gift from Uncle Steve and Aunt Julie. Isn't it nice?" She grinned, seeing his pain.

"Turn it off! Shut it off!" He shook his head and grabbed the back of his neck, rolling his eyes around. Suddenly, he began to tremble. "I said shut it off, bitch!" He reached down on the floor and picked up an empty bottle of rum, then whipped it across the room at the clock. The fine glass enclosure shattered at the impact. The clock stopped, and he stood upright, his eyes glowing in fury. "I told ya to shut the damned thing off! What are ya, deaf?"

He swung his arm into her face, slapping her with a resounding *whop*. "When I tell ya to do somethin', woman, I mean it!" He grabbed her by the collar and slammed her against the wall.

"Jonas! What are you doing?"

He reeled back and punched her directly in the nose.

She cried and slumped over, blood gushed from her face. "No, Jonas! Please!" She held her head down and covered it up in defense.

"Oh, you ignorant bitch! You did that on purpose!" He grabbed her hair and slung her against the wall, cutting the back of her head.

She flailed her arms wildly, attempting to block his fists.

He pulled back to hit her again when she tucked in her chin and dove at him, making contact with his stomach, just as he was about to throw a punch. He coughed and let out a bellyful of air. His eyes dilated and he stumbled backwards, trying to catch his breath.

She didn't hesitate. On the first inclination of his loss of balance, she bolted for the door, holding her head as she went. She was in hysterics.

He fell down in one of the chairs at the table and doubled over in shock, then got up in more than a fury. As he staggered to the door to catch her, he could hear the car start and the tires squeal on the way out of the driveway. He gave up and sat back down, rubbing his stomach.

She drove as fast as the car could go, wiping her eyes and her face in transit. She arrived in the parking lot of the cabins within minutes, still in tears. Quickly, she ran to Charles's place and knocked voraciously at the door.

Charles opened it instantly and saw her bleeding, then exploded. "What the hell? I knew it! Come on now!" He placed one arm around her and helped her inside.

She was blubbering incoherently. "I ... I ... I stopped by the house." He guided her to a chair and set her down easy.

Chad and Katherine both jumped off the couch and ran toward her. "Ma!" Chad yelled. "What's the matter?" Katherine shook her head in disgust.

"Don't talk now!" Charles said as he wiped the blood from her face with his shirt, then gripped her head with both hands, examining the damage. "Just relax. Do you feel O.K.?"

She nodded. He reached over to the table and took a tissue from the holder, handing it to her. "Here," he said, "wipe your eyes and I'll get a cloth to remove the dried blood and clean up the wound on the back of your head. Man, he got you good, didn't he?"

Chad ran through the inside of the cabin screaming. "He's going to get it! He's really going to get it!"

Charles tried to calm him down. "Please, Chad, can't you see that your mother doesn't need your screaming?" The cloth he was searching for lay in front of him at the counter by the sink, and he shoved it under the faucet, wetting it down. "Can't you give her a break?"

The boy kicked the table. "I'll give her a break, all right! I'll break Dad's head!" His body was a tense ball of emotion. "He'll get his!"

Katherine stood still.

"O.K., Chad, you made your point. Let me take care of your mom right now." He placed the cloth on the back of her head, on the spot where she had hit the wall.

She cried unremittingly.

"It's O.K., it's all right. Take it easy and we'll have this all cleaned up in a second. Don't worry." He tried to comfort her, and her sobbing slowed. "Well, you're not going to need stitches, and that's a blessing! I have some bandages in the car that work like band-aids. That should work. I'll get them in a minute. You just take it easy!"

"I ... I ... I only wanted to pick up that clock. It was my uncle's, and he enjoyed it so much. Then ... then ... then he gave it to me!" she wailed from her chest, and held the tissue to her eyes. "It's from him!"

"O.K., now, relax." The final phase of wiping off the dry blood was complete, and he looked for further damage but found none. He sat down. "You know, I should take you to the hospital." He sighed.

She turned to him, with the tears welling up in her eyes. "No! No, I don't want that. I'll be fine." She stared at him with bleary eyes. "I'll be fine!"

He stood and growled, "I'm sorry, but I'm going to have to report this! You need the protection of the State. This can't continue. Don't you see what you're doing to yourself?" He was rattled even though the injuries had been contained. "I don't like it!"

"Please, Charles, no!" She wiped her eyes.

"I'm sorry!" His response was demanding. He walked over to the table and picked up the phone book. While he thumbed through the book, he grabbed the telephone. Once he had gotten the correct information, he dialed.

"Please, Charles, no!" She sobbed more. "I don't want any trouble. It's not that big a thing. Just let it go!"

"I can't! I'm getting a restraining order!" he responded, then pulled the phone closer to his ear. "Hello, is this the Department of Human Services?"

Chapter 25

It wasn't easy getting up that morning, but the rippling effects of the sun through his window proved to Charles that this Maine climate had the subtle promise of what he was told: 'Get up early, go to bed early!'

He despised it but woke and stretched in bed. He had sent Elena and the kids back to the cabin but felt a bit guilty by calling the state on her behalf. It really wasn't his concern. He glanced out the window and saw that the skies were bright blue, with no clouds in sight.

It was about time that he checked his traps. How long had it been? He couldn't remember. Was it a week? It had to have been. Elena's car was still outside, and he was happy with that. The Department of Human Services had issued a restraining order against Jonas due to his phone call and explanation. The incident with Chad sealed the case. That was documented.

The whole thing was getting so bizarre! He had arrived only less than two weeks ago and had already seen so much. He had to talk to Janet, but it was too early yet.

He looked at his watch. It was nearly 8:00 a.m. "Whoo!" he thoughtlessly uttered. "Boy, did *I* sleep in!" He picked up his clothes and quickly got dressed, then stepped outside to check on Elena and the children.

He knocked on the door of their cabin, and Elena answered, wearing just jeans and a T-shirt.

"Hi!" he said, politely.

"Good morning, Charles," she replied. "Please, come on in and have a cup of coffee." Her spirits were chipper and her demeanor was upbeat.

He stepped inside. "Thank you, that sounds good!" He looked around, and only Chad was there. "Where's Katherine?" he asked.

Elena poured coffee into a cup on the counter then handed it to him. "Charles! It's Monday. She goes to school, you know! I just got back from driving her there." He took hold of the cup. "Now, I don't know how you like it, but there is sugar and cream if you want." She smiled politely.

"Thank you, no. This is fine!" He took a sip. "Hey, look, I've got to go out and check my traps today. It's been a long week for me. I can only hope things get better." He looked at her wounds, but they had cleared up, mostly. Chad jumped up off the futon and walked to the two of them.

"Hey, Charles, if you go check traps today, can I go?" he pleaded, with passion.

Charles laughed. "I don't see why not. That is, if it is all right with your mother." He turned to her, searching for her opinion. "I only have five traps. It shouldn't take too long."

She smiled at him. "That's fine."

"I don't want you going back to the house while I'm gone. I can't see the reason. I mean—"

She patted him on the back. "Don't worry! I'm not going anywhere. God knows!"

He turned back to Chad. "O.K., then, go get ready and we'll be off. I have to make one phone call. Why don't you come over to my cabin when you're all set, O.K.?"

Chad nodded heartily, "Yeah, sure! It will only take me a few minutes."

Charles gulped his coffee. "Then, I'll be there!" He pointed his finger at Elena, like the local school nurse. "Now, you stay here today, get it?"

She gleamed. "Yes. Thank you, Charles!"

He set his cup down and went back to his cabin. It seemed like a good idea, that is, Chad going with him, and it would keep him out of trouble. The boy was a time bomb, he figured as he stepped inside and went to the phone. It had been a long time!

He dialed his home phone. "Hello?"

Janet answered. "Charles! What is happening up there? I'm worried to death! Lord, Charles, I've been trying to get in touch with you for a week! I can't deal with this! The children are wondering who their father is!" Her attitude was not conducive to a happily married woman.

"Well, Janet, it's a long story. Oh, Lord, I miss you, too! Have a little bit of patience. I want to know what's going on with Dean Groton. I can't get hold of him."

"You mean old rotten Groton? He's called here about a thousand times. For what, I don't know. All of a sudden, he won't answer my phone calls. I tried to get in touch with you. Where are you? There's no record of your being there. What's going on, Charles?"

He stalled. "You mean to tell me that he's tried to get in touch with you?" He seemed concerned.

"Well, yes!" The phone went silent. "Does that surprise you?"

"No, no. You have to know, I'm staying under an alias. I'm not Charles Ritter here, now, I'm John Twimbell!" He chuckled under his breath.

"Ha! John Twimbell! Ha! I could have picked a better name than that!" She laughed. "No wonder why I couldn't get you. Oh, Charles! Where are you staying?"

"I have a cottage on the bay. It's really quite nice!"

"I'm coming down there, Charles, and I need the address."

"Janet! Oh, all right! Wait a minute and I'll give you the directions."

"Oh, by the way, honey, we're getting billed for all your hotels. I thought the school was taking care of that!"

"What? They are! That is, they're supposed to!" He thought to himself. "Oh, no! I have to get in touch with Dean Groton. There's a glitch in this whole thing! He went on vacation at the same time that Ben did, and there is no record of my class!"

"Charles, are you safe?"

"Yes, yes, yes, don't worry. All that is all over now! Look, I'll get the directions for you, then I have to leave. I'll call you later tonight. I love you!"

"I love you, too, dear. I've talked to Mrs. Hauser, and she's willing to take the kids for a couple of days. I'll see you tomorrow, sometime." She hung up.

It was very warm out for this time of day as Charles and Chad backed the trailer down the ramp and unloaded the skiff into the bay. The water surged at the docks in an irregular pattern, and the waves lapped up the small rocks. Chad was eager to get going and hustled into the bay, neglecting his own attire.

The regular two old men stood on the end of the long pier, and he could overhear their conversation, but they stopped talking and watched as he and Chad loaded the boat.

"Mornin', flatlander," Sam said. "We ain't seen you in a while."

Charles nodded to them, "Good morning, gentlemen. No, I've been busy." He glanced out at the moorings and saw Jonas's boat still there. "Hey, guys, have you seen Jonas today?"

They both shook their heads. "Nope!" Andrew said. "Looks like he took the day off! I see ya got his son. Hello, Chad." He waved to him.

Chad bobbed his head up and down. "Hi!" he said. He saw a starfish just below the water and leaned in to pick it up, then placed it in the boat.

The old man turned his attention to the bay. "The police are out there, though!" He glared at the sea.

Charles drew back, distracted from what he was doing. "What? Why?"

"Don't rightly know! There's talk about the chief havin' a boatin' accident. I heard he was in trouble for cheatin' the State. Or maybe he's on the lam."

"Nope," Sam corrected, "I heard he was out chasin' a skirt! Ah-yup, had enough of his wife, 's what I heard."

Charles knew the truth but scratched his head. "Then, they have the patrol boat?" he asked, insincerely.

"They found it!" Sam said.

"Found it?"

"Ah-yup!" Andrew interposed. "Out by Hog Island. It was just floatin' there. I s'pose he's off to tend to his own temptations." He pointed his index finger to his head. "He ain't all there, you know." He then pointed to his crotch. "It's all there!" He laughed, and Sam joined in. The two of them went on in their ridiculous fashion. Charles turned his head, got into the skiff, and pulled it up to the wharf where Chad got in.

"Gentlemen, we'll see you later." The two old men waved.

They took off to the mooring, tied up the dinghy and climbed aboard the boat. "Now, Chad, I'm going to show you what traps are mine and where they are. I can't let you pull one up on your own, though."

"Dad let me!" Chad yelled over the roar of the engine. "I know how to do it!" The ripples from the ocean splashed up on the side of the boat as they slithered out into the inner harbor.

"No, Chad. I can't. This is my last time on this bay, I think. I'm not allowed to have anybody but me to do that. Do you understand?"

Chad hung his head, disappointed. "Yes, I guess!"

The ocean rocked the boat as they went. "Now, Chad, I have to point out my colors." They went out past the minefield of lobster buoys outlining the bay until they got up to the first set of traps at the channel buoy. It rolled sideways with their approach. He pointed to the objects floating in the water. "These are mine. I have three here and two up there." He flung his finger north, in the direction of the other two. "I'm going to start here, and make it to those. You got it?"

"Yes. I can pull this in for you, if you want." He formed on a weak smile.

"Chaaad! I already told you, no!" Charles reminded him, then set the boat into neutral as he approached the buoy. "I'll haul this one up, and you keep your eyes open." He leaned over the side of the boat and grabbed the top of the buoy then proceeded to haul it up. He brought in the toggle and set it on the deck, then pulled the warp up into the hauler. He could feel the weight of the trap and thought it was much heavier than he expected, but the pulley served its function, and he placed the trap on the sideboard. There were six lobsters inside!

"Wow!" Chad exclaimed when he saw the goods. "That can feed a family!"

Charles turned to him and nodded. "That's exactly what it is going to do! We'll have lobster tonight! I must have left the trap in there for a week, and this is what you get!" He pulled off the crabs from the outside of the trap and threw them back into the water then opened the top of the trap, carefully removing the lobsters and tossed them into the bin in the boat.

"Oh, oh! Well, we have company!" Chad leaned to his right, signaling to Charles. "It's the police!"

Charles lurched sideways and looked over the starboard side of the boat. The police patrol roared up along the side, with Red sitting at the wheel of the vessel and Danny Lipowski riding beside.

"Just stay right there, Mr. Ritter. We've finally got to ya." He held his pistol in the air. The boat drifted and came to rest beside his. "Keep your hands up so that I can see 'em." He waved his gun recklessly, then pointed it inside the boat, cocking back the hammer. "What'd'ya got in there?" he asked, staring down.

Charles looked at him with trepidation. "Lobster!" he answered. "Why? What did you expect?" He turned the motor off and the patrol idled into position beside him then Danny stood up and held the two boats together. He stepped over the side of the patrol and into Charles's boat. "What's going on? What do you want?"

"I'll decide that, flatlander!" He inspected the inside of the boat, and the bin where the lobster lay. "Ya got any weapons on board?" He curtly snarled at Charles.

"Weapons? No, why?" He was flabbergasted. "I'd like to know what's going on!" He slapped the wheel.

The deputy ruffled through all he could, in a very short period of time. Red turned his vessel off and stared at him. "It appears that the chief has been missin' for a couple a' days. We'd like to know what you know about it. That's all."

Charles coughed. "Nothing. I don't know anything."

"Is that right?" Danny insisted. "Well, then. I guess ya won't mind comin' down to the station and answerin' a few questions, then, would ya?" He leered at him.

"No. I don't mind, but I would like to reset this trap, first. That is, if that's O.K. with you."

Danny turned to Red. "There ain't no weapons here. What d'ya think?"

Red shrugged. "I guess that's O.K." Danny turned back to Charles.

"Ya follow us." He waved the pistol around. "I don't know what you're here for, but I don't like it! Nope, not at all!" He kicked the bin beside him and placed his gun back into his holster. "I got questions!" He stepped back

LOBSTER TRAPPED!

over the edge of Charles's boat, and into the police boat. "We'll keep an eye on ya on the way in. Now, let's go!" Red started the engine again.

There was nothing left to do but obey their demand. "What do they want?" Chad asked, and Charles started the engine, then followed the police.

"I don't know!" he exclaimed. "But we do have dinner when we get back! Sit down!" He stayed within audible range of the police boat, when Chad jumped up.

"Hey, what's that?" he screamed, pointing to an object in the bay. "It looks like garbage!" Charles knelt on the cushion at the helm and peered over the side. There was something there, but it wasn't garbage—it was the chief of police's body, drifting past the police boat. He quickly sat back down.

"Damn idiots didn't even see it" he said aloud. "Keep that to yourself, Chad!"

The interrogation was brief, and there was nothing that they could hold him for, so they released him while Chad waited in the other room. "I can go now, and get you back to the cabins. They're satisfied that I had nothing to do with the disappearance of Chief McFagan, but Lord knows, they tried to accuse me of it. I'm hungry."

Chad leapt off the wooden bench and shouted back, "Me too!" They exited the station and got back into the vehicle. They were polite enough to allow him to moor his boat, remove the lobster and drive to the station on his own. They questioned him about his presence in town, and he told them, point blank. There was nothing mentioned about the bell or any of the other victims. It was purely for information, of which Charles offered none. He simply spoke off the cuff.

It was the middle of the day when they released him, and he got out of there as quickly as he could, then rushed back to Belfast. He was happy to see Elena's car in the lot when they returned. Chad had to mention the police when he ran into the cabin. Charles carried in the lobster, and she greeted him at the door. "Well, what do you have here?" she asked, knowing full well what it was. "And what is this about the police?" She helped him bring the buckets inside.

"Oh, it's nothing, really. They're concerned about the chief, who's missing, and wanted to know if I knew anything."

She spun around. "Do you?" she asked.

"Ah, ha! I'd rather not talk about it. Hey, look, I brought an early dinner for everybody. Can you cook them?"

She glanced down into the bucket she held. "I sure can! These are beautiful!"

He stammered and kicked the ground. "I've never had lobster before. I don't know how to cook them. I was hoping you could help."

She laughed. "Of course!" she said. "I only hope that there is a big enough pot in here." He followed her inside. "Now that I think about it, there is. You're in for a treat!"

He smiled politely back to her. "Thanks."

They had a large meal that day, with Elena finding some canned vegetables in one of the cupboards and preparing the entire feast, after having Charles run to the store to get some corn on the cob and butter. Charles was stuffed, partly due to the lobster and partly due to the butter. He had not enjoyed such a meal. Soon, they all grew fatigued. Elena cleaned up as the rest wiped their chins and lay back. "Whew!" she said. "I think I'll take a little nap!"

Charles stood up. "I agree!" He tossed the napkin in his hand down into the trash bucket. "Me too! Thank you for cooking that for me, but it happens after every big meal for me. I think I'll take a nap, myself." He started to walk outside, when he heard a loud crack of thunder. The skies turned pitch black. "Oh, oh!" he said.

The rain poured down in a matter of seconds, and the deluge pummeled the parking area. He covered his head with his arms. "I'll talk to you later, Elena." He ran out the door, and over to his cabin.

She shook her head while the children turned on the television, then she scraped off the excess lobster from the table. "Kids, I'm going to lie down for a little while. Do you think you can behave?"

They nodded and went back to the television. Lightning shot through the sky outside, and the cabin shook. "Wow!" she said. "I hope I can get in a nap!" Another resounding crash of thunder burst in the air, and the rain poured ever harder. She looked outside and saw that Charles had made it inside his cabin. She went to the bedroom to lie down when another bolt of lightning streaked across the sky and then the thunder followed, pushing her forward. She glanced over and saw Katherine was sound asleep while Chad was just nodding off.

The windows of the cabin rattled with the next passing thunder, and she looked back to Chad, who had now fallen asleep. She walked into the bedroom and placed her robe on. "I just wish I had taken everything from the house," she said, remembering why she had the robe.

She lay down, and the sound of the rain, tapping against the roof, made it easy for her to fall to sleep in a mere second. Her mind wandered in fantasy, thinking again of Peter and of the house. *How pleasant!* she thought as she fluffed the pillow of the bed and dreamt.

LOBSTER TRAPPED!

The next thing she heard was a faint voice: *"No sleep! No sleep until you hear me!"*

She wrestled in the bed then placed her head back down on the pillow.

"No sleep! I whisper in the night, but I speak!"

"Huh?" She got up in a half sleep and rubbed her eyes. "Who's there?" she yawned out. The rain continued to rattle off the building, and her vision was blurry with the humidity in the air, that seemed to creep through the walls. "Who is it?" She blinked many times, attempting to focus.

"It is I, your father!"

A figure appeared before her, at the end of the bed. It became clear now. It was a man wearing a blue navy suit, handsomely trimmed. He held a very grim countenance.

She sat up in bed. "Dad?" she asked, shaking off the cobwebs. "Dad, is that you?"

He glared at her. *"It is I!"* He leaned forward.

"Dad? How? Aren't you ... are you ... dead?" She pulled the blankets up to her chin.

"Oooooh, yes! I am dead! I died, and am dead!" The response was instant, and the figure never changed. The voice was mellow and smooth, and it echoed.

She studied him from head to toe. He was immaculate. His white hair was well groomed and seemed to glow in the dark of the room. His large handlebar mustache was exactly as she remembered. He placed his hands behind his back.

"Dad? But how?" she stuttered in shock.

"It is for a reason!" The voice was so real.

"Reason, Dad? What? Why?"

"Oooooh! My murder will be revenged!" He suddenly spoke tersely. *"Oooooh! No sleep until I see it. I cannot sleep, and you will not sleep! Oooooh! Unsaintly! So shallow! The water is shallow!"* he moaned.

"Your murder? Dad, you died in a fishing accident! You weren't murdered!" She spoke in a thin, squeaky voice.

"Oh, no! It was no accident! Oooooh, noooo!" He twisted his body in a show of pain. *"Oooh, I suffer! No sleep! Noooo sleep!"* He groaned slowly. *"Oooooh!"*

She shook her head and shuddered. "Who murdered you, then?" She pulled the blankets around her neck.

He quickly pointed to her, scaring her. *"You know! You have always known! Oooooh, no sleep!"* His eyes burned into her like daggers. *"Nooo, no sleep! You are the apple of my eye! Oooh!"*

"Dad, what are you talking about? Jonas said it was an accident; that you banged your head and fell overboard. It was just an accident, Dad!" She shivered.

"Accident! No! It was no accident! Oooooh! My tortured soul!" The figure rolled his body in anguish. *"I was to sell my boat and quit fishing. I was to retire in peace. Oooh, no peace! No sleep!"* He clenched his fist up to his mouth. *"Now the boat is yours!"*

She shook her head in bewilderment. "You mean that Jonas...." She stopped when a flash of lightning appeared at the window, and the thunder banged above. The storm was directly above them. She was startled by the flash of light.

"Oooh! No accident! No! They called it an accident! Oh! How untrue!" The apparition shook with emotion. *"I was the pilot then and now I must meet my pilot! Oh!"*

"But how then?"

"Oh! Where the water is shallow, the human is shallow!" The lightning flicked again and he turned to watch it pass. *"That day was much like this night! I was confronted, and an oar came to the back of my head. The sea is unforgiving! Oh! Ungodly! How unfair! Oh! I cannot sleep until I have my revenge! Oh!"*

"You mean *me*, Dad?" She winced curiously then cowered. "I am a Christian and worn by the tenets of our faith to love and care!"

"No! Not you! It will not be you that gains my revenge, but those from you! Oh!"

She tilted her head, "Those from me? You mean Chad?"

"You will see!" The boom of thunder pealed through the room with no sign of lightning. *"The heavens call me."* He glared deeply into her bosom. *"Time runs out! Time runs out. Time!"* The vision faded, and instantly, the rain ended.

She gasped and stared around the room, perspiring profusely. Her hands shook and her heart beat violently! She wiped her dripping brow and looked out the window. "Oh, God! That must have been a dream! What did it mean?" She sat on the edge of the bed, allowing her legs to drape over the side then touched her feet on the floor. "He mentioned time! Time? What does that mean?"

It came to her. "Aha! The clock!" She shook her head once more to wake up. "I have to get the clock!"

She looked at her watch and saw it was only 3:30 a.m., and Jonas would not be up yet. She got dressed, knowing she should get back before anyone here got up and found out that she was gone.

Chapter 26

Maybe it was a dream, and maybe it wasn't. It must have meant something, and it certainly made sense. Her father had wanted to get out of the fishing industry for years but told Jonas that he was going to leave the boat to him. They had a falling out during the period just before her father's death, and Jonas was quite upset with him. When her father told him about selling the boat, instead of leaving it to him, it was very plausible that he could have killed him. He was capable of many odd things, including murder. She wanted to get to the house and retrieve the clock quickly; that must have been why he mentioned time. At least, that was all she could think of it meaning. Plus, the clock meant so much to her.

She raced through town and arrived early enough to be sure that Jonas was still asleep. This was confirmed, because the lights of the house were off. She glanced at her watch and checked the time. It was 3:45 a.m. She had to move quickly. The car came to a stop in the driveway and she stared inside. There was no motion within the building, so she carefully turned the ignition off, to remain undetected. She eased out from the door of the car and gently shut it, but not completely, keeping it ajar. She stepped up the drive, to the front door, and slowly turned the knob on the door of the house, to gain access. She twisted it very, very slowly, holding her ear on the outside of the door. There was still no sound inside. The door opened and she slid in, holding the knob.

She whispered, "Hello?" There was no response; it was safe enough to enter. She tediously pulled the door out and glanced around inside; it was still trashed and pitch black inside, when she reached around and took hold of the doorknob from the inside, then turned it slowly, to close the door. She squinted and could see that empty bottles of rum outlined the floor, clothes were strewn about and the dishes were piled up hastily on the counters—all dirty. She peeked to where the clock was standing, but still broken after his last outburst. She gently pushed the door back to shut it. "What a mess!" she whispered to herself then tiptoed over to the clock. The glass on the door was broken, and an empty bottle of rum lay inside the pendulum compartment, wedged against the edge of the cabinet and the pendulum itself. She carefully picked broken glass out of the cabinet and, afterwards, pulled the rum bottle out.

The pendulum swung freely! The clock was not totally ruined, and this brought a wide smile to her face. She leaned back and folded her arms, watching the clock work. It ticked with each swing of the arm.

Unexpectedly, she heard a voice! "Well, ya come back?" She jumped in terror!

She looked over the clock, to the bedroom. Jonas stood at the door, half naked, and half asleep.

"Oh, Jonas, did I wake you?" She cupped her hands over her mouth and gasped.

He swaggered up to the clock, and she could detect a strong odor of alcohol on his breath. He was unshaven and unkempt. "Yeah, ya woke me!" As the clock continued to tick, he placed his hands over his ears. "That damned clock woke me!" He dropped his arms and snarled, "I couldn't go anywhere yesterday, 'cause of ya!"

She started back, seeing his anger, then frowned. "What do you mean, because of me?"

He gritted his teeth, "I had to talk to Social Services all day. They told me I can't see ya or the kids now."

She sighed. "Oh, my! Charles called them, not me!" she spoke defensively.

"Yeah, ya got that boy by the scrotum! What are the two of ya doin' together? Huh?" He pulled his pants up and grunted loudly. "Huh?"

"Oh, no! It's not like that. He's only helped me out, that's all!" Her face wrinkled in worry. "We're just friends."

"Friends my ass! Ya move in with him and drag the kids away from me, then ya call the damn State! You're shaggin' him, aren't ya?" he screamed.

"Oh, no, no. It's not like that, Jonas. Not at all!" She slapped her hands to her cheeks while the clock continued to tick.

"Ya used me just like ya father did!" He grabbed his ears again, blocking out the clicking of the clock.

Suddenly, she stopped and stared at him; thinking. "You *killed* my father, didn't you?" Her mouth dropped open, anticipating the answer.

He spun, avoiding the question.

"Didn't you?" she demanded.

"Huh? Ha! That old jerk?" He smiled fiendishly and put his hands down. "Ya can't prove it!" He started to laugh. "It was an accident!" He laughed louder.

"It was no accident!" she yelled back.

"Now, how the hell would ya know that?"

"He told me!" she revealed.

He laughed boisterously, keeling over and holding his hands on his hips. "He told ya? Don't make me laugh!"

"And you raped your own daughter! It was bad enough that you forced yourself on me, but she's just a child! You've beaten Chad to his limits! You're despicable! You're an insult to the human race! You disgust me! This is it! I filed for a divorce yesterday; and I want you out of my life!" She stomped her foot in anger. The clock ticked away.

He stared at her then rolled his eyes in a fanatical way. "Ha! Ya think ya got me all figured out, don't ya?" He pointed to his groin. "This is what ya want, ain't it? Ya want this *little* Jonas, don't ya?" He rocked his head, nodding as if answering his own question. "Yeah, that's what it is! Ya want a piece of this, don't ya?" He laughed lowly then shook his head. "Ya whore! Ya're a stinkin' whore! C'mon, I'll give ya what ya want!"

Tick, tick, tick; the clock never stopped. "Jonas, no! Please, Jonas, no!"

He covered his face with his hands then rubbed the top of his head. "You're screwin' that guy from Rhode Island, aren't ya? Ya whore! I know ya are!" He swung at her, but she avoided the blow and ran back towards the door. "Ya screwin' him, ain't ya?" He crumbled with pain. "And stop this damned clickin'!" He leaned back and shifted his foot, holding it up for a second then sent it back down on the side of the clock. It crumbled at impact. The pendulum stopped, and he stared at her. "Ya got this comin'!" he ranted. "Ya did this on purpose!" He lunged at her.

"My clock! No, Jonas, please!" She covered her body up with her arms as he stretched over the damaged timepiece to grab her.

Chad awoke upon the termination of the rain and sat at the edge of his bed. The aftermath of the storm had woken him; it was the silence after the storm, he guessed, but he thought he heard something. He got up, quickly got dressed and stepped into the living room, but as he examined it, he could tell that it hadn't changed. He strolled to the refrigerator to find what he could eat at this early hour.

It was too early to turn the lights on, lest he wake the rest of the family. It had just passed 3:40 a.m., and he imagined that he had heard voices earlier, but it must have been the rain. The light from the refrigerator nearly blinded him, but he found some leftover corn on the cob and decided he would have a piece. He took one ear out and shut the door to the appliance, chewing on the cold corn.

The rain had left dampness inside the cabin, giving the atmosphere a slight chill that ran through his bones. He walked over to the couch and sat down. The voices he heard sounded so authentic! It was only his imagination, he figured.

Then he glanced over at his mother's bedroom door. It was open! He jumped up and ran to the bedroom to look inside. The bed was unmade, and his mother was gone!

Where was she? He began thinking, what could have happened to her? The possibilities ran rapidly through his mind. Could it be that his father had come back? Could Jonas have taken her? Or did she and that guy from Millinocket run away together? Or was she really still here, somewhere? Those voices he heard—who were they?

He hustled to the window and looked out. The car was gone! Something was definitely wrong!

His eyes widened. *The house*! She went back to the house to pick up things! There was no time to waste, he concluded. Oh, no, what was she thinking? How foolish! He realized that the only way to find out was to go there, but how? He sloppily slid on his sneakers and ran around the room trying to think. *Of course ... Charles!*

He ran out the door without tying his shoes and skipped through the rain-soaked soil, splashing the water from the puddles all over his pants. Once he got to Charles's cabin, he wailed wildly on the door, screaming his name. Eventually, Charles opened the door, wearing just his bathrobe and adjusting his glasses. He rubbed his eyes. "Chad? What's the matter with you? It looks like you just saw a ghost!"

Chad panted deeply and his voice was shrill. "My mom! It's my mom!"

Charles adjusted his robe. "What about your mom?" he asked sincerely. "What's the matter with her?"

He pointed to the parking area. "She's gone!"

They both turned to look, and Charles could see that the car was not there. "Where did she go?" he asked.

Chad struggled to catch his breath. "The house! I'm sure of it. Oh, help me, Charles. Give me a ride there, please!" His eyebrows curled, pleadingly. "*Please!*"

Charles rolled his eyes. "I'm sure she's all right, Chad. Don't you think you're being a little bit paranoid? You know, she is a big girl now, and it's kind of early." He glanced at his watch. "No! It's really early!"

"No, Mr. Ritter, I know! She's gone back to the house, I just know it!"

"What for?"

"I don't know, I just know it! You don't understand. My dad raped her!

My dad raped Katherine!" He began to cry and clenched his fists tightly.

"What? You're kidding me, right?" He suddenly changed his attitude. Chad shook his head. "You *are* kidding me, right?" He demanded the answer, but Chad kept shaking his head. "Oh, my Lord!"

"Hurry, Mr. Ritter, I have a funny feeling!" he shouted. "I know she's in trouble!"

Charles held his hand up in the air. "Give me a minute, and we'll take a ride. I just hope it's not what you think. What the hell is she doing that for anyway? Oh, God, let me get dressed."

"Hurry! Hurry, Charles!" Chad was bouncing up and down.

"So ya think ya so smart, ya whore! Ya want a divorce, do ya?" he ranted.

"My aunt and uncle left me their money. I don't need you anymore, Jonas!" She turned and ran to the door, which she had left slightly ajar, but he was upon her in seconds. She grabbed the doorknob with one hand and held her other arm out to block her attacker.

He grabbed her arm and yanked it, then pulled her away from the door.

"Ya screwin' him, ain't ya?" He pulled her up to his chest. "AIN'T YA?" he roared in a tone that echoed into her brain, causing her to nearly faint. "Ya want some of me? Huh, do ya?" He swung her by the arm then shoved her against the far wall, which shook when she hit, with a loud *Bang*. The fishing net and the series of gaffs bounced with the impact and got tangled together. The ten-inch gaff caught in the net in such a way as to protrude from the wall with the point facing away from the wall.

Jonas grabbed her by the arm again and whipped her in a full circle then released his grip. "Ya lyin' whore!" he shouted, gritting his teeth and flexing his muscles.

She hit the wall face first with her arms outstretched and landed directly on the exposed gaff, impaling her in her midsection. She moaned softly; her figure fused in that position, with blood pouring out of her body. Her neck flipped back and to the side with blood trickling out of her mouth. Her arms fell limply to her side, palms facing upward. She remained stuck in the air.

Jonas stood and stared; his eyes wide open, and his mouth agape. Everything stopped.

At that moment, he heard the door creek open and Chad walked inside. He turned and looked at Chad, then back to his wife. Hastily, he ran out past the boy, who was standing near the door in shock.

"Ma!" Chad yelled and ran to her, propping her up with his shoulder.

Jonas stumbled out of the door, and into the drive, where he saw Charles waiting in the minivan. He snapped his head to face his own truck and climbed inside quickly, screeching out of the driveway. Charles watched him leave and, after hearing Chad's scream, ran up to the door and peered inside. He witnessed the gruesome scene and jumped over the broken clock, across the room, grabbing Elena at the shoulders. "Give me a hand, Chad, and we'll get her down from here." He turned her slightly and could see the gaff had entered her just below the chest, with the hook firmly embedded. He gently turned her back to the original position and pulled up on her shoulders then back off the hook. Chad removed the hook from her torso.

The two of them eased her down to the floor. Charles placed her head in his hand and lowered it down. Blood covered her entire frame and blood dripped off the gaff, as well as the wall.

"Elena! Elena, can you hear me?" he asked, slapping her gently on the cheek.

"Uh, uh, what, what happened?" she hoarsely answered.

"She's in a traumatic shock, but she's still alive, Chad!" He pressed down on her wound to alleviate the tremendous bleeding. "Quickly, get me a cloth and I'll apply a pressure dressing. I'll call the hospital to let them know we're coming, then let's get her to the van. Hurry, now!"

Chad swiftly retrieved a fresh towel from the bathroom while Charles called the hospital. They informed him that it would be better to have an ambulance pick her up, but he told them that they would bring her in, because time was of the essence. He hung up and placed the cloth Chad handed him over her wound, pressing down. "Now, Chad, you hold this on while we take her to my van."

He lifted her under her armpits and dragged her to the door, then to the van. Chad held the dressing, crying relentlessly. They lifted her inside, and cautiously laid her down, so as not to injure her further. The two men jumped into the van and rushed to the hospital at breakneck speed.

Chad constantly talked to his mother between tears. "Oh, ma! I knew something like this was going to happen! Oh, God, Ma, talk to me!" He was babbling in hysterics. "He's going to pay for this, Ma! He's going to pay for this, I promise!"

She pointed up with her index finger, but her eyes rolled back into her head, as she slowly slipped into unconsciousness.

Chapter 27

Jonas hastened along the road with no compunction for his actions; he just wanted to stay clear of the police. What happened wasn't intentional, he felt, and after all, she was the one who came to him; it wasn't as though he tracked her down. He tugged at his beard, still only half dressed. He didn't care. There was no time to waste in finding the treasure, knowing that the cops would eventually catch up with him.

"Damn woman!" he exclaimed as he drove, making futile glances in every mirror on the truck. There was no one behind him while he powered his way to the Searsport pier, but he checked nonetheless. His head still hurt from the clicking of the clock. "Her damned aunt and uncle! That damned Rhode Islander! The damned boy!" He gurgled. "I gotta stay clear of the cops!"

The ride took only minutes, and he pulled into the parking lot off Steamship Avenue and backed the vehicle down the ramp, leaving the engine running. He panted in the front seat, and set his head down on the steering wheel, breathless, then he slapped the wheel. "Damn!" He hollered. "Damn bitch!" He pivoted his head all around, but the yard was deserted. It was still early, and he worked with meticulous speed getting the skiff off the back and into the water. He waded in and pulled it over to the side, where he tied it up, then returned to the driver's seat, pulled the truck into a typical parking spot near the rock wall and turned the engine off. He hurried down to the dinghy and climbed aboard, still checking the area for onlookers. He saw none.

The moon was full, and the dim light gave him some vision for his flight out of the harbor. The boat moved swiftly in the still waters and he arrived at his boat very quickly. Once he climbed onto the *Stinger* he pushed the throttle to full speed, ignoring the other moorings and buoys. He headed to Cape Rosier.

Charles arrived at the hospital and zipped into the emergency ward's semi-circular driveway, then slammed the van into park. The hospital was ready and had a team outside to greet them. He stood and watched while Chad was pushed away by the hospital team; against his wishes, trying to stay by his mother's side. They pulled out a gurney and laid her down on it tediously. Intravenous was immediately applied, although it was ambiguous as to its make-up.

Charles sighed heavily, knowing that there was nothing more that he could do. He shook his head and breathed in and out several times. Chad followed the stretcher into the hospital, wailing as he went. They stopped him once more, but he persisted to follow her inside, grabbing on to the edge of the gurney. The attendants, who were not directly monitoring her, motioned to Charles to come and get him.

He nodded to them and strode up to the gurney. "Come on, Chad, we're just going to have to wait. Let them do their jobs." He spoke solemnly and held Chad by the arm.

Chad struggled with him. "Ma! Ma!" He cried. The technicians had taken the towel off her and replaced the dressing with a sanitary one. They strolled down the corridor while Charles kept Chad still. "Ma!" he screamed as they took her away. His efforts ceased, and he slumped down into a fit of unrepressed crying.

"Why?" he stammered. "Why?"

Charles gave him a hug, and he wept into his shirt. "He'll get his!" He blurted out. "He'll get his!" The tone was obvious, and his anger was apparent. The crew vanished down the hallway to one of the operating rooms.

Charles drew Chad to his chest and he also wept. "We'll wait and see." He patted him on the back. "We'll see. Sit down on the bench here and we'll talk."

Chad squatted onto the seat and slumped. "He'll get his!" he kept on repeating.

"Now, look, Chad. I'm going to have to go back to talk to Katherine, and let her know what happened." He glared at him in a caring fashion. "Do you want to go with me, or do you want to stay here?"

Chad shot his head into Charles's face, then pointed to the floor. "Here!" he stated with no hesitation.

Charles grinned. "O.K.," he said. "I'll be back." He patted him on the shoulder and exited.

Jonas reached Cape Rosier relatively quickly and set the boat into idle. He had put on a pair of pants and his boots along with a T-shirt when Elena woke him, but he was wearing no socks. His hair and beard were tangled and flew haphazardly in the breeze. He was sweating from fear but did not see anybody else near him, yet. It was fully light out at the time that he reached the area where he had killed the Rat. He cut off the engines of the boat and took out one of the wooden oars that he kept on board, then mindlessly poked it into the water at random locations, hoping to get lucky and hit the treasure. He wasn't even sure what he was looking for, but he plugged away regardless. At least he was far enough away from Searsport that the cops wouldn't find him. His mind wandered in a million directions.

If it was a sunken ship it should be pretty obvious, he thought, *but if was so damned obvious, how come nobody else has found it?* The waves rocked the boat while he pondered the possibilities. *Maybe there is no ship. This could all be a game—but wait! If Kenny and the Rat had put so much effort into this, it has to be.*

He prodded into the bay uselessly, and now the other fishermen and boaters were arriving in large numbers, far away from his boat.

That's it! That's where I'll find a clue. I saw them lookin' at a map! Of course! He laughed to himself. *I'll just have me a look inside their boat. I don't think they'll mind too much!* He threw the oar into the boat and started the engines.

Charles pulled up to the hospital's visitor parking lot this time with Katherine inside the van. The two of them entered the facility. He had not told her the whole story; just that her mother had an accident. He didn't dare.

Chad greeted them as they walked into the waiting room, with tears in his eyes. "Katherine!" He shouted and ran over to give her a huge embrace. "He's really done it this time!" He rocked her in his arms.

"Huh?" she replied. "What are you talking about? I thought this was just a minor accident." She looked over to Charles, who shrugged.

Chad pulled away from her and held her at arms length. "Dad tried to kill her!" he explained, wiping the tears from his face.

She gasped and jumped back. "What? What do you mean by that?" Her face turned white.

He sobbed while he spoke. "I found her stuck to one of the gaffs on the wall at home. She was stuck there with a big hole in her belly. There was blood everywhere! He did it! He took off when we got there! He'll pay, Katherine! I swear, he'll pay!"

She fell back against the wall, still staring at Charles. "Why didn't you tell me?"

Charles drew his shoulders up to his ears. "I really didn't want to get you upset. It'll be fine, don't worry. We'll just have to wait for a word from the doctor."

She cringed and held both hands over her mouth. "Oh, my God! She's going to die!"

Charles snapped back. "No, no, no! Don't jump to conclusions, you two. I'll check right now and see how she is. The two of you just sit quietly until I get back." He pointed to a row of chairs in the room and walked away.

Katherine staggered over to Chad, and they hugged; both of them crying in each other's arms.

The air was warm, and the sky shone brightly. Jonas pulled up alongside Kenny's boat, where he had hidden it on Spectacle Island in a small, little-known harbor. It was the same as he left it. He turned his engine off and banged up beside the other craft, then jumped on board of it with his bow rope in his hands. He tied up his boat to one of the cleats on Kenny's. He could see the splattered blood of Souharat's on the inside rail of the vessel before he began looking around for the maps.

It didn't take long for him to find what he was looking for; except there was only one. He picked it up off the deck and studied it. The map was only slightly wet from the rain but had been placed below the pilot housing's protection and was still readable. It held the grid that the Rat had so carefully detailed, showing the Head of the Cape and a rectangular pattern which spread over a large area.

This was it?

It could take forever to pinpoint the location, and the color patterns made no sense. He blew out air in disgust and frustration.

But wait a minute! He drew the map closer to his face and grinned. The color pattern ended, and where it ended, had to be the location where they were when he came upon them!

He folded the paper up and shoved it into his pocket then re-boarded his own boat He clenched his fist and threw it into the air as he sped away, back to the spot.

A gentleman in a light blue gown and cap entered the waiting room where Charles stood. When the children saw him approach Charles, they jumped up from their seats and pressed up closely to him. "How is she?" Chad yelled. "How's my mom?" He was nearly bouncing.

The man turned to Chad. "She's going to be all right! Don't worry." He looked to Charles. "Are you her husband?"

He shook his head. "God, no!" he stated. "That's how she got here! But these are her children." He tipped his head at the two kids. "I brought her in here."

The man smiled at them. "Well, then, I guess it's all right to talk to you.

May we speak alone?" He stared at Charles, and he nodded, stepping off to the side, but the children followed.

He was an average-height man with graying hair protruding from the edges of his cap until he removed it, and the top of his head was balding. He wore thin bifocal glasses, which he pulled at while he spoke. He stood erect and had a slight pouch around his waist. He sighed. "Well, I guess it's O.K. if they know, also. First of all, my name is Doctor Cote and I'm only assisting on the operation." They shook hands. "We have her stable right now, but she's suffered from an acute puncture of her rectus abdominal muscle, near the top." He paused and collected his thoughts. "Do you know what happened to her? I mean, it looks as though she has been impaled by something." His thin eyebrows squeezed together above his nose, inside his glasses, and he stared at Charles.

"She *was* impaled! I don't know exactly how, but we found her stuck on a large fishing hook at her house. Is she going to be all right?"

Doctor Cote flashed his teeth. "I think so, but it's still too early to say for certain. She sustained damage to the muscle that will be relatively easy to repair, but I'm afraid...." The children stared at him anxiously. He looked down at them then continued. "I'm afraid she had lost a lot of blood. She's actually quite lucky that this didn't hit any organs." He rubbed his chin. "Extremely lucky!"

Katherine turned to Chad and smiled. They each bobbed their heads with the news, so far.

"But I'm afraid she has ruptured her splenic artery. I don't know how long it took you to get her here, but if you were a minute later, she wouldn't be with us, now!" He clasped his hands. "She also has torn part of the renal artery and vein. If you could tell me what happened, I could explain what she's going through. She must have had that hook pulled up on her, because the wound barely missed her heart!"

Charles stood silently, listening. "Wow!" He rubbed his head in relief. "She actually slid down on the hook. I got her here as quickly as I could!"

"It's a good thing!" Doctor Cote exclaimed. "The laceration barely missed her abdominal aorta but did cut into her stomach. She's very lucky to be alive!" He stopped and crossed his arms. "Like I said, we've stabilized her."

Charles glared at him. "When can we see her?"

"Yes, when?" Chad interrupted huskily.

He placed his hands on his hips. "Whenever she wakes up. The operation is still ongoing, but the major repairs have been completed." He sighed. "She fell into a slight coma prior to arriving."

Charles stepped back. "A coma?"

The doctor reeled back and forth between Charles and the children. "It's normal, but I expect a full recovery. It's amazing that the damage wasn't worse. It was so close to the organs! But we should be done in about an hour. You won't be able to speak with her, but you can see her up in ICU after we're done." He smiled sympathetically.

"I want to see her now!" Chad insisted.

"I'm afraid you can't now, lad. Try to relax if you can. The cafeteria is on the basement floor, if you like. I'll let you know when she's out of danger."

Charles winced. "Thank you, Doctor." He pointed to the chairs again, suggesting patience to the kids. The three of them went over and sat down while Doctor Cote turned around and stepped back down the hallway.

Jonas returned to the Head of the Cape and took the chart out from his pocket, opening it with one had while steering with the other. The sun beat down fiercely now and the inside of the boat dried rapidly. He began glancing back and forth between the map and the shore but was having trouble with the scale of the chart, which, he realized, wasn't the same as the ones he used.

Other boaters had gone out past him, but none came close to him. Then, out of the corner of his eye, he saw a boat, well off in the distance; heading directly at him! He placed the map down and picked up his binoculars from the side pocket near the wheel then looked through them at the incoming vessel. It was the police patrol boat! Damn!

His heart raced. *This will have to wait,* he thought. *I just hope they didn't recognize me.* He threw the ship into full throttle, heading around the cape. He would hide at Bakerman Beach until the trouble passed.

He waited nearly all day. He knew the patrol boat would only be out for so long, because the cops don't get overtime. He needed to get his scuba suit anyway to look in the water, so he would call it a day and return to the house to gather up his gear.

When he returned, it was late, and he notice a note posted on the door. He looked at it closely; it was a search warrant! He stepped inside and saw that the place had been turned upside down, with the furniture scattered all around. The table had been flipped onto its side, and even the couch was pushed out and knocked over. The chairs for the table were strewn throughout the place. It was a war zone!

"I'd better just grab my gear and get out of here before they come back." He spoke out loud to himself then he glanced at the wall. The gaffs were all gone. "Damn!" he said. "I'd better hide out for the night and sleep in my truck. I got a spot near Mack Point where they won't find me." He hustled through the house, gathering up what he needed, including his scuba gear, and then left.

Charles walked up to the children, who were both asleep in the chairs at the waiting room. They both woke up when they heard him approaching. "Did you guys get a good nap?" he asked.

Chad stretched and yawned. "I did!" he replied. Katherine simply nodded.

"I spoke with the doctor, again. She's fine, but you still can't talk to her. She's still in a light coma. He figures she should come out of it at any time. We just have to wait."

"What about Dad?" Chad asked in disgust.

"Well, I went to the house and he wasn't there, so I went down to the piers and saw his truck. He must have gone out on the bay looking for the treasure."

"Treasure?" Chad inquired. "What treasure?"

Charles laughed. "Oh, it's a long story! He'd better not go back to the house. I went to the police and filed a report, and they've gone through the house completely. If I know him, he'll wait until daylight and go back to search in the water then." He yawned. "I've had a long day! There's nothing to do here but wait and sleep. The doctor will tell us when she comes out of the coma. Try to get some more sleep, you guys." He patted Chad on the head.

The three slept peacefully through the night until Chad woke up well before sunrise. He leaned over and woke up Katherine. She opened her eyes slowly. "What?" she asked.

"Shhh!" Chad said, holding his index finger up to his pursed lips. "Don't make any noise!" he whispered. "I've got an idea. I'm going to take off and get the bastard! I'm not going to wait for the cops. If Charles wakes up, tell him I just went to get something from his van." He winked at her then tiptoed over to Charles and gently picked out his keys from his pocket, careful not to wake him.

"Chad! I hope you know what you're doing!" She was concerned.

"I'm not sure, right now," he answered.

"Be careful!" she stated.

"I will!"

"And good luck!"

He nodded and left the hospital.

Chapter 28

It was still pitch black out when Chad sat down in the driver's seat of Charles's van. He adjusted the seat and the mirrors as best he could, to fit his frame. He had driven his father's truck many times in the past and felt quite comfortable in this vehicle; it was much cozier. He slipped the key into the ignition after he acclimated to his surroundings and turned the van on. He was barely tall enough in the seat to see over the dash, but he could. He fumbled around with the instruments until he found the lights and turned them on. He put the car into gear and drove away, very slowly.

There were virtually no other cars on the road, but he still took his time and made it to the Searsport landing within ten minutes. As he pulled down Steamship Avenue, he gawked everywhere and saw that his was the only vehicle in the area. He pulled up to the landing and tried to back the van up with the trailer attached, but he couldn't get the hang of it, hitting the concrete guides twice. The trailer didn't go where he intended, therefore, he finally gave up, jumped out and removed the skiff onto the pavement by hand, cautious not to damage it. He pulled it along the parking area, scraping the bottom as he went. It didn't matter; he was in a hurry!

Eventually, he got the boat in the water and tied it to the pier then ran back into the van that he had left running. He drove it down Cottage Street a little ways and parked it on the side of the road so that Jonas wouldn't be able to see it when he arrived. He knew that he would! It was a devious plan he had developed. He exited the van and ran back to the pier, where he climbed on board the dinghy, started the engine and headed for Charles's mooring. He arrived in no time, having been there before, even though it was almost impossible to see in the darkness. He pulled the skiff up beside the lobster boat, climbed onto it and tied the smaller boat to the mooring, then lay down, nestling up to the edge of the rail. It was a little bit chilly, and he huddled, waiting.

It was still dark out, but he expected his father to show up before the sun. He stayed stationary, knowing it would be difficult for his father to see him there.

LOBSTER TRAPPED!

It was a very unpleasant sleep Jonas had. The front of the truck wasn't big enough to afford him a comfortable station, and his back hurt. He tried to see what time it was by looking at his watch, but it was too dark, and he didn't want to turn the dome light on to see. *What a night!* he thought. He sat up and leaned forward in the driver's seat, then rubbed his teeth with his finger. It had been a long time since he took his last shower, and he stunk; not to mention the nasty shape of his body. He still had no socks.

The moon was out, but blocked by clouds, rendering it impossible to view very far this morning. He glared through the windshield and could barely see the tops of the evergreens that surrounded the truck. He had found an inconspicuous spot off the road, near Mack Point, where he made his bed. He played with his hair to remove it from his eyes and face, then stretched, placing the key in the ignition.

He felt he had to move quickly to avoid being discovered, so he started the engine immediately and drove up the short path, indifferent to the brush in his way, until he reached Trundy Road, then onto route #1. He arrived at the landing and placed his skiff in the water, complete with all his gear.

The birds provided the only sounds this early in the morning, and the slapping sound of the water off of the piers. It was peaceful when he rowed out to his mooring. Even though it was difficult to see, he had done this so many times that it was second nature to him, and he reached his lobster boat in a whisker. He climbed inside after tying up the dinghy to the mooring, then started the engines to the boat and slithered out into the harbor with his lights on. When he had a problem seeing anything, he would snap on the flashlight he brought, just in case. It didn't take long until he had cleared the buoys in the harbor and could relax. He tooled along at a steady pace.

Chad heard the boat engines roar as he lay hidden on the deck of Charles's boat. He climbed onto his knees and watched as his father took his vessel out of the harbor. He craftily stood and started the engines in the boat he was in, then leaned over and untied the mooring. His plan was a simple one; once his father stopped his boat, he would ram him with Charles's boat, tossing him into the bay, and allow him to drown. He clenched his fist with determination, and his face glowed in the mist of the early morning. He rubbed his shoulder, recalling his trip down the stairs. *He did this to my mom! He did that to Katherine!* he thought. *Why did I lie to Mrs. Blake and tell her it was an accident?* He was working himself into a tizzy. He became possessed with hate! He monitored his father's wake and followed it closely, still not turning on the lights on the boat. He had watched enough of Jonas and Charles to know how to operate the vessel and maintained his course masterfully. He kept his distance from the other craft, only keeping visual contact with his father's boat.

Jonas never even heard the other boat start up. He was concentrating on his mission and the treasure, constantly checking his gear to make sure he had brought everything he needed. He had his underwater flashlight, his scuba gear and some burlap sacks, in case he found what he was looking for. He was so engrossed in his own efforts that he didn't notice the boat behind; albeit a long distance away.

Chad didn't have to stay very close once they got into the open water. It was easy to follow the only other boat on the bay this morning, especially when it had its lights on. He kept his distance, but not too far. The water was absolutely still as the two boats headed to Cape Rosier.

The boat glided to a rest when Jonas cut off the power to the motor. He looked at the shore near the Head of the Cape and tried to recall where he was when he killed the Rat. It was quite dark, and he had trouble making out the exact location. The bay was calm, and this helped, but it was difficult in the darkness. He turned his flashlight on the shore and rolled its beam from side to side on the beach. He knew it wasn't far from shore where they had been, but he didn't want to hit any projecting rocks. He began to give up hope when he figured that something might have fallen out of the boats the other day. Without any other option he could think of, he flashed the beam of light on the water around his boat. That's when he noticed an object floating not far from him. It looked like a buoy! Here? Who would put a buoy this close to the shore? He directed the light to it and leaned over the boat to get a better view.

Then, he heard the thunderous roar of another boat to his port side, behind him. Still leaning over the rail and looking over the starboard side, studying the buoy, he tried to glance over his shoulder, but it was too late!

Chad had opened Charles's boat to full throttle, bearing down on his father, and it hit Jonas's boat directly at mid ship, creating a reverberating *BOOM* in the still morning air. The collision caused Jonas to fall sideways over the starboard rail of his vessel.

He screamed as he fell. "Whaaaat?" He splashed into a small whirlpool the reeling boat had produced and went directly underwater with the beam from his flashlight creating a mini rainbow above him.

The jolt of the impact knocked Chad into the windshield of the craft, and he banged his head. The boat stalled and bounced backwards in the water. When he picked his head up, he could hear his father's scream and watched him tumble.

"Success!" he yelled jubilantly. He quickly restarted the engine and set it in reverse, then throttled it away from the scene of the accident. Like a seasoned sailor, he piloted the boat back to the piers; this time with the lights on.

Neither boat suffered much damage, except for some non-threatening cracks near their tops, but these vessels weren't built to be torpedoes. Jonas's ship continued to rock in the waves made by its sudden shift, but it did not capsize.

Jonas's heavy body caused him to sink quickly, and he found himself struggling near the rocks at the bottom of the bay when his head hit something. He was upside down in the water, but turned over to gain his balance. He was a proficient swimmer, and that little bump didn't bother him. He spun and pointed his flashlight on the object. It was a wooden pole—or was it? He rubbed his head and pointed the flashlight towards the object. It was a pole, but not just a regular pole. It was the bowsprit from an old sailing vessel, sticking out of the bottom of the bay, barely exposed.

It had to be the remains of the pirate ship!

He nearly wet his pants! He was not very far below the surface of the water and close to shore. He flashed the light around the area and could see the partial hull, exposed to view. He held his breath and swam into the rocks nearby then saw the culmination of his efforts—the treasure!

Jammed in between the rock arrangement, protruding from the bottom of the bay in an underwater Alp-like formation, lay the chests!

"Success!" he gurgled, below the waves. Suddenly, he shifted his focus to the left, where he saw something floating by him. He tried to focus while he stared at the treasure, but he didn't want to take his light off the object of his desire. The first chest he saw showed that it possessed jewels and coins, and he was struggling not to breathe.

He swam as far as he could, until the object he noticed out of the corner of his eye bumped into him. It wasn't a fish—it was a boot! He shone the light on it. The boot held a human foot! Veins and flesh spurred out from the top of the boot and he shuddered in shock, then swam away from the horrific sight. The tumble into the water had knocked some of the breath out of him, and he swam upwards. When he surfaced, the buoy was floating near his head at the top of the bay. Now he knew where it was, but it would not be easy retrieving it alone. He tried to think as he swam back to his boat, still teetering in the waves. He climbed back onto the transom and boarded. He was panting excessively and coughed out the water he had consumed. He saw that the treasure was mostly confined in chests and what he needed to do was to remove the entire load. *How?* he wondered, and he ran his fingers through his drenched beard.

Well, that takes care of my shower! he thought. *Aha!* He turned his attention to the shore. It was close enough to run a series of chains from the trees to the chests and pull them out. He would need a come-along and a lot of chain, but he knew where to get it. The spot was marked with the buoy, which must drop out of sight at high tide, and that would be the reason he hadn't noticed it before. *All the better,* he thought, *that nobody else would be curious to find its meaning. That is, if they can't see it. I gotta act quick, and get the hell out of Dodge!*

A nurse wearing a short, white jacket shook Charles to wake him. "You have a visitor, sir," she said. She had a pleasant smile and demeanor.

"Huh?" He woke up grumpy. "What? I have a visitor? Who?" He stretched and turned to Katherine, lying beside him. "Where's Chad?" he asked to no one.

Katherine woke at the voice but remained in her fetal position. "Oh, he went to your van to get something," she stated wobbly.

"Get what?" he asked.

"I don't know. You'll have to ask him."

The nurse interrupted, "Ahem, sir, your visitor." She tilted her head over her shoulder, where a tall, good-looking gentleman stood then leaned forward, holding his hand out.

"Hi. You must be Charles Ritter. My name is Peter Arnold. I, uh, heard about Elena." His face was clear but glum.

Charles sat up straight and accepted the handshake then released his grip. "Hi. I don't think we've met." He continued to wake up by blinking his eyes rapidly and rolling his shoulders.

"No, sir, we haven't. I'm an old acquaintance of Elena, and I came over here after hearing of the incident. It's a shame that this continues." He forced a smile.

"It's Peter?" he said as he placed the back of his hand over his mouth to suppress a yawn.

"Yes, sir, Mr. Ritter. I'd like to see Elena, if I could."

Charles stared at him curiously. "How did you find out about Elena being injured?" He leaned back.

"Chad called me yesterday," he returned brusquely.

Charles pivoted his head to and fro. "Where is Chad?" he demanded.

"Right here," Chad spoke from the door of the room. He was in a cold sweat but held his head high. He was carrying a pair of socks in his hand. "I just ran out to the van to get these," he lied, handing Charles the keys. He had removed his own socks he to sustain the ruse.

"I see," Charles said, totally unaware of where he really had been.

"I heard outside that the police got Dad!"

"Good!" Charles stated emphatically.

Doctor Cote entered the room with a wide grin, the fluorescent lights shining off his balding head. "She's awake!" He smiled triumphantly, and the smile was contagious.

"Ma!" Chad screamed. "Can we see her?" He nearly jumped to the doctor, his eyes beaming. Katherine leapt off the chair where she lay. Charles stood, stoically, with Peter remaining at his side.

"I think you can," Doctor Cote responded. "She's rather weak, so please keep your stay to a minimum. She will need her rest today. You can follow me." He turned around, happy to deliver the news.

Chad and Katherine ran up behind him. Peter turned to Charles. "May I?" he asked.

Charles nodded. "Of course. You probably know her better than I." He swooped his arm in a gesture to suggest that the man go before him. He did.

Elena lay propped up in her hospital bed when they stepped into her room. The children ran up to her and gave her a hug. She cried in their embrace.

"Easy, now!" Doctor Cote spoke to them, shaking his finger in the air. "Careful you don't cause any more damage," he spoke sternly.

Elena sat up in the bed. "It's all right, Doctor. I feel fine." She smiled politely then turned to see the two gentlemen who had entered behind the children. "Hi, Charles." She waved to him weakly. "Peter, what are you doing here?" Her voice was hoarse and the equipment strapped onto her body made it difficult to maneuver.

He smiled at her. "I've come to ask you something." He was wearing a brown suit and a yellow tie. "First, though, I want to see how you are doing. You know, you gave everyone quite a scare." He walked up to her and gave her a kiss on the forehead.

She blushed. "Oh, Peter, I'm just a little sore, that's all." He placed her hand which was not attached to the I.V. in between both of his hands and dropped down on one knee.

"Elena, I know what's been going on. I despise it! You deserve better than that. I know it's been a long time, but...." He stopped and tucked in his chin, then patted her hands.

"Peter? What are you trying to say?" She wriggled in the bed, staring at him with wonder.

"Oh, Elena! Chad called me yesterday and told me what happened. He also told me that you and your husband were separated, and your marriage would be dissolved."

She spun to Chad and stared at him coldly. He stutter-stepped and hung his head but smiled brightly. She turned back to Peter. He sighed, "Elena, I still love you, you know that!"

"Oh, Peter!" she exclaimed.

"What I want to ask you, is, well ... would you make me the happiest man on earth, and marry me?" He picked his head up and drew his face close to hers, staring her directly in the eyes.

She gasped and began to cry uncontrollably. She just nodded. "Oh, yes, Peter! I filed for divorce already!"

They kissed a long and seductive kiss. Once the embrace was stalled, she wiped the tears from her eyes. "Maybe I can start a new life." She looked at him. "I've inherited my aunt and uncle's house and money. Oh, Peter!" She continued to weep then turned her attention to Chad. "And you, boy! You take care of everything, don't you?" She spoke harshly, but there was a smile on her face.

Chad turned to Katherine, who was standing beside him, and winked. "I sure do!" he stated.

Katherine grinned.

Jonas tied his boat up at his mooring and threw all his gear into his skiff. "How stupid!" he said aloud. "All I had to do was take this damned boat over to Cape Rosier instead of this big clumsy dinosaur, and rowed out to where I met 'em." He rubbed his head. "I'd like to know who the hell rammed me!" He was rambling to no one in particular.

"All I have to do is to drive up to Ames Cove Road and drop this little boat in the water there. I know what I'll do. I'll gather me up some chains and come-alongs and start to pull those chests out. The cops won't even be on to me, over there. How stupid of me!" He jumped into his skiff and headed for shore.

The day was just beginning!

Chapter 29

Doctor Cote cleared his throat. "Ahem!" It was an attention getter. "I'm sorry, but she will need her rest right now. I can't have all of you in here. As you can see, she's recuperating well." He walked up to her bed and placed his hand on her forehead, then turned back to the four. "I'm going to take some tests, and then I can allow two people to stay, but not all four. I don't want her to have too much excitement in one day. I hope you understand." He stood and waited for a response.

Charles spoke up first. "Well, I'd like to go out and check my traps. It's been quite a while since I tried to pull them." He shrugged. "Plus, I don't think I will be of any use here." He walked over to Elena's bed and gave her a peck on the cheek. "I'm happy to see you're doing well."

She pulled his head to her mouth and whispered in his ear. "Thank you!"

He snapped his head back up. "Oh, you're welcome."

Chad poked his head up. "I'll go with you, Mr. Ritter." He wrapped his hand together behind his back. He was anxious to see if he really killed his father and the anticipation, on the sly, was exciting to him. He wanted to see the corpse. The hate for his father was that intense.

Peter turned to Elena, "I'd like to stay, if you don't mind."

"Yes, of course, Peter," she replied.

"I want to stay, too, Ma," Katherine spoke.

Elena smiled. "Of course, dear!"

Doctor Cote pushed everyone away from her bed and pulled the curtain which encircled it around the bed. "Well, that's decided. Now, I have my work to do. Excuse me, but the two of you can wait in the other room, if you don't mind."

Charles twirled his head to the boy. "Ready, Chad?"

"Yes!" he exclaimed. They all exited the room. Peter and Katherine went into the waiting room, and the other two left the hospital.

As they walked out of the door to the infirmary, Charles mentioned, "You know, Chad, I don't remember you leaving a pair of socks in the van." He shook his head.

Chad cringed. "Yes, when we went out to check traps the last time, I left them in your van. My feet were wet after the rain, so I figured I'd change them." He looked up at Charles with such a serious expression that Charles couldn't doubt his word.

The calm of the early morning led into a blustery day, and they had to rush to the van to avoid the gale.

The two old men were at the docks, gossiping to each other when they arrived minutes later. Chad looked around in confusion; his father's truck was not there! His boat was tied to the mooring! He wasn't dead! Damn!

The two elderly gentlemen turned, hearing the approaching vehicle. "Mornin', flatlander," Andrew said.

"Mornin', Chad," Sam added.

Charles leaned out of the window of his van. "Good morning, gentlemen," he answered as he backed the trailer down the ramp to the bay.

He guided it in perfectly and set the van into park. "You know, it looks like I scraped the bottom of this thing on something," he mentioned as he walked to the pier. "I've got to be more careful—it's not really my boat." The breeze tossed him sideways.

"Ay-yup, I hear they got a competition out there today," Sam responded, holding on to his hat. "But 't ain't good weather."

Sam was correct, and the wind gusted. "Said it was for stripers! Ain't too many people out there."

"I seen it windier than this!" Andrew argued, grabbing the edge of the rail. "Hell, I remember one year it took my uncle's clothes right off him, walkin' down Searsport Ave. Took 'im a week to find it all." He laughed.

"Oh, yeah? I seed a sailboat leave from here and make it to Damriscotta on just one good zephyr. Ay-yup! That were a bad storm brewin'." Sam had to outdo Andrew.

"Damriscotta! How the hell could ya see Damriscotta from here?"

"I dunno, I s'pose 't was a real good wind!" Sam explained. The two old men laughed at each other and mumbled to themselves.

Charles had set the boat in the bay and Chad climbed inside. After parking his vehicle, he climbed in also and they departed. "Those two guys can really tell a story!" he said.

The ride was extremely bumpy as they pulled out of the harbor. "Mr. Ritter?" Chad asked. "Do you mind if we check your traps way out in the harbor?"

Charles glanced at him. "Why?" he asked.

"Because I've never been out far in the bay, and I don't think you'll be hauling in all your traps today; it's just too windy."

Charles contemplated his suggestion. "You know, I think you're right. We'll check the traps I set near Castine." He turned the wheel in that direction. The water splashed up onto the both of them, traveling sideways to the surge, and the waves were relentless. "This is too choppy," he said as they powered past Turtle Head. The boat had a mind of its own.

"Can we just go for a ride then?" Chad asked, determined to see the fate of his father.

"Actually, that sounds like a good idea. Where would you like to go?"

"Around Islesboro!" he responded with enthusiasm.

"Sure. Why not?" He turned the boat south, around the island. Chad sat down, satisfied. When they got just west of Cape Rosier he stared towards the shore. If his father was there, it wasn't in his boat.

"May I borrow your binoculars, Mr. Ritter?"

Charles pointed down, bothered by the breeze and the waves. "There in the side pocket."

Chad picked them up and looked to the Cape. There, he saw Jonas's dinghy rolling back and forth in the water at the shore line. He focused them in closer and saw his father on shore struggling with a crate. He had found the treasure Charles spoke of!

Jonas had retrieved the items he needed to pull the treasure out of the water and returned to Ames Cove Road, into Cape Rosier. He parked his truck in a wooded area off of the road, where the spruce trees emitted a fine aroma, and he enjoyed the smell from the evergreens but had no time to waste. He slid into his scuba gear in a brief instant while the wind whistled through the trees. The amount of equipment he brought was tremendously awkward, but he packed the gear into the skiff and hurried to get his small boat into the bay to begin his quest for the fortune he had seen. The paddling out to the buoy was a quick one, even though the waves played havoc with the small craft, the gear inside gave him ballast. He could have swum out to the chests, he thought, but using the boat would be more proficient; he had too much to carry. He had calculated the length of chain he needed would be nearly seven hundred feet.

He stole two full drums of 5/16" zinc-plated chain; that totaled five hundred fifty feet, but it was all he could do to lift those into his truck. He then took three pails of the same chain, which was much easier to handle. The total length he stole, after snapping the lock of the Searsport hardware store, was 826 feet. The drums weighed 256 pounds each, but the pails only weighed 85 pounds each. He carried just one pail with him on the skiff, assuming he would only tie up to one of the chests on his first dive and then roll out the rest of the chain to hook up with it. It was going to take all day to remove the three chests he saw at the bottom of the bay. He made sure, during his burglary, that he included hooks and binders.

The choppy seas may have benefited him, he guessed, because there were very few boats on the water today. He had only seen one pass as he tied the skiff to the make-shift mooring Souharat had set. He watched it pass. It was a fishing vessel. "Headed out to the Maritime," he said. The police patrol boat was nowhere in sight, and this was most likely to do with the weather.

The seas didn't delay him as he pulled out most of the chain from the pail and dropped the end into the bay. He lowered enough to hit bottom, then he adjusted his gear and jumped into the water, holding his flashlight. This time he knew where to go. He stared at the partially buried parts of the ship he had seen before. He took hold of the end of the chain, then swam over a huge trench, which he guessed held more parts of the ship that sank. He ignored it and continued on to the rocky area where he had seen the chests. As he swam, he studied the area to find the best way to haul the cargo away from the rocks, in the direction of the shoreline. Most of the bottom of the bay was sand in this area, and dragging the crates should be simple once he got them to clear the obstructions. He got to them and gazed at the half-opened chest, showing its vast fortune inside. He was nearly drooling at the prize he would soon have. In a moment of glory, he dreamt of the life he could lead once he disposed of this loot. It was his, after all—finders keepers! He met a man, when he was in Boston, who would buy some of the gems he had seen, and that man had connections in New York, who could sell the coins to collectors. Even if he only sold a few at a time, he would be rich in a very short while, and he could travel to any place he wanted.

The greedy visions lasted only a moment; there was work to be done! The beam from the flashlight scanned the area within the rocks, until he could see a narrow gap through the stones, leading directly to the beach. It would be a smooth glide to shore! He swiftly hooked on to the first chest, nearest the shore, and ran the chain from the boat to the voided area of rock along the bottom. He tugged at the box to make sure it was secure and, satisfied with that, ran the chain its full length. One chest was ready to be removed!

He returned to the truck and snatched the next pail, then rowed back to the temporary mooring. He leapt into the water with the flashlight in one hand, and the end of chain in the other, then swam to the end of the other chain, tying the two together in a tight knot using the hooks. This time he would run the length of chain from the dinghy, dropping it as he went. He strung it out to its full length then left it on the bottom, as it was.

LOBSTER TRAPPED!

The rest could be done without the skiff, he realized. There had been no other traffic on the waters since he started, so he wasn't afraid of being caught.

He returned to the shore and let the boat float on the surface, rocking in the waves. He ran to the truck and backed it up on shore as close as he could to the bay without the possibility of getting stuck in the sand. After opening the container, he pulled out as much chain as he could and laid it on the beach, then walked into the bay, up to his waist, with one end of the chain in his hand. He dove in and pulled the chain along until he came to where the very end of his last installment lay. He hooked the lines together and swam back, but the end of his line was short of the beach. He dragged the next container to the edge of the truck's bed and pulled out the chain by hand, returned to the water and waded in to tie it to the last piece.

Once that was complete, he could stand up in the water and do the rest from shore. He had brought two come-alongs, in case one gave out, and enough chain to hook up to almost any tree on the peninsula. He followed the line from the buoy Souharat had set to the shore and eyed in the direct path to the nearest tree; a tall oak standing alone. He fixed the come-along to it and tied the chain to the end of the apparatus, using the hooks he stole. It was tedious work and it took him nearly an hour, but he hauled the first chest onto the soft sand on the beach. Wrenching on the fixture locked on to the tree was nearly complete when he saw another boat pass by. It was too far away to see who it was, or even whose boat it might have been, but it still caused him some concern. He waited until it passed to tow the chest all the way up to the tree. From there, he had to disconnect the come-along and attach it to another tree. He would hide the treasure chests in a spot he found, where no one else could detect them, and cover the booty with branches and leaves until he could figure out a way to load it onto his truck. One was nearly complete, and he leaned against the spruce tree beside him, heaving out a huge sigh of relief. It had begun!

Chad looked at Charles, while his eyes watered from the wind in his face and the splash of the water coming at him. "Mr. Ritter, I have a question." He acted naïve.

Charles, managing the speed of the boat against the bouncing of the waves, answered. "Yes, sure, what?"

"That treasure you mentioned. What is it?"

"Well, if my theory is correct, it is a pirate's treasure that was abandoned here a few centuries ago. Why?"

"Well, what would it be carried in?"

"Oh, most likely, chests or lockers. Some sort of large container. Why?" He turned to him with an odd, speculative stare.

"Oh, no reason, really. I was just curious." He sat back down on the seat. He had a plan!

Chapter 30

Oh, how sweet the music was! Peter had bought Elena a compact disc player to help her pass the time at the hospital. When Charles and Chad entered the room, it was a symphony of Brahms, emanating throughout the establishment. It was certainly soothing for the patients, as well as the hospital staff. Elena was wide awake and quite coherent when they advanced to her bedside. She sat up and ogled the two of them. Katherine sat in one of the chairs in the room, monitoring her mother's progress. Chad leaned to his mother and gave her a kiss on the cheek. She smiled at him. "How was your day, dear?" It was obvious that she was out of danger, and in good spirits.

"It was O.K.," he stated. "But it was too windy to haul any traps, so we took a ride on the bay." He gleamed back towards her.

She never lost her smile but turned to Charles. "I can't even begin to thank you," she said sincerely. "Peter and I will be getting married after the divorce is final. I heard what you've done for me. I'm just so indebted, I can't think of a way of paying you back. I did receive an inheritance—"

He stopped her. "No, no, no! That's not why I did that. I'm glad you'll be all right, but I couldn't possibly take anything from you. Never! I did it for you as I would for anyone else in your situation. I'm happy you're O.K." He spun to Peter. "I think you're in good hands now. I'll take the children back to your cabin, if you like. I think they might need a little rest, just like you. It's awful hard to sleep here, believe me." He stretched and grabbed his neck, twisting it around.

She nodded and looked at the children. The two of them looked quite fatigued and agreed with a head nod.

"Well, that's decided. I have to get back to the cabin and find out what's going on with my job. I only have another day or so here, and I'm leaving, one way or the other. I've seen quite a bit in a short period of time. Please get better, and I'll bring the kids over tomorrow. Until then, I'll say goodbye."

"I'll be leaving tomorrow!" she explained.

He stood, stunned. "Already? You just had major surgery, why would they let you leave?"

Chad walked over to Katherine and whispered in her ear. "I thought I got rid of Dad, but he's still alive. I have an idea, if you want to be a part of it."

She listened attentively.

They arrived back at the cabins shortly before the last light of day fell, and there was Janet in the doorway. She stood beautifully, with her arms folded and a bunch of papers in her hand. There were two bags on either side of her. He pulled up close to the cabin and stared at her.

"Janet! What are you doing here?" His smile was a fake one, knowing his own negligence.

"Well, well, well, Mr. Ritter!" she answered with a long face and shaking the papers in her hand. "I see you're still alive!" She grinned. "It would be a good idea if you let your wife know that once in a while."

"I'm sorry for not calling you." He stopped the van, and the children got out. "This is Chad and Katherine. I worked for their father. Kids, this is my wife."

The two children said, "Hi," and ran into their cabin. Janet threw both of her arms around him. The two of them embraced with a long, tender kiss. He shifted his head back. "Oh! How I've missed you! I love you so much!"

"I've missed you, too! The kids miss you. I thought all of this foolishness here was supposed to be over and you would be home by now." She kissed him once more, holding the papers behind his back, then pulled away from him, and shook the paperwork in his face. "See this?"

"Yes, what is it?"

"It's the bills for your little vacation," she answered sarcastically. "How can we afford to pay this? Look at them!" She held them out for him to take.

"What? The school is supposed to take care of everything. Dean Groton told me so." He was perplexed as he took the papers out of her hand and began to look through them, one at a time.

"That Dean Groton is another thing. He wouldn't answer my phone calls. The school said you quit!"

"Quit? Something is funny about this. These bills have all been forwarded by the school," he said, looking directly into her eyes, then a long, wide smile shot across his face, and he put his arm around her. "This can wait until later. Right now I have more important things on my mind!" He kissed her and led her inside his cabin.

Chad and Katherine went inside their cabin and turned on the television. "Tonight," Chad said, "just before Charles goes to sleep, I'm going over to his cabin. I'll make up some sort of excuse, then I'll steal his keys. I know where Dad is going to be!"

She smiled at him, nodding emphatically.

LOBSTER TRAPPED!

It was dark now, when Jonas pulled the last of the chests up to the spot in the trees where they would least likely be found. He had removed his scuba gear earlier. The chests had to be pulled from one tree to another in the wooded area behind the shore, to the spot he chose. He began covering them up with branches and leaves, anything he could find. He stared down the crates and smiled at his achievement, then he heard the snapping of twigs. *Click, click, click.* The sound came from both sides of him. He held his hand over his ears to block the sound.

Suddenly, a figure stepped out into the clearing in front of him. "Chad!" he screamed in shock. Chad was holding one of his rifles in his hands.

"Don't move, Dad." He pointed the weapon at his father.

"What do ya think ya gonna do with that?" he asked with hesitation.

"You raped my sister. You threw me down the stairs on purpose. Now, you nearly killed my mother!" There was anger in his words. "I hate you!"

The sounds of snapping branches continued, but this time, from the opposite edge of the woods. Out from the trees behind him stepped another figure. He spun around to look. "Katherine! What are ya doing here?"

They had taken the minivan back to their house to pick up a few items. The rifle was one, and the meat cleaver in Katherine's hand was the other.

She stuck the cleaver into a tall spruce tree beside her. "Hi, Daddy!"

There was fire in her eyes!

Chapter 31

Charles stretched in bed and woke Janet. "I guess we have to go back to Rhode Island today and stop into the university to find out what's going on. This is all very strange, indeed."

She yawned and sat up. He had told her about all the bizarre incidents he had been subject to. She shuddered when he told her about Elena and Katherine. "Poor creatures!" she said.

He stood up and got dressed while she remained in the bed. "I'm going to take the kids to see their mother today and say goodbye. I'll call Randy Thompson when I get back from picking up the traps, to let him know that I'll be leaving the boat on the mooring in Searsport. I'll let him know what the school's up to when I find out. There's nothing much more I can do."

"Oh, Charles! Do you have to pick up those traps? Can't you just leave them there?" She was disappointed.

"No, I can't. I'm the only one that is allowed to pick them up, plus, it won't take long. A couple of hours or so. You can stay here while I'm gone." He leaned over and gave her a peck on the cheek.

"All right, I guess," she answered. "I really don't want to leave Mrs. Hauser with the children more than a couple of days. She gets cranky after a while." She smiled and lay back down.

He stepped out of the cabin door and patted his clothes pockets. "Where are my keys?" he asked himself. "Huh!" He became worried. "Maybe I left them in the van."

He walked over to the van and looked inside. The keys were in the ignition. "That's funny, I don't remember leaving them in here. I don't think I've ever done that before." He shrugged and left them there, then walked over to the other cabin he had rented for the Hales and knocked on the door. There was no response so he knocked again, this time much louder.

Katherine came to the door in her nightgown. "Come on in. Chad's still asleep." She yawned.

"Still asleep? It's nearly eight o'clock. I'm going to be leaving today and I wanted…." Chad stepped into the room. He had huge bags under his eyes.

"Good morning, Mr. Ritter," he said, barely keeping his balance.

"My Lord, you look like you've been up all night!" Charles said.

"I didn't sleep very well," he answered.

"Well, let's get dressed and I'll take you to the hospital to see your mother. I'm headed to Rhode Island today after I pick my traps up." He shook his head as he studied Chad's face.

"We'll be ready in a minute," Chad responded.

They arrived at the hospital a half hour later and went directly to Elena's room. She was standing up beside the bed with Peter holding on to her. "Good morning," she said as she saw Charles walking inside the room. The kids ran up to her and put their arms around her.

"Ma! You're O.K.!" Chad exclaimed.

"They are letting me go home today!" she boasted.

"That's great!" Charles said. "That makes me very happy, but where are you going to go?"

Peter spoke up quickly. "With me! She inherited her aunt and uncle's house, so we'll be moving in there today. It seems that they don't want you to stay in the hospital for very long. Their theory is that the best recovery is at home."

"Plus, they need the beds!" Charles laughed. "That is wonderful news. Hey, look, I'm leaving today after I pick up my traps, and I just want to say goodbye." He forced a smile.

"Oh, Charles! That's too bad!" Her face drooped.

Chad interrupted, "We can meet you at the piers and say goodbye there. It's such a nice day! Can we, Peter?" He batted his eyes for sympathy.

"You have a mooring in Searsport, right?" Peter looked at Charles, who nodded to the affirmative. "Well, I don't see why not, then. We have to go right by there, anyway."

"O.K., I'm headed down there now. How long do you think it will be before they release you?" He turned to Elena.

"Just a few minutes. I have to wait for the doctor, he just left to sign me out and write up my prescriptions. He said it would only take a minute." She smiled.

"I guess, I'll wait for you there," he said as he turned around and walked out the door.

Chad was right, it was a beautiful day! Seagulls swarmed around the piers while Charles placed the skiff in the water, and tied it to one of the cleats on the dock. The sun shone brilliantly in the cloudless sky. The water was as calm as he had ever seen it. He pulled the van into one of the parking spots.

He had to find out where Randy wanted him to leave the trailer and the skiff when he left for Rhode Island. Peter's car pulled into the parking area right after he got out of the van. He walked up to the passenger's side window, where Elena sat. "You're looking good!" he said then leaned inside and gave her a hug.

She hugged him back. "Thank you so much for everything you've done for us. I couldn't have made it if it wasn't for you. Goodbye, Charles." She gave him a kiss with a tear in her eye.

"Oh, you're welcome. Goodbye, Elena." He stood up erect, and the children got out of the backseat of the car. They both ran up to him and gave him a hug, while he leaned down to accept it. "Goodbye, kids. Good luck, and take care of your mother, you hear?"

"We will!" they said in unison.

"Goodbye, Mr. Ritter. Thank you!" Katherine was on the verge of crying.

"You're welcome, dear," he answered. She got back inside the vehicle.

"Goodbye, Mr. Ritter," Chad said then placed his hand to his mouth and whispered in Charles's ear, "I left you a present!"

He jumped back into the car.

"Huh? What do you mean?" Charles was puzzled at the comment.

"You'll see!" Chad yelled as the car sped away.

Charles scratched his head. "I wonder what he meant by that. Oh, well." He walked down to the skiff.

The first trap came up with difficulty. He had not checked this one at all, yet. Once he got it on the edge of the boat, he could see that it was loaded with lobster. He threw all the warp and buoys into the boat, including the trap with the lobsters still inside. There was no real reason to take them out, since he wasn't going to reset the trap. He wanted to get back to Janet as soon as possible, and that would only hold him up, he thought.

He idled by his second buoy and hauled it up onto the table on the side of the boat. It was much heavier than the first one, which was very heavy. There was something different, he noticed, as he pulled it onto the side of the boat. The trap had a huge red cloth covering it, and when he finally placed it on the table, he could see the words "Thank You!" written on the cloth, which entirely surrounded the trap. There was a wire tied around it, holding the cloth on with a small bottle secured to the wire. As he stared at it, he could see a piece of paper inside the bottle.

This must be Chad's surprise, he figured. A cork was plugged the top of the bottle, and he removed it, then picked the paper out from inside.

It was a note which read:

LOBSTER TRAPPED!

Thank you, Mr. Ritter for everything you've done for us. We very much appreciate it. To show our gratitude, we will give you the location of the treasure that you mentioned.
   Chad and Katherine Hale.

Below the words was a map of Cape Rosier with an 'X' signifying the location of the chests. He laughed. "That Chad, what a guy! I'll have to check that area and see if this is really true!" He placed the paper into his pocket and tossed the bottle onto the deck of the boat.

He then removed the wire from the trap and the cloth draped over it. He swooned!

There was no lobster in this trap! There was the severed head of Jonas Hale! It was white with blued lips and the full beard and mustache still attached. Arteries and veins stuck out of the neck where it had been cut.

He fell backwards against the other side of the boat in absolute horror! His head felt light, and he nearly passed out.

Chapter 32

He cowered in the bosom of the boat on the edge of the far deck, staring at the gruesome object in the trap that he had extracted from the depths. His body quivered and his lips shook uncontrollably. He was in a near state of shock, then he glanced back towards the shore to see if he could detect Chad. He could not but knew that this had to be his work. He smiled an understanding smile, realizing that the course had come to its fruition. Their vengeance was complete, and there was nothing left to do but the obvious. He stared back inside the trap and the head was fresh, perhaps preserved by the salt water of just recently severed. Either way, it didn't matter. As Jonas would have said, "It don't make no never mind."

He was going to simply cut the line to the trap and let it fall to the bottom on its own. He wasn't involved in this sort of behavior, or this aspect of the kids' actions.

He began to rise up from his crouched position when he heard a bang at the back of the ship, on the transom. Then another bang. "What the heck?" he blurted out.

Suddenly, he saw a hand reach up from the water and grab the back of the boat, then a second hand. They were both clutched firmly onto his vessel, and quickly, a figured emerged.

His mouth dropped, and he slumped back into his original position. Two legs straddled over the right arm of the figure, and the complete image rolled onto the deck. Charles crawled up to the pilot house, his face was completely white, and his eyes were wide open, staring at the figure. It appeared to be a man, except for one thing—it had no head!

He fell against the control board. "Who … who … who are you? What … what are you? What … what do you want from me?" His voice quivered, and his body trembled in fear.

The figure stood. It was clothed in black shoes with one buckle each, a set of pantaloons to his waist, and a belt holding two pistols and a sword. One hand reached down to the hilt of the sword and removed a triangular hat from it, holding it in one hand. It wore no shirt, and its chest was covered with wounds of one type or another.

Charles nearly fainted at the sight. "What sort of specter are you? What do you want of me?" His breathing had become irregular. "Can you speak?"

The figure reached into the sheath attached to the belt and drew the sword out. It stepped forward, moving towards Charles, very slowly, then raised the sword in the air.

Charles cried "NO!" and covered his head.

The apparition stuck the sword into the deck of the boat with both hands on the hilt. Charles peeked through his arms, not believing what he saw. The sword stood erect.

The ghastly figure turned to the lobster trap on the table and opened the top, pulled out the severed head and shoved it in between its shoulders.

Charles held his hands over his eyes and watched through the cracks in his fingers.

The hand of the figure twisted the severed head into place. Somehow, by some freakish act of nature, the skin around the head of Jonas Hale and the neck of the apparition adhered, bonding together, as if it were a new man! A moment passed, and the eyes of the figure blinked; one at a time, then both. The chin rotated in one direction, then the other. It tilted the head back and forth—it was secure! Its mouth rotated, and it smacked its lips together. "There now! That be better!" It spoke!

Charles's chin dropped, and he thought of jumping overboard before the spirit. "Who ... who ... who are you?" he said in astonishment.

The figure placed the hat it held onto his new head, then pulled the sword from the deck and lightly set it back in its sheath. "I be called Teach! Edward Teach!" He pointed to his head. "Do ye know how long it takes to find one o'these in the sea?" he answered brusquely then laughed and twisted his head around. "Ha! Ha! Ha! Ye be scared o'me?"

Charles reeled back and rubbed his eyes. "Blackbeard?" he asked.

"Aye! Some call me that!" He placed his hands on his hips and stared at Charles. He played with the whiskers of his newfound head. "A fine shank'a'hair!" he commented. "Good and easy fer lightin'!" He fondled the mustache. "What be this rig?" he asked, turning to the lobster trap, where he found his new head.

"It's a lobster trap," Charles answered, terrified.

"A lobster trap? What be a lobster?"

"Oh, it's a crustacean, that is.... Well, you really wouldn't understand! But ... but ... but...." He was at a loss for words.

Blackbeard looked around the boat, then back at Charles. He placed his hands on his hips. "Where be ye sails?" This time, it was he who was confused.

Charles couldn't speak.

"I ain't gonna hurt ye, lad. I just came for what be mine!"

Charles placed his arms around his legs in his sitting position. "There are no sails on this boat," he stated.

"No sails! How does she work?" The pirate looked up and down. "Where are ye masts?"

"There are no masts, either. This boat runs with an engine."

"Huh? Engine? What's that?" He turned back to Charles. "Ye got oars?"

"No, you don't understand," Charles stopped him. "This is a motorized boat. I'll show you." He stood up, more comfortable that the pirate meant no harm, then started the engine and pulled the boat forward a bit.

Blackbeard fell back on his heels when the boat shifted. "Well, I be bludgeoned!" He held his hat tightly.

Charles idled the boat. "You said what you wanted was what was yours. What is that?" He was curious.

Blackbeard leaned back, laughing loudly. "First!" he said. "Be this!" He pointed to his newly attached head, then stuck the sword into the deck with both hands. "And me treasure! I know it be here! Where be the map?" He held his hand out to Charles.

Charles nodded in agreement. He had never seen a ghost before, but this was the strangest of all. "Yes, sir." He chortled and handed him the map in his pocket.

"Now where be ye Hollands?" he shouted.

"Hollands? Hollands? I don't have any here." Charles shook.

"Ah, well!" The pirate studied the map and handed it back to Charles. "This be where me treasure is? Find it!" he yelled.

"Yes, sir!" Charles answered, and he turned the boat in the direction of Cape Rosier.

Chapter 33

They pulled up on the beach near where the treasure was hidden. Charles cut the engines. "I'm afraid I don't have my skiff here to get to shore." He tilted his head and grimaced.

Blackbeard drew in a deep breath. "Well then, I guess ye be the one to check for the booty, and I be holding the ship. When ye find it, let me know!" He held his belly.

"Uh, huh. I see!" Charles acted hesitantly. "That means I have to swim to shore."

"Ain't a long swim, lad. Now, get to it!" He patted one of the pistols in his belt.

Charles nodded and climbed over the rail of the boat, lowering himself into the water. "Brrr!" he exclaimed as he dropped into the bay. "The water temperature is really cold here, not like in Rhode Island!" He proceeded to swim to shore, and stood, prior to reaching it. He looked again at the map and headed towards the tree Chad had pointed out on the parchment. There were drag marks along the beach where Jonas had pulled the crates to their final destination, so the trail was well marked. He put the map back into his pocket and followed the indentations in the sand.

When he got to the tree line, the trail was just as obvious though the brush. He walked into the wood, going along the well-defined route until he came to the large covered crates. It was so clear to him that he had found what he was looking for, he only brushed off a few leaves to see the top of one of the chests.

That was it! He turned around and headed back to the boat to tell Teach.

Out of the blue, he heard a voice. "Well, thank you, Charlie!"

He spun around and saw Dean Groton standing in front of him with a revolver in his hand. "Dean Groton, what are you doing here?" He jumped with the break of silence.

The dean waved the pistol back and forth. "I knew you could do it! I had the utmost faith in you, my boy." Ben pulled up beside him, grinning. "You remember Ben, don't you, Charlie?" He smiled with an evil eye.

"What's going on? Why the weapon? What are you doing here? I have some questions for you!" He stamped his foot on the ground. "I've gotten billed for all these expenses that the university was supposed to cover!"

"Oh, boy, are you that naïve, Charlie?" the dean responded. "You really think anyone wanted to take a class on maritime history with a practical aspect?" He laughed. "No, no, no! That was *my* idea. You see, one of my graduate students saw the two fishermen who had discovered the treasure and called me to let me know. He thought it would be a good idea if we sent up a team of experts to pull it up and help." He stepped closer to Charles. "I didn't think it was a good idea! If they found it, they would give it to a museum. It would be of no use to me that way. Instead, I sent you up here. I knew you could find it for me."

Charles spit on the ground. "You mean the whole thing about the class was a ruse? You tricked me!" He was extremely agitated. "That's not right!"

The dean laughed. "Perhaps not, but I don't care. The treasure belongs to me now! I set you up with the most despicable man I could find, to get you to lead me to the location of the fortune. You think that guy, Hale, is the best lobsterman they have here? Ha! He's probably the worst! I knew about him, and how greed would take him to find it. Now it's mine!"

Charles lurched back. "What about the school board that authorized my class and helped me with my license."

Ben laughed loudly. "I made the phone calls." He turned to Charles and with a thick German accent said. "Ya, I vould love to take da class!" He spoke in a thick French accent "Ey! De class sound good to me!" He slapped his thigh with his hand. "Hell, Charlie, I wrote the letters to the school board with several different handwritings!" He continued to laugh until he had to grab his stomach. "We got you!"

The dean was still laughing with all his might. "I convinced the school board to install the class and send you up here. When it was time for school to open, they realized there was no such class, and they shut off all the funding. I didn't care! I knew I would be rich in a short period of time. Now I am, thanks to you, Charlie! Sorry about that, but I don't think you'll have to worry about the bills." He gritted his teeth, sinisterly.

"Why shouldn't I worry about the bills?" he asked, shaking with the anticipated answer.

"Why? Because you'll be dead! You know I can't share this with you, Charlie. Sorry!" He pulled back the hammer of the gun and took direct aim at Charles.

Charles closed his eyes, expecting the worst, then he heard a yell. The blade of Blackbeard's sword swung though the dean's torso at mid-height, cutting him in half. The body of Dean Groton hit the ground; one piece here and one piece there. Ben turned to the pirate and held his hand high in the air.

"Ayeah!" He couldn't come up with an English word.

"Get ye out of here, a'fore ye get the same treatment!" He shoved his head forward at Ben, who spun and took off as fast as he could through the trees. Blackbeard watched him prance though the woods. "Ha! Ha! Ha!" He turned back to Charles. "Now, let's have us a peek!" He sheathed his sword and walked to the chests, with Charles following. He brushed off the top of the first chest and opened the top. It was full of jewels and coins of every type. Blackbeard scooped up two handfuls and gave them to Charles. "It be fer the boat, and whatever expenses ye be speaking about!"

Charles nodded his head and took the goods. It would certainly pay the bills! "Thank you," he said.

"Now I got other things to do!" the pirate shouted.

"What is that?" Charles asked, stuffing the fortune into his pockets.

"I got more a' this on Smuttynose!" He placed his hands on his hips and looked up to the sky, scratching his beard.

"But first, laddie, ye gotta show me how to run that ship!"

"It's a boat!" Charles sighed.

THE END

Printed in the United States
32237LVS00003B/37-48